BRUTAL VOWS

OTHER BOOKS BY J.T. GEISSINGER

Queens and Monsters Series

Ruthless Creatures

Carnal Urges

Savage Hearts

Brutal Vows

Standalone

Pen Pal

BRUTAL VOWS

J.T. GEISSINGER

BRAMBLE

TOR PUBLISHING GROUP | NEW YORK

BRUTAL VOWS

Copyright © 2022 by J.T. Geissinger, Inc.

A Bramble Book
Published by Tom Doherty Associates / Tor Publishing Group
120 Broadway
New York, NY 10271

www.torpublishinggroup.com

Bramble™ is a trademark of Macmillan Publishing Group, LLC.

The Library of Congress Cataloging-in-Publication
Data is available upon request.

ISBN 978-1-250-38825-4 (trade paperback)
ISBN 978-1-250-34665-0 (ebook)

Our books may be purchased in bulk for promotional, educational, or business use. Please contact your local bookseller or the Macmillan Corporate and Premium Sales Department at 1-800-221-7945, extension 5442, or by email at MacmillanSpecialMarkets@macmillan.com.

Previously self-published by the author in 2022

First Bramble Trade Paperback Edition: 2025

Printed in the United States of America

0 9 8 7 6 5 4 3 2 1

To Jay, my HEA

Many a good hanging prevents a bad marriage.

—WILLIAM SHAKESPEARE

BRUTAL VOWS

ONE

REY

*T*he weight of memory can sometimes be so heavy, it's suffocating.

Take now, for instance. I'm standing across from my brother's oak desk in his enormous wood-paneled study, staring at his face and struggling to breathe around the invisible hand squeezing my lungs. There's also a rock in my throat and a vat of acid churning in my stomach.

All inevitable results whenever the word "marriage" is mentioned in my presence.

No four-letter curse word could ever be so vile.

Uncomfortable under my stare, Gianni glances down at the desktop. He fiddles with the edge of the blotter, then runs a finger under the collar of his white dress shirt.

"Don't look at me like that. You knew this was coming. Lili's of age now."

"She's been eighteen for all of two weeks, for fuck's sake. And what about college? You promised you'd consider it."

He lifts his gaze to meet mine. He has our father's eyes,

coal black and lifeless. Everyone else finds them—and him—terrifying.

But my father didn't scare me, and neither does my older brother. For that matter, neither does anyone else.

After what I've been through, the devil himself could show up demanding my soul, and I'd tell him to kiss my sweet ass and fuck off back to hell.

Gianni says, "No, *you* insisted I consider it. And as usual, when you got an answer you didn't like, you ignored it."

When I only stand there glaring at him, he adds, "I vetted him. He's not Enzo."

At the sound of my late husband's name, a shudder goes through me. The acid churning in my stomach sears a burning path up into my throat.

I stand still for several moments, struggling to regain my equilibrium. Then, so I don't start breaking furniture, I start to pace.

Gianni watches me silently for several moments before trying a new approach.

"We'll get territory. Trade routes. Important allies we desperately need. The match will make us a substantial amount of money. Tens of millions at least. Potentially hundreds."

I mutter, "You sound like a pimp."

He brushes that off. "Not to mention garner us influence over the other families. You know how desperate everyone is to make an alliance with the Mob. If we can pull this off, I'll be named capo. The stakes are huge, Rey. We can secure the family's position for generations."

"You keep saying 'we' and 'us.' I don't want anything to do with forcing my niece into slavery."

With exaggerated patience, he says, "Lili was always going to be matched for the betterment of the family. You know it. She knows it. Everyone knows it. This is nothing new."

I stop pacing and look at him. "She's still a child."

"At eighteen, she's now an adult. And you were two years younger than she is when you were married."

I say bitterly, "Yes. And look how well that turned out."

His expression sours. "You inherited Enzo's fortune. You gained your freedom. I'd say it turned out rather well for you in the end."

"You conveniently skipped all the carnage in the middle between our engagement and his death."

"Lili isn't you, Rey."

"No, she's my niece. And my goddaughter. And one of the sweetest, brightest girls I've ever met. She doesn't deserve to be married off to some horrible old Irishman!"

"I never said he was old."

"Who probably stinks like cooked cabbage!"

"I promise you, he doesn't smell like a vegetable."

"And has a kiddie porn habit! Any man who wants to marry a teenager *has* to be a pervert!"

Careful not to raise his voice, though it's obvious he's annoyed with me and wants the conversation to be over, Gianni says, "I don't believe he's the type for child pornography, but you can judge for yourself. He'll be here any minute."

I recoil in disgust. "He's coming here?"

"To meet Lili."

"Now?"

"Yes."

I narrow my eyes in suspicion. "Why are you only telling me about this marriage contract seconds before the Irishman sets foot in the house?"

After a short pause, he says carefully, "Considering your temper, it seemed like a good idea to give you as little time to start smashing things as possible."

That might be a reason, but I can tell it's not the main one. I know my brother well.

"You son of a bitch. Lili doesn't know yet, does she?"

Gianni rises from his desk. Smoothing a hand down the front of his bespoke navy blue suit jacket, he walks toward me. He stops in front of me and gently grasps my upper arms.

"I was hoping you could tell her."

I say flatly, "I will kill you where you stand."

He examines my expression, then drops his hands to his sides and takes a step back.

Smart move.

"This is why I didn't tell you sooner. I'm sorry this brings up bad memories for you, but it's happening. The terms have already been negotiated. The only thing left is for the Irishman to meet Lili. If she pleases him, the contract will be signed and the date will be set."

He doesn't elaborate on what will happen if Lili fails to please, but I know it won't be good.

For Gianni, failure on even the smallest scale is unforgivable.

He continues in a softer tone. "And her *zia* will explain to her how this is all for the best, and how family comes first, and how, if her new husband proves to be anything like her *zia*'s late husband, Enzo, he'll find himself the victim of an untimely death, too."

He pauses. "A meticulously planned death with no witnesses or evidence of foul play. An 'accidental' death so well executed, it even fooled the police."

Without missing a beat, I say, "I didn't kill my husband."

He smiles. "I've never met anyone who can lie as well as you do."

"It's a gift."

His smile grows wider. "One of many."

"Stop trying to flatter me so I'll do your dirty work for you."

"She won't listen to me, Rey. You know how she is."

"Yes, it's very inconvenient for the men in this family when the women have minds of their own."

I can tell he wants to sigh, but he doesn't. He simply stands and looks at me beseechingly until I give in.

It's not like I have a choice, anyway. As the head of the Caruso family, Gianni calls all the shots. Someday, there will be a female head of one of the five Italian crime families in New York. It's a dream of mine that I'll live long enough to see it.

Until then, all I can do is exert as much influence as possible. It helps that my brother's afraid of me.

"I want final approval about this Irishman. I'll tell Lili for you, but if I don't like him, the deal is off."

Gianni runs his tongue over his teeth. He's probably counting silently to ten in his head or cursing, wishing he had a sister more like his best friend Leo's. A docile, dim bulb of a girl with no opinions about anything except what her father and brother tell her to have.

Instead, he's got me.

A woman with a bad reputation, a chip on her shoulder, and a sword for a tongue.

"Agreed?" I prod.

"You won't think anyone is good enough for her," he counters. "We'll be having this same conversation over and over again for the next twenty years."

"Untrue. I can be reasonable."

He lifts a brow.

"Don't make that face. I simply want to make sure he's not a monster."

"I assure you, he's not a monster."

"This would be a good time to point out that you liked Enzo, too."

Gianni winces. "Enzo was a sociopath. They're very good at pretending to be charming."

"Exactly. Which is why I need to have the final word. If any-one can spot a psycho a mile away, it's me."

He doesn't have an argument for that. How could he? It's the truth.

I earned my monster radar the hard way.

Gianni gazes at me with an unreadable expression for so long, I think I've lost. But then he surprises me by saying, "Fine. If you don't like the Irishman, the marriage is off."

Relief floods my body. I exhale, nodding.

"But you still have to tell Lili."

At the sound of car tires crunching over the gravel of the circular driveway outside, Gianni and I turn to the windows. Sounding amused, he says, "And I think you better do it quick."

My ears burn with anger. "You're a shitty father, Gi."

He shrugs. "It runs in the family."

I turn and walk out before I grab the letter opener off his desk and do something I'll regret.

I take the stairs up to the second floor two at a time. At the landing, I make a sharp left and head down another corridor, the opposite direction from my bedroom. Grim ancestral oil portraits framed in gold glower down at me as I pass.

Ignoring the hand-painted frescoes on the walls, Venetian glass chandeliers sparkling overhead, and a startled housekeeper dusting the leaves of a potted palm, I stride quickly toward the room at the end.

I don't have any time to waste.

I stop in front of the heavy oak door and pound my fist on it. "Lili? It's me. Can I come in? I have to talk to you."

"Just a second, *zia*! I'll . . . I'll be right there!"

From behind the door, Lili's voice sounds faint. And panicked.

Maybe she already knows. She's very clever for someone who's been sheltered her entire life.

I hear some scuffling noises, then an odd thud. Concerned, I lean closer to the door. "Lili? You okay?"

A few long, silent moments later, my niece pulls open the door.

Her cheeks are flushed. Her long dark hair is disheveled. The white T-shirt she's wearing is wrinkled and untucked on one side from a pair of black yoga pants. She's barefoot and looks disoriented, as if she just woke up.

Which would be strange, considering it's four o'clock in the afternoon.

"I'm sorry, were you sleeping?"

"Um . . . working out." She points over her shoulder to the television on the wall on the opposite side of the room. On the screen, a woman in hot-pink spandex is doing jumping jacks. "If you don't mind, I'd like to get back to it."

She's about to close the door, but I push past her into the room. "This can't wait."

Like the rest of the house, her bedroom is overdecorated. There's not a spare inch of space where the gaze can rest that isn't bedeviled with velvet, gilt, mirrors, ornate wallpaper, elaborately carved wood, or stained glass.

At least in here, the colors are muted pinks and greens. My bedroom is all black, burgundy, and gold. It looks like a bordello inside the Vatican.

Gianni's late wife was big on the Catholic church school of interior design. She died giving birth to Lili, but her unique taste in décor lives on.

I grab the remote control from the top of the dresser, click a button to mute the TV, then turn back to Lili. She stands in the same spot, looking nervous.

"What's up, *zia*?"

"There's no good way to say this, so I'm just going to say it." When she starts to wring her hands, I add, "Maybe you should sit down."

"Oh god. Who died? Is it Nonna?"

"Your grandmother's fine. She made a deal with the devil to live long enough to annoy the rest of us to death first. Now listen, we don't have much time." I walk closer to her, take her hands in mine, and look her in the eye. "I'm going to tell you something. You won't like it."

Her face pales. "Oh shit."

"Yes. And you know how I feel about you cursing."

"Judging by the look on your face, I'm going to be cursing a lot more in the next few minutes."

"You make a good point."

"Plus, you curse all the time."

"I don't want you to turn out like me."

"Why not? You're a bad bitch."

"Exactly."

"No, *zia*, being a bad bitch is *good*."

"Oh. Thank you. I think. Back to what I need to tell you. Are you ready?"

"No. Tell me anyway."

I give her hands a reassuring squeeze before letting her have it. "Your father negotiated a marriage contract for you. You're meeting the man today. As in right now. His car just pulled up."

Lili falls still. She swallows. Other than that, she has no reaction.

"You took that better than I expected. Brave girl. So that's the bad news. The good news is that if I don't approve of his choice, the contract will be canceled."

She closes her eyes, exhales, and says faintly, "Holy fucking buckets of cat shit."

"Very creative. Anything else?"

She opens her eyes and stares at me in panic, clutching my hands so hard, it hurts. "I don't want to get married, *zia*."

"Of course you don't. You're sane."

Her voice rises. "No, I mean, I *can't* get married!"

She pulls away from me, crossing the room to stand defiantly in front of the big wooden wardrobe near her bed.

The thing is huge, a floor-to-ceiling antique made of shiny carved mahogany. It's always reminded me of the magical wardrobe from *The Chronicles of Narnia* that can transport a person to a land of talking animals and mythical creatures.

She props her hands on her hips and declares passionately, "I'd rather die than marry a man I don't love!"

From inside the wardrobe comes a distinct thud, as if a body just fell to the floor.

Afterward, there's silence.

I stare at my niece. She stares right back at me, her normally sweet brown eyes on fire with defiance.

I say calmly, "Lili?"

"Yes?"

"What was that noise?"

She lifts her chin and folds her arms over her chest. "What noise?"

I look at her mussed hair, her untucked shirt, her bare feet, and her rebellious expression, and know in my bones that we have a big fucking problem.

I cross the room in several long strides, headed to the wardrobe.

Lili tries to stop me, jumping in front of the wardrobe doors and pleading, but I push her aside and yank open the door.

And come face-to-face with the young man standing inside.

Hiding inside, between a mink coat and a beaded evening gown, shrinking back as far as he can against the back wall.

He's good-looking, I'll give her that. With liquid brown eyes, full lips, and a chest that could be featured on magazine covers, the boy is undeniably attractive.

He's wearing nothing but a pair of tight white briefs, through which his erection is clearly visible.

He can't be more than eighteen.

I slowly close the wardrobe door. Then I turn back to Lili.

She stands with her arms crossed over her chest and her lips pulled between her teeth, her shoulders rounded. If she had a tail, it would be tucked between her legs.

I say quietly, "You know what would happen if your father discovered this."

She doesn't bother with lame denials. She simply nods.

But it has to be said aloud. Things gain a certain gravitas when they're spoken.

"He would kill him, Lili. Whoever he is, the boy standing in this wardrobe would die. Slowly. Painfully. And most likely, you'd be made to watch."

Lili's eyes well with tears. She nods again, swallowing hard, her face contorted with misery. She whispers, "I know."

My heart breaks for her.

She's a fool. A young, reckless fool, but I understand her completely.

I was young once, too. I had dreams once, too. I had needs and desires and a wide-open future that stretched out ahead of me like a golden, glimmering dream.

Until all the beautiful dreams were destroyed by the cold, killing weight of a wedding ring.

I gather her into a hug, pulling her close and wrapping my arms around her shoulders.

"I don't know how you got him in here," I murmur into her ear, "but make sure no one sees you when you get him out. I can buy you ten minutes, maybe fifteen, but no more. Meet me in your father's office. Wear your blue dress, the one with the pearl buttons. Smile and look sweet. Let me do the rest. Deal?"

Nodding, she sniffles. "Deal. Thank you, *zia*."

Hearing voices drifting up from the courtyard below, I release Lili and hurry to the bedroom windows. I nudge aside the curtain and peer out.

Below on the circular driveway, a shiny black Escalade is parked in front of the fountain. Two of my brother's armed guards stand several feet away from a man I don't recognize.

He's big and barrel-chested, larger than both of the guards, but he has a friendly smile and manner. Clad in a black suit and shiny black oxfords, he cuts an imposing figure.

The guards and the man continue to speak. One of the guards pats him down, searching for weapons, then all three of them nod. The guards step back, the driver rounds the car and opens the passenger door, and another man clad in black exits the vehicle.

My breath catches.

This man is leaner than the first. Just as tall and wide-shouldered, but not as bulky. A quarterback to the other's defensive lineman.

His hair is dark gold. It looks carelessly styled, as if he dragged his fingers through it instead of using a comb. His beard is a darker shade, closer to bronze, covering an angular jaw. One of his nostrils is pierced with a small metal ring.

He's incredibly handsome. Half aristocrat and half bare-knuckled street fighter, he exudes a kind of raw, brutal power, unmistakable even from this distance.

Clearly visible above the collar of his starched white dress shirt is a spiderweb tattoo.

He glances up at the window and catches me staring.

Our eyes lock.

My heart skips a beat.

And in that instant, I know with dark certainty that I'm gazing into the eyes of the man who will tear my family to shreds.

TWO

SPIDER

I get only a glimpse of the woman in the window before the curtains fall back into place and she disappears, but the image of her is seared onto my retinas.

Dark hair, red lips, olive skin.

A black, low-cut dress.

Acres of cleavage.

And eyes that glittered silver in the afternoon sun like the flash of coins at the bottom of a wishing well.

She can't be Liliana, the lass I'm here to meet. I've seen pictures of her. She has a sweet, innocent face. A shy, lovely smile.

The woman in the window looks like she'd only smile if she were slitting your throat.

Mindful of the armed guards, I say in Gaelic to Kieran, "I thought the lass's mother died?"

Standing beside me, he follows my gaze and looks up at the blank window. "Aye. Why?"

"Who else lives here?"

He shrugs. "Dunno. From the size of the bloody place, probably a thousand people."

She's not a servant, that much I know. There wasn't a hint of servitude in those flashing eyes. She looked more like a warlord about to lead an army of soldiers into battle.

Irritatingly, I'm intrigued. The last thing I want to deal with is a strong woman. I learned the hard way that the stronger a woman is, the more likely she is to break a man's balls.

Or his heart.

"This way," says the guard nearest to me. He nods toward an arched opening in the brick wall that leads from the circular driveway into an interior courtyard.

Dismissing the thought of the mystery woman, I button my suit jacket and follow behind the guard as he leads Kieran and me away from the car. The other guard walks behind us. We're led through the lushly landscaped courtyard to a set of enormous carved oak doors, flanked on either side by towering marble columns.

The main house looms over us, three sprawling stories of beige limestone with elaborate balustrades and scrolled iron balconies, topped by a line of Roman centurion statues gazing down at us from a ledge on the red-tiled roof.

Inside the main foyer, the décor becomes even more ostentatious.

Naked cherubs frolic with hairy satyrs and woodland nymphs in colorful frescoes on the walls. Instead of one drop-crystal chandelier overhead, there are three. The floor is black marble, the carved mahogany furniture is edged in gilt, and my eyes are starting to water from the kaleidoscopic glare of stained-glass windows.

Under his breath, Kieran says, "Jesus, Mary, and Joseph. Looks like Liberace hurled his lunch all over the bloody place."

He's right. It's fucking awful.

I have to force myself not to turn around and walk out.

"Ah, Mr. Quinn!"

I turn to my right. A man approaches with his hands spread open in greeting.

He's fit, of average height, and somewhere around forty. His dark hair is slicked back with pomade. Wearing a navy blue pinstripe suit I can tell is custom made, a powder-blue tie with a diamond tie pin, a chunky diamond watch, and a gold pinky ring on each hand, he oozes wealth, privilege, and power.

His cologne reaches me before he does.

His smile is blinding.

I hate him on sight.

"Mr. Caruso, I presume."

He grabs one of my hands in both of his and pumps it up and down like he's a political candidate campaigning for my vote. "It's a pleasure to finally meet you. Welcome to my home."

"Thank you. It's a pleasure to meet you as well."

He hasn't stopped grinning or shaking my hand.

Ten more seconds of this shite, and I'll break those Chiclets teeth of his.

"This is my associate, Mr. Byrne." I extract my hand from Caruso's death grip and gesture to Kieran, who inclines his head respectfully.

"Sir."

"Mr. Byrne, welcome. And please, both of you, call me Gianni. I prefer if we're all on a first-name basis, don't you?"

I'd rather blind myself with acid, you wanker.

Kieran politely offers his name. I offer nothing. There's an awkward pause while Caruso waits, but he gets the hint and suggests we retire to his study to speak in private.

After what feels like a death march through miles of echoing corridors, we arrive at the study. It's probably larger than the law library at Notre Dame. We sit across from Caruso in a pair of leather chairs so uncomfortable, they had to be designed by sadists.

I haven't been here ten minutes, and I'm already regretting the fuck out of this.

Until *she* walks in the door.

Dark hair, red lips, olive skin.

A black, low-cut dress.

Acres of cleavage.

Not only cleavage, but long legs and an hourglass figure that would make any man stupid with lust.

If he wasn't too busy being turned to stone by the ice in her eyes, that is.

I've never seen an attractive serial killer, but I bet this is exactly what she'd look like.

"Mr. Quinn, Kieran," says Caruso, gesturing to each of us in turn, "this is my sister, Reyna."

I'm on my feet before I consciously make the decision to rise. Kieran stands, too, murmuring a greeting.

Reyna returns his hello and smiles at him, but when she turns her gaze to me, her smile dies.

She looks me dead in the eye and says, "Good afternoon, Mr. Quinn."

It sounds like *I'm going to eat your spleen for supper.*

I'm not sure whether to laugh or ask what her bloody problem is but go with a neutral greeting instead.

"Good afternoon to you, Ms. Caruso."

My gaze drops to the ring finger of her left hand. It's encircled by a small black tattoo, some wording in cursive too tiny to read from where I'm standing. "Or is it Mrs. something?"

I glance back up at her face to find her stony gaze turned to withering heat.

It's a look that could melt steel. I've never seen such hot, wordless fury. It makes the burning lakes of fire in the deepest pits of hell look like cozy bubble baths in comparison.

All that heat and hate she's blasting at me goes straight to my dick, which throbs in excitement.

Figures. The fucker only ever wants what he can't have.

When she doesn't answer my question long enough to make it uncomfortable, her brother answers for her.

"My sister is a widow."

"I'm sorry for your loss."

Like a switch has been thrown, all the heat in her eyes cools to ice. "Thank you."

She turns and walks stiffly to the windows behind her brother's desk, where she gazes out with her arms folded over her chest, sending a wintry chill over the courtyard below.

I'm surprised the windowpanes don't crackle with frost from her nearness.

Kieran and I share a look, then take our seats again.

Caruso says, "May I offer you a drink, gentlemen?"

Kieran declines. But I think I'm going to need liquid fortification to get through this meeting, so I accept.

From a bottom desk drawer, Caruso removes two cut crystal glasses and a carafe of ruby-colored liquor I assume is wine. By the time I've swallowed a mouthful of the bitter shite, it's too late.

It sears a path down my windpipe, singeing all my nose hairs in its wake.

Caruso smiles at me with toothy anticipation. "It's Campari. You've had it before?"

A shake of my head is all I can manage. If I tried to speak, I'd retch.

Over her shoulder, Reyna throws me a glance. She sees the look of disgust on my face and quickly turns back to the window, but not before she can hide her small, satisfied smile.

Maybe I'll burn the house down after I marry the daughter. The neighbors would thank me, no doubt.

Caruso's still rattling on about the Campari, how it's famous in Italy, blah blah fucking blah, but I interrupt him to ask when I'll meet Liliana.

"Oh. Yes. Liliana."

For a moment, he looks disoriented, like he lost the plot. But he pulls himself together and plasters on his shite-eating grin again. "She'll be right down."

He turns slightly toward Reyna for confirmation.

She remains silent but nods.

In his smarmy politician's way, Caruso says, "In the meantime, Mr. Quinn, allow me to extend my gratitude to both you and Mr. O'Donnell for the visit. I'm looking forward to getting to know both of you better as we join our families—"

"Let's not get ahead of ourselves," I interrupt, setting the glass of foul liquid onto his desk. "After I meet your daughter, we'll have plenty of time to talk about the future. As of right now, this deal hasn't been inked."

"Yes, of course," he says, his voice subdued. "Please forgive me."

Reyna turns from the window again, this time to send her brother an outraged, tight-lipped glare.

She's thinking he's a pussy for acting so weak. In his own bloody house, no less.

She's right.

I rise from my chair, gazing at her. "Actually, I'd like to speak with your sister first for a few minutes. Alone."

Caruso looks startled by the request.

Reyna looks like she's wondering where the nearest hatchet is so she can bury it in my skull.

I have no idea why this woman hates me so much, but it's starting to get annoying.

Regardless of what my dick thinks about her, she's pissing me off.

Kieran stands, already knowing my request will be granted. Caruso follows, sending a nervous look in Reyna's direction.

"Certainly. We'll give you a moment. Kieran, why don't I show you my collection of Fabergé eggs?"

With a straight face, Kieran says, "Can't think of anything better, mate."

They leave. As soon as the door closes behind them, I look at Reyna. "All right. You've obviously got something to say to me. Say it."

She turns from the window, blinking. "I'm sorry, I have no idea what you mean."

Her hand rests at the base of her throat. Her eyes are wide and guileless. She's the picture of innocence, and she's entirely full of shite.

I say, "Too late, woman. I've already seen the swamp witch you're trying to hide under that human skin suit you're wearing."

"*Excuse* me?"

"You're not as good an actress as you think."

She stares at me in blistering silence for a few seconds, then says icily, "Number one: don't call me 'woman' like it's a pejorative. It's not. Number two: if you're not bright enough to know what the word 'pejorative' means, ask your sidekick. He seems like he might have actually read a book once. Number three—"

"Will this take long? I've got a meeting to get through."

Her nostrils flare. Her lips thin. Her body trembles with impotent fury, and I think I'm starting to have fun.

She says tightly, "Number three: I have nothing to say to you."

"No?" I let my gaze travel the length of her body, down and back up again, relishing every dangerous curve. "Because it bloody sure seems like you do."

With what appears to be a huge effort of will, Reyna holds back whatever vitriol is burning the tip of her tongue. She smooths a hand over her dark hair, straightens her shoulders, and forces a tight smile.

"If you insist."

"I do."

"But it won't be pleasant."

"I doubt you're capable of pleasantries, wee viper."

Her eyes flash. "Insulting me won't win you any points."

"I'm not the one here who needs to win points."

That makes her even angrier. Her cheeks turn scarlet. "Why are you deliberately baiting me?"

"Because you're better than your brother," I say, holding her infuriated gaze. "You don't need to pretend to be something you're not. Now talk to me. I need to know why you're so angry, and I won't get the truth from him."

She's taken aback by the compliment and by my forthrightness, both of which she obviously wasn't expecting.

I get the feeling there isn't much she doesn't anticipate, so that's gratifying.

When she doesn't speak for too long, I prompt, "You don't like that I'm Irish."

"I'm not that petty or prejudiced," she says crossly. "I don't judge people by where they were born."

The way she says it, I believe her. She's genuinely insulted by the suggestion.

Which is interesting, considering most of her kin would rather be burned alive than befriend an Irishman.

Our families might do business together when it suits us, but it's a point of pride that we hate each other's guts.

"So what, then?"

She gazes at me in silence, measuring me up. Then she shakes her head.

"You know I can't possibly be honest with you. There's too much at stake for my family."

"There's too much at stake if you're not honest with me."

"Such as?"

"I'll walk out of here without meeting Liliana and without looking back, because there are plenty of other lasses in the Cosa Nostra who'll happily spread their legs for me and gain advantage for their families if she doesn't."

She stares at me. Her eyes are an unusual color, a pale greenish-gray, like a mermaid might have.

On a woman without the urge to murder me and bury my dismembered body in a shallow grave, they could be mesmerizing.

"I hate you for saying that."

"Add it to your list."

My smirk is the thing that finally breaks her.

"Fine. You want the truth? I'll give it to you. My niece is a good girl. She deserves so much better than to be sold off to the highest bidder without a damn say in the matter. She deserves so much better than a man who'd marry for money, position, or power. She deserves to be loved, cherished, and respected for everything she is. What she doesn't deserve is to not have a voice. Or a choice. Or a life of her own!"

"What makes you assume she won't have a life of her own if we're married?"

Reyna blinks. Once. Slowly. As if what I've just said is the stupidest thing she's ever heard.

"Or that I wouldn't respect her?"

She quirks her lips. "Now you're toying with me, Mr. Quinn."

"Spider."

After a beat of confusion, she says, "Pardon?"

"Call me Spider."

"Why on earth would I do that?"

"Because it's my name."

She laughs. It's a lovely sound. It also seems to surprise her, because she stops laughing abruptly, looking as if she has no idea how she allowed something so pleasant to pass her lips.

"Your name is . . . *Spider*?"

"Aye."

"Did your mother hate you?"

"No."

"But she named you after an insect?"

"It's a nickname. And spiders aren't insects."

She furrows her brows and stares at me.

"Why are you gaping at me like I've got a horn growing between my eyes?"

"Because I think I must've fallen out of bed this morning and gotten a concussion."

I chuckle. "That would explain why you're eatin' the head off me."

She opens her mouth to say something but closes it again. It feels like a victory, which pleases me, which then annoys me, because I shouldn't be feeling anything for this woman at all.

"Oh, look. The wee viper lost her words. Bet that doesn't happen but once in a donkey's years."

Through gritted teeth, she says, "If you'd speak English instead of idiot, we wouldn't be having this problem."

"Ooo, the fangs are out."

Her mermaid eyes glitter with malice. "Stop. Mocking. Me."

"Or what? You'll bury that letter opener in my chest?"

Her gaze slices to the blotter on her brother's desk, then back to me. The way her lips turn up at the corners, I can tell she's relishing the idea of stabbing me.

"Have a go. I'm in the mood for a good laugh."

"You wouldn't be laughing for long. I think this meeting is over."

"Sorry to break it to you, lass, but you're not the one in charge here."

That really gets her goat. A flush of red rises up her neck to merge with the burn in her cheeks. She says stiffly, "We obviously have nothing more to say to one another."

"Now that's the silliest thing you've said since you walked in."

"If you don't stop smirking at me, I won't be responsible for what happens."

I cock my head and consider her. "It's men in general, is that it? You hate men."

Her evil smile would look right at home on Satan himself. "Only a deserving few."

I know we could go back and forth like this until hell freezes over, so I decide to get to the point.

"I admire your loyalty to your niece, Ms. Caruso, but I want a wife, not a slave. If Liliana and I marry, she can do as she likes, as long as it doesn't interfere with my business or reflect badly on me."

She studies me, no doubt trying to decide if I'm lying. Then in a challenging tone, she says, "She could go to college?"

That surprises me. "Does she want to go to college?"

"She was accepted at Wellesley. It's an all-girls school—"

"I know what it is."

"—so you wouldn't have to worry about her being around other boys."

My gaze drops to her mouth. Her full, lush, scarlet mouth, which seems mainly to be used for hurling insults.

Pity. It would look beautiful stretched around the head of a stiff cock. I force myself not to imagine it's mine.

I say softly, "I'm not a boy."

When I lift my gaze to hers again, she looks flustered, but as if she's trying not to show it.

"What else? Might as well air all the dirty laundry while we're at it."

"All right, then. Do you drink?"

"Not to excess, if that's what you're asking."

"Do you have a temper?"

"All men have tempers."

She scoffs. "Don't I know it. What I mean is are you violent?"

"I'm second-in-command of the Irish Mob. What do you think?"

She swallows, glances away, then meets my gaze again. She moistens her lips. "I . . . I meant with women."

And here we have it.

I glance down at her left hand, at the circle of black ink on her ring finger, and finally understand what this inquisition is all about.

My voice low, I say, "I'm not your dead husband."

She starts as if she got an electrical shock. Her eyes widen. She steps back, then catches herself and stands in place, squaring her shoulders and lifting her chin.

"I don't know what you mean."

"That's the third time you've lied to me, wee viper. Don't do it again."

Our held gazes feel electrified, as if there's an invisible wire connecting us, sending bolts of energy snapping back and forth on a loop. We stare at each other in crackling silence while my dick stiffens and the vein on the side of her neck throbs.

In a carefully controlled, freezingly polite tone, she says, "I don't take orders, Mr. Quinn. I also don't address grown men by ridiculous nicknames, nor do I appreciate being given one. Though I have to admit the 'viper' is accurate, but the 'wee' is completely off mark. I'm as big as they come."

She turns and walks away, hips swaying. At the door, she stops and turns back to me. When she smiles, those mermaid eyes of hers glitter as icy cold as diamonds.

"You should also keep in mind that vipers are venomous . . . and they eat spiders for lunch."

She opens the door and walks through it with her head held high, leaving me standing alone in the study.

Alone and grinning.

For the first time since entering the house, I'm glad I came.

THREE

REY

*B*y the time Kieran and Gianni return from the salon where his Fabergé egg collection is kept in sealed glass cabinets, I've wrestled my boiling murderous rage down to a more manageable black fury.

I lived with black fury for most of my married life, so I know I won't be committing bodily harm to a smirking, arrogant Irishman in the immediate future.

I almost lost it when he mentioned the letter opener, however. I almost went full Jack the Ripper on his sorry ass.

It was an extremely close call.

"Everything all right?" Gianni inquires, nervously eyeing the open door of the study.

I exhale and try not to look like the axe murderer I feel like inside. "Yes. Mr. Quinn and I were finished speaking, so I thought I'd wait for you here. How did you enjoy the collection, Kieran?"

"Er . . ." He coughs into his hand. "It was dead brilliant."

Gianni beams, not understanding that if someone had handed

poor Kieran a noose during the tour, he would have seriously considered hanging himself from the nearest rafter.

"It really is, isn't it?" I say mildly.

We share a look. Kieran tries to hide his smile by chewing the inside of his cheek.

The sound of footsteps echoing over marble makes my pulse quicken.

Lili appears from around the corner of the corridor in the blue dress I instructed her to wear, her color high and her eyes darting. When she sees Kieran, her step falters, but she recovers quickly, plastering a smile on her face.

At her sides, her hands are clenched to fists.

Steady, tesoro. *You're not marrying anyone, especially not that bastard in your father's study.*

I still can't believe what he said. *"I'm not your dead husband."* As if the son of a bitch could read my mind.

I haven't been that shaken in years.

Lili's nervous gaze finds mine. I incline my head slightly, make a small motion with two fingers of my right hand, and watch her exhale in relief.

"Ah! Here she is now!"

Gianni holds out his arms. Lili hurries to him. He kisses her on both cheeks, then turns to Kieran. "Mr. Byrne, I'd like to introduce you to my daughter, Liliana. Lili, this is Mr. Byrne."

Smiling shyly, Lili murmurs a hello.

"Please, call me Kieran. Pleasure to meet ye, lass."

He extends his baseball mitt of a hand. Startled, Lili looks to me for guidance.

She's never touched a man outside her immediate family.

Excluding the boy hiding in the wardrobe in her bedroom, that is. Judging by his state of undress, they've been doing quite a bit more than touching each other's hands.

A problem I'll address as soon as I'm finished with this one.

When I nod, Lili hesitantly stretches out her hand. It's swallowed by Kieran's, disappearing into his meaty grip.

Looking somber and respectful, Kieran says, "Don't ye worry, lassie. He looks a fright, but he's a pussycat, I promise ye."

I stifle a snort. *Pussycat, my ass. Your friend's a rabid dog.*

Catching the expression on my face, Lili says, "Um . . ."

"Yes, I'm sure Lili will very much enjoy making Mr. Quinn's acquaintance. Won't you, *bambolotta?*"

Gianni says his nickname for her like a threat.

I'd like to punch him in the throat.

"Yes, Papa."

"Shall we go in, Reyna?"

I take one of Lili's hands. Her father takes the other. We lead her into the study between us, a lamb to slaughter.

God, how I despise the tradition of arranged marriage. Knowing she'll be spared the indignity of having to marry this particular Irish lout who calls himself an insect helps me feel better, but it will be someone else someday.

No matter how much I might want to, I won't be able to protect Lili forever.

In the Cosa Nostra, it's still the Dark Ages. Women are valued only for our ability to bear heirs, how well we can cook, or as cum dumpsters. We're not even allowed to vote.

It's enough to drive any woman mad.

Or to murder.

"Mr. Quinn," Gianni is saying, his smile so bright, it could be seen from outer space. "Please allow me to present my daughter, Liliana."

Spider—I cannot believe I allowed myself to call him that— looks at Liliana with no trace of emotion on his face. He could be looking at a block of cheese in a refrigerated deli case for all the interest he shows.

It surprises me. Lili's an extremely pretty girl. Most men start salivating the moment they set eyes on her.

Not this one. He merely looks her up and down and murmurs a dismissive, "Hullo."

Gianni glances at me in panic, but I can't look at him because I'm too preoccupied trying not to break into song.

It will be so much better for me if Quinn is the one to call off the contract.

Though Gianni agreed to allow me the final vote in the matter, I'd never hear the end of it. He'd alternate between sulking and lashing out until he found another suitor for Lili. He'd make my life hell. A price I'd willingly pay, but hell nonetheless.

If Quinn doesn't want Lili, however . . .

Maybe there is a God.

Ha! Don't be ridiculous.

"Lili, this is Mr. Quinn," says Gianni, his voice slightly too high. He clears his throat, then snaps, "Say hello."

Gazing demurely at his feet, Lili says, "Hello, Mr. Quinn. It's very nice to meet you."

When the Irishman only stands there looking at her, mute as a statue, his eyes narrowed, Gianni elbows her sharply in her ribs.

"I . . . I, um, hope we can get to know each other better. I look forward to . . . visiting with you. Um. Today."

Quinn is silent.

Gianni clearly would like to slit his wrists.

This is turning out to be a good day after all.

Giving Lili a little shove toward Quinn, Gianni says, "Why don't you two lovebirds have a nice chat over there on the sofa? Reyna and I will give you some privacy—"

"We can't leave them alone together," I interrupt, my voice hard.

The Irishman looks at me with a cocked eyebrow.

I smile my best don't-mind-me-I'm-only-a-silly-woman smile.

"Lili isn't allowed to be alone with a man. She requires a chaperone. Correct, Gianni?"

Since he's the one who made the damn rule, he can't contradict me.

He'd still like to smash something into my face.

"Correct," he says, forcing it past his teeth. "I'm sure you understand, Mr. Quinn. My apologies, but we're old-fashioned."

"Are you?" he drawls, looking at me.

His hazel eyes are half-lidded. His lips are faintly curved. He looks like he's enjoying some private joke that I'm the butt of.

The boiling rage I'd managed to beat down comes roaring back, searing a path along all my nerve endings and setting my face on fire.

He sees it and smiles.

Then he takes Lili by the arm—*by the arm! Like a possession!*—and leads her away from us without another word.

As soon as they're out of earshot, Gianni turns to me and hisses, "*Che palle!*"

"Cool your jets, brother. There's no way we could leave Lili alone with that . . ." I think of his hungry eyes, the way he looked at me earlier like he might eat me alive. "Predator."

Besides, I've already decided this marriage will happen over my dead body.

"We can't risk insulting him!"

I think of our little verbal sparring match and have to suppress a grin.

Too late.

Seething, Gianni adjusts his tie and glances over to where Lili and Quinn are seated on the velvet divan on the opposite side of the room. Her hands are folded in her lap, her legs are crossed at the ankles, and her gaze is directed at his feet, as if she's fascinated by his shoes.

His enormous, black leather oxfords, which he surely has to have custom-made because they're so large.

The size of them is startling. But now that I think of it, he has enormous hands, too.

My husband had small hands and even smaller feet. They were the size of a doll's in comparison. To go along with his teeny-tiny cock.

I refuse to consider what it might mean that the Irishman has feet the size of skis.

"Anyway," I say, flustered, "at least he's not wearing that awful face now. Did you see the way he looked at her when they were introduced?"

"I thought he might walk right out the door," says Gianni, shaking his head in disgust. "What the hell is wrong with him? Lili's beautiful!"

"Maybe he's gay."

"Pfft. Look at him. The way he carries himself, the way he swaggers . . ."

The way he looked at my lips.

I swallow, my mouth suddenly dry.

"That's a lion king," Gianni continues. "Not a *fanook*."

I wince. "Please don't use that word. It's extremely offensive."

Gianni rolls his eyes, muttering, "You and your love of pole smokers."

"That's even worse! For the love of God, Gianni, how about trying not to be such a bigot for once?"

He waves a hand dismissively at me. "Look, she's laughing. That's a good sign, *giusto?*"

Lili's tinkling laugh carries the distance between us and them. I can tell it's genuine, not forced. She isn't trying to be polite, she actually thinks whatever the Irishman said is funny.

He probably tried to tell her that he's intelligent.

At that moment, he looks over, catches me watching him, and winks.

He fucking winks.

Then he grins, revealing a set of perfect white teeth.

I'd like to carve out his liver.

Gianni mutters, "Well, he certainly seems to be in a better mood now." He blows out a hard breath and looks up at the ceiling. "Don't stare at him, for Christ's sake."

But suddenly it has become impossible not to stare at him. His laughing eyes are tractor-beams, dragging me in.

No one laughs at me. *No one.*

Ever.

They're all too busy avoiding my gaze, as if I'm Medusa and they're afraid they'll be turned to stone with one glance.

But this golden lion who's named after a bug and looks like a comic book superhero doesn't avoid my gaze. He grabs it and holds it hostage.

And he's definitely not afraid to laugh at me. In fact, I think it might be his new favorite thing.

I don't quite know what to make of that.

Maybe the Irish are all crazy? I haven't really known any before. All I think of when someone says Ireland are four-leaf clovers, leprechauns, and green beer.

Now I can add to that rude men with huge feet.

Though Kieran seems sweet. He isn't rude in the least.

I glance over my shoulder to find him out in the corridor, his hands shoved in his pockets and his nose scrunched as he gazes up at the frescoes on the wall.

He shakes his head and mutters, "Bloody daft altogether."

I turn away. It's too bad he's not higher up in the Mob's hierarchy. He might actually be tolerable as a spouse. But he seems to be a bodyguard or a driver, a rank too powerless to be of use to Gianni.

Though Quinn is only second-in-command, Gianni knows very well how quickly leadership changes in our world. Our own father was once the top dog, until a ruthless rival replaced him. All it would take is a single bullet to put Quinn on top.

Or take him out.

The thought makes me smile.

When I do, the Irish lout still staring at me licks his lips.

I rip my gaze away from his and wonder if I remembered to reload the gun in my nightstand after I cleaned it last week.

Lili and the lout spend another twenty minutes chatting while Gianni and I wait patiently near the door. Then he stands, gesturing for Lili to do the same.

"Here they come!" Gianni blurts as they start to walk toward us.

Lili's expression is calm. I can tell she's being careful not to show any emotion. She'll tell me everything about their conversation, of course, but for the moment all I can do is hope that it wasn't too horrible for her.

The Irishman's face is also emotionless, but there's a look in his eyes that I don't like.

If he asks for proof that she's a virgin right in front of her, I'll tear off one of his giant feet and beat him to death with it.

Jesus, Reyna. Get a grip!

Honestly, I haven't felt this unhinged in years. The man brings out the animal in me.

Thank God I made sure to get the final word on the approval of this match, because if he married into the family and I had to interact with him on a regular basis, I'd start climbing the walls and shrieking like a baboon.

As Lili approaches, I hold out a hand. She quickly comes to my side and takes it, gripping it tightly and standing so close, it's as if she wants to hide under my dress.

Quinn strolls to a stop a few feet away and looks at Lili from under his lashes.

Then he looks at Gianni.

Then at me.

His smile comes on slow and hot. Then he scowls, as if he's angry with himself for smiling.

"Mr. Caruso," he drawls, still looking at me. "Thank you for allowing Lili and me a moment to speak privately."

He's calling her Lili? Nobody calls her that but her family!

The nerve of this beast.

Gianni is so excited by the change in the Irishman's manner that he's practically shitting himself. "Of course! I trust everything went well?"

The Irishman lets him hang on his anxiety for a moment before nodding.

Shit.

Gianni exhales an audible breath of relief. Then he claps his hands together, making Lili jump. "Excellent!"

"If I may have a word with you, however. Alone."

"Certainly!"

In his rush to get Lili and me out the door, Gianni gives us both a shove. He regrets it when I growl at him, but not enough to dampen his excitement.

"Go. Go!" he hisses, waving us out. The moment we cross the threshold, he slams the door behind us, rattling the picture frames on the walls.

Kieran looks at my livid face and chuckles.

"I'll give ye lasses a wee bit of space. There's a painting of the baby Jesus 'round the corner that I'm dyin' to have a gander at." Whistling, he strolls away down the hall.

As soon as he's out of sight, I turn to Lili, give her a hug, and start apologizing.

"Are you okay, *tesoro*? I'm so sorry you had to go through that. I should've prepared you better for this moment. If only I'd known he was coming, we could've talked first. I could've given you some support—"

"I'm fine," she interrupts, pulling away. "It wasn't that bad, I promise."

I look at her in disbelief. "I know you're only saying that so I don't worry."

"No, I'm not. He was actually nice."

I almost topple sideways and fall to the floor. *"Nice?"*

She shrugs.

"Well, what did he say to you?"

"He asked me about my hobbies, what kind of music I like, my favorite food. Stuff like that. Oh, and college. He seemed really interested in what I wanted to study. When I told him criminal law, he laughed."

"He mocked you!" I say, heated.

"I don't think so. He said he liked the irony of it. He said he thought I'd make a good attorney."

Someone is going to have to assist me with getting my jaw off the floor.

"If he was so nice, why did you skitter over to me like a scared baby mouse?"

She pauses. "I mean . . . have you seen him? The guy's totally intimidating. Like big and . . . I don't know . . . *all that*. I thought I might get pregnant just sitting next to him."

Horrified, I make the sign of the cross on my chest. "Don't even say that word out loud."

"I know you have it handled, anyway. You have the final word about this, right?"

"Right."

"And it's obvious you hate him and you're not going to let Papa marry me off to him, right?"

"Right."

"So why are you so worked up?"

That is a very, very good question.

"I'm . . . not." I smooth a hand over my hair and smile at her reassuringly.

She rolls her eyes. "*Zia,* please. You're foaming at the mouth."

Dismissing that, I lower my voice and say, "Did you take care of the situation in the wardrobe?"

Lili's cheeks flush. She glances down and nods, smiling a secret little smile.

"How did you get him out?"

"The dumbwaiter."

I gasp. "You wedged that poor boy into the dumbwaiter? Did you break all his joints first?"

The flush in her cheeks deepens, and so does her smile. "He says it's worth it."

I say sarcastically, "I bet he does." Then something else occurs to me. "Oh, no. This isn't the first time, is it?"

She glances up at me and makes a face.

"Never mind, I don't want to know. Just promise me it's the last time."

When she hesitates, I say vehemently, "Lili, you cannot allow him back into this house. Your father will hang his stuffed head on the trophy wall in his study."

"I know," she whispers, her smile dying.

"Who is he, anyway?"

"Timo's son."

I have to think for a moment. "Timo? The gardener?"

"The pool man. Juan Pablo helps his dad clean the pool sometimes. That's how we met." Her secret smile reappears. "I was lying out getting sun in my yellow bikini."

Dear God. The daughter of a mafia don is having an affair with the Latino pool boy.

We're a telenovela.

I'm about to interrogate her about birth control when the door to Gianni's study opens. The Irishman and Gianni walk out.

"Thank you again for the visit," Gianni says, avoiding my eyes. "It was a pleasure."

"The pleasure was mine."

The Irishman stops in front of me and Lili. Formal and serious, he says to her, "I appreciate meeting you, Lili. Thank you for speaking with me."

She inches closer to my side. "You're welcome. And thank you, too."

The Irishman nods, then turns his gaze to me. His hazel eyes start to burn.

"And Reyna," he says, his voice so soft it gives me a shiver. "It's been . . . interesting meeting you." He extends his hand.

I look at it. A crocodile's toothy open snout would seem more inviting.

But I slide my hand into his and meet his gaze unflinchingly, because queens aren't afraid of dumb reptiles.

Or spiders, either.

"Goodbye, Mr. Quinn. And safe travels. The roads around here can get dangerous after dark."

I know he received the threat when he smiles.

He holds my hand and my gaze for a beat, then wipes the smile off his face and turns abruptly to Gianni. "I'll show myself out."

"Oh, no, I'll walk with you!" Gianni protests. But it falls on deaf ears because the Irishman is already striding away, his shoulders squared and his chin up, as cocky as a bullfighter.

When he disappears around the corner, I say flatly, "I don't approve. The marriage is off."

Sounding triumphant, Gianni says, "Unfortunately, *sorellina*, that's impossible."

Beside me, Lili stiffens.

My voice turns sharp. "What are you talking about?"

"The contract has already been signed. We did it just now . . . and set the wedding date as well. Lili and Mr. Quinn will be married next month."

Lili cries out in horror and slaps her hands over her mouth.

Infuriated, I step toward my brother. "You said I'd have final approval! You promised me I could choose!"

His lips curve upward at the edges. "You're not the only one in this family who's a good liar."

Then he turns on his heel and locks himself in his office, leaving Lili and me alone in the hallway, her anguished wails echoing off the walls.

FOUR

SPIDER

*T*he moment we pull out of Caruso's driveway, Kieran starts to laugh.

"What are you cackling about, you bloody gombeen?"

He snorts. "Only yerself, wearin' a face that would drive rats from a barn when ye first met Mr. Goodfellas back there. I thought ye were gonna slap him silly!"

"Aye. Almost did. I've never met such a tool in my life."

Kieran pounds a fist on the steering wheel in glee. "Ah, it was grand! Him almost soilin' his knickers every time you took a breath, bowin' and scrapin' like he had an audience with the bloody queen of England. Nearly had a nervous breakdown, he did. I can't wait to tell Declan all about it. Pure craic."

He sighs happily, shaking his head, then suddenly turns serious.

"Ach, but the sister was a fine thing, eh? A trifle scary, what with how much she wanted to outright slaughter ye, but fine nonetheless." He whistles low. "Wouldn't want to get on that woman's bad side, but I'd pay a pretty penny to see her in her kex! Got chubbed up just lookin' at her."

You're not the only one. My dick is still rock-hard.

"Put a sock in it, mate. I've got a brutal headache."

He ignores me.

"I feel awful bad for the wee *cailin,* though. The poor sweet lass. Imagine havin' the kind of father who'd trot out his own bairn to be sold like a prize pony!"

He makes a sound of disgust. "But I suppose it's their way, isn't it? Savages, the whole lot. Well, good riddance to those Italian buggers and that pile of shite they call home. Glad we're seein' the last of 'em."

"We're not seeing the last of them."

Startled, Kieran looks over at me. "Whaddya mean?"

"I mean I signed the contract. Liliana and I will be married in thirty days."

Kieran almost drives off the road. He shouts, "Are ye off your rocker?"

"Watch out for that light pole."

He veers sharply back to the center of the lane, cursing under his breath, then starts in on me again.

"Ye can't be serious, Spider! The idea of marryin' into that family is entirely daft!"

"Why is it daft?"

"Did ye not just attend the same bloody meeting I did? Caruso's a colossal lickarse! The sister wants to cut out yer tongue! They live in a place with scenes hand-painted on the walls of fairies and devils effin' each other!"

He's so worked up, I wouldn't be surprised if his head exploded.

"None of that matters. Lili's a sweet lass. She'll make a fine wife. And the terms of the contract are excellent. I'm going ahead with it."

I close my eyes and rest my head on the back of the seat so I don't have to see Kieran gaping at me.

I can still hear him, however, sputtering in protest.

"But . . . did you even like the wee lass? I mean . . . were you attracted to her?"

No. Which is why it's so perfect. The last thing I want is a wife I'm attracted to.

Like Reyna, for instance.

I'd never be able to focus on anything else if I were married to a woman like that. All I'd be able to think about would be that fine arse and those gorgeous tits and holding her down so I could shove my hard cock inside her beautiful wet cunt.

It's already difficult not to think about it, and I only met her an hour ago.

"Unbelievable," Kieran mutters.

"Don't say it."

"This is about Riley, isn't it?"

"I said, *don't say it.* Drop the bloody topic."

He ignores that as well, as I knew he would.

"Yer a right prick to marry a lass to try to get over a different one!"

My sigh is heavy. I open my eyes and look at him. "I'm not *trying* to get over her, I'm already over her. But thank you for your unsolicited opinion. Now shut your gob. You're making my headache worse."

Kieran huffs. "Jesus, God, and all the saints. Ye stubborn barmy bastard."

"If it makes you feel any better, arsehole, think of it this way: at least with me, the lass will have her own bloody life. If she married one of her own kind, she'd be chained to a stove in the kitchen. Or worse, chained to a bed and forced to be a baby-making machine."

He eyes me. "Uh-huh. And what about the baby makin' between the two of ye?"

"What do you mean?"

"I mean if yer not attracted to the lass, how're ye gonna get yer flute to play a tune for her?"

Maybe I'll think about her beautiful, homicidal aunt.

Jesus Christ, you bloody wanker, get control of yourself! What's the matter with you?

I close my eyes and rest my head on the back of the seat again.

There's a long, loaded pause. "Ye can't be tellin' me yer not gonna have sex with yer own wife."

"She's only eighteen fucking years old. I'd feel like a pedophile."

"So what's the plan? Ye'll wait until she's old enough to order a pint at a pub?"

When I remain silent, he heaves a sigh. "Yer the biggest eejit in all the land, and that's a fact."

"Listen, you tosser, it wouldn't do you any harm to show me a little more respect. Technically, I'm your boss now."

He cackles. "Oh ho! That's a mighty high horse ye got there, lad! Do ye want a wee crown to go along with yer lofty new position, my liege lord?"

I picture myself in a Shakespearean period outfit with pouffy sleeves and a belted tunic, a bejeweled crown on my head as I haughtily survey the peasants toiling over my land, and can't help but smile.

"Aye. Give me a bloody crown, would you? Even better, I'll borrow the diamond tiara Sloane wore when she married Declan."

"Why not go the full monty and borrow her red dress, too?"

"I do look smashing in red."

"Always knew ye were a little light in the loafers, mate," he says, still laughing.

"And what does it say about you that you're my best friend?"

"That I'm the second-biggest eejit in all the land, obviously."

"For once, we agree. Now shut the fuck up, you gas bag. I want to catch a few winks before we get back on the plane."

Try as I might, however, I can't sleep.

All the way to the airport, memories of furious greenish-gray mermaid eyes keep me awake and churning.

"So you went ahead with it."

"Aye."

Declan grunts. I can't tell what it means. I know he thinks I'm as daft as Kieran does to agree to an arranged marriage with a complete stranger, but I also know he's pleased as punch with the deal itself.

Which means everything to me. Not only is Declan O'Donnell the head of the Irish Mob, he's one of the finest men I've ever met. I wouldn't be alive today if it weren't for him. My loyalty to him is unshakable.

It's a small price to pay to marry a lass I don't love to prove it.

"And?"

"And what?"

"What's she like?"

I think about it for a moment. "Bright."

Declan makes a face. "Light bulbs are bright. What's the lass bloody *like*, Spider?"

We're sitting in his home office in Boston, drinking scotch. It's late, past midnight, but Declan doesn't ever seem to sleep much. When I texted him from Logan that we'd landed, he instructed me to come to his house after supper so we could talk.

Now here we are, talking, but I can't come up with much to describe my future wife.

I barely know the lass, for fuck's sake.

"What difference does it make?"

He snorts. "Only the difference between misery and happiness."

"Not everyone can have what you have with Sloane." I add drily, "Or would want it."

His blue eyes twinkle at the mention of his wife. "Are you saying my dear bride is a handful?"

"Handful doesn't even start to scratch the surface. Your woman's a bloody force of nature. Had us all eating out of the palm of her hand within a day after you kidnapped her."

His look sours. "I'll have you know, I was in complete control the entire time."

I chuckle. "Aye, it sure looked it as you were tearing out your hair and screaming."

His wife, Sloane, could easily rule the world if she wanted to. They met under unusual circumstances—he abducted her with a mind toward interrogation after she caused a shootout between our men and the Bratva (long story)—and he instantly fell under her spell.

As everyone does, man or beast.

When I said she was a force of nature, it was accurate. She's an erupting volcano, a category 5 hurricane, and a magnitude 10 earthquake, all wrapped up in a body made for sin.

Like someone else I recently met.

Who I am not fucking thinking about, goddammit.

Except I am, because Declan says, "Did you meet Caruso's sister?"

I glance up to find him looking at me with expectation. "Aye. Why?"

He lifts a shoulder. "Only that I've always wondered what the notorious Black Widow is like. Does she have the arse on her they say she does?"

"Whoa, hold on a minute. *Black Widow?*"

"Aye. According to the rumors, she killed her husband in cold blood." He takes a swallow of scotch. "Not that he didn't deserve it. Word is he was violent with her. By all accounts, he was a gigantic prick."

I think of Reyna's face when I asked if she was Mrs. something, the way she grew so angry. I think of how she was so upset about her niece not having a choice about getting married. How she scoffed when I asked what made her think the lass wouldn't have a life of her own after we were wed.

Then I wonder about that tattoo on her ring finger, the small black line of script in the place where a wedding band would be.

I feel a sudden powerful urge to know what that script says.

I say absently, "Aye, she's got the arse. And a pair of tits that could give a man a heart attack. And eyes like thunderclouds over a stormy sea."

After a moment lost in thought, I realize Declan hasn't said anything. I glance over at him to find him staring back at me with his brows raised, an amused expression on his face.

"Made quite an impression on you, did she, boyo?"

I scowl. "No."

"Really? You're sitting there spouting poetry about her dreamy eyes, and she didn't make an impression?"

I drag a hand through my hair and shoot the rest of my whiskey. Then I admit reluctantly, "Aye. But only because of how much she hated me."

"Hated you?"

I nod. "Wanted to douse me in petrol and light a match. And would've danced a jig as she watched me burn."

"Why? What did you do?"

"Excuse me, but I didn't do a bloody thing!"

"So she's just a bitch, then."

"Aye, she's a bitch!" I pause, thinking of our encounter. "Can't really blame her, though. She seems awful fond of her niece. Protective of the lass, almost like a mother. Couldn't have been easy for her to have some strange Irishman clomping about the place and grilling the lass like she was up for an important job interview."

"Which, technically, she was."

I exhale heavily, suddenly exhausted. "And she passed. Let's talk about something else now."

"Are you joking? I'm having far too grand a time watching you squirm. Tell me more about the Black Widow. What's her real name?"

I look at the ceiling, biting my tongue and knowing there's no way out of this but through. My voice comes out gruff. "Reyna."

"Hmm. Suppose it fits, what with her reputation."

"You lost me."

"Reyna means queen."

Queen. Why that should send such a jolt of lust through my veins, I have no idea.

I close my eyes and clench my teeth, trying to banish the thought of her.

My dick laughs at me and sends me a memory of her full, scarlet lips instead.

Suppressing a groan, I pour myself more scotch.

Watching me closely, Declan says, "You better not make that face outside this room, lad, or you'll be begging your new wife not to cut your prick off."

"I'm not making a face."

"Your cock is."

"Aye, well, he's not the boss of me."

"Let's hope not. Stick him where he shouldn't be, and you could start a war."

I say through gritted teeth, "I'd never do anything to risk that. I know how important this deal is to you. To us. I won't fuck it up over a piece of arse. Besides, like I said, she hates me."

Declan lowers his voice. "Funny thing about women, though, Spider, is that it's never as simple as it first seems."

"Don't I fucking know it," I mutter, then take another big swallow of scotch.

I have a feeling I'll be finishing the bottle.

FIVE

REY

For six entire days, I don't speak to my brother. I can barely look at him, either.

Which is lucky for him, because if I look at him long enough, I'm liable to scratch out his eyes.

The heartless bastard.

In the meantime, he's been floating around on cloud nine, bragging about the match to anyone and everyone who'll listen. He's already had a meeting with the heads of the other four families to announce the news. I'm surprised he hasn't taken out a full-page ad in the *New York Times*.

And Lili, my poor darling Lili, has been locked in her room, crying.

I'm concerned about how hard she's taking this.

Of course it's horrible being no more to your own father than a pawn on a chessboard to be moved around to his advantage in Mafia war games, but it's never been a secret that she'd be matched to a husband the way all the women in our family are.

Though I suppose cold, stark reality is always worse than the theoretical.

A man of flesh and bone is worse than the idea of one.

And an arrogant, swaggering Irishman is exponentially worse than them all.

I haven't been able to wipe the memory of his smug smirk from my mind. The way he looked at me. The way he *laughed* at me.

The way he pulled me in with his eyes.

Those long-lashed, half-lidded eyes that burned and brutally mocked me.

If he's anything less than an absolutely ideal partner to Lili, a Prince Charming she can eventually learn to tolerate if not love, I'm going to kill him.

Which basically means I'm going to have to kill him, because that insufferable toad of a man couldn't be less of a Prince Charming if he tried.

"Reyna! *Sei fuori!* You've ruined it!"

Startled out of my thoughts by my mother's sharp rebuke, I look down at the pot of boiling water in front of me. I'm standing at the stove in the kitchen with a wooden spoon in my hand and no idea how long I've been off in la-la land, brooding about Lili and the lout.

Long enough to overcook the pasta, evidently.

Leaning on her cane at the stove beside me, my mother crossly pokes me in the arm.

"Look at that soggy mess. Put it down the drain and start over."

"Sorry, Mamma," I say, sighing. "I'm preoccupied."

Her gaze stays on me as I pull on a pair of oven mitts and take the heavy stockpot over to the sink. She watches me as I dump the pasta, refill the pot with hot water, and bring it back to the stove. She continues silently watching as I salt the water and turn up the heat.

This hawkish focus is nothing new. My mother is like one of those creepy paintings in a haunted house whose eyes follow you everywhere, looking right at you no matter where you're standing.

Or where you try to hide.

"You're right to be upset," she says abruptly. "The Irish are despicable. To give one of them such a jewel is . . ." She curses in Italian, gesturing angrily.

"It's not that he's Irish. It's that he's a *canaglia* and a *mascalzone* with the manners of a barnyard animal. You should've seen the way he strutted around, pompous as a peacock."

A peacock with size-sixteen feet.

Shaking off the unwelcome memory, I continue. "I've never met anyone so horrid. He barged in here like he was Julius Caesar at the Colosseum, expecting us to shower him with rose petals and virgins."

Under her breath, my mother says, "Not that he'd find any of those in this house."

I look at her sharply.

She waves a hand at me like she's swatting away a fly. "Oh, don't give your own mamma such an evil glare. It's not like I'm a *ragazza stupida,* you know." She taps her glasses with a finger and waggles her eyebrows. "I see what goes on around here."

I know she isn't talking about me, because literally nothing is going on around here where it concerns me.

Unless she found my collection of sex toys and erotica.

No, that can't be it. She'd already have had a stroke and keeled over dead if she found those.

"I don't know what you mean."

She smiles. "No? You haven't seen that pretty boy Lili sneaks into her room at all hours of the day and night?"

I'm scandalized. I simply can't believe the matriarch of the

Caruso crime family would allow her granddaughter to have illicit liaisons in the house, let alone with the son of the pool man.

"You *knew* about that? Why didn't you say anything?"

"To who? Your brother? And get the poor boy shot?"

"To *me*!"

"Why, so you could ruin all her fun by putting an end to it?"

"Yes!"

She clucks. "The *piccolina principessa* is going to be married to the same idiot for the rest of her life, Reyna. She deserves to live a little first."

When I only stand there staring at her in disbelief, she says more softly, "It's one of my great regrets that I didn't allow the same freedom for you."

After a moment of profound shock, I say faintly, "Please hold. My brain has melted."

She turns and makes her way to the kitchen table, hobbling with the help of her cane, then drops into a chair and sighs.

Dressed all in black—as all widows in the family dress, regardless of how long their husbands have been dead—she looks much older than her sixty-five years.

She's never colored her gray hair and wears it shorn close to her head like a man's. The style of dress she wears is frumpy and unflattering. She's not overweight, but she refuses to do anything whatsoever to make herself even slightly attractive, including wearing makeup or updating her eyeglasses to a style from this century.

After my father was killed, she simply gave up.

I know it wasn't from grief. I think it's that she never wanted another man to notice her again.

Life with my rageaholic Sicilian father was hell for all of us.

Especially after she was diagnosed with MS and he brought his twenty-two-year-old mistress to live in the guest cottage so he didn't have to "fuck a cripple," as he put it.

Watching my mother hold her head high and grit her teeth through all his cruelty and indiscretions taught me to have the same strength when my own husband turned out to be worse than my father ever was.

So much worse, I never could have imagined it.

Gazing at me fondly, Mamma says, "You're the best thing I've done with my life, *stellina*. I'm very proud of you."

I have to turn back to the pot on the stove so she doesn't see the water welling in my eyes.

My mother giving me a compliment is an event as rare as a UFO sighting.

I murmur a thank-you, staring at the water and willing it to boil so I'll have something to do other than struggle with this awful feeling in my chest.

Anger is so much easier for me to deal with than tenderness.

Anger gives you armor. Tenderness strips you naked to the bone.

"You would've made an excellent mother," she continues in a thoughtful tone. "It's a pity you couldn't have children. Or should I say . . . made sure you couldn't."

When I glance at her, startled all over again, she chuckles.

"I don't blame you, *tesoro*. Enzo as a father?" She shudders. "You were smarter than I was. Not that I'm saying I regret my children, mind you. You're the love of my life." She thinks for a moment. "Your brother, meh."

I laugh. "I know you don't mean that. He's the firstborn and a boy. It would be a crime punishable by death in Sicily if you didn't love him the most."

She shrugs. "Then it's lucky we're not in Sicily."

I scoff. "Oh, Mamma. You've been at the wine again."

"No, but that reminds me," she says, perking up to look over at the wine cooler next to the refrigerator. "How about a nice Pinot Noir?"

"Since when do you drink anything but Chianti?"

"Since I started watching this charming young man on You-Tube with his own channel all about wine."

"You're watching YouTube?"

She nods as if her deciding to get on the internet isn't as monumental as the moon landing. Up until last year, she'd still been using a rotary phone.

"Pinot is his favorite. He drinks it by the gallon. Let's have some with the tagliatelle."

"Wow. Wonders never cease. Okay, Mamma, you're on."

I head to the wine fridge, select a bottle, and bring it over to the counter to open it, when a man walks through the kitchen door.

It's the Irishman.

My heart clenches. My face goes hot. I draw in a sharp breath and freeze.

"Hullo," he says in a throaty voice, gazing at me.

Past my shock, I manage to say, *"You."*

He sends me his signature smirk. "Aye. Me."

He's holding a wrapped bouquet of white roses. He's wearing a black suit again. Armani, by the looks of it. His tie and shirt are black, too. On any other man, that much black would make him look like a game show host or an undertaker.

This man in head-to-toe black looks like a runway model who moonlights as an assassin, the smug fucker.

And oh, sweet Jesus have mercy on my soul, I am not noticing how tight the suit is around his crotch area.

I do not see that substantial bulge.

I do *not.*

I say stiffly, "What are you doing in my kitchen?"

His heated gaze takes a leisurely trip over my body, head to toe and back again. He licks his lips.

"I was in town. I wanted to see Lili."

I exhale hard and set the bottle of wine on the counter with such force, my mother jumps in her chair.

"If you'd like to see Liliana, Mr. Quinn, you'll have to make arrangements prior to showing up at our home unannounced. Regardless of how things are done in the Mob, this family has certain standards of conduct."

"Oh, come now, lass," he chides, enjoying my agitation at his sudden, unwelcome appearance. "A man should be able to see his fiancée without penciling it in on a calendar."

Knowing there's nothing I can do to stop him from showing up any damn time he likes, he smiles.

He's so lucky I don't already have the wine opener in my hand. He'd have a corkscrew shoved up his ass before he could speak another word.

Into the ensuing silence, my mother says, "Hey. Irish."

Quinn looks at her. Judging by his expression, he's surprised to see someone else in the room. She points to a cabinet behind him.

"The vases are in there. When you're done arranging the flowers, you can open the wine." She smiles. "If you can pry it out of Reyna's hand, that is."

"Pardon my manners," Quinn says. "I didn't see you sitting there."

"I know. You were too busy annoying my daughter."

"Mrs. Caruso?"

"The one and only." She chuckles. "Well, now. The rest of them are worm food."

God, my mother has a dark sense of humor.

Quinn crosses the kitchen and extends his hand to her. He says respectfully, "It's my honor to meet you, ma'am. I'm Homer."

I nearly fall face-first onto the kitchen floor.

First, because Quinn is acting like a human for once—not the ape I know him to be—and second, because . . . *Homer?*

Mamma accepts his outstretched hand. He clasps it gently for a moment, inclining his head, then releases it and straightens. She gazes up at him through her glasses with narrowed eyes.

She says bluntly, "What kind of name is that for an Irishman?"

He doesn't take offense. He only chuckles. "My mother was an art student. Winslow Homer was her favorite artist."

Mamma cackles. "Good thing it wasn't Edvard Munch."

"If I tell you the name everyone else knows me by, you'll laugh even harder."

"What is it?"

"Spider."

She doesn't laugh. Instead, she looks over at me. "You didn't tell me he was a comedian."

"He's not," I say through gritted teeth. "But he is leaving."

"Not before he pours me my wine!"

Quinn's smug smile reappears. "And puts the flowers in water."

I mentally telegraph a murder threat to him, which he ignores, turning instead to the cabinet behind him to select a vase from the collection of crystal.

As my mother and I watch him, he brings the vase and the flowers to the sink, tears the plastic and tissue paper wrap from the bouquet, fills the vase from the tap, then says calmly, "Your pot's boiling."

I look over at the stove. The pot of water is at a full rolling boil, about to spill over the edges.

Cursing, I abandon the bottle of wine and jump over to the stove. I switch off the heat, turn back to Quinn, and demand, "How did you get in here?"

"Through the front door."

Cocky bastard. "I mean who let you in?"

"The housekeeper. Nice lass. Bettina, I believe? Couldn't have been sweeter."

I bet she couldn't. One look at Mr. Supermodel Assassin here and she most likely fainted.

"Why didn't she announce you?"

"I told her I wanted it to be a surprise." He sends me a smoldering glance. "Surprise."

I feel that look all the way down to my toes.

Flustered, my cheeks hot, I snap, "I hate surprises."

Mamma mutters, "Somebody around here is about to get a surprise in the form of a smack if I don't get my wine soon."

Quinn drops the flowers into the vase of water, fusses with them for a moment until he's satisfied they're just so, then crosses to the counter and picks up the bottle of Pinot Noir.

He examines the label. "Hmm."

Mamma says, "I'm sorry we don't have any beer to offer you."

His smile is faintly amused. "I don't drink beer."

"Then why are you looking at the wine like that?"

He glances up at her. After a pause, he says, "I don't want to insult you by telling you the truth."

"It's never stopped you before," I say, furious that I can't get him out of my kitchen.

He smiles at me, his hazel eyes burning. "Corkscrew?"

He managed to make that sound lewd, the pig.

I point to the drawer next to the dishwasher, then say, "Liliana is at the movies with her girlfriends tonight, so unfortunately, you won't be able to see her. And my brother is in the city for business. If you call tomorrow morning, we can set up a time for later in the week."

"The movies?" Quinn repeats.

"Yes," I lie, nodding. "You've heard of feature films, I presume? Perhaps they don't have them in Ireland. Too many other important things to do, I imagine, what with the sheep shearing and the river dancing and all the dart-throwing championships down at the local pub. But she goes every Thursday. She won't be home until late. So you should leave. Now."

He gazes at me in silence for a while, then says, "Sea Smoke."

I blink. "Excuse me?"

He turns his gaze to my mother. "If you like Pinot Noir, you should try Sea Smoke." He holds up the bottle in his hand. "It's better than this cheap bloody shite."

My mother says, "My YouTube boyfriend drinks that. It's too pricey for me, though."

"I'll buy you a bottle."

She brightens, clapping her hands. "Ah, *grazie mille*. I can't wait!"

Am I having a stroke? What the hell is happening?

"Mr. Quinn—"

"Spider." He smirks at me. "I'd let you call me by my real name, but you haven't earned the privilege yet."

I gather all the raging anger in my body and concentrate it into my glare, which I direct to a superheated laser focus on his handsome, hideous face.

He smiles wider and opens the wine.

SIX

REY

Mamma and I sit with my archenemy at the kitchen table, watching in silence as he devours his pasta.

I've never seen a man eat like this. He fell on his plate and started inhaling the tagliatelle with meat sauce like he'd been adrift at sea in a raft for six months.

I'm equal parts fascinated and disturbed.

"Mmmpf," he mutters around a mouthful, rolling his eyes heavenward and chewing lustily. "God almighty. Mrs. Caruso, this is the best bloody food I've had in my entire life."

"Looks like the *only* food you've had in your entire life. And thank Reyna, she's the cook."

He stops eating long enough to glance at me in surprise. "You made the meal?"

As if he wasn't sitting right in that damn spot watching me the entire time.

"From scratch," Mamma supplies when I only sit there glaring daggers at him. "The pasta, the Bolognese, *and* the focaccia. And that Caesar dressing on your salad is homemade, too. Reyna does all the cooking for the family. Once my husband died, I hung up my apron for good."

Quinn grunts.

Somehow, it encapsulates his disbelief that I'm able to put together an edible meal along with an acknowledgment of my father's passing. Though I shouldn't be surprised, considering most of his vocabulary is probably composed of such nonverbal expressions.

Barnyard animals aren't known for their witty discourse.

I take another swig of the Pinot from my glass. My plate of food remains untouched. My stomach is unsettled and my armpits are damp, and I can't wait for him to finish his supper so I can smash his plate with a hammer and dump it into the trash, ensuring no civilized person can ever eat from it again.

That fork he's using will have to go, too.

There isn't enough bleach in all the world to clean his germs off it.

Tearing into a piece of focaccia bread with his teeth, Quinn says, "Does Lili cook?"

Mamma glances at me, waiting to hear how I'll handle the question.

I go with a neutral-sounding "Yes."

"This well?"

I hesitate, not wanting to admit that Lili has been banned from the kitchen for starting not one but *two* fires, one in the microwave and one on the stove.

"She's learning. I'm sure in time she'll master it. If you recall, she's only a teenager."

I say the last part acidly. I'm gratified to see it gives Quinn pause.

He looks at me steadily for a moment, a lump of bread bulging in his cheek, then chews and swallows, wiping his mouth with his napkin.

He sits back in his chair, takes a swallow of wine, then says somberly, "Aye."

Then he exhales heavily, as if he's troubled by her age.

Mamma shoots me another wordless glance, her eyebrows raised.

Before I can pounce on the opportunity to shame him for wanting to marry a child, he says to me suddenly, "How old are you?"

Mamma cackles. "Ah, *gallo sciocco,* you have a death wish, *sì?*"

Setting my wineglass down carefully on the table—so I don't break it—I hold his penetrating gaze and say, "What charming manners you have, Mr. Quinn."

"Nearly as charming as yours, Ms. Caruso."

"I'm not the one asking impolite questions."

"Why is it impolite to want to know my future aunt's age?"

"Aunt-in-law," I correct, wanting to wash my mouth out with soap just hearing it. "And it's *always* impolite to ask a woman's age."

"As impolite as it is to shower a new relative with such . . ." He regards my withering gaze and my stiff posture. "Warmth and hospitality?"

Mamma says, "Don't take it personally, Homer. She doesn't like anyone."

"I like some people just fine!"

She looks at me. "*Tch.* Name two."

The Irishman grins, leaning over his plate and setting his elbows on the table. He props his chin in his hands and says, "Thirty-eight."

My inhaled breath is sharp and loud. "I am *not* thirty-eight years old."

He pauses to take a leisurely, half-lidded inventory of my face and chest. "Thirty-six?"

I say flatly, "That butter knife can also be used as a carving tool."

"Five? Four?"

"I think it's time we called it an evening, Mr. Quinn." I shove my chair out from under me and stand.

He lounges back in his chair and smiles, folding his hands over his stomach and stretching out his legs, the very picture of the lord of the manor at ease.

"But we haven't had dessert yet."

Mamma—the traitor—seems to find the entire exchange highly amusing. In fact, she seems to find Mr. Quinn himself highly amusing, something that outrages me.

She's the one who said the Irish are despicable!

I grit out, "We don't have any dessert."

"Except for that panna cotta you made this morning," says Mamma. "There's some tiramisu left, too."

Quinn's smile blossoms into a huge grin. He flashes all those nice white teeth at me, not knowing or caring that he's in mortal danger.

I glare at my mother. "How *kind* of you to remember, Mamma. Isn't it time for you to go to bed?"

She looks out the kitchen window, then back at me. As it's only six thirty and the middle of August, it's still light outside. But since she's chosen the wrong side of this fight, she needs to leave.

She stands. Quinn stands, too.

"It was lovely to meet you, Mrs. Caruso," he says.

His smile appears to be genuine. Not the shit-eating, fuck-you smile he's always gifting me.

Mamma says, "Nice meeting you, too, *gallo sciocco*. Good luck."

She hobbles out of the kitchen, chuckling to herself.

Smug, Quinn looks at me. "Took to me like a duck to water, don't you think?"

I say flatly, "It's the dementia."

"No, lass, your mother's as sharp as a tack."

"Which is why she kept calling you a goofy rooster."

"Admit it. She likes me."

"She likes maggot cheese, too."

He grimaces. "What the bloody hell is maggot cheese?"

"Look in the mirror and find out."

He gives me a sour look, then takes his seat again and glances pointedly at the refrigerator.

"Mr. Quinn, I'm not serving you dessert. Please, go now."

"Why would I want to leave when we're having so much fun?"

"You're as much fun as gangrene."

"Ouch."

He pretends to be serious, but I can tell he's trying not to laugh.

I grab my plate of uneaten pasta, stride over to the sink, and dump it down the drain. I run the water and the garbage disposal at full blast, hoping the racket will deafen him.

He leans over the table, picks up my empty glass, and refills it with Pinot. Over the din of the garbage disposal, he shouts, "I'll try the panna cotta *and* the tiramisu. And I love mango ice cream, if you've got it." He smirks. "If not, I'm sure you could whip up a batch, since you're such a walloping good cook."

I turn off the water and the disposal, grip the edge of the sink, close my eyes, and take a deep breath, praying for strength and for the ceiling to give way and collapse onto his head.

When I open my eyes, Quinn is staring at me with such burning heat, my heart flip-flops.

"Are you afraid to be alone with me, lass?"

"Don't be ridiculous."

"You sure? You look a bit flustered."

"This is how I always look before I throw up."

He pulls his lips between his teeth. His eyes sparkle, and his chest starts to shake.

He's laughing at me again.

What a big fucking surprise.

"Mr. Quinn—"

"Spider."

I glare at him, heat burning my cheeks and my heart pounding. "I will never call you that stupid nickname. Now please. *Go.*"

He tilts his head and examines my expression. His eyes are still hot, but there's something soft in them, too. Something . . . unexpected.

He points at my empty chair and orders, "Sit."

My back stiff, I answer through clenched teeth. "I don't respond to commands. I'm not a dog."

"God knows you're not," he says hotly. "Now get your fine arse in that chair, woman. Don't make me tell you a third time."

That sounded distinctly like a threat. I snap, "Or what?"

He growls, "Or I'll take you over my knee and teach you some bloody manners."

This bastard just threatened to spank me!

My heart takes off into a thundering gallop. My hands start to shake. My breath is shallow, and there's a high-pitched ringing in my ears.

I can't remember the last time I was this furious.

Oh, wait. Yes, I can.

The last time he was in my house.

I glance longingly at the wooden block of sharpened kitchen knives on the counter.

Quinn says softly, "Reyna."

I look at him. Big, masculine, and handsome, taking up all the space in the room. His gaze like a forest fire and the faintest hint of a smile hovering on his full, sculpted lips.

Suddenly, I can't wait to get out of here.

But I already know enough about the Irishman to realize that the only way that will happen is if I give him what he wants first.

So I sit.

I grab my glass of wine and guzzle it.

Then I look at him in nervy silence, waiting.

He sits there and smolders back at me, a whirlwind of unspoken questions in his eyes.

I'm about to jump back up and run out of the room when he says abruptly, "Why do you live with your brother and niece?"

"Why do you have a spiderweb tattoo on your neck?"

It's out before I can stop it. I had no idea I was curious about that stupid tattoo until just now.

He sets his forearms on the table and leans closer. "I'm the one asking the questions."

"I know you think you're in charge of everyone in the universe, Mr. Quinn, but you're deluded."

"I'm not in charge of everyone in the universe. Only everyone in this house."

God, how I hate him for that. How I hate his dominating confidence and his pathological maleness, his assumption that he—and only he—is the one in control.

I hate it more than anything that he's right.

Because in our world, men are in charge.

And alpha males like him are the very top of the food chain.

My poor sweet Lili. He's going to eat her alive.

"I won't hurt her," he says suddenly, startling me.

"What?"

"I said I won't hurt her. I know you're worried about that, but I've never laid a hand on a woman in my life." He laughs softly. "Well, not in anger."

I look away, unnerved that he can read my mind so easily, and also by the vivid image my mind unhelpfully provided me of him on top of a naked woman, thrusting between her spread thighs as she arches and cries out in ecstasy.

My face flushes hot again. It seems to be happening with concerning frequency.

"Let's try again. Why do you live with your brother and your niece?"

I flatten my hands on the tabletop and stare down at them as I gather the necessary mental armor to answer.

"When my husband died, I . . ." I stop to clear my throat. "I'd never lived alone before. I went straight from my father's house to Enzo's. After the funeral, I went home to that big, empty house, and I couldn't stand it. The awful silence."

And the awful memories. Lurking goblin memories that haunted me at every turn.

"So I packed a bag and came here. I've been here since. I'll get a place of my own eventually. I just . . . haven't yet."

"How long have you been a widow?"

"Three years."

Three blissful, broken-bone-and-bruise-free years.

I notice my hands shaking, so I pour myself the last of the wine from the bottle and gulp it down. Quinn watches me silently, his gaze intense.

"How long were you married?"

"Too fucking long."

"And how long is that?"

I draw a steadying breath and glance at the ink on my ring finger. It's black and comforting, a visual reminder of the promise I made to myself that no man would ever own me again.

"Fourteen years."

"That's a long time."

To spend in hell.

Aloud, I say, "It felt longer."

Neither of us speaks after that for a while. Then he says, "Tell me about the rest of the family."

"Like what?"

"Like how many of you are there?"

"It's just me, Mamma, Lili, and Gianni."

"No grandparents?"

"All dead."

"Cousins?"

"There's no one. Just us."

"I thought all Italian families were big."

"I thought all Irishmen were drunks."

He chuckles. "You have a smart comeback for everything, don't you?"

"It's easy to win a war of words when your opponent is a donkey."

Surprised by how viciously that came out, I look up at Quinn. "I'm sorry. That was rude."

But he doesn't seem offended at all. He's chuckling again, shaking his head.

"Why are you laughing?"

"I've been called a lot of things, but a donkey's a first."

I'm taken aback by his reaction. If Enzo were sitting in his place, my jaw would already be broken.

"Well . . . it's not that it's untrue. I just shouldn't have said it."

He laughs harder.

Despite my utter hatred for him, I smile.

My smile fades when he rises from his chair, crosses to the wine fridge, and removes another bottle.

"What are you doing?"

"What does it look like I'm doing?"

"Like you're going to open another bottle of wine."

"Aye. And here I thought you were nothing but a pretty face and a forked tongue. You can actually make correct assumptions, too."

Something about the familiar way he's teasing me, the way he's smiling at me from under his lashes and especially the thing about my pretty face, sets my teeth on edge all over again.

"How about my assumption that you're going to make my niece's life hell? Is that correct?"

He pauses before saying softly, "Not every marriage is awful, lass."

I scoff. "Really? What fairy tales have you been reading?"

He grabs the corkscrew from the counter, peels off the top of the label from the bottle, and opens it with swift efficiency. Then he crosses to the table and refills my glass.

Standing over me, he's all heat and muscle, a powerfully potent male presence in a black Armani suit.

"Don't know how many times I'll have to repeat this, but I'm not your dead husband."

I glance up at him. His expression is serious. His hazel eyes are soft and warm.

My mouth goes dry. My mind goes blank. I can't think of a single thing to say to him.

He picks up the wine and hands it to me. "Here. Drink this. It'll give you something to do with your mouth other than spit venom at me."

He glances at my mouth and licks his lips.

This is when I realize I'm at eye level with his crotch.

And that enormous bulge straining the seam of his trousers.

Dear God. I'm going to have to let Lili borrow my Greedy Girl XL dildo. That pool boy she's been fooling around with is no match for this monster.

Breaking out in a sweat, I grab the wine from him and drink the entire glass in one go.

He drawls, "Do I make you nervous, wee viper?"

I cough violently, my eyes watering. "You make me wish for a stroke."

"Why do you dislike me so much?"

"Because you have the personality of a festering wound."

His lashes lower. He considers me in blistering silence for a moment, then leans down and murmurs into my ear, "Liar."

He inhales deeply against my neck, raising goose bumps all along my arms.

I stiffen. He exhales, making a low sound of pleasure deep in his throat.

Then he straightens and stares down at me.

"Tell Lili I'll be back tomorrow at five o'clock. Or would you like me to go up to her bedroom and tell her myself?"

Startled, I glance up at him to find his smirk back in place and his hazel eyes mocking.

He knows she's here. He's known the entire time.

Without another word, he turns on his heel and walks out of the kitchen, leaving me sitting alone at the table with my heartbeat throbbing and a million questions swimming in my head.

The most important one being that if he knew Lili was in the house all along, why did he stay and eat supper with me?

"Oh my God," I say aloud, horrified. "Does that son of a bitch think he's getting a two-for-one special?"

SEVEN

SPIDER

She's smart, she's sexy, and she's got an arse on her I'd like to bite, spank, and fuck.

Even worse, every time I look at her too long, my dick gets hard as a rock and my mouth starts watering.

That settles it.

I'm never speaking to Reyna fucking Caruso again.

EIGHT

REY

I wait until morning to tell Lili the bad news that her lecherous pig of a fiancé will be paying her a visit.

She takes it like any rational female should and starts crying.

"*Zia,* please!" she wails, clinging to my arm. "Can't you do something? Can't you get Papa to call it off?"

"If I could, I already would have. Now dry your eyes. We've got to talk, and I need you to pay attention."

I shake her off and start to pace the length of her bedroom, over to the dresser and back to the door, wringing my hands in anxiety.

I didn't sleep at all last night. I lay wide awake in bed, staring at the ceiling, remembering the way that beast Quinn sniffed my neck like I was a candy bar.

And that *noise* he made.

That low, rumbling, masculine sound of pleasure that came from deep in his throat.

I'm shivering right now just thinking about it.

In disgust, of course. The man is absolutely revolting.

"Okay, here's the thing." I pause to gather my chaotic thoughts. "Quinn is a man. Right? A very masculine sort of man. He's very . . . manly."

What the hell are you saying? Pull yourself together!

Sniffling, Lili sits on the edge of her bed and chews on her thumbnail as she watches me pace.

"He's going to be difficult to handle. Impossible, really. He's obviously extremely stubborn. And used to getting his own way."

And arrogant. And gorgeous. And hung like a damn horse.

I turn and pace the other way, dragging my hands through my hair in aggravation.

"And unfortunately, *tesoro* . . . you should prepare yourself for the reality that he won't be faithful to you."

"Who cares if he's faithful? I'm going to stab him to death in his sleep!"

I pull up short and stare at her in horror. "Don't ever let me hear you speak such nonsense again."

"Why not? You killed Uncle Enzo!"

I close my eyes, draw a breath, count to ten, then open my eyes again. I say calmly, "Do you want to die in prison?"

"Did *you*?"

I was willing to, if it meant I'd never be whipped bloody again.

Instead of saying that, I say, "I didn't kill my husband."

"Quit lying, *zia*! Everybody knows! Why do you think they're all so scared of you?"

"People are scared of any woman who speaks her mind and doesn't put up with their bullshit. Now, listen. You said Quinn was kind to you when you spoke. He took an interest in your life. And I think we may be able to convince him to allow you to go to college. So though he has the charm of a rotting carcass, he might prove to be endurable."

Who am I kidding? Her life's going to be one long nightmare Groundhog Day.

Lili leaps to her feet and cries passionately, "I *can't* marry him, *zia*!"

My heart goes out to her, but I can't waver on this. I make my voice firm. "I completely understand your feelings, but the contract is inescapable. If you don't marry him, it will ruin the family. Your father's life will be over. Literally, I mean. The Mob will put a bullet in his head for the disrespect."

I pause, hesitating to tell her this and upset her even more. But she needs to know exactly what's at stake.

"They'll do something terrible to you, too. Something *worse* than death, especially if Quinn discovers you're not a virgin. We'll talk about how you can fake that later, but the bottom line is that you'll marry the Irishman."

"No, I won't! I'm in love with Juan Pablo!"

This is when I notice the small dark bruise on the side of her throat.

Except it's not a bruise. I know a love bite when I see one.

Feeling sick, I stride over to the wardrobe and throw open the doors.

It's empty.

Lili is sobbing behind me. "I'm in love with him. I don't care about the stupid contract or what anybody thinks. I'd rather die than marry anyone else. *I'd rather die!*"

I turn and look at her tearstained face. At the agony in her eyes. At all her shaking, frenzied fervor, and feel a twinge of jealousy.

At least she had this. At least she loved once. The memory of what she shares with Juan Pablo will help sustain her through all the dark and lonely years to come.

The only thing I had to sustain me was the hope that one of Enzo's violent rages would end in my death.

They never did, though. He beat me near to it many times, but death never came to rescue me.

I had to rescue myself instead.

I cross to Lili and take her in my arms. She clings to me and sobs against my chest, her shoulders shaking. Smoothing a hand over her hair, I hold her and make soothing noises until she's calmed down a little and is only hiccuping.

"*Tesoro,*" I murmur. "My beautiful girl. You're the daughter I never had, and I love you."

Lili whispers, "I love you too, *zia.*"

"I know you do. And I want you to know that however I can support you through this, I will. I'll always be here for you. I'll always take care of you. I'll never abandon you, do you understand?"

She whimpers.

My voice hardens. "And I promise you that if your new husband ever lays a finger on you in anger, I will end his life."

That's as close to an admission of my capabilities as I've ever come, but these are dire circumstances.

She lifts her head and stares at me through watering eyes. My heart aching, I wipe the tears from her cheeks with my thumbs.

"Now dry your eyes. Lift your chin. Steel your spine. Caruso women are strong and proud. We keep our moments of weakness private. Your fiancé is coming to see you today, and you need to be prepared."

Her chin quivers. She shakes her head, clearly traumatized by the thought of having to face him.

"Don't ever let him see you cry, Liliana. No man deserves your tears, especially not that one. Just remember what I've told you."

I sigh, gathering her into my arms again. She tucks herself into me and sniffles.

After a long time, she whispers, "Maybe we'll get lucky and he'll get shot before the wedding."

I close my eyes, imagining Quinn lying still and silent on the ground in a widening pool of his own blood.

For the first time in forever, I feel happy.

Then I leave Lili alone with her thoughts and get ready to deal with the next important task on today's agenda.

Firing the pool man.

He's punctual, the smug Irishman. I have to give him that.

Precisely at five o'clock, Quinn rings the doorbell. Lili and I are already waiting, standing hand in hand in the foyer in tense silence. Beside us stands Gianni, vibrating happiness, practically wagging his fucking tail.

Bettina opens the door and lets the Irishman in.

His ego takes up so much space that instantly, the house feels smaller.

"Mr. Quinn!" Gianni steps forward with his hands extended. "Welcome. So good to see you again so soon."

Quinn gives him a cursory nod. They shake hands. Quinn glances at Lili and sends her the same disinterested nod he gave my brother.

He doesn't look at or acknowledge me.

It feels deliberate.

Whatever the reason for it, his snub loosens the vise around my lungs, allowing me to breathe easier.

Maybe I was being paranoid when I thought he was coming on to me in the kitchen. It's so rare that a man outside my family even dares to look at me, let alone flirt with me, I can't remember what it feels like.

Gianni says, "Let's go to my study and have a drink, shall we?"

"No. I'm here to see Lili."

I can tell Gianni's offended by the rude dismissal, but he keeps the pleasant smile on his face. "Of course. Would you like to visit with her in the salon, or—"

"We'll go for a ride," Quinn interrupts coldly.

Lili glances at me in panic.

I frown. *He wants to take her for a ride? In his car?*

When I grasp his motivation, heat flashes over me. It crawls up my neck and settles in my cheeks, where it burns.

He doesn't want to take her for a ride, he wants to *take her for a ride.*

This *testa di cazzo* thinks he's going to sample the merchandise before he buys it!

Keeping my tone tranquil though I'd like to rip out his intestines through his nostrils, I say, "That will be lovely. I adore afternoon rides in the summer. So refreshing."

When Quinn sends me a blistering scowl, I smile. "Of course I'm sure you remember that I'm Lili's chaperone."

If looks could kill, I'd already be dead. Quinn's gaze is a thousand incoming arrows shot from enemy bows.

My smile grows wider.

The Irishman glowers at me like he'd give his left nut to make me invisible. "Aye, I remember. Let's get on with it, then."

He turns on his heel, yanks open the front door, and disappears through it. I listen to his footsteps echo angrily off the courtyard tiles and wonder if perhaps he has bipolar disorder.

It would explain a lot.

Gianni turns to me and mutters, "Brought up in a fucking barn."

"A barn is too civilized. That Irishman was brought up in a slaughterhouse."

Lili whispers nervously, "What do we do?"

"Follow him!" hisses Gianni.

I give Lili's hand a reassuring squeeze, then lead her out the door. We walk out to the driveway, where Quinn is standing beside his big black Escalade.

The driver's door is open. His sidekick, Kieran, is nowhere in sight.

Lili and I walk to the rear door of the SUV and stand there, waiting.

Quinn realizes we're waiting for him to open the door for us and mutters, "Fuck."

He stalks around the front of the vehicle, yanks open the back passenger door, and growls at me, *"In."*

Then he opens the front passenger door and looks at Lili. "Sorry, lass. I've got a lot on my mind today. Up you go."

He helps her get settled in the passenger seat, makes sure she buckles her seat belt, then closes the door. Without another glance in my direction, he hops back into the driver's seat and guns the engine.

Clearly, I'm on my own managing to climb up into the truck.

Regretting that I didn't think to bring my handbag—the one with the secret compartment for my .38—I gingerly step on the Escalade's running board and reach up to grab the handle on the roof inside the door. I'm in heels and a dress, so hauling myself up onto the seat is a production.

Why the man couldn't drive an adult vehicle like a sedan is a mystery.

I've barely got the door closed before he peels out. Gravel sprays from under the spinning wheels. Lili yelps in surprise and grabs onto her door handle. I topple over sideways onto the bench seat, cursing.

"Mr. Quinn! Will you please slow down?"

In the rearview mirror, he sends me a look of murderous rage that exactly matches my own. But he does take his foot off the accelerator, allowing the car to slow to a reasonable speed.

With four of Gianni's armed guards following in a car behind us, we pass the guard gate in silence.

We drive through the wooded area surrounding the house in silence.

Miles of country lanes pass in the same stiff, uncomfortable silence.

It isn't until we pass the lake and enter the highway that I break it.

"Mr. Quinn?"

Gazing straight out the windshield, he grunts at me.

"Where are we going?"

He shakes his head as if I'm annoying him. I certainly hope I am.

And what the hell is his problem today?

I glance behind us to make sure Gianni's guards are still in sight. I have no idea what this crazy fucking Irishman is up to, but when I see the black Mercedes following us, I feel better knowing we're not alone with him.

We speed down the highway as Lili clings to the handle on her door.

I'm so angry that he's frightened her, I want to take off one of my heels and stab him in the ear with it.

After another few miles, he takes an exit off the highway and turns left. He steers the car toward the country carnival off in the distance.

Wait . . . when he said ride, did he actually mean a PONY ride? Does he think she's six years old?

We park in a dirt lot. Quinn exits the car and helps Lili from the passenger seat. Then he leads her away by the hand. He doesn't look back.

When the guards pull up, I've already jumped out and slammed the door behind me.

Luigi, the driver, rolls down his window. He makes a questioning gesture with his hand.

"Who fucking knows?" I say, aggravated. "Maybe the idiot wants a cotton candy."

I hurry to follow the receding figures of Lili and Quinn as they head toward the ticket booth. I catch up with them just as they're going through the main gate.

"Ma'am! Ma'am, you need a ticket!"

Ignoring the pimply young man calling out to me from the booth, I follow behind Quinn and Lili as he leads her through the small crowd. She glances over her shoulder in a panic, looking for me. When she sees me marching behind her with my executioner's face on, she looks relieved.

I almost break an ankle trying to keep up with them. He's got long legs and is making good use of them, striding through the crowd with purpose as he drags Lili along. I'm starting to think he's going to march us around in circles until one of us drops from exhaustion when he suddenly veers left, toward the carousel.

What on earth . . . ?

There are about twenty people standing in line. Quinn pushes past all of them, shoves a ticket to the gawking girl at the gate, and walks straight over to the slowly spinning carousel.

He picks Lili up by the waist and hoists her onto the platform.

She spins away from him, looking utterly confused.

I gasp and lunge forward, pushing past people until I reach the gate. The ticket girl is about to ask me for my ticket, but takes one look at my face and shrinks back.

Quinn turns just as I reach him.

I shout, "What the hell do you think you're doing?"

He grabs me around the waist with one arm and yanks me roughly against his body.

His big, hard, unyieldingly masculine body.

For a long, breathless beat, he stares down at my face. His brows are knit. His eyes are dark. His full lips are pressed into a narrow, angry line. When his gaze drops to my mouth, a muscle in his jaw clenches.

Then he meets my eyes again and growls, "Whatever the fuck I want, viper."

He leaps onto the moving platform, taking me with him.

A scream catches in my throat.

He grabs a bar on the edge of the platform, swings me around, and sets me on my feet, then releases me abruptly. Off-balance in my heels on the uneven, moving metal platform, I stagger, flailing for the nearest stupid colorful carousel horse moving lazily up and down on its pole.

I throw my arms around its neck and hang on.

Quinn glares at me.

I glare right back.

Then he stalks off through the field of undulating carousel ponies while I shout curses in Italian that the brassy calliope music does nothing to drown out.

I kick off my heels and follow him.

It's a Herculean task. He appears to have zero problem navigating a crowd of people riding moving fiberglass animals on a spinning disc, while I'm slipping and sliding all over the place, bumping into everyone and starting to feel sick.

When I finally catch up to him, he's lifting Lili onto a purple-and-gold pony, holding her carefully, but managing her weight easily, as if she's a doll.

She sits astride the pony, grasps the gold pole coming out of its neck, and looks at Quinn with wide eyes.

I'm about to drive a fist into his kidney when she smiles.

Thank God. She's not afraid.

I stand one pony away, watching them in relief, until he turns his gaze to me and it sharpens.

When he steps toward me, I know exactly what he has in mind.

"Don't you dare," I warn as he approaches. "I mean it, Quinn! I am *not* getting up on this thing!"

But of course I am.

Because he wants me to.

He picks me up by the waist and lifts me onto the horse so I'm sitting on it sidesaddle, clinging to his broad shoulders, my bare legs and feet dangling helplessly as I stare down at him.

He gazes up at me, his hands still gripped tightly around my waist.

The horse drifts down on its pole. Quinn's hands drift up from my waist to my rib cage.

Another inch and those huge hands will be cupped around my breasts.

I suck in a breath. My nipples tighten. My entire body erupts into flames. Our eyes lock, and suddenly, the carousel, the music, and everything around us disappears. It's as if nobody else in the world exists but the two of us.

The two of us and my aching vagina, which just now arose from the dead to start howling with need.

For *him*.

This awful, arrogant Irishman.

Who's betrothed to my beloved niece.

Who's madly in love with the pool boy.

I understand with chilling clarity in that moment that none of this is going to end well.

NINE

SPIDER

The viper stares at me with her red lips parted and her mermaid eyes wide, her dark hair falling around her face and her lush tits straining for release from the deep V neckline of her dress as she clings to my shoulders.

The hem of her dress has ridden up, exposing her bare thighs.

Thighs I want to kiss, bite, and bury my face between.

Right here on this fucking carousel. Right *now*, I want to make this fiery, dangerous woman come with my mouth. I want to hear her moan my name and feel her pull my hair as I finger fuck her and lick her clit until she's screaming.

Then I want to fuck her, deep and hard.

Heat rushes to my dick. It throbs, stiffening. I almost groan with need.

I knew I shouldn't have come back to New York.

I should've stayed in Boston until the wedding, then moved Lili into my home and avoided her lethal, luscious aunt for the rest of my bloody life.

But it's like my dick has become one of those divining rods, always pointing right at her hidden treasure. It's obsessed with her.

After our first meeting, I left with a hard-on that kept returning despite repeated attempts to jerk it to satisfaction. I woke up in the middle of the night every night that next week with a dick so rock-hard and aching, I couldn't go back to sleep unless I made myself come.

Thinking of the viper, of course. Imagining in carnal detail every single filthy thing I'd like to do to her.

The list is endless.

Those full, red lips I'd force my swollen cock past.

That long, dark hair I'd wrap around my wrist twice and use to pull back her head.

Those plush, soft tits I'd lick and fondle, sucking her nipples until they were deep pink and rigid in my mouth.

And that sweet, hot pussy I'd fuck in every goddamn position, over and over again.

I want it.

I want it all.

Except I convinced myself I didn't. I convinced myself the burning lust I felt was all in my imagination. Especially after Declan's warning. How could it have possibly been that obvious?

It couldn't.

So, determined to prove to myself that I was totally in control, I threw myself into the shark tank once again.

I strolled into her kitchen, took one look at her standing at the stove glaring at me, and got so hard so fast, I was embarrassed for myself.

I came back today more determined than ever to keep it together, but she wrecked me with a single glance. She stood in the entryway burning me to ashes with her eyes, and I had to restrain myself from grabbing her and throwing her over the nearest chair so I could fuck her from behind in front of everyone.

In front of the lass who's going to be my bloody goddamn wife!

I'm no stranger to sexual chemistry. I've felt desire before, many times. But this is something different.

This is the strike of the match that lit the raging forest fire.

This is dark, intense, and dangerous.

This is *need*, not want . . . and I don't like it at all.

In fact, I fucking hate it.

Maybe even as much as Reyna hates me.

And I better find a way to handle it, because there's too much on the line to screw up.

I can't back out of the marriage to Lili. Not that I even want to—the lass is sweet as could be. She'll make a wonderful wife. A wife I would never obsess over. Be distracted by. Be consumed by, which is the last fucking thing I want.

I don't want to *feel* anything—that's the whole bloody point! I wanted an arranged marriage so I'd never have to feel anything for a woman again.

The last woman I felt something for was kidnapped because of me.

She was shot because of me.

She wound up in Russia, impregnated by her Bratva assassin fucking kidnapper, all because I failed to keep her safe.

With my cursed luck with women, I know better than to ever let feelings get involved in my relationships again.

Yet here I am with my bloody idiotic divining-rod dick blasting at full speed in the direction of a woman they call the Black Widow.

A woman who's like a mother to my soon-to-be bride.

A woman who hates me with a burning passion.

A woman who can never, ever be mine.

I yank my hands from her body and turn away, wondering what the fuck I ever did to make God hate me so much.

TEN

REY

Quinn stalks away from me, leaving me gasping.

Gasping and shaken to my core.

I can count on the fingers of my left hand the times I've experienced true attraction in my life. None of them were anything like this.

My nipples are hard, my hands are shaking, and my damn clitoris is tingling.

Tingling.

To match all the fireworks going on inside my uterus. I never imagined I'd one day actually feel my ovaries throb and pulse like they were hooked up to electrodes, but here we are.

I have to get off the carousel before I throw a leg over this pony and start grinding against the poor thing.

I slide off the horse, landing awkwardly on the metal platform with a thud. I have to take a moment to allow my quaking knees to settle down. Then I take a deep breath, put my shoulders back, and shakily retrace my steps to where I discarded my heels.

I grab them and jump off the merry-go-round.

Barefoot, I make my way to the entry gate to wait for it to stop.

I stand there with my dry mouth and my pounding heart and my utter confusion, which is only slightly less severe than my guilt.

I wanted Lili's awful fiancé to kiss me.

I groan, covering my eyes with a hand, glowing with shame that what I really wanted was so much more than that.

I wanted his mouth on every inch of my skin.

And I know in my bones he'd know exactly what to do with that mouth of his, too. He'd know exactly how to make me moan and beg, how to make me delirious with pleasure.

He'd let his big, rough hands roam all over my body while he lavished my pussy with his tongue, then he'd flip me on my belly and pull my hair and growl filthy things into my ear as he fucked me.

Fucked me hard and deep, because that Irishman is nothing if not powerful.

If I wasn't already going to hell for all my other sins, I'm definitely going for this.

The carousel eventually slows, then stops. Lili and Quinn get off along with everyone else. They make their way to me as I try to look anywhere but at Quinn's face.

He walks Lili past without glancing at me once.

Thank God. I prefer his silences and scowls over the other side of his personality. The swaggering, smiling, flirtatious one.

The one that constantly makes me flush with anger.

Except now that my sad and lonely vagina started howling like a wolf when he touched me on the carousel, I have a terrible suspicion that it wasn't anger that made me flush before.

I think maybe my anger has been covering up something else.

Something unimaginable. Inexcusable.

Insane.

"Zia!"

I whirl around at the sound of Lili's call. She's being dragged along by the hand by Quinn, looking back over her shoulder and waving frantically at me.

Shoving my heels back onto my feet, I lurch away from the gate and follow them. Quinn is moving so fast, it's impossible to catch up, but I keep them within sight as they walk straight through the crowd, forcing people to skitter out of their path or risk crashing into them.

We're headed back to the parking lot. Gianni's guards follow me, two behind and two ahead, spread out at a short distance. In their dark suits and mirrored sunglasses, they stand out from the casual summer crowd, but not as much as Quinn does. With his height and his golden-god good looks, he's winning lustful stares from left and right.

And not only from the women.

By the time we reach the Escalade, I'm sweating and out of breath.

Quinn opens the front passenger door for Lili and helps her in. He closes her door and reaches for the back passenger door handle just as I do.

Our hands touch.

A crackle of electricity snaps white-hot over my fingertips.

Gasping, I snatch my hand away from his.

He's staring at me with hard eyes, a hard jaw, and an expression of pure fury.

Instead of angering or scaring me, that look sets every nerve ending in my body on fire.

My insides go liquid. My nipples harden as if he pinched them. My heart starts to pound, and I break out in a cold sweat. I'm so turned on, I'm breathless.

Clearly, I can never go near a carousel again.

He opens the door. Through gritted teeth, he commands, "Get in."

It takes a great deal of effort to keep my voice steady when I speak. "I don't know why you're acting so strange today, but I've already told you I don't take orders."

Leaning close to me, his jaw still clenched, he stares into my eyes.

"Get your arse in this car. No questions. No sass. You don't speak again unless I give you permission to. Which I won't. Understood?"

His voice is low and gruff. His body heat burns me. I can smell him, the warm, masculine scent of his skin, and count every fleck of gold in his gorgeous hazel eyes.

My mouth goes dry. I can't manage an answer, so I simply climb up into the car and sit.

He gazes at me for a beat, then his gaze drops to my mouth. He exhales, nostrils flaring.

Then he withdraws and slams the door so hard, the whole car is rocked by it.

"Zia?" whispers Lili from the front seat, terrified.

"I don't know what's wrong, but if he does anything dangerous, I'll handle it."

Quinn leaps into the car, slams his door, and guns the engine. He sits there in blistering silence, breathing hard and staring straight out the windshield. He closes his eyes for a moment.

When he opens them again, he seems more in control of himself. He drives out of the carnival's parking lot and back onto the highway at a reasonable speed. But his hands are gripped so hard around the steering wheel, his knuckles are white.

By the time we arrive back at the house, I'm wrung out from all the tension in the car.

Quinn pulls to a stop in the driveway, kills the engine, and hops out. Ignoring me, he helps Lili out, holding her hand. Then he leads her into the courtyard without glancing back.

I slouch down in the seat, cover my face with my hands, and exhale.

I'm still in the same position when Quinn returns ten minutes later.

He opens the door and stands there silently until I drop my hands and look at him.

"What?"

"What are you doing?"

"Maybe I'm meditating."

"Are you?"

"No. Go away."

He shifts his weight from foot to foot. He still seems agitated, but not as furious as before. "I have something to say."

This should be interesting. I lift my brows, waiting.

He clears his throat and glances at the boxwood hedge around the driveway. He tugs on the knot in his tie, then drags a hand roughly through his hair. A muscle flexes in his jaw. "I owe you an apology."

"Are you talking to that shrub or to me?"

His gaze slices back to meet mine. "I'm talking to you, smart-arse."

"And I'm allowed to speak to you now? Because I distinctly remember something about getting permission. I wouldn't want to get in trouble or anything."

His lids drift lower. His eyes grow hot. He says gruffly, "Aye, viper, you have my permission."

That sounded so sexual, I have to swallow before speaking again.

"What exactly are you apologizing for?"

"The same thing I just apologized to Lili for. Losing my temper."

I say tartly, "Yes, I remember asking you about that the day we met. Do you remember what you told me?"

"That I wasn't your dead husband."

We stare at each other. I could fall into those gorgeous hazel eyes and drown.

This is a fucking disaster.

My voice low, I say, "No one could be as bad as him. And I can handle your little tantrums, but I won't allow you to frighten Lili."

"It wasn't a tantrum," he snaps, insulted.

Ignoring that, I continue. "And if you *keep* frightening her by acting rude, inconsistent, and aggressive, there will be consequences for you."

He laughs abruptly. "Are you threatening me, viper?"

"Yes."

His laughter dies. He huffs in disbelief. Then he runs a hand over his beard, studying me intently.

The way he's looking at me makes my entire pelvic floor clench like I'm doing Kegels.

I should call my gynecologist first thing in the morning and schedule a hysterectomy. My reproductive organs have gone insane.

"Now it's my turn to apologize to you."

He cocks a brow. "Changed your mind on that threat so soon, have you?"

"No. The threat stands. What I need to apologize for is not giving you a chance. I was a bitch to you from the minute you first walked in the door." I pause, a smile hovering at the corners of my lips. "I should've waited until I knew what a *culo* you are first."

"*Culo* means handsome warrior, right?"

My smile grows wider. "Riiight."

He grins. We stare at each other until our grins slowly fade and we're somber.

He says gruffly, "You have my word I won't lose my temper around Lili again. You're another story, but . . . I'll try."

I glance away, unable to look at his face one second longer. "Thank you. May I ask why you did?"

His pause is short but charged. "No. Now come inside. Your brother promised me you're going to make me dinner."

"My brother has the IQ of a tadpole."

"You will, viper," he says softly. "You'll feed me."

I look back at him and find him gazing at me with burning intensity.

My heart skips a beat, but I keep my voice light. "And why would I do that, Mr. Quinn?"

"Because it's suppertime. Because you're a good hostess." His pause is almost too brief to notice, but the drop in his voice isn't. "And because I'm ordering you to."

My heartbeat goes from skipping like a silly schoolgirl's to pounding with anger. I say coldly, "You seem to be under the mistaken impression that when you tell me to jump, I'm supposed to ask how high."

He smirks. "You are."

"Oh, look. The man who thinks he's Main Character of Earth is back."

"So's the woman who could freeze off my balls with one look."

"Tiny things freeze so easily, don't they? And thank you for disabusing me of the silly notion that you can sometimes act human. Now get out of my space. You're sucking up the oxygen with all that mouth breathing you do."

I grab the door handle and try to pull the door closed, but he blocks it, stepping closer.

"I'm not done with you yet," he snaps.

"Then let me borrow your gun. I'll only need one bullet."

"You want to shoot me now?"

"The bullet's for me."

When he growls, I can't help but send him the kind of smug, shit-eating smile he's always sending me. "Careful. You're dangerously close to breaking your promise about your temper already."

"That's because you could turn Father Christmas into the Grinch, woman."

"What did I tell you about using the word 'woman' as a pejorative?"

"Something I couldn't hear over how loud your resting bitch face was screaming."

My smile dies. Breathing hard, we glare at each other in blistering silence.

After a pause that feels endless, he says tightly, "You don't have to like me, Reyna. But you do have to show me respect."

"Right back at you, Quinn. And let me make it perfectly clear for you in case it already isn't: I *don't* like you. And I especially don't trust you."

"And why is that?"

I answer without thinking, saying the first thing that comes to mind.

It's something I believe absolutely.

"Because a man who'd marry a woman for any reason other than love has the soul of a monster."

He clenches his jaw. He stares at me, visibly restraining himself from speaking, until finally he says from between gritted teeth, "You ever consider you're not the only person on this fucking planet who's been hurt before?"

"Of course I know that."

"Aye? Because you've got a stick shoved so far up your arse about how bad marriage is that it's blinded you."

Exasperated, I say, "Blinded me to *what?*"

After a long, blistering pause, he growls, "Forget it. It'd be a waste of my fucking breath."

"No. No way, Quinn. I'm not letting you off the hook so easily. If you think I've got a stick up my ass about marriage, you're right. You know why? Because a man gains everything when he takes a wife. A maid, a cook, a housekeeper, a social manager, and a toy he can fuck whenever it suits his convenience. But for a woman, a wedding is where her life ends."

"If you really believe that, you've been hanging out with the wrong women."

I scoff. "I was raised in the Cosa Nostra. All the women are in the same situation I was. That Lili is. We're auctioned off like assets to men who don't know how to love."

"Or ones who just can't bear to be broken again."

He lets that hang in the air between us, crackling like a live wire.

I stare at him, speechless. I simply can't find any words.

Not only because of the raw vulnerability of it—something I never would have believed him possible of—but also because I know in my heart of hearts that what he said is the truth.

His truth.

He's not like Enzo, or any of the other made men I know who take young brides in exchange for power, money, or family gain without a second thought to the girls' feelings about it.

For Quinn, marriage isn't part of a bigger game. It's not about positioning his pawn on a chessboard like it is to my brother, or to have someone weaker to rule over with an iron fist like my husband did.

It's about escape.

He wants to escape *into* marriage with the same longing I wanted to escape *from* it.

For me, marriage vows were the beginning of a long, horrible tumble into the dark.

For Quinn, they're the end of it.

He's been hurt so badly, he doesn't think he can survive it again.

Everything I thought I knew about him was wrong.

I'm about to make another apology when he snaps, "Do us both a favor and get someone else to be Lili's chaperone from now on. You're too bitter a pill for me to swallow."

He turns and walks away, shaking his head.

"Wait. Quinn, wait!"

I hop out of the SUV and hurry after him. He ignores me, striding quickly through the courtyard toward the front door. He throws it open, barging inside. I catch up to him in the foyer and grab his arm.

"For fuck's sake, you stubborn Irishman, hold on! I want to tell you something!"

He whirls around, takes me by the shoulders, and pulls me against his chest. Staring down into my eyes with burning intensity, he growls, "Listen to me, viper. I'm marrying Lili, whether you like it or not. I'll be good to her, whether you believe it or not. And I'll thank you to keep your fucking opinions to yourself from now on."

He pauses, nostrils flared and jaw clenched. He gazes at me with such searing intensity, it's as if he's trying to commit my face to memory.

"In fact, this is the last time I want to see you, ever again."

Dear God, this man is impossible! "You're overreacting."

"Incorrect. If I were overreacting, I'd have Gianni throw you out of this house and onto your arse in the street for being so fucking disrespectful to me."

My cheeks flame with heat. "My brother would never do that."

"No? You want to bet on it?"

I'm about to say yes, but rethink it. There's a good possibility

Gianni would do anything Quinn asked. No matter how afraid of me he might be, he's far more afraid of the Mob.

"That's what I thought."

I blurt, "I'm sorry. That's what I wanted to tell you. I shouldn't have—"

"Save your apologies. I don't believe you, anyway."

My hands are pressed flat against his chest. Underneath my palms, his heart pounds wildly. Instead of giving me the hard shake I know he'd like to give, he holds me captive against his body, glaring at me with the burning heat of a thousand suns.

And here I am once again, melting under his pure masculine beauty and wishing with all my heart this macho, swaggering idiot would kiss me.

But he just gave me an out from this madness. An out I can't pass up, unless I want to make myself miserable and betray my niece in the meantime.

Lusting after another woman's husband is unforgivable.

Especially if the woman is a blood relative.

Gazing up into his eyes, I say, "If you really don't want to see me again, I'll respect that. But at least let me attend the wedding. Lili will need me there. After that, I'll be gone."

Inhaling slowly, he stares at me in silence.

"Please, Quinn. She's the only thing in the world that means anything to me. I know you don't care about what I want, but I believe you do care about what she wants. And if she finds out you banned me from the wedding, she'll be devastated. She'd never forgive you."

"The only way she'd find out is if you told her."

I snap, "She knows very well the only reason I wouldn't be with her on her wedding day is if I were in a coma!"

"That can be arranged."

I know it isn't a threat, because the corners of his mouth turned up.

He's teasing me.

Relieved, I roll my eyes. "So we're agreed?"

His gaze drops to my mouth. His hands tighten around my shoulders. My heartbeat goes haywire.

Then, in a weary voice that sounds like he's a thousand years old, he says, "Aye, viper. We're agreed. The wedding is the last time we'll see each other."

"Okay. Oh . . . wait."

"What?" he growls, aggravated.

"What should I tell her about all the rest of the times?"

"What times?"

"Birthdays. Anniversaries. Holidays." I gasp in horror. "*Christmas!* Oh, God, Quinn, what am I supposed to tell her about why I can never come visit her for Christmas?"

"Maybe you should've thought of that before you unleashed your demon tongue on me."

"But—"

"You'll think of something!" he interrupts loudly. "Jesus Christ on a fucking crutch, you're enough to drive a man to drink!"

He releases me, drags both hands through his hair, emits a sound a rabid bear might make, and turns to head in the direction of the kitchen.

Halfway down the corridor, he turns back abruptly and shouts, "Don't forget about my bloody supper, woman!"

He turns around and continues down the hall, leaving me seething.

He's ordering me around again? He just banned me from seeing my own niece, and now he's hollering commands at me about making his goddamn dinner?

And he's calling me WOMAN?

Glaring with narrowed eyes at his retreating back, I mutter, "I hope you like spider stew."

ELEVEN

———————

SPIDER

*O*nce in the kitchen, I head straight to the wine fridge, pull out a bottle of Cabernet, and bring it over to the big marble island. I grab a corkscrew and open the wine, all the while breathing deeply to try to calm my throbbing heartbeat.

That fucking female could give me a heart attack.

And not only because of those perfect tits.

"Hey. Irish."

I'm so startled by the voice, I drop the corkscrew and curse. "Christ! I didn't see you there."

Reyna's mother sits at the kitchen table, squinting at me from behind her glasses.

It's unnerving how she does that. It's as if the woman can materialize out of thin air, like Dracula.

I exhale hard and add in a more civilized tone, "I'm sorry, Mrs. Caruso. I'm not myself today."

She snorts and says something in Italian.

I don't know what it is. I also don't want to know. I grab two wineglasses from the cabinet and bring them and the bottle over to the table.

I sit down across from her, open the wine, pour us both a glass, and raise mine. *"Sláinte."*

She makes a sour face. "Same to you."

That makes me chuckle. "It means cheers."

"Oh. Well, why didn't you say so?" She picks up her glass. "To what?"

Looking at her, the woman who spawned Reyna, Queen Devil Bitch of All Existence, I say sourly, "Birth control."

"Heh! I'll drink to that."

We clink glasses and drink. When I set my glass down, she's smiling at me.

Somehow, it's not comforting.

She says, "So. Homer-who's-named-after-a-dead-artist. You kill people for a living, *sí?*"

I debate about how to answer but decide to go with the truth. She seems like someone who doesn't tolerate bullshit.

"I wouldn't say it's my primary role, but it's definitely in the mix."

She nods, grunting. "My husband killed people, too. So did Reyna's. It's a way of life for all made men."

She peers at me over her wineglass as if she's waiting for me to respond.

"If you're asking if I enjoy it, the answer is no." I stop and think for a moment. "Actually, strike that. I can recall several times I did enjoy it. But those particular men were savages."

"All men are savages," is her instant response. "It's simply a matter of degree."

I say drily, "I'm starting to see where your daughter gets her love for the opposite sex."

"If you were married to the devil for fourteen years, you'd see a lot better."

The way she says it, in a low voice laden with pain and regret, makes my skin crawl. "He was that bad?"

She meets my gaze and holds it for several silent moments, then sighs and takes a deep swallow of her wine.

"I wouldn't have survived him. To be honest, I've never known anyone who could. But Reyna did. Would you like to know how?"

She doesn't wait for my answer before saying firmly, "Grit."

When I only gaze at her in silence, she adds, "She might not be sweet. All that was carved out of her. But once a heart has been hollowed out by knives, it can withstand anything."

"What about Lili? Does she have grit?"

She looks me over for a long moment. "I guess we'll have to wait and see."

I'm about to protest that I'm not anything like Reyna's dead psycho husband when the crack of gunfire rings out from somewhere behind the house.

"Oh, listen," says Mrs. Caruso calmly, glancing toward the kitchen window. "They're playing your song."

I leap to my feet, kicking the chair out from under me and crouching low. Pulling my gun from the holster inside my suit jacket, I snap, "Get under the table!"

"No can do. I've got wine to finish."

As another volley of shots rings out, she sips her wine and smiles at me.

Bloody hell. The whole fucking family is bonkers.

I make my way swiftly to the wall next to the windows. Leaning in, I take a quick scan of the backyard. The yard is surrounded by massive maple and oak trees and a tall hedge of arborvitae that blocks the view of the property from outside.

There's still enough daylight left for me to see the long stretch of lawn leading down to the pool, the formal garden with its rosebushes and fountains, and the pool house off in the distance.

And the fast-moving line of men dressed in black combat gear making their way toward the main house, snaking in and out between the trunks of the trees, tactical rifles held at the ready.

I also see four men lying facedown on the lawn, scattered around like discarded dolls.

Gianni's guards.

"We've got company," I tell Mrs. Caruso.

She chuckles. "Thank you, Captain Obvious."

I turn and glare at her. "Will you get under the bloody table, please?"

"I can get shot there as easily as I can right here. And you should be worrying about Lili, not me. She's up in her bedroom, in case you were wondering. Turn left at the top of the staircase, last room at the end of the hall."

Shaking my head, I pull the revolver from my ankle holster and set it on the table in front of her. Then I switch off the lights in the kitchen and leave Mrs. Caruso with her wine.

I head swiftly down the corridor outside, where I encounter Gianni coming out of his study with a shotgun in his hands.

"I counted six," I tell him. "There may be more."

"Where?"

"North side of the yard. Headed in fast. How many armed guards are on property?"

"A dozen."

"You're down to eight. You have a safe room in the house?"

He nods. "In the basement."

"Lili's in her room. Get her and take her to the basement. I'll deal with our visitors."

"I've already put everything into lockdown mode," he protests. "The doors and windows are bulletproof and the walls are reinforced. There's no way they can get in the house."

"There's always a way."

As if proving my point, an explosion somewhere nearby rips

through the house, setting the chandeliers swinging and plaster tumbling down in chunks from the frescos on the walls.

"Any idea who your friends might be?" I ask Gianni, eyeing the marble statue of Apollo teetering dangerously atop a column nearby.

"Maybe they're *your* friends," he retorts. "We've all got targets on our backs."

"Fair enough. Where's Reyna?"

Glancing around, he mutters, "Probably off somewhere sharpening her claws and boiling the skulls of her enemies."

If we weren't in the current situation, I might actually laugh at that.

"Get Lili and get to the basement. Don't open the door for anyone but me."

Without waiting for his response, I head toward the explosion, moving swiftly and staying away from the windows. After turning down several corridors, I find the one with smoke drifting in the air and rubble scattered over the travertine.

I back up a few steps, crouch low against the wall, and listen.

It's silent for several seconds. Then I hear the crunch of broken glass under a boot.

I lean around the corner and open fire.

A hail of bullets screams past my face, missing my nose by inches. Jerking back to safety, I'm gratified to hear the heavy thud of a body dropping against the floor.

There's a low groan, a wet gurgle, then silence.

Another quick peek around the corner reveals one of the intruders lying flat on his back, staring with sightless eyes at the ceiling.

Other than him, the hallway is empty.

They split up.

I run to the corpse, crouch beside him, and do a quick search of his jacket and tactical pants. He has no ID, phone, or wallet.

The only things I come up with are spare cartridges of ammo for the rifle.

I pull off his gloves and shove up his coat sleeves, looking for tattoos, but his skin is bare. So is his stomach and chest when I yank up his T-shirt.

Interesting.

All made men have tattoos that declare their family affiliation. The only lads who don't wear ink are those who don't want anyone to know who they are.

In other words, they're hired help.

Mercenaries.

Gunfire erupts at the front of the house, outside in the courtyard. Most likely it's Gianni's other guards putting up a fight to the newcomers in black. I'll worry about them as soon as I deal with whoever else is inside.

Heading down the corridor again, I come to a ragged hole blown through the exterior wall. The floor all around is littered with debris.

It's about a six-by-six opening. A substantial size, which means substantial firepower. This mess was made by something with much more oomph than a hand grenade, especially considering the walls are reinforced.

The echo of heavy footsteps catches my attention.

I duck into a niche in the wall and listen as the footsteps move farther away. I can tell there's more than one man, but not more than three. Holding my handgun at low ready and keeping my footfalls as light as possible, I walk farther down the corridor until I come to a break in the wall, beyond which is an enormous sitting room with a glossy black grand piano in the corner.

Two men with rifles move swiftly among the clusters of sofas and chairs. The scopes of their weapons are held to their masked faces, the muzzles pointed at a figure standing still on the other side of the room.

It's Reyna.

Her hands hang loosely at her sides. Her expression is impassive. She watches the men approach with an eerie detachment in her eyes, as if the scene unfolding in front of her is happening to someone else.

She's in shock. Fuck. Reyna, run!

I raise my weapon, take aim, and fire.

Brains splatter the wallpaper in a chunky vivid patchwork of red. The intruder the brain belonged to drops heavily to his knees. He falls face-first onto the carpet.

The other one spins on his heel and jerks the muzzle of his rifle in my direction.

Before he can get off his shot, Reyna pulls a knife from a pocket in her dress and embeds it in his neck.

He screams, staggering sideways and dropping his rifle. As he grapples with the blade jutting out from the side of his neck, desperately trying to dislodge it, I put a bullet between his eyes.

He jerks and falls, landing backward on a velvet sofa. Blood squirts erratically from the wound in his neck. Then he slides slowly to the floor and remains still, his mouth hanging open.

Reyna looks at me with undisguised irritation.

"I had it handled, Quinn."

This woman. Jesus, God, you really broke the mold when you made this one. She's fucking magnificent.

"You were about to get your bloody head shot off! And you're welcome!"

Rolling her eyes as if she thinks I'm being ridiculous, she kneels down next to the body in front of the sofa. She yanks the knife from his neck, wipes the blade on his jacket, and stashes it back into the hidden pocket in the skirt of her dress. She picks up his rifle, checks to make sure there's a round in the chamber, and stands.

"You know these guys?"

Impressed by her utter calm, I say, "No. You?"

She shakes her head. "Where's Lili?"

"Gianni's taken her to the safe room."

"And Mamma?"

"In the kitchen alone, drinking wine in the dark."

She nods, as if what I've just told her is entirely normal. When more gunfire erupts outside, she says, "Any idea how many of them there are?"

"I counted six. Killed one in the hallway. Plus these two, that leaves three left."

"Two."

"How do you figure?"

"I killed another one on my way in here."

"Of course you did."

With a toss of her head, she flips her hair over her shoulder. "Flashed my tits at him. He froze like a deer in headlights."

Funny how I can be insanely jealous of a dead man I've never met.

"How creative."

"Men are annoyingly predictable."

"Tits are our Achilles' heel. Now get down to the basement with your brother and Lili. I'll clear the rest of—"

"Oh, shut up, Quinn," she interrupts crossly, then spins around and strides out of the room.

I have to take a moment to press a hand over my heart, which is having a seizure.

No matter how long I live, I'll never forget the image of Reyna Caruso in a black dress and stilettos, carrying a high-caliber rifle at the ready as she heads off to hunt armed intruders, her full hips swaying and her long dark hair flaring out behind her like a flag.

I leap into action again when I hear the staccato pulse of shots fired.

Weaving around the velvet chairs and tufted divans, I head

out of the room. I search five more rooms on the ground floor, each bigger than the last and seemingly used for nothing more than display of hideous furniture and frightening, religious-themed art.

All are empty.

Near the staircase in the foyer, a man clad in black combat gear lies facedown in a pool of blood. His weapon is missing. The front door stands wide open. I see three of Gianni's guards sprint past outside, in pursuit of someone running on foot.

Several seconds later, there's more gunfire, then some shouting in Italian that sounds celebratory.

If there were only six men who entered the property, there's one more to go.

Reyna's nowhere in sight, so I run up the stairs and go from room to room, checking them one by one to ensure they're empty. When I've confirmed they are, I trot back down the stairs, then hurry through the remaining rooms on the ground floor. They're all empty, too.

Then I hear an angry voice coming from a nearby salon, the last one still unsearched. It's a voice I'd recognize anywhere.

"Go ahead, fucker. You'll be doing me a favor. But I'll see you again in hell, and then I'm going to cut off your balls and choke you with them."

Reyna.

My heartbeat surges into overdrive. Moving fast but quietly, I stride over to the salon, gun in hand, and slow just outside the doorway.

When I glance in, my pounding heart skids to a dead stop.

Reyna stands in front of an unlit fireplace, eyes flashing with fury, chin lifted in defiance. A man stands across from her, about six feet away.

He's pointing a semi-automatic handgun at her chest.

A rifle lies on the floor beside him.

I think it's the one she was carrying. He must've surprised her somehow and pulled it from her grip.

I say loudly, "Oy. Dickface."

He jerks his head to the right.

I squeeze the trigger and put a bullet in his temple. He collapses like a rag doll into a heap on the floor.

Then something kicks me in the shoulder from behind.

"What the . . . ?"

I spin around to find another masked guy in black crouched on one knee in the corridor, arms outstretched, holding a Glock semi-auto in his grip. Before I can raise my weapon, a shot rings out.

Blood mists from his mask in a spray. He topples sideways, gun clattering against the marble, then lies still.

Breathless, Reyna runs up beside me. "It's too bad you can't count, Quinn. There were seven of them, not six."

Too stunned to argue, I stare at her holding the rifle in her hands. "Did you just shoot a man to protect me?"

She looks at me, blinks, then winces. "Shit. Must've been a reflex."

"Or maybe you were feeling gratitude for both times I saved your life in the last ten minutes."

She scoffs. "Please. I didn't need your help." Then she gasps and her eyes grow wide.

"Don't tell me. You just remembered you didn't make me supper yet."

"No, Quinn . . ." She reaches out and lightly touches my shoulder. "I think you've been shot."

I look down at where she's touching. A wisp of smoke rises from a small hole in the fabric of my jacket. The acrid smell of scorched silk hangs in the air.

Watching a ring of wetness grow larger around the hole, I sigh.

Fuck. This is my favorite suit.

TWELVE

REY

*L*et me take a look," I tell Quinn, reaching for his lapel.

He brushes me off impatiently. "It's fine."

"It's *not* fine, idiot. You have a hole in you. You're bleeding. I can help."

"I don't need a nurse. Especially one who's likely to stab me in the neck when I'm not looking."

Realizing that arguing with him will get me nowhere, I give up. "Okay, Macho Man. Good luck with that nasty infection."

He glowers at me. "I don't have a nasty infection."

"Not yet. But it'll set in soon from the debris that entered the wound along with the bullet. You know, threads from your shirt and suit, bone fragments, burnt powder, all that fun stuff. The wound needs to be irrigated, disinfected, and stitched up or things will get ugly fast. You could end up dead."

I try not to look too pleased by the thought, but I'm sure I fail.

He pauses to consider me for a beat. "Have much experience with bullet wounds, do you, wee viper?"

Irritated by that heinous nickname, I grind my molars. "I've lived all of my thirty-three years in the Mafia. What do you think?"

He quirks a brow. It turns to a smirk. Then he drawls, "So you're thirty-three. Hmm." He looks me up and down. "You don't look a day over forty."

"At least thirty-three is my age and not my IQ."

"And at least *I* don't have the personality of a cold toilet seat."

"God, I wish you'd fall onto a hive of murder hornets. In the meantime, why don't you go outside and see if you can miscount any more intruders? I'm going to check on my mother."

As I walk away, headed to the kitchen, he calls out, "How do I get to the safe room?"

"Make two right turns at the end of that hall. You'll hit a set of double wood doors. The stairway to the basement is behind them."

I walk into the kitchen and flick on the overhead lights. Mamma sits at the table with an empty glass and a bottle of wine on the table in front of her. She's got a small silver pistol in her left hand.

"Ah, *stellina*! Just in time—I'm out of wine." She sets the gun down and pushes the empty wineglass toward me. "And no Cabernet, please. That stuff Homer likes is too dense."

I mutter, "Like the man himself."

Setting the rifle on the island, I pick up the house phone and dial down to the safe room. Gianni picks up on the first ring.

"It's me. You've got Lili?"

"Yes, she's safe."

"I haven't checked the cameras yet. What can you see?"

"The grounds are clear."

"Good. So's the house."

"Leo's on his way with more men."

"How long until they get here?"

"Any minute." A short pause follows. "Mr. Quinn saved your life."

I can't tell by his tone if he's going to thank him or hate him for that. "I would've been fine without his help."

He chuckles. "From what I could see, it didn't look like it, *sorellina*."

Little sister, little star, little viper . . . why does everyone insist on calling me *little*?

I'm fucking BIG!

And I certainly don't need a bossy, overbearing, overconfident man-child with a dumb nickname and an even dumber matching tattoo to save my life. I can do it all by myself, thank you!

I blow out a breath, push my anger aside, and focus. "So who do you think they were?"

Gianni's voice hardens. "I don't know yet. But I'll find out. What did they say to you?"

Both times I was confronted by the intruders, they spoke to me, which Gianni obviously saw as he watched on the security camera bank in the safe room. But there's no audio feed, so he wouldn't have been able to hear.

"They asked me where Lili was. Said they'd shoot me if I didn't take them to her."

Gianni curses under his breath. "I should've known."

"Known what?"

"This joining of our families, the Mafia and the Mob . . . it's made Lili a high-profile target."

Realizing what he means, my stomach turns over. "For kid-napping."

"Yes. Now I'm not the only one who'd pay a fortune to get her back. Mr. Quinn has a vested interest in her safety, too. Someone wanted to double his money."

He pauses. His voice drops. "Or prevent the match com-pletely."

I know what he means without him having to spell it out.

There are plenty of people who'd be glad if the Mafia and

the Mob remained enemies forever. By joining our houses, we've made powerful allies, but also put ourselves in the sights of those who'd be happier if we stayed at odds.

Lili's not only in danger of kidnapping. She's in danger of something far worse.

Murder, for instance.

My blood runs ice-cold.

Gripping the phone so hard it shakes, I say, "Russians?"

"Doubtful. Declan O'Donnell has a tie to them. By blood."

"The king of the Mob is related to the Russians? How?"

"His wife's sister is pregnant by the boss of the Moscow Bratva."

That's shocking news. The Mob and the Bratva have been at each other's throats for as long as I can remember. "How did *that* matchup ever happen?"

"By force. She was taken."

"Oh, shit."

"Exactly."

Wonderful. So not only is Lili in danger of being kidnapped and held for ransom or killed to prevent the alliance altogether, she's also in danger of being stolen and purposely impregnated so an alliance with some other third party would be forced.

She's now on every mobster's radar in the States.

And probably worldwide.

Fuming, I say, "Christ, Gianni! I told you not to make the match with this Irishman!"

"Don't be so shortsighted. We'll gain far more in the long run than the danger we face now. It's just a turbulent period we have to navigate until the venture pays off."

"You know this is your daughter we're talking about, right? Your own flesh and blood? She's not an investment in the damn stock market!"

Bored by my concern for his offspring, Gianni sighs. "We'll

come up when Leo arrives. Don't let Mamma drink too much
wine. She gets mouthy when she's tipsy."

He hangs up, leaving me growling.

"I'm dying of thirst over here, *tesoro*." Mamma taps her empty
glass with a fingernail.

I slam down the receiver on the phone and glare at her. "You
raised an absolute asshole, you know that?"

She pauses to purse her lips. "Are we talking about your
brother?"

"Do you want your wine or not?"

"*Sì.*"

"Then we're talking about my brother!"

She *tsk*s. "I'm only teasing you. *Mamma mia,* you're so tense
lately!"

Crossing to the wine fridge, I say, "Gee, I don't know why,
could be that home invasion we just had."

Under her breath, she says, "Or something a little more hung."

I whirl around and stare at her. "I'm sorry, what did you just
say?"

She blinks innocently. "What?"

"Did you just say the word . . . *hung*?"

She pretends to think. "Did I?"

"You know what? I don't want to know. I'm getting you your
wine. Now please never speak again."

She shrugs and holds out her glass.

At that exact moment, Quinn saunters into the kitchen.

Mamma cackles. "Aha! The plot thickens!"

He looks at me. A furrow forms between his brows. "What
did I miss?"

I snap, "The entire period after childhood when you were supposed to grow into an adult."

He looks at Mamma.

She says, "You can try to respond to that, but it will be *molto* dangerous."

After a moment of thought, he simply sits down across from her and shrugs off his jacket, draping it over the back of the chair beside him.

Mamma chuckles. "Good call."

I grab a bottle of wine, get the wine opener from the drawer, and hack away at the foil on the top of the bottle until it's shredded. Then I stab at the cork with the corkscrew until Mamma says to me softly in Italian, "It isn't the home invasion that's got you so worked up."

I stop what I'm doing and glance up at her.

She nods, holding my gaze. "Now take a breath and calm yourself. You're my daughter. You're made of iron, like me. Forged in fire. Unbreakably hard. You can withstand anything."

She inclines her head in Quinn's direction. "Including your attraction to him."

It's a humbling thing, having someone who knows you so well. Someone who sees past all the walls you've erected, past all the smoke and mirrors you've thrown up to protect yourself and lead everyone else astray from the truth.

I set the corkscrew down slowly on the countertop, close my eyes, and exhale.

Into the ensuing silence, Quinn says, "Maybe I can get that for you."

When I open my eyes, he's pointing at the bottle, a questioning look in his eyes.

"You're shot, you fool."

"I'm used to operating under less-than-ideal circumstances."

That makes me laugh. "I'm sure you are. By the way, why are you in here? I thought you were going to the basement."

"I did. Everything's fine down there. Gianni wants to stay

there with Lili until his men arrive, and I agreed with that. So now I'm back up here." His voice drops. "With you."

Ignoring Mamma's piercing stare, I say, "If you're staying, you're getting stitched up."

He wrinkles his nose.

"No arguments. I don't want your blood all over my clean floor. I'll pour us all some wine, then have a look at your wound. Whether you like it or not!" I add loudly when he starts to protest.

He holds up his hands in surrender. "How about if we make a deal? You can stitch me up, but after that, I'd like you to make me supper."

I arch an eyebrow. "Oh, the master of the universe is issuing a request? And here I thought you only knew how to bark orders."

"I've noticed that you don't respond well to orders."

When I don't say anything, he adds softly, "Please?"

We gaze at each other for a moment as Mamma looks back and forth between us. Then she raps her wineglass against the table, muttering, "Prisoners get better service than this."

Quinn sends her a fond smile. "I'm glad you said it and not me."

"If the two of you are going to gang up on me, *nobody's* getting wine!"

Irritated by their easy camaraderie, I pour Mamma her wine, then get two more glasses from the cupboard. I serve Quinn his, then stand beside the table and guzzle an entire glass of Chianti in one go.

Watching me, Quinn is silent.

When he stands and loosens his tie, I'm still under control. It isn't until he unbuttons his black dress shirt and pulls it off that I almost topple over backward in a dead faint.

The muscles. Good God, the muscles.

His chest is broad and rock-hard. His nipples are pierced with small silver studs. His abs look like they were carved from marble. His shoulders are wide and his biceps bulging. Everything is hard, defined, and tight. There isn't an ounce of fat on him.

And the tattoos.

Mercy, the tattoos.

How can a collection of colorful ink be so devastatingly sexy?

His right arm has a full sleeve, shoulder to wrist. An elaborate scrolled font in a language I don't know snakes in an arc across the top of his chest, from shoulder to shoulder, just under his collarbone. There's some kind of tribal symbol decorating his left biceps, and another on his left shoulder.

And that spiderweb on the side of his neck, of course.

Somehow with him stripped naked to the waist, even that damn spiderweb tattoo has taken on a seductive allure. I want to trace every line with my tongue.

Where he isn't tattooed, his skin is smooth and golden, like he works shirtless outdoors in the sun.

This man could be a pinup model.

At least my vagina thinks so. A five-alarm blaze has erupted in my underpants. I'm going to have to go in search of a fire extinguisher to put these roaring flames out.

Quinn's brows draw together. Examining my expression, he says, "What's wrong?"

Mamma and I share a stunned look before I pull myself together. "That bullet wound is serious."

He glances down at his arm. There's a ragged gash on the top outer part of his shoulder. It's surrounded by bruised tissue darkening to purple, and it's leaking blood.

He says, "It's barely a scratch. He only clipped me."

"A few inches lower and that bullet would've torn straight through your heart."

"But it didn't. Luck of the Irish, I suppose."

I'm shocked by how casual he sounds. He could be discussing a hangnail for how nonchalant he seems.

"Have you been shot much?" asks Mamma.

"Depends on how you define 'much.'"

"More than once."

"Then, aye. This makes . . ." He pauses, thinking. "Five? Six?"

I'm astonished. "You're not sure?"

He cocks a brow at me, smirking. "You seem impressed."

"Only you would think that. It's unfortunate your maker decided to finish you without giving you a brain. Sit."

He winks at Mamma. "Look who's barking orders now."

She smiles knowingly. Then she rises and grasps her cane in one hand and her wineglass in the other. "I won't stay for the gory part. I don't have as strong a stomach at the sight of blood as Reyna does."

A stomach I earned through years of cleaning my own blood from clothing, carpet, and my skin.

As Mamma hobbles out, Quinn watches me, his hazel eyes sharp as an eagle's.

"You okay?"

"Yes. No. I don't know. Today has been . . ."

"All sorts of fun," he says, chuckling.

"Be quiet now."

I turn away and head to the sink, where I pull a bottle of hydrogen peroxide from the cabinet beneath. The first-aid kit is in a cabinet over the dishwasher, with clean gauze pads, antibiotic ointment, bandages, gloves, and tools inside.

I set the kit on the table, then stand over Quinn and pull on the latex gloves. As I gingerly clean and disinfect the wound, he drinks his wine and smolders as only he can, glancing up at me from time to time with hooded eyes.

I can tell he's deep in thought, but I'll be damned if I'll ask him about it.

After a while, he says abruptly, "I still don't want to see you after the wedding."

"You made that clear earlier. I don't want to see you, either. Your mood changes require medical intervention. Now shut up, or I'll make your stitches look like they belong on Frankenstein's monster."

"You can just glue it."

"With what? Elmer's?"

"You don't have any skin glue?"

"Do I look like a fucking pharmacy?"

His gaze rakes over me, head to toe. He growls, "No, viper. You look more like a fucking land mine."

"If that was an insult, I didn't get it. Now please. Shut. *Up*."

A low sound of aggravation rumbles through his chest.

Working as quickly as I can, I thread a needle with unwaxed dental floss and make small, even stitches across the wound to close it. Instead of tying a knot at the end, I snip the floss with an inch left over, then tape it to his skin on both ends.

When I feel him looking at me, I know he's about to demand an explanation, so I beat him to the punch. "It will heal better if the sutures aren't pulled too tightly. Knots make them pull."

"How do you know that?"

I mutter, "Years of personal experience on my own body."

I'm about to draw away, but he grasps my wrist and holds it, his grip firm but not tight.

Startled, I look into his eyes.

They're blazing with emotion.

He says gruffly, "I'd like to kill him."

"Who?"

"Your husband. If he were still alive, I'd kill him for you. And I wouldn't make it quick."

That takes my breath away.

I stare at him with my lips parted and my heart hammering like mad, feeling as if I'm balancing on the edge of a high cliff, gazing down into an endless abyss below me, dangerously close to tumbling over.

Before I can say another word, Quinn releases my wrist, rises, yanks his shirt and suit jacket from the back of the chair he folded them over, and walks out of the kitchen.

THIRTEEN

REY

*T*wo hours later, there are two dozen more armed guards patrolling the grounds. Leo, Quinn, and Gianni are locked
in the study, strategizing. I'm in the kitchen, making dinner.
Mamma is upstairs, asleep, and Lili is in her bedroom, doing
God knows what.

She's probably still in shock. When she came up from the
basement with Gianni, she was white as a ghost and shaking
badly.

This was her first experience with the darker side of Mafia life.

She's been pampered and protected since she was a baby, attending only exclusive all-girl private schools with other children
of wealthy families, surrounded by bodyguards and watchful
eyes. Scarsdale is less than an hour from Manhattan, but has only
about twenty thousand residents and almost no crime.

She hasn't been exposed to death in any meaningful way. Her
grandfather was killed before she was born, her mother died in
childbirth, and her *zio* Enzo, well . . .

She didn't see him die, either.

The point being that she's never seen this kind of violence. I thought she might faint when she saw the bloodied body lying facedown in the middle of the foyer when Gianni brought her up to her bedroom.

This has been quite the day for her.

For both of us.

I can still see Quinn's face when he said, *"I'd kill him for you."* I still hear that rough, urgent tone in his voice, see his burning, beautiful eyes.

All of it will be seared into my mind forever.

No one ever tried to help me. Everyone knew what was happening, what Enzo enjoyed doing to me, but nobody ever intervened. I was his wife and therefore his property, and in the Cosa Nostra, you can do with your property whatever you like.

Even my own mamma could only offer her shoulder for me to cry on.

After a while, there were no more tears left, so I didn't even need that.

But Lili's Irishman wishes he could've helped. I believe he would've, too, had he been around then to see it.

Maybe she'll never love him. And maybe he'll be moody or irritating or a slob, but now I believe he won't hurt her beyond the petty ways husbands and wives can hurt one another, those small moments of unkindness, words spoken thoughtlessly or small deeds of neglect.

Quinn killed four men today. Protecting me—us, our family— he took four lives.

He would've taken on an army by himself if he had to.

Which convinced me, more than anything he could say, that she'll be safe with him. It might not be a love match, but a man who will protect a woman with his own life is a rare thing.

So rare, I've never seen it before.

So although I might have wanted someone different for Lili, this Irishman will do.

"*Buona sera,* Reyna."

I look up from the stove to see Leo entering the kitchen. He's the same age as Gianni, and looks about the same, too. Slicked-back dark hair, custom suit, pinky rings. With their close height, build, and coloring, they could be brothers.

"*Buona sera,* Leo. Thank you for coming."

He waves that off. "You look well. Not a scratch, eh?"

"Not a one."

He chuckles, shaking his head. "I suppose you can't scratch titanium."

As is the way with all Gianni's friends, he never looks right at me. He addresses me directly, but his gaze lands anywhere but on my face. I used to think it was respect, but now I think it's fear.

Men don't like unpredictable things they can't control. Which is why they prefer dogs over cats.

"How's your mother?"

"The same ray of sunshine as ever. And yours?"

"Her arthritis is worse."

"I'm sorry to hear that. Please send her my regards."

"I will."

Gianni walks in, nodding at me and clapping a hand on Leo's shoulder. "Smells delicious, *sorellina.*"

"I made enough for an army, so Leo's men can come in and eat in shifts during the night."

Leo looks surprised. "Thank you. They'll appreciate that."

"Soldiers can't focus when their stomachs are growling."

Gianni says proudly, "She would've made a good general in the army, eh?"

I know by the compliment that he's getting ready to ask me to do him a favor. Otherwise, he'd be taking credit for teaching me everything I know about cooking.

He taught me nothing, of course. The man doesn't even know how to boil water. Between Mamma, his late wife, and now me, he's never made a meal in his life.

Quinn enters the kitchen, instantly making the room feel crowded. I have no idea how his presence takes up so much space, but it's a gift. He pulls up a chair and sits at the table.

He doesn't look at me, but I sense a huge change in him from when we last spoke. He's glowering and agitated, drumming his fingers restlessly on the tabletop, a thundercloud of temper settled over his features.

Honestly, the man should see a doctor about his mood changes. A girl could get a broken neck trying to keep up.

Gianni glances at him as if waiting for permission to speak. When it doesn't come, he says abruptly, "We've decided to move up the wedding date. For Lili's own safety and—"

"I agree," I interrupt, calmly stirring an enormous pot of carbonara sauce.

Quinn's sharp gaze snaps in my direction. My body temperature rises several degrees. No one says anything for several moments, then Gianni clears his throat.

"Well . . . good. She needs a gown. And she'll have to be all packed and ready to go to Boston. Her clothes and belongings, whatever she needs."

"Of course. I'll take care of everything. How much time do I have?"

"A week."

My stirring falters for only the briefest of seconds before I start up again. "I see. The venue?"

Quinn says gruffly, "The Old North Church in Boston."

Shocked, I glance up at him, meeting his penetrating gaze. "A church? Is that safe? Somewhere so public?"

"It's our home parish. If the head of the Mob can be safely married there, so can his men."

When I look at Gianni, he nods. I suspect they've had in-depth discussions about the exact safety precautions that will be put in place for the ceremony. Discussions I won't be privy to, so I'll just have to trust they know what they're doing.

I don't, but I'll have to try.

"What about the rehearsal dinner? Where will that be held?"

Looking stumped, Gianni glances at Quinn. "Do we need a rehearsal dinner?"

Quinn examines my face for several seconds. "What do you think, Reyna?"

I almost drop the spoon in surprise but manage to compose myself in time. "We definitely need a formal meeting between the two families before the wedding."

Gianni says, "I'm making the trip to Boston tomorrow to meet Mr. O'Donnell."

"That's fine, but you've got to get the women involved, too."

Gianni looks irritated by that. "Why do we have to get the women involved?"

Leveling him with a stony stare, I say, "Because we're joining our families, and it's respectful to include us in something so im-portant. Because it will help Lili adjust to her new life in Boston if she's already met some of the women she'll be spending time with. And because we're the ones who decide if your home lives are heaven or hell, so you should accommodate us once in a while."

Sighing, he says, "Fine. We'll have a rehearsal dinner."

"Thank you. Quinn, will you please put me in touch with your contact at the church so I can make arrangements for flow-ers, music, and the other ceremony details?"

"Aye."

"What about the guest list? Who's handling that?"

I get a bunch of blank stares in response to that question.

Seriously, how are men in charge of anything? They're totally incompetent with logistics. Did they think we'd send out carrier pigeons?

Trying to rein in my temper, I say, "How many people does the church hold?"

"Four hundred max," says Quinn.

"So we'll say two hundred per side, is that fair?"

Gianni protests, "We'll need more than that!"

"Why, if you have such a small family?"

Gianni looks at Quinn with his brows drawn together. "Who said we have a small family?"

When Quinn sends me a pointed, disapproving glare, I smile. "I might've fibbed about how many relatives we have."

"Among other things. Are you a pathological liar, or is it more like a hobby?"

"It's closer to a protective evolutionary adaptation, like the stripes on a tiger."

After a beat, he says, "You live in a jungle, you learn to camouflage yourself."

I shrug. "Survival of the fittest and all that."

He says darkly, "Aye. And you're one bloody fit tiger, aren't you, woman?"

Leo and Gianni are looking at us like we're two psychiatric patients babbling to each other in a padded cell.

Ignoring them, I say, "So two hundred a side. I'll handle the invitations for our side. I trust you have someone you can delegate that task to for yours?"

Looking pensive, Quinn nods.

"Good. Any suggestions where you'd like the rehearsal dinner to be held? I'm not familiar with Boston."

"I know a place."

"We'll keep the list for the dinner limited to the immediate families and whoever's in the wedding party, so it doesn't have to be as big as the church. What else?" I think for a moment. "Marriage license."

Quinn says, "It's already taken care of."

"What about the wedding reception? Where will that be?"

More blank looks.

"You know what? Leave it to me. I'll find somewhere close to the church that can hold four hundred gangsters and has good security. Maybe there's a federal prison nearby."

Quinn shakes his head. "Let me handle that. I know someone who can put together big events on short notice." He pauses. A crack appears in his stormy demeanor. His smile is faint, but it's there. "She's a boss. Reminds me a lot of you, actually."

"Really? She runs a zoo, too?"

"Aye. Keeps all us monkeys in line."

"I'm sure we'll have a lot to talk about. What about the ring?"

Gianni and Leo look at Quinn, who's looking at me with his brows drawn together.

"What about it?"

As if I'm speaking to a toddler, I say with exaggerated patience, "You'll purchase one, I assume?"

"I suppose."

"You *suppose*? Do you want everyone laughing at you during the part in the ceremony where you should be putting a ring on your bride's finger, but you can't because you forgot to buy her one?"

He looks at the ceiling, as if calling on a higher power for patience. Then he scowls at me again. "I'll buy a ring."

"A nice one," I insist. "Not just a simple gold band. Make sure it has diamonds."

Leaning back in his chair, he crosses one leg over the other and gazes at me in silent, tight-lipped fury.

Finally, his teeth gritted, he says, "Any particular carat size you'd like, Madam Queen?"

My smile is so sweet, it could cause cancer. "The bigger the better. She'll need something to show off to her friends, and it certainly isn't you."

His look turns black. The thunderclouds over his head start to boil.

I'm about to move on to the next item on my list when he says suddenly, "You'll come with me to pick it out."

I stop stirring the carbonara sauce to grimace at him. "It's too personal. You have to choose something you think she'd like."

A muscle in his jaw flexes. He stares at me in brooding silence, then says gruffly, "I don't know what she bloody likes, do I?"

"For God's sake, it's not rocket science. Just pick out a pretty ring!"

Seeing that Quinn's about to become unhinged, Gianni snaps, "You'll go with him. It's decided."

"First thing in the morning," agrees Quinn darkly.

A judge handing a prisoner a death sentence couldn't sound more threatening.

"Fine. What time should I expect you?"

He snaps, "I'm staying here tonight!"

Fed up with his bearish attitude, I say flatly, "What a treat."

I lower the heat under the pot and remove my apron. Then I put together a plate of spaghetti and sauce for Lili, along with a slice of the garlic bread that came out of the oven just before they walked in.

I turn away and head toward the door. Gianni looks at me quizzically.

"Where are you going?"

"I'm taking your daughter her dinner and delivering the news about her new wedding date, which you hadn't gotten around to badgering me into yet."

He's aghast. "What about *our* dinners?"

"None of your arms are broken. Help yourselves."

I feel Quinn's eyes burning holes into my back as I walk out.

When I get upstairs, I knock lightly on Lili's closed bedroom door. "It's me. I thought you might be hungry."

There's no response for so long, I think she might be asleep. But then the door cracks open, and she's standing there in her pajamas, red-eyed and pale.

"Hey, *zia*," she whispers.

"Oh, sweetie, I know. A little food might help."

She backs up, letting me into the room, but she's shaking her head. "I can't eat. I feel sick."

She crosses to her bed, crawls under the covers, and pulls them over her face.

I set the plate of food on the nightstand, perch on the edge of the bed, then gently pull the blankets down. Smoothing a hand over her forehead, I say, "You want to talk about it?"

She sniffles. "Which part? The shootings, the explosion, the dead bodies, or that angry Bigfoot Papa wants me to marry?"

"Any of the above."

She blows out a hard breath, puffing out her bottom lip, then closes her eyes. "Not really."

"Okay. But there's something I have to tell you."

Her eyelids fly open. She stares at me in panic. "Oh God. What now?"

I'm about to tell her about the wedding being moved up when the ringing of a phone interrupts me.

The sound is coming from somewhere under the blankets.

This wouldn't be strange, but Lili doesn't own a cell phone because she's overprotected and her father thinks all teenage girls do on their phones is take pictures of themselves in their underwear to post on the internet.

As the ringing continues, Lili slowly pulls the covers back up over her face until only her wide, horrified eyes are showing.

I say firmly, "Give it to me. Where is it, Lili? Hand it over."

When she doesn't respond, I stand and whip the covers off

her. She immediately starts scrambling around, searching for the phone that's tangled somewhere in the sheets.

I find it first and snatch it up. It's a cheap, old-school Nokia with a small screen and a pixelated readout.

A burner.

She didn't get this on her own.

As Lili whines and grapples with me, trying to grab it back, I hit the Answer button but don't say anything.

"Hello? Lili? *Corazon*, are you there?"

The voice is young, male, and has a slight Spanish accent, and of course I know who it is.

"Hello, Juan Pablo," I say, walking away from the bed so I can hear over Lili's pleas. "This is Lili's aunt, Reyna. We need to talk."

"*Zia*, please! Give me the phone! Let me talk to him!"

I go into her bathroom and lock the door behind me, ignoring her muffled pleading.

On the other end of the line, Juan Pablo is silent. I sit on the closed toilet seat, lean over and prop my forehead in my hand, and sigh.

"Look. I have nothing against you—"

"You fired my father," he interrupts, sounding indignant.

"You deflowered my niece," I shoot back.

"We're in love!"

"I know you think that means you should be together, but it's not going to happen. Her father won't allow it. I need you to promise me you'll leave her alone."

He says flatly, "No. You can't keep us apart."

Surprised, I huff out a breath. *The balls on this kid.*

I'm inclined to like him, but considering he'll be a corpse if Gianni discovers any of this, I'll save my affection for the living.

"Maybe I can't, but her father and the rest of the Mafia can. Do you have any idea what will happen if they find out about you?"

His voice rises. "You think I care what a bunch of racist goomba fucks think about me?"

"This isn't about your race."

"Bullshit!" he hollers. "That's all it's about! Your kind hate us!"

I listen to his angry breathing for a while, feeling bad for him, but also stung that he assumes I dislike him based on his race . . . but also completely understanding why he'd make that assumption.

A person only has to hang around Gianni for half an hour to get a solid education in what prejudice looks like.

Keeping my voice low, I say, "I don't hate you. But even if you were Italian, you couldn't be together."

His breath hitches. "Because I'm poor?"

"No, sweet boy. Because she's engaged to be married."

"To someone she doesn't love! She was forced into it! If you care about her at all, how can you let that happen?"

He's so impassioned, so furious and desperate and so obviously sick with love, I'm moved.

So I tell him the truth, even though it gains me nothing.

"I wish I could help her, Juan Pablo. I wish you could be together, because I believe you'd make her happy. But in the world Lili and I live in, we don't get a choice. And if you try to interfere with this marriage, my brother will kill you. That isn't an empty threat. He'll kill you, and it won't matter to him at all."

In an anguished, theatrical burst, he cries, "I'd rather die than live without her!"

Jesus Christ, these kids are a Shakespearean tragedy waiting to happen.

"Keep this up, and you will die. I don't know what else to say."

"You can say you'll help us!"

"Okay, enough. You seem like a good kid. I don't want you to get hurt. So this stops. *Now.* If you really do love Lili, you have to end this. It's making her miserable." My voice hardens. "It's putting her in danger, too."

Into his fraught silence, I say, "Or do you think men like my brother and her fiancé won't care if they find out she isn't a virgin? Because let me tell you, Juan Pablo, you won't be the only one to pay a price. And what they'll do to her . . . death would be preferable."

When I disconnect, my hands are shaking.

I stand, set the phone on the floor, then stomp it under my heel as hard as I can. It splinters into pieces.

I open the door and look at Lili, standing there with her hands over her mouth and her eyes filled with tears.

"It's over, Lili. This is the end. You'll never speak to Juan Pablo again. And because of what happened today, your father has moved up the wedding. You're marrying Quinn in a week. I'm sorry."

There's nothing left to say, so I pull her into my arms and hold her tight as she sobs.

I'm not sure whose heart is more broken, hers or mine.

FOURTEEN

SPIDER

I don't sleep at all that night. Hypervigilant, I prowl the dark halls of the house, checking and re-checking rooms I've already cleared a dozen times.

Gianni and Leo's men are lurking around the grounds and patrolling the perimeters, but it gives me no peace of mind.

Every bit of that I might have had flew straight out the window when Caruso told me what the intruders said to Reyna. I knew it was one of his enemies who set it up—we've all got them.

But when the enemies are more interested in taking your daughter than killing you, that's a whole different problem.

So here I am again for the second time this year, pacing hallways and gnashing my teeth over a female under my protection who's a target for kidnapping.

Only this time, it's not the target I'm worried about.

I should be. Lili's going to be my bloody wife. She's a lovely girl, and she's going to make a lovely wife. But the moment Caruso said he believed the armed intruders were here for Lili, I could think of nothing else but the safety of her aunt.

Reyna.

Queen Devil Bitch of All Existence, who makes my blood boil and my dick hard and speaks to me with the kind of disrespect no man would dare to, because it would get him killed.

Reyna who hates me.

Reyna who challenges me.

Reyna who has the guts of a Viking and the body of a fertility goddess and the attitude of a feral cat.

I shouldn't be worried about her. If anyone ever did kidnap that woman, he'd regret it within the hour. He'd throw her back through the front window with an apology note and speed away as fast as he could.

If she didn't drive a dagger through his heart first.

She's a witch! Demon spawn of the devil!

But she shot a man for me. She had my back—literally—and killed a man.

Why did she do that if she hates me so much? She could've simply let me get killed and dusted off her hands. Good riddance to a man she insults at every opportunity and only ever calls by his last name.

And lies to like it's her favorite hobby.

A man who made her look like she wanted to puke when she saw him without his shirt.

But why was she so concerned about my wound? Why would she care if it got infected? Why would she offer to stitch me up?

Why would she *insist* on stitching me up, then take such care as she did, biting her lip in concentration?

And why, oh fucking *why*, can't I stop thinking about her?

We don't even like each other, for fuck's sake!

No. That's not true. I do actually like her. Despite her sharp edges that could cleanly shear off a limb, I like how smart she is. How quick-witted. How funny, though I'm usually the punchline of the joke. I like the way she lobs an insult like a tennis drive, then hits me again when I lob one back.

I like how protective she is of Lili. How tender she is with her. Like a mama bear with her cub.

It means she's not all razor blades and barbed wire. Somewhere underneath all that armor she wears beats a soft heart.

A soft heart that learned how to hide from a cruel hand.

I meant what I said when I told her I'd like to kill her dead husband. I'd even be happy to exhume his rotten corpse and have a go at that.

I also meant what I said when I told her I never wanted to see her after the wedding. That was the God's honest truth.

Because every second I spend in that woman's company is a reminder of all the reasons I agreed to an arranged marriage in the first place.

Christ. I wish a few dozen more of those intruders would show up.

I'm going to need to shoot a lot more people before all this is over.

FIFTEEN

REY

*W*hen I rise early in the morning and head to the kitchen to make breakfast for the men, I find Quinn already there, standing in the middle of the room like he's been waiting in that spot for centuries.

Surprised, I stop short in the doorway and look at him.

His eyes are bloodshot. His hair's a mess. He's wearing the same shirt he had on yesterday, the one with the rip through the shoulder and bloodstains down the sleeve.

He looks strung out. Dangerously wired. As if he was up all night mainlining cocaine.

"Good morning," I say cautiously.

His gaze drags over me like a rake over hot coals. His voice comes out rough. "You all right?"

"Yes. Why, did something happen while I was asleep?"

He shakes his head, then shoves a hand through his hair. He stares at me for a moment, then turns away abruptly and starts to pace back and forth in front of the island with his hands propped on his hips and his brows drawn down.

This is normally where I'd make a smart remark about his calm and cheery personality, but there's something different about him today. His thunderclouds have a heavier aspect. He's all charged nerves and crackling tension, and it makes me worried.

I take a few hesitant steps into the kitchen. "Quinn?"

He makes a sharp cutting motion with his hand and growls.

I put my hands up. "Okay."

Ignoring him, I set the oven to preheat. Then I head to the fridge and start pulling things out. Next, I hit the pantry. I put everything on the counter by the stove, start a pot of coffee, and begin to chop veggies and prep for the meal.

Behind me, Quinn paces back and forth. Every so often, he huffs, sounding like a bull pawing the ground before it charges.

I fight the almost overpowering urge to turn around and give him a hug.

He drops heavily into a chair, exhales in a gust, then groans. The sound is low and full of misery.

When I turn to look at him, he's got his elbows propped on the kitchen table. His eyes are closed and his head is gripped in his hands, his hair sticking through his fingers.

Without saying a word, I pour coffee into a big mug, add a teaspoon of sugar, and set the mug in front of him. Then I go back to cooking and ignore him again.

After a while, he says in a low voice, "How did you know I take my coffee black with sugar?"

Beating eggs in a mixing bowl, I smile to myself. "You seem like a man who likes a little sweetness but doesn't want anyone to know it."

Grouchy as hell, he snaps, "Aye? Any other witty observations you'd like to share?"

"Drink your coffee. It's too early to argue."

For the next ten minutes, we don't speak. With words, anyway.

He sits and throws lightning bolts at my back, which I deflect with a calm that only seems to incense him more.

I can tell he's spoiling for a fight, but I won't give it to him.

Twice, he jolts up from the table and refills his mug from the coffeepot, only to return to the table, fling himself into a chair again, and recommence brooding.

After he lets out his third loud grumble in as many minutes, I've had enough.

I stop what I'm doing, cross to the table, pull up a chair beside him, and say quietly, "What is it? I'm worried about you."

Stunned, he blinks at me.

"I'm serious, Quinn. I want to know what's wrong. Please tell me."

He blinks again. "Did . . . did you just say 'please'?"

"Cut the bullshit. What's happened?"

When he only sits there staring at me like I just landed from outer space, I prompt, "Did you argue with Gianni? Did you find out something about those men? Has there been a change of plans?"

"The wedding's still on, if that's what you mean," he says crossly.

I gaze at him for a moment, then sigh. "I'm sorry I've been so negative about that. I'm sure you can understand why, but . . . well, I was thinking that I've been really hard on you. Unfairly hard. After what you did yesterday . . ."

"What did I do?"

He says it as if he really has no recollection that he went full John Wick mode and hunted down and killed the men who blew a hole in the side of the house and wanted to kidnap Lili.

"You protected us. All of us. And you saved my life."

He swallows, his Adam's apple bobbing. His burning gaze never leaves my face. He says gruffly, "You saved mine."

"Probably not. I mean, that guy was a terrible shot. You would've blown a hole in his forehead before he could've gotten off another round. If it were *me* shooting you in the back, you'd be dead. Not that I would shoot you, because I've decided I don't hate you anymore, but you know what I'm saying."

When I smile at him, he exhales a small, astonished laugh.

"Just like that, you don't hate me anymore?"

I make a screwy face. "Let's say I've downgraded it to intense dislike and leave it at that."

"And all it took was a few murders," he says, looking dazed. "Had I only known that sooner."

"Ha. But seriously, all joking aside. Are you okay?"

He stares at me for a long moment in silence, then demands angrily, "Who *are* you right now? Where's the swamp witch?"

"Why can't I be a swamp witch *and* a sweetheart? Hecate had three forms, and everybody worshipped her. Also, you're one to talk, Dr. Jekyll." I stop to think. "Or is it Mr. Hyde? I can never remember which one's the monster."

Appearing exhausted, he sags back into his chair and passes a hand over his face. "Every time I have a conversation with you, I feel like I'm going insane."

"I take it that means you're not going to tell me what's wrong."

"I can't!"

That leaves me deflated. "Because you don't trust me."

"No, because I don't want to be telling secrets to the soul eater who replaced Queen Devil Bitch with this reasonable person." He waves a hand at me in irritation. "Whoever she is."

I raise my brows and stare at him. "Excuse me . . . *Queen Devil Bitch*?"

"Aye," he says without missing a beat. "No, wait. That's not it—it's Queen Devil Bitch of All Existence."

I'm horrified. "That's what they call me? How awful!"

He chuckles. "No, that's what *I* call you. God only knows what the other lads call you, but whatever it is, I'm damn sure they'd never say it to your face."

Deeply insulted, I say, "That's because they're afraid if they did, their wives would be picking out their caskets. Quinn, a swamp witch is one thing, but . . . *Queen Devil Bitch of All Existence*? Seriously?"

"Have you even met yourself, lass?"

"I'm not that bad!"

He snorts and scratches his beard. "Aye. And vipers aren't that poisonous."

I cross my arms over my chest and smile at him. "Oh, that reminds me. It wasn't sugar I put in your coffee. It was arsenic."

"You're only proving my point!"

The oven timer dings. I rise, pour the egg casserole mixture into six greased baking dishes, and put them in the double ovens. Then I turn back to Quinn.

"Fruit?"

"Pardon?"

"Would you like some fruit with your egg bake, or are you strictly a proteins kind of guy?"

He quirks his lips. "You mean you don't already know?"

I tilt my head and look at him from under lowered lashes. "I'd say you're a big-time fruit eater."

A faint tinge of pink stains his cheeks. He swallows. "What I really need is scotch."

"No, what you really need is a shower and a new shirt. I'd give you one of Gianni's, but you're much too big across the chest and shoulders to fit into anything of his."

"Was that . . . did you just give me a *compliment*?"

"Oh, stop gaping at me. I was only saying you need a change of clothes. We can't go ring shopping with you looking like you crawled out from under a bridge."

His face falls. "Ring shopping. Right."

He looks utterly depressed by the mention of it, which is confusing, considering he's the one who's so insistent on this marriage.

"Quinn?"

He glances up at me.

I hesitate, but decide I have to say it, no matter how much he won't like it. "Lili's going to need patience from you. Your marriage, at least at the beginning, will be very hard on her."

When his look sours, I quickly add, "I'm not talking about your dizzying mood changes now. I'm talking about the fact that she's young and naïve."

Not to mention madly in love with someone else.

My voice drops. "She's scared, okay? Please be gentle with her. If I won't be around to hold her hand, you're going to have to. And I know you can, because I've seen the human side you try so hard to keep buried. Give that side to her, and you'll make her happy."

He stares at my face with an expression on his own that's indescribable. If I didn't know better, I'd say it was anguish.

He says gruffly, "Goddammit, woman. Just when I think I've got you figured out, you grow another Hydra head and knock me on my arse again."

I throw my hands in the air. "Will you please stop calling me 'woman' like it's a bad word? I hate that!"

His piercing gaze on mine, he replies softly, "I've never said it like it's a bad word. It's the most beautiful word in the language."

Then he stands and walks out of the kitchen, leaving me staring after him in stunned silence.

An hour later, I've fed the men, checked on a still-sleeping Lili, and splashed enough cold water on my face to cool it from scorching to merely warm.

No such luck with my panties. They're still on fire.

Quinn called me beautiful.

I mean, I think he did. In a roundabout sort of way.

Didn't he? Or am I making it up in my head? Has my vagina hijacked my intellect and held it hostage so that it makes everything the man says now sound suggestive?

I hate myself for not knowing. I hate myself even more for wanting to know.

I hate myself most of all for hoping I'm right.

When Quinn reappears in the kitchen in a fresh shirt and says he's ready to leave, I can't look him in the eye. I just nod and keep rinsing dishes.

He stands there vibrating tension until he growls, "Any time this century."

I turn off the water, dry my hands, and walk past him, out of the kitchen.

"Where are you going?"

"To get my handbag, if that's all right with you, Prince Charmless."

He grumbles something under his breath that I ignore. Ten minutes later, we're in his big black Escalade, headed into the city.

The silence in the car is deafening.

When I can't take it anymore, I try to make polite conversation. "So where will you honeymoon?"

He looks at me as if he's unfamiliar with the word.

"Don't tell me you're not taking her on a honeymoon!"

He glares at the windshield, gripping the steering wheel so hard, I'm sure he's wishing it were my neck. Through clenched teeth, he says, "I really can't wait until I never see you again."

I stare at his stupid, handsome profile, forcing myself to refrain from dragging my nails down the side of his cheek. I don't want Lili to have to look at his gouged face during her wedding vows.

"You should take her to Ireland," I pronounce, then stare out the passenger window because I can't look at him one second longer.

After a while, he says gruffly, "Why Ireland?"

Resisting the urge to make a crack about the joys of drunken pub yodeling, I say instead, "So she can see where you were born, Quinn. Get to know you better. You know, meet all your relatives from the motherland and whatnot."

"I don't have any relatives left in Ireland."

The dark way he says it makes me glance over at him. His jaw is hard and his thunderclouds are gathering, but I have to ask.

"Because they're all in the States now?"

"Because they're all dead."

"Oh. I'm sorry to hear that."

Don't ask. Don't say it, Reyna. Be smart and leave it alone.

Into my ambivalent silence, he says, "Aye, lass, all of them. And no, I don't have anyone here, either."

"So it's just you?"

"Aye."

"No parents? Siblings? Cousins? No one?"

"No one," he repeats gruffly, then sends me a pointed look. "And that's the truth."

"You're the last Quinn?"

"There are a million Quinns," he says with a flick of his fingers. "Just not any I'm directly related to." After a pregnant pause, he adds, "Which was the point."

That sounds ominous. But he doesn't offer any further explanation, so I say, "I don't understand."

He closes his eyes briefly, shakes his head as if he's regretting the entire conversation, then heaves a sigh. "In the Old World, when someone really wants to send a message, they wipe out an entire family tree, top to bottom. Grandparents, parents, children, husbands, wives . . . every living generation related by blood or marriage to the one who caused the offense."

And here I thought the Cosa Nostra was brutal.

"That's what happened to your family?"

Instead of answering, he switches on the radio.

I reach over and switch it off. "How did you survive?"

He glances at the tattoo on my left ring finger. "How did *you* survive?"

I look out the window again, at the passing suburban landscape creeping toward the city. "Day by day. Any way I could."

"Then you already know. The details don't matter."

He switches on the radio again, ending the conversation.

I close my eyes and allow the sudden and intense longing to get to the dark heart of this strange changeling of a man to pass through me until it's only a faint, bittersweet taste on my tongue.

The wedding can't come soon enough.

He's a riptide and I'm swimming far out in dangerous waters, getting pulled under fast no matter how hard I fight to stay afloat.

SIXTEEN

SPIDER

*I*t becomes clear I made a massive mistake ordering Reyna to accompany me on the ring-buying excursion the moment we walk into the Cartier store in Manhattan and the store manager greets us with a big smile, open arms, and an enthusiastic, "Congratulations on your engagement!"

Reyna stares at the manager as if she's planning his murder.

She says icily, "How kind. Thank you. Now please show me the biggest diamond you have for sale."

"Do you have any preference for shape?"

"Whichever one's the most expensive."

The manager almost wets himself in excitement. "Right this way!"

Someone please fucking kill me now.

I follow behind them as they walk to a lighted glass display case near the back of the store. We're the only customers, as Declan called and arranged a private showing for us.

I didn't tell him I was bringing Reyna instead of Lili, because

I didn't want to get a lecture. Now I'm thinking I could've used a good lecture to talk me out of such a dumb idea.

I have no doubt that by the time we leave, I'll be flat broke.

The manager, who still hasn't introduced himself, hops behind the case and makes spokesmodel hands at the rows of glittering rings nestled in white velvet below.

I hear words like "flawless" and "exquisite," but I'm too distracted to pay attention to anything else.

Reyna has leaned over the counter. Her posture and the way the fabric of her dress clings emphasizes the perfect rounded swell of her arse. Inspecting the goods in the case below, she lifts a hand to her jaw and slips a pinky between her lips, biting the tip of it in concentration.

Good God, that mouth. How I want to fuck that luscious mouth.

I have to force myself to look away so the front of my trousers won't get tented.

"The pink ones are gorgeous. Lili would love those."

"You have excellent taste," the manager says, sounding awed. "Pink diamonds are among the rarest of all gems."

"Probably the priciest, too," I mutter.

"They sell for between one to five million per carat, depending on clarity and cut."

When I send him a sour glance, he smiles like a used car salesman. "But who can put a price on true love?"

"Me," I say flatly. "And it isn't five million bloody quid."

The manager glances at Reyna, who's giving me a look that could melt solid steel.

"But *darling*," she purrs, slinky as a panther. "Aren't I worth it?"

I narrow my eyes at her.

She smiles.

Sensing a power play between us and an opportunity to profit from it, the manager says to Reyna, "If you're looking for something *really* unusual, try this."

He opens the back of the case with a key from the chain on his wrist, removes a clear acrylic stand, and sets it on the glass counter. On the stand sits a ring composed of a simple rose gold band with an enormous bloodred stone set in the middle. It glitters and flashes under the light like it's alive.

"Is that a ruby?" says Reyna, frowning at it.

The manager replies in a hushed voice. "It's a red diamond. One of only a few ever mined. It contains zero impurities and is absolutely flawless."

It's also the exact color of Reyna's lush lips.

I stare at it, mesmerized by the vivid hue.

"Try it on," the manager urges, pulling the ring off its stand.

"Oh, no, I couldn't," Reyna starts to protest. But the manager has seized her hand and is already sliding the ring onto her left ring finger.

She yanks her hand away, but it's too late.

The ring sparkles on her finger like a big, brilliant drop of blood.

She holds her hand out as far away from her body as it will reach and gapes at it with wide, unblinking eyes. She's pale, and her hand is trembling.

I'm not sure, but I think she's about to vomit.

Very gently, I grasp her wrist and slide the ring off her finger. The tattoo on her skin appears somehow darker, the slanting script seeming to crawl like hissing snakes.

I blink, and the illusion is gone.

Reyna murmurs something in Italian, then exhales a shaky breath.

"It is, isn't it?" says the manager, beaming.

I hand the ring back to him. "You know Italian?"

He nods. "My mother was born in Rome. I never lived there, but we were brought up as kids speaking it at home. I took some college courses as well."

Reyna pulls her arm from my grip. "Please excuse me. I need to use the restroom."

"Yes, of course. Just through that archway. Second door on your left."

Nodding distractedly, she hurries away without looking back.

As the manager is putting the ring back into the case, I say in a low voice, "Did you happen to see the tattoo on my fiancée's ring finger?"

"Yes, Mr. Quinn, I did."

"What does it say?"

When he looks at me quizzically, I smile at him. "She's too shy to tell me herself."

He chuckles. "Well, I suppose that makes sense. It is a little awkward."

"How so?"

"Anyone with the words 'never again' tattooed where a wedding ring would sit probably has some strong feelings about matrimony. You must've been very persuasive."

Never again.

It hits me like a kick in the gut: a powerful urge to unalive her already-dead husband.

With a new sense of urgency, I ask, "What did she say to you about the ring?"

His smile is smug. "That it's the most beautiful thing she's ever seen in her life."

He whips out a business card from his suit pocket and writes something on the back. Then he slides it across the glass case toward me.

I pick it up, read the price of the red diamond, and almost laugh out loud.

Twenty million dollars.

Flipping over the card to read his name, I say, "Tell me, Lorenzo, if you were an eighteen-year-old girl, which of the pink ones would you like?"

He frowns in confusion. "Eighteen?"

"It's a long story."

On the drive back to the house, Reyna is silent.

She has an expression on her face that I've never seen before. It's a mix of longing and loneliness, pain and sadness.

A kind of sadness that makes her look lost.

"You want to talk about it, viper?"

She glances at me, then turns away, shaking her head. "Talking never helps anything."

"I know a few therapists who'd disagree with you."

"You say that like you actually know therapists."

"I do."

I feel her attention sharpen, but she doesn't look at me. "Personal friends of yours, or . . . ?"

I shrug. "I went to counseling for a few years. Tried a few different ones."

Now she does look at me, swinging her head around to stare at me in shock. *You?*

I grumble, "Don't make it sound so bloody implausible."

"Not implausible, impossible."

"Why?"

"Because you're you!"

"Whatever the fuck that means."

"Did these therapists know what you do for a living?"

"No. I never talked about my work."

"What did you talk about?"

After a moment to gather my thoughts, I say, "The meaning

of life. The futility of revenge. How forgiveness isn't for the other person, it's for you. How to go on when you don't have a reason for living."

Her silence is profound. I don't risk looking at her.

I can feel her looking at me, though, and that's enough.

Dragging a hand through my hair, I exhale heavily. "When I was a young man, there was a time when all I did was think about dying. I wished for it, every day. I'd put myself in all these crazy situations, tempting fate." My chuckle is dark. "I was suicidal."

"Why is that funny?"

"Because I could easily kill another man, but I never found the guts to kill myself."

She says softly, "Oh, Quinn. Not killing yourself wasn't an act of cowardice. It was an act of courage. It takes so much more bravery to keep living when you're in pain than it does to give up."

When I look over at her and our eyes meet, it feels like I plugged myself into a socket. Electricity, snapping hot, courses through my veins. Even the air feels charged with a current. My hair is probably standing on end.

She murmurs, "And for what it's worth, I'm glad you're alive."

I can tell she immediately regrets that, because she closes her eyes, shakes her head, and turns away.

We don't speak for the rest of the ride. As soon as I pull up into the circular driveway and stop, she jumps out of the car and hurries into the house. I sit there with the engine running, fighting the need to run after her.

Then I text Declan that I need something to keep me distracted for the next week.

Preferably something violent.

SEVENTEEN

REY

*T*he rest of the week flies by.

A rep from the Vera Wang atelier in Manhattan comes to the house with wedding gowns for Lili to try on. Since we don't have enough time to have a custom dress made, we have to buy something off the rack and have it fitted. Luckily, Mamma is an excellent seamstress and can do the adjustments.

Lili runs to the restroom twice to throw up and breaks down into tears three times while trying on dresses. But we get through it and decide on a gorgeous A-line chiffon-and-lace gown. The skirt is flowing with a short train, and the bodice is detailed with sequins and seed pearls. She looks like an angel in it.

A teary, miserable angel.

When I ask her how she's holding up, she says darkly, "You don't want to know."

The last time I felt this helpless, a premeditated murder was right around the corner.

On Friday, the day before the wedding, we fly to Boston on Gi-anni's jet. I've packed everything Lili will need to start her new life. Except for antidepressants.

She has a wild, desperate look in her eyes that I don't like.

With a dozen armed guards in tow, we check into the Four Seasons under an assumed name, taking the presidential suite for the four of us. The rest of the rooms on the floor are empty, because Gianni made sure to book them all.

Paranoia is driving him crazy.

He still doesn't have any idea who the men were who invaded the house. Despite all his power and his contacts in the under-world, he hasn't been able to unearth a clue.

The lack of information is unnerving. There's always someone willing to talk for a price—or be persuaded to, under threat—but not this time. No one seems to know anything.

Most chilling of all is that the forensic technicians working on the bodies at the morgue came up with nothing identifiable about any of the men.

The pads of all their fingers had been burned off with acid. Dental records showed no matches. Their faces weren't in any law enforcement database.

They were ghosts.

I tried not to admit to myself that I would've felt better if Quinn had stayed at the house the rest of the week, but my sub-conscious knew better. The house felt emptier without his ex-pansive presence in it. The Mob sent armed reinforcements to take his place and provide supplemental protection to Gianni and Leo's men, but it didn't make me rest easier.

A hundred Irishmen couldn't give me the same peace of mind.

He might be grouchy, bossy, and altogether aggravating, but Quinn's the one to have around when things get bad.

I hate that I think that. But for Lili's sake, I'm glad. If someone tries to kidnap her again, they'll have to deal with his crazy-but-fiercely-protective ass.

And I know they'll regret it.

In the car on the way to the rehearsal at the church the night before the wedding, Gianni sweats like a pig.

"Why are you so nervous?" says Mamma, frowning at him. "Your daughter's the one getting married."

Sitting next to me in the back seat of the limo, Lili rests her head on the back of the seat and closes her eyes. I squeeze her clammy hand, but she doesn't squeeze back.

Mopping his forehead with a silk pocket square, Gianni says, "But I'm the one who'll be up shit's creek if anything goes wrong."

"What could go wrong?"

I say, "Don't tempt fate by making a list, Gianni."

Mamma cackles. "As if fate has anything to do with anything. It's all God. He's the one with the mean streak."

To Lili as much as Gianni, I say soothingly, "Nothing will go wrong. Boston belongs to the Mob, and everyone knows you don't cross Declan O'Donnell."

Mamma says, "She's not marrying Declan O'Donnell."

I send her a pointed look. "She's marrying his right-hand man, which is almost as good."

"Almost isn't the same thing."

"Mamma, stop! You're scaring her!"

She looks at Lili, sitting passively beside me with her eyes closed and face pale. "That child isn't scared. She's in mourning."

Gianni frowns. "Mourning over what?"

"Don't listen to her," I interrupt, giving her a hard stare. "She's already had half a bottle of wine."

She smiles back at me. "The night's still young."

I might have to lock her in a coat closet.

When we arrive at the lovely old brick church, Quinn is

already there. Dressed in his usual black Armani suit, with his hair combed and his eyes burning, he's breathtaking.

Lili takes one look at him smoldering inside the vestibule doors and lets out a whimper.

"Mr. Quinn," says Gianni, rushing over with his hand and his panic outstretched in front of him. "So good to see you again. Are we late?"

"No. I've been here for hours." He shakes hands with Gianni, nods at Lili and Mamma, then looks over at me.

The sheer force of his gaze knocks me back onto my heels.

"Reyna," he says gruffly.

"Quinn."

His gaze scorches me up and down. He licks his lips, straightens his tie, and shifts his weight from foot to foot. Then he looks away, jaw muscles flexing.

"Everyone's already inside."

I can tell Gianni's horrified that we're the last to arrive, but he tries not to show it.

"Wonderful! Shall we go in?"

Quinn gestures toward the doors. Gianni takes Lili's hand and drags her through them. Mamma follows, chuckling to herself and shaking her head. I'm following her, wondering if she's starting to lose her marbles, when Quinn reaches out and grabs my arm.

Startled, I look at him.

His voice low, he says, "I've been thinking."

"Really? Did you borrow someone else's brain?"

"Very funny, viper."

We gaze at each other for a moment as his fingers tighten ever so slightly around my upper arm. When I inhale, I smell him. Skin, heat, and masculine musk. Just his essence, undiluted by cologne.

My mouth starts to water. I think that faint moaning I hear is my ovaries.

He says, "It wasn't fair, what I said about you not seeing Lili after the wedding. She's welcome to go see you in New York anytime she wants."

I'm so surprised, I almost laugh. "Are you sure? I thought you couldn't stand the sight of me."

His reply is stiff. "That's why I said she could go see you, not that you could come see her."

Why is he holding my arm? Why is my heart pounding? Why are we standing so close?

I say, "It's good you came around, because I wasn't going to obey that ridiculous order anyway."

His lashes lower. He drawls, "What a shock."

"I didn't think you'd be surprised. May I please have my arm back now?"

His gaze takes a leisurely trip over me again, skimming every curve. "Why do you always wear black?"

"Says the man who always wears black."

"I'm a mobster. It's the uniform."

"It's the uniform for widows, too."

"You've been a widow for three years. Black's only traditional for the first year."

Surprised he remembered that detail, I say, "I'll wear black as long as I'm a widow. Which will be forever, so I'll always wear black. Is this the best time to be having a conversation about my wardrobe? You're supposed to be marching around an altar right now, practicing for tomorrow."

Ignoring me, probably because I'm making too much sense, he says, "You won't be a widow anymore if you remarry."

My laugh is soft, but full of bitterness. "I'll *never* remarry."

"Never say never. What if you met the right lad?"

"I'm disappointed you decided to smoke something hallucinogenic before your own wedding rehearsal, Quinn, but 'never' is the correct choice of word. It means not ever, at no time, absolutely not. The threat of my own death couldn't compel me to walk down the aisle again."

Staring deep into my eyes, he says in a throaty voice, "I said never again once, too. Turns out I was wrong."

My heart starts to beat faster. I become aware of all the skin on my body at once, because it's overheating. I feel like I'm being roasted from the inside out.

I try to sound normal, but my voice comes out faint. "What was your never about?"

His gaze drops to my mouth.

He's about to say something when we're interrupted by a woman's voice.

"There you are! I thought we'd lost you."

I look over to see a stunning brunette in a tight white dress standing a few feet away, smiling at us, her hands propped on her hips. She's tall and curvy, with a glint in her green eyes that's equally self-confident and mischievous.

Quinn drops his hand from my arm and steps back. "Hullo, Sloane."

"Hiya, Spider! Introduce me to your friend."

"Reyna, this is Sloane, Declan's wife. Sloane, Reyna."

Sloane and I shake hands while she smiles and looks me over with unabashed interest.

"So this is the infamous Black Widow. Babe, have I been dying to meet you. I have *so* many questions."

Horrified, I glance at Quinn. "*Black Widow?* What happened to Queen Devil Bitch of All Existence?"

He sighs. "I didn't dub you that, viper. It's what everyone else calls you."

Sloane says, "I like Queen Devil Bitch of All Existence *way* better! How badass! If you don't want to use that one, I'll take it. I can already see the tattoo, a sexy red demon with horns, a long tail, and a black diamond crown, sitting on a throne of skulls in the middle of a lake of fire. Right?"

She's still grinning at me, shaking my hand. I'm starting to feel like I'm being filmed for one of those reality shows where they punk unsuspecting fools for laughs.

"Sure. We'll get matching ones. I'll put mine right above the spot where my heart's supposed to be. You know, if I had one."

When I smile at her, she throws back her head and laughs. "Ooh, I like you. I'd say let's be besties, but I already have one of those. You can be next in line, though."

I deadpan, "My life will be complete."

She links her arm through mine and leads me into the church, throwing a glance over her shoulder at Quinn. As soon as we're out of earshot, she murmurs, "A word of advice? Stay away from Boston for a while after the wedding. Like, forever."

I'm not sure I want to know what she means, but I ask anyway. "Why?"

"Because, babe, any man who looks at a woman the way Spider looks at you is already thinking about how he's going to ruin his life."

EIGHTEEN

REY

The rehearsal goes off without a hitch, but for me, it's thirty minutes of absolute hell.

I don't look at Quinn. I want to, badly, but I don't. If what Sloane said is true, then this insane carnal attraction I feel toward him is mutual.

And very obvious.

Which means we're standing on top of two tons of dynamite, and it's only a matter of time before someone strikes a match.

I beg off the dinner afterward by claiming a stomachache. The limo drops me off at the hotel, and I go straight to the bedroom and lie down. I get up after five minutes and raid the minibar.

When I pour the vodka into a glass, my hands tremble.

Two hours later, Gianni, Mamma, and Lili return.

Lili goes into her bedroom and locks the door. Mamma heads to the sofa in the living room and lies down. Gianni whips off his tie and tosses it onto the back of a chair in the dining room, shaking his head and muttering.

"How did dinner go?"

He stops his muttering to glare at me. "How did it go? I'll tell you how it went. Quinn didn't speak a goddamn word to me the entire time."

From the sofa, Mamma calls, "He didn't speak to anybody else, either."

Gianni nods in agreement. "Not even his own boss! You should've seen him, sitting there grinding his molars in silence while everyone else tried to make conversation around him. Who does he think he is, king of the universe?"

Actually, yes. But I don't say that out loud. "He's probably just nervous about tomorrow."

"What does *he* have to be nervous about, the rude son of a bitch?"

I say cuttingly, "Only that his new bride was the target of kidnapping a week ago. Maybe he's worried about what might happen at the wedding!"

Mamma chuckles. "If he shows up. That man has feet colder than the iceberg that sunk the *Titanic.*"

"Don't even suggest it! On Monday, the families are holding a vote for the new capo. If that Irish bastard doesn't show up for the wedding . . ." Gianni shudders, unwilling to even finish the thought.

"Jesus, Gianni. Do you care about anything else but becoming capo?"

He looks at me as if I've lost my mind. "What a stupid question. Of course not."

I pour myself another vodka, then go knock on Lili's door. She doesn't answer.

"Lili?"

"Go away, *zia*. I need to be alone right now."

"But—"

"This is my last night of freedom!" she screams from behind the door. "Leave me the fuck alone!"

I close my eyes and bang my forehead gently on the door several times. Then I shoot the rest of the vodka and go to bed.

I wake in the morning with a sense of dread so powerful, it feels like a premonition.

I run to Lili's bedroom in a panic and bang on her door. When she opens it, I'm so relieved to see her, I almost collapse into a pile at her feet.

"Thank God," I say breathlessly, pressing a hand over my hammering heart.

She makes a face at me. "Did you think I escaped out the window in the middle of the night?"

"No. But now that you mention it, yes."

"We're on the nineteenth floor. The only thing I'd be using the window for is to throw myself out of it. Now please leave me alone. I have to put on my shroud and get ready."

"It's not a shroud, it's a wedding dress."

When she only stares at me in baleful silence, I say, "You're right. It's the same thing. Are you okay? Scratch that, what I meant was do you need me for anything?"

"Yes."

"What?"

"Tell me how to kill my husband and get away with it."

I close my eyes and draw a breath. "I'm going to pretend I didn't hear that."

"Then you can't help me with anything. Knock on my door when it's time to leave. Until then, I'm holding a candlelight vigil for my lost future."

She shuts the door in my face.

At four o'clock, we head to the church. In the limo, everyone is tense and silent. Even Mamma looks unhappy. When Lili sees the huge crowd milling around on the steps outside the church, she turns white.

I murmur, "Steady, *tesoro*."

She doesn't respond. Nobody else says anything, either.

Surrounded by a barrier of bodyguards, we go inside the church. The coordinator, an elderly woman in a red cardigan who has stooped shoulders and a sweet smile, shows us girls into the bride's dressing room while Gianni heads off to make sure Quinn has arrived.

In her wedding dress, Lili drops heavily into an overstuffed chintz chair in the dressing room and stares blankly at the wall. Her bouquet is already here, waiting on the coffee table in a white box with tissue paper. My bouquet is with it, a smaller version of hers.

"I'm sorry your father wouldn't allow you to have any other bridesmaids besides me," I say gently, touching an orchid in my bouquet.

"It doesn't make a difference," she says, her voice lifeless. "I won't be seeing my friends again, anyway. I'll be living here in Boston from now on. And you know they won't be allowed to come visit me."

I'm about to protest that Quinn will let her have friends when Gianni bursts into the room in a rush of excitement.

"He's here! Quinn's already here and everything's fine and I think I'm having a heart attack!"

Sounding bored, Mamma says, "You can die after you walk me to my seat. I don't want to navigate that crowd alone."

She gives Lili a kiss on the cheek and hobbles out on her cane. An exultant Gianni follows behind, leaving me alone with my grieving niece.

Before I can think of something appropriate to say, she asks me to leave her alone until it's time for us to walk down the aisle.

My heart aching for her, I leave, quietly closing the door behind me. Ignoring the guards stationed outside and avoiding the crowd of people in the vestibule, I find a deserted ladies' room in a back hallway and lock myself in a stall for a few minutes to try to catch my breath.

I can't. I sit there hyperventilating for long, awful minutes until finally, the church bells start to ring. Then I head back to the dressing room, feeling like a cement block has been dropped on my chest.

When I open the door to the dressing room, I freeze in horror.

Lili is on her knees in the middle of the floor, sobbing.

She's clinging to a young man with dark hair dressed in a brown leather jacket, jeans, and a white T-shirt, who's standing protectively in front of her, using his body as a shield.

Juan Pablo's dark eyes burn with defiance and fury.

Gianni stands six feet away, pointing a gun at his chest.

Reacting purely on instinct, I slam the door shut so the guards can't see what's happening and order, "Gianni, put down the gun."

He spews curses in Italian, then shouts in English, "You cocksucker motherfucker piece of shit! You crawled in through the window like a cockroach? Say your fucking prayers, *coglione!*"

Lili must've called him from the hotel. She called him and told him where she was getting married, and he came here to stop the wedding.

Despite kicking myself for leaving her alone in a room with a telephone, I have to admit I feel a deep sense of admiration for Juan Pablo's bravery.

He's brave, but so, so stupid. Gianni will never let him walk out of this room alive.

"Papa, please! Please listen to me!" wails Lili, crying so hard, her whole body shakes.

"Why should I fucking listen to you? You've dishonored your whole family!"

Creeping closer to Lili, I say, "Everyone calm down. Take a breath, Gianni. Don't do anything stupid."

He looks at me, his eyes wild and his face bright red. "She's been fucking this kid, Reyna! She just admitted it! She thinks she's in love with this . . . this . . . son of a pool man! She's ruined! And she's ruined *me*!"

When he lurches a step closer to them, waving the gun like a lunatic and shouting about how Juan Pablo's about to meet his maker, Lili screams in terror, "You can't kill him! I'm pregnant!"

Gianni freezes. His eyes widen. All the blood drains from his face.

Pregnant.

Beyond my shock, there's a dawning anger. Lili would've married Quinn if Juan Pablo hadn't shown up. She would've married Quinn and tried to pass off their baby as his.

Would she have ever told me? Would she have expected me to keep that from him, that the child he believed to be his own was, in fact, another man's?

Pretending to be a virgin on your wedding night is one thing. Lying for an entire lifetime about the real identity of your child's father is quite another.

My anger gets sidetracked when Gianni hisses, "Then you *both* have to die."

Before he can pull the trigger, I jump in front of Juan Pablo. "No!"

"Get out of the way, Reyna," Gianni snarls.

Holding out my hands, I say, "You don't have to do this! There's another way!"

"There's no other fucking way! There are four hundred people out in that church waiting to see a wedding. When Lili doesn't walk down the aisle, who do you think will be blamed? What do you think will happen to me? To *us*? Quinn will be humiliated. The contract will be canceled. We'll lose our standing with the other families, I won't be named capo, and we might as well start digging our own graves. It's all over for all of us unless Quinn gets a wife!"

Unless Quinn gets a wife.

Oh shit. I knew today was going to be a nightmare.

I drag a deep breath into my lungs and give my life away.

It's not the first time I've done it, but it is the first time I've done it for a noble cause.

Saving three lives counts as noble, right?

Staring straight into Gianni's wild eyes, I say quietly, "Lili isn't the only single woman in the Caruso family."

It takes him a moment before he understands. Then he puffs out an astonished breath.

"Now put the gun down and send someone to go get Mamma."

"What do you need her for?"

I exhale, barely able to believe the words about to come out of my own mouth.

"She has to alter a wedding dress."

NINETEEN

SPIDER

*S*tanding beside me on the steps leading up to the altar, Declan glances at me so many times from the corner of his eye, I'm getting annoyed.

I try to keep my voice as low as possible because there are four hundred bloody people staring at me. "Stop that, for fuck's sake. I'm solid."

He smooths a hand down the front of his tux and smiles at our audience. A woman on the bride's side of the aisle near the front smiles back coyly and starts to fan herself with the wedding program.

Barely moving his lips, he murmurs, "Aye? As solid as you were last night during dinner when you were acting like a mute gorilla? Or as solid as you've been all morning, wearing a face like you've got a date with a firing squad?"

Through gritted teeth, I say, "Stop worrying about me."

"It's not you I'm worried about. It's your blood pressure. You're wired to the moon, and your head's about to explode. I don't want brains all over my tux."

From Declan's other side, Kieran leans in and whispers, "Ye do look a wee bit frightful, lad. Like maybe there's ants in yer pants, nibblin' on yer willy."

"Thank you. Arsehole."

The organ music sounds tinny and grating in my ears. The smell of flowers and women's perfume is overpowering. I'm sweating in my tux, there's a metallic taste on my tongue, and I could really use a stiff nip of scotch to settle my stomach.

I just have to get through the ceremony. Then I'll be better. Then I can stop regretting the fuck out of this god-awful decision and get on with my bloody life.

Like every other man who gets married.

Except Declan. He doesn't regret it for a second. He'd marry Sloane every day if he could, the mad bastard. She's sitting in the front row on the groom's side, beautiful and beaming like one of Raphael's Madonnas, making all the other women around her look like dowdy pensioners.

Only Reyna could eclipse her.

Reyna with her scarlet lips and acid tongue and body that men and gods would gladly die for. Reyna with her tender heart and easy lies.

Reyna who *I'm not fucking thinking about.*

Again.

Forcing the thought of her from my mind, I concentrate on the row of stained-glass windows lining one side of the sanctuary. It immediately makes me think of the stained-glass windows at Reyna's house, so I change my focus to the restless crowd.

My gaze lands on an unfamiliar woman sitting on the aisle about half a dozen rows back. She's wearing a navy blue dress with a pattern of pretty flowers that are the exact pale greenish-gray shade of Reyna's mermaid eyes.

I'm so fucked.

When the music changes to the bride's processional, I'm relieved at the distraction.

My relief lasts about two seconds, until Declan says, "Why are they playing this? It's the wrong music. The matron of honor is supposed to come down before the bride."

He's right. That's how we rehearsed it last night. Reyna should walk down the aisle before Lili and Gianni and take her place opposite the groom and groomsmen on the steps of the altar. Then "Here Comes the Bride" starts, which is everyone's signal to stand. Then the bride comes down the aisle, arm in arm with her father.

But there's no Reyna. And there's no Gianni.

Instead, walking slowly out alone from the narthex, is Lili. Wearing a lovely white gown and holding a bouquet of white flowers. A long lace veil obscures her face.

My first thought is that something bad has happened to Reyna. I know bloody well she'd never disappoint Lili by not showing up for the wedding, so whatever's happened, it's major.

My blooming panic stalls when Kieran whispers in confusion, "Is it just me, or did the wee lass grow a whopping pair of melons overnight?"

I peer more closely at the slowly approaching figure.

He's right.

Those aren't Lili's tits.

That's not her nipped waist, either, or her generous hips.

Lili has a girl's figure. The person walking down the aisle has the full, dangerous curves of a woman.

My heart makes one final, painful squeeze inside my chest, then drops dead.

Declan says, "Sweet Mother Mary. Looks like there's been a change of plans."

Murmurs arise from the Italian side of the aisle. People are starting to whisper, rustling in their finery as they crane their necks and gawk at the bride passing by who they can obviously tell is the wrong one.

Everybody on the Irish side has confused looks, trying to figure out what's happening.

"Spider? You want to tell me how we're going to handle this?"

I'd answer Declan's question, but I'm unable to speak. I'm blank with shock. My brain's in a jumble, my ears are ringing, and my central nervous system can't decide if it's about to shut down altogether or burn through a lifetime of adrenaline reserves in the next ten seconds.

The only thing that's working—big surprise—is my dick.

Watching Reyna walk toward me down the aisle in a wedding gown has me sprung so hard and so fast, it's got to be some kind of goddamn erection record.

She gracefully passes the first row of pews, walks up onto the altar steps, and faces me. Behind the veil, she's tense, unsmiling, and very beautiful.

The only thing that manages to make it past my lips is a hoarse "What the fuck?"

She says quietly, "You wanted a wife, Quinn. You got one."

The murmurs from the guests grow louder. I sense things are about to get even more banjaxed than they already are.

So I turn to Declan and say, "Don't let anyone move. I'll be back in two minutes."

I grab Reyna by the arm and pull her away.

She allows it without fighting me or saying a word. I stalk past the startled priest and across the chancel, headed toward the sacristy at the back. I yank open the door, pull Reyna through it, and slam the door shut behind me.

She backs up several steps until she hits the wall and can't go any farther.

Surrounded by racks of priest's vestments in the small, office-like room, we stare at each other in blistering silence.

I growl, "Start talking, viper. And whatever comes out of that mouth of yours better be the bloody truth."

She licks her lips nervously. She inhales and briefly closes her eyes. Then she opens her eyes and looks straight into mine.

"Lili's in love with a boy named Juan Pablo. He came here to stop the wedding. Gianni found them together in the dressing room and was going to kill them both."

I try to unfuck my brain long enough to piece a sentence together. "How does that end up with you in a wedding dress?"

She knits her brows. "Because of the deal you made with Gianni. What other Caruso female did you think would take Lili's place? My mother?"

When I don't say anything, she begs softly, "Please, Quinn. Please don't hurt them. They're good kids. They're just in love."

I huff out a laugh that's part surprise and part anger. "Why the fuck do you think I'd hurt her for being in love?"

Caught off guard by that, she blinks.

Now I'm *really* insulted.

I demand, "Do you really think so bloody little of me?"

"I . . . I didn't know what to think. Everything happened so fast. All I knew was that Gianni was about to start firing his gun, so I proposed an alternative."

We're staring at each other again. Both of us are breathing hard. She's got anxiety written all over her, I'm about to choke in my bloody bow tie, and my dick is painfully straining the zipper of my trousers, throbbing with need just from looking at her.

Looking at her and thinking *Fuck me, how bad I want to be balls-deep in that.*

I lick my lips and step closer.

"So you thought I'd just accept this little switch of yours? You thought I'd have no problem substituting you for Lili?"

She gazes at me for a moment, then pulls the veil back over her head, exposing her face.

And her chest. And her cleavage. And her shoulders. And her lovely long neck, on the side of which a vein erratically pulses.

Christ, she's fucking magnificent. I almost groan out loud with desire.

Examining the expression on my face, she says, "Yes."

Because I'm no longer in complete control of my body, I step closer until we're only inches apart and I'm staring down into her wide, beautiful eyes, watching her fight not to give in to the urge to run.

"You told me last night not even the threat of your own death could make you walk down the aisle again."

"It was the threat of Lili's death that changed my mind."

"So this is about Lili? That's all it's about?"

When she glances away, I take her chin in my hand and force her to look at me. "It's truth-telling time, remember?"

She nibbles on her lower lip for a moment, hesitating. "I'm not comfortable answering that."

"And I'm not comfortable taking a wife who thinks she's not going to have to sleep with me."

She closes her eyes and mutters, "Jesus Christ, Quinn, you're killing me."

Leaning close to her ear, my heart pounding like mad and my dick aching, I murmur, "If I marry you, Reyna, I get to fuck you as hard and as often as I want."

"Oh my God."

"That's the deal, or there's no deal."

She says sarcastically, "Should we add it to the contract?"

I pull away and gaze down at her. "I've wanted you since the first second I saw you, stabbing me to death with those eyes from the bedroom window at your house. This fake marriage includes sex, or it doesn't happen."

She glares at me. "Your charm could sweep a girl right off her feet, you know that?"

"Wait till you see my cock. Then you'll really be swooning."

Her whole face turns red, from her neck to her hairline. She presses her lips together into a thin line.

I know that isn't a rejection. She's not saying no, which means she's saying yes.

But she has to say it out loud.

"So? Do you agree?"

Sounding as if she'd like to shove her bouquet down my throat, she says, "Yes, Quinn. I agree."

"Good. Then go ahead and ask me."

"Ask you what?"

"To marry you."

Her mouth drops open. She stares at me in shock for a moment, then says flatly, "You're joking."

I point at my face. "This isn't my joking face. Ask me. And do it nicely, or I might say no, because I'll be taking my own life into my hands."

"How so?"

I smirk at her. "Any man who marries a Black Widow has to sleep with one eye open."

Oh, how she hates it when I smirk. Her eyes glitter with anger. She says through stiff lips, "That's a very smart idea."

Then she draws herself up to her full height, looks at me with withering disdain, and grits out, "Mr. Quinn . . . will you marry me?"

I reach out and stroke my fingertips over her cheek. "Aye, viper," I murmur, feeling my blood pump fast and hot through my veins. "I'll marry you. But if you decide to kill me, wait until tomorrow."

She arches a brow. "Because?"

"Because I need to feel those sharp claws of yours dig into my back at least once before I die."

I grab her hand and lead her out of the room and back to the altar.

TWENTY

REY

*W*hen we exit the room, half the church is on its feet. The sanctuary echoes with sound. Whispering voices, muffled laughter, the rustle of clothing. The instant we're spotted, however, the noise dies and everyone turns to stare at us.

Quinn commands loudly, "Everybody back in your bloody seats."

He drags me to my position, says to Declan, "Full speed ahead, mate," then snaps his fingers at the priest, indicating he wants him to get a move on.

The priest looks at Declan for direction.

Sending an amused glance toward the astounded guests, Declan says, "Maybe we should skip the mass and get straight to the vows, Father."

"Yer bang on," says Kieran, chuckling. "This rowdy lot's about to start throwin' eggs."

I still haven't caught my breath when the priest says to me in a heavy Irish accent, "What's your name, lass?"

"Reyna."

"Lovely. Best of luck to you."

Cradling the Bible against his chest, he looks up at the crowd and lifts a hand. He keeps it lifted until everyone has taken a seat again and the sanctuary is silent. "Dearly beloved, we are gathered here today to celebrate the union of Homer and Reyna in the blessed sacrament of marriage."

More than one person on both sides of the aisle whispers, "Who?"

Ignoring them, Quinn growls to the priest, "Get to the kissing part."

He's staring at me when he says it, wearing an expression of hunger and hot impatience, his gaze darting back and forth between my eyes and my mouth.

My hands tremble so hard, all the flowers in the bouquet quake.

The priest sighs, shaking his head. "Very well. Do you, Homer, take this woman—"

"I do."

"Hold your horses, lad," the priest mutters. "This isn't a bloody race." He exhales hard and starts again. "Do you, Homer—"

"I do."

"—take this woman, Reyna—"

"I do."

After pausing for another aggrieved sigh, he continues. "To be your wedded wife. To have and to hold from this day—"

Quinn interrupts vehemently, "I do. To all of it. Now get to the kissing part."

"You can't kiss her until she says her vows!"

"Then get on with it!"

The priest looks at the vaulted ceiling for a beat, then turns to me. "Do you, Reyna . . ."

That's all I hear. After that, everything is drowned out by the high-pitched buzzing in my ears and the roar of my pulse underscoring it.

I'm sweating. Trembling. Hyperventilating so badly, I'm in danger of passing out. This must be a dream or a nightmare, some impossible fantasy world I'm trapped in where I agreed to marry a stranger to save my niece's life.

Except Quinn's not a stranger. Not a total stranger, anyway.

But he is the one who described this union as a "fake" marriage.

A fake marriage specifically including sex.

So we're both here by obligation, but he's already got an advantage. He's gained a concession from me, but I haven't gained anything.

Except another lifetime commitment I didn't want.

Suddenly, I realize the sanctuary has gone dead silent.

There's an air of expectation, like a collective held breath. I look around in panic, unsure what's happening because I've been lost in my thoughts, when the priest gently prompts, "This is where you say 'I do,' lass."

Panicking, I blurt, "Where's the ring?"

A ripple of laughter goes through the crowd.

Quinn's glower indicates he doesn't find anything funny.

Declan reaches into the jacket of his tux. He pulls out a folded white silk pocket square. He unwraps it and hands Quinn a ring.

Quinn takes my left hand in his and slides the ring onto my finger.

It glitters there, big and bold, red and brilliant, as vivid as a drop of fresh blood.

Shocked to see the red diamond, I whisper, "You said you bought one of the pink ones."

"I did. I returned it for this one."

"Why?"

He gazes down into my wide eyes with the full force of his potent masculinity engulfing me.

"I decided I needed something to remind me every day that my heart can't be trusted. What could be better than a stone the exact color of your lips?"

That makes me lightheaded. "It's lipstick, you big dummy. Also, that makes not one iota of sense."

He growls, "Maybe I'm lying. You're familiar with the concept. Now say 'I do,' viper, and give me that goddamn mouth."

I draw my final breath of freedom. I make a silent prayer for strength. Then, so softly it's hardly even a breath, I say, "I do."

Quinn knocks the bouquet out of my hands, yanks me against his body, and kisses me.

It's hard and demanding at first. I can tell he expects me to resist or twist away, but when I wind my arms up around his shoulders and sink into him, his mouth gentles. Cradling me in his arms, he sweeps his tongue against mine, the pressure as soft as his lips are.

Within seconds, I'm lost to it.

My fingers creep into his hair. All that soft, silky golden hair. I tug on it, wanting him even closer. Wanting him to devour me with his mouth.

The low sound of pleasure that rumbles through his chest makes me shiver.

The kiss goes on and on, going from sweet to hungry and back again. I'm floating and flying and falling, all at the same time. His mouth is decadently lush. His taste, delicious. I don't care at all that we have four hundred witnesses, or that my life is over, or that I've traded my freedom for Lili's.

I've never been kissed like this before.

Muscles I didn't know I had are waking up and stretching. Desire unfurls like a heated lotus under my skin. A steady pulse beats between my legs, my breasts feel heavy, and my nipples ache. I feel a wild, animalistic urge for him to throw me onto the altar, hold me down, and fuck me.

When he finally breaks away, I'm gasping and unsteady, woozy as a drunk.

My eyes drift open. I find him gazing down at me with blazing eyes, panting, his parted lips stained red with my lipstick.

He breathes in astonishment, "Fucking hell, woman."

There's a swell of noise. Clapping. Hooting and laughter, stomping feet. I turn my head and blink at the riotous crowd, unable to understand what's happening because my brain is still floating somewhere in outer space.

Then Quinn's handing me a ring. It's an unembellished band of dark matte metal, black on the outside and gunmetal gray within.

He says, "I took the liberty of buying my own wedding ring, considering nobody asked me what I wanted. Put it on."

Concentrating hard on maintaining consciousness, I take it with shaking hands and slide it onto his left ring finger.

He stares at it for a moment, his expression pensive as he examines it.

Then he looks up at me and grins. "I just wifed a viper."

My laugh is faint and disbelieving. "And I just married an insect."

"Arachnid," he corrects, eyes sparkling.

"Excuse me. That's *much* better."

He kisses me again, grabbing my face between his big hands.

The priest lifts his voice to the congregation. "Dearly beloved, I give you Mr. and Mrs. Quinn!"

The roar from the crowd is deafening.

That's when my knees finally give out.

Before I can hit the ground, Quinn sweeps me up into his arms and carries me off, hollering for Declan and Kieran to follow us.

To me, he says, "Take me to your brother and Lili. I need to get that sorted."

I can't find my words, so I point in the direction of the dressing room.

Quinn strides down the aisle with me in his arms, nodding at people in the crowd as we pass. I consider the possibility that I've been drugged, or that he put me into that coma he teased me about, but decide I wouldn't feel quite so much if this were all just a hallucination.

I didn't know my body could contain so much emotion. It must be bursting out of me, seeping from my pores, visible for everyone to see. I feel achingly alive and sick and terrified, and I long for somewhere to hide so I can think all this through to try to make sense of it.

But there's nowhere to go.

Not now. Not ever.

If there's one thing I know about Quinn, it's that he'll never let me run away and hide. He'll be in my face, challenging me and forcing me to expose myself to him for as long as we're together.

A little voice inside my head whispers that if things get too bad, I know how to get rid of him, but I push that aside and focus on giving directions to where I left my family in shambles before heading out to get married to the Mob.

Quinn sets me on my feet outside the door. Then he bursts into the dressing room with me, Declan, and Kieran right behind.

We startle Gianni, who's leaning against the wall, glowering at Lili and Juan Pablo, who are huddled together on the sofa. She's wearing his brown leather jacket over my black dress.

Mamma, nodding off in a chair by the window, sits bolt upright with a snort. She sees the four of us and cackles.

"Ha! *Now* we're having fun!"

"Be quiet, Mamma. Lili, Mr. Quinn wants to talk to you."

He says, "I understand your father threatened to kill you. Tell me exactly what he said."

Gianni looks at Declan, Kieran, and Quinn in flat-out horror.

"No, no, no," he starts to protest, but Quinn shoots him a lethal glare that makes the words shrivel up and die in his mouth.

He snaps, "When it's your turn to talk, I'll tell you. Now shut your piehole before I shove my fist in it."

Gianni looks to Declan beseechingly. "Mr. O'Donnell, please let me explain—"

Declan interrupts with a hard "Guess you didn't hear my lad tell you to shut your piehole, Caruso, but if you don't hear me, I'll put a bullet straight through that unibrow of yours."

Gianni wants so badly to shout something about disrespect, but he wisely keeps it to himself. He sags against the wall, crossing his arms over his chest and seething.

Meanwhile, Juan Pablo is on his feet.

"She doesn't have to tell nobody nothing!" he shouts, glaring at the three Irishmen. "She doesn't take orders from you!"

I'm about to start pleading with him to be reasonable, but Quinn steps forward, holding up a hand to silence me.

He tilts his head, looking Juan Pablo up and down. He gestures to Lili, cowering behind him. His voice calm and low, Quinn says, "You're in love with this girl?"

"Yes! And I don't fucking care who knows it!"

"*Tranquilo,* amigo. *Cálmate.* We're only talking."

Clearly confused by Quinn's gentle tone, Juan Pablo glances at me. I nod encouragingly.

Quinn looks at Lili. "And you're in love with him?"

Tears streaming down her face because she probably thinks they're both about to die, she says in a broken voice, "Yes. I'm sorry."

"You don't have to apologize to me, lass," says Quinn softly. "I'm not angry with you. The heart wants what it wants."

Declan chuckles. "Isn't that the bloody truth."

"So what's the plan? You want to marry her, or are you just fucking around?"

Juan Pablo pulls his shoulders back and lifts his chin, sending Quinn a look of defiance. "Yes, I want to marry her. She's my life."

Quinn nods. "Good answer. Okay, then. Take your girl and go."

Lili cries out in happy disbelief. Juan Pablo looks around the room as if he has no idea what's happening.

Aghast, Gianni starts to sputter. "She can't leave with him!"

"Why not?"

"I forbid it, that's why!"

"She doesn't need your approval. The lass is eighteen, which makes her legally an adult. She can do whatever the fuck she likes."

Gianni stabs his finger in Juan Pablo's direction, shouting, "She won't leave with this fucking loser! I won't allow it! No daughter of mine will be with a—"

His rant ends abruptly when Quinn spins around and punches him square in the face.

He crashes to the floor and lies there, bleeding and gasping, clutching his nose.

Glowering down at him with both hands fisted and his jaw clenched, Quinn growls, "It's not nice to call people names."

Controlling his anger, he smooths a hand down the front of his tux and turns back to Juan Pablo. "Lili's in danger. Do you know about what happened last week?"

"Yes, she told me."

"You need to get away from the East Coast. Preferably out of the country altogether, at least until we find out who was behind the attack."

Juan Pablo nods. "I have family in Mexico."

"Good. We'll get you on a private flight with bodyguards and security. Once you're there, keep a low profile. No social media posting, no talking to your friends. You're off the grid."

Holding his bleeding nose, Gianni stumbles to his feet, using the wall for balance. Breathing hard, his hands shaking, he looks at Juan Pablo with pure hatred in his eyes. Then he turns his vicious glare to Lili.

"If you leave with this boy, you're dead to me. Do you understand? I'll never speak to you again. You'll be cut off. You won't have a dime of my money."

Juan Pablo snaps, "She doesn't need your money. She'll have mine."

Gianni's laugh is cold and hard. "From what, your newspaper route?"

"My family's probably richer than yours, *ese*."

"Really? Cleaning pools is a big moneymaker, eh?"

"No. But drug trafficking is."

The air in the room goes static. Nobody says anything. The silence has a strange, dangerous weight.

Into it, Declan says quietly, "Anytime you'd like to explain that, feel free."

"My uncle is El Mencho."

Gianni makes a strangled noise, like a cat trying to expel a hairball. His face turns sheet white.

With lifted brows, Declan says, "Alvaro?"

Juan Pablo nods. "My father and I aren't in the business. We don't want nothing to do with that. But he's family. My mother's brother. He makes sure we don't want for anything."

A confused Kieran says, "Who's Alvaro?"

"Head of the Jalisco cartel," answers Declan, assessing Juan Pablo with a new look in his eyes.

"Oh. We friends with them?"

"Never met them. But they're Sinaloa's biggest rival."

"And Sinaloa's our enemy," finishes Quinn. A hint of a smile lifts his lips.

Juan Pablo says, "If you want, I'll make an introduction."

Declan nods. "It would be appreciated. Thank you."

"No, thank you. You didn't have to do this for me and Lili."
He looks at me. "You, too. I know you're only wearing that dress
to protect us."

Gianni appears as if he's having a stroke at hearing the news
that not only has he lost control of his daughter, he's lost out on
leveraging a blood tie to the second-largest cartel in the world.

Desperate not to lose anything else, he shouts at Declan, "Our
families negotiated a contract in good faith!"

Declan smiles. "And the contract stands. Christ, I love weddings."

Quinn says, "I hope you love receptions, too. You can tell me
all about it tomorrow."

"What do you mean?"

Quinn turns his attention to me. His eyes darken and his voice
takes on a husky edge. "I've got a date with my wife tonight."

He licks his lips, leaving no doubt as to his intentions.

TWENTY-ONE

REY

We're in a limo. I don't remember exactly how we got here. The past hour of my life has been such an overwhelming whirlwind of emotion, I can't think straight.

I don't know if I'll ever be able to think straight again. My brain is broken. There's a network of cracks all over the poor thing that looks exactly like my new husband's dumb spiderweb tattoo.

Sitting beside me, Quinn stares at my profile in broody silence. Then he reaches over and drags me onto his lap.

"What the—"

"Easy," he murmurs when I yelp in surprise. He winds his arms around me and holds me in a tight, possessive grip, gazing at me with hooded eyes. The skirt of the wedding dress poufs all around us like a cloud.

"Quinn, I'm not sitting on your lap!"

"Funny, but it looks like you are."

"Let me go."

"No. Now, listen. No, don't start cursing at me. *Listen.*"

He takes my chin firmly in hand and turns my face so I'm forced to look at him. His voice low, he says, "You're in shock."

My laugh sounds crazed. "You think?"

"Aye. I've seen you stab a man in the neck without batting a lash and hunt armed intruders with the enthusiasm of a big-game poacher, but saying 'I do' seems to be beyond your stress threshold."

"Marriage is beyond any rational woman's stress threshold."

His lips thin in displeasure. "I'm not your bloody dead husband."

I try to look away, but he doesn't let me. He keeps those fingers clasped around my jaw, holding my head in place.

Looking into my eyes, he demands, "Say it."

I frown. "Say what?"

"That I'm not him."

He's deadly serious, his expression dark and his eyes darker. I don't know why it's so important to him, but I don't have the presence of mind to figure it out. Or to argue.

All I really want is to take a bath, go to bed, and wake up tomorrow with someone else's life.

"You're not him."

"Say it again."

"For fuck's sake!"

"Indulge me."

I sigh and close my eyes, too tired to fight. "You're not him. I know you're not. Honestly, I do."

When he remains silent, I add softly, "You're ten times the man he was. That doesn't mean my feelings about this situation are illegitimate."

He strokes his thumb along my jaw and murmurs, "Thank you."

"You're welcome."

"Are you ever going to look at me again?"

When I crack open an eye, he smiles at me. Then he turns serious and businesslike.

"We need to talk."

"Why do I have a bad feeling about this?"

Adjusting my weight in his lap, he spreads his legs wider so my butt is resting on the seat and his thighs are open around my bottom. He pushes on the mass of white chiffon so it's out of his way and slides his hand up my thigh, pulling me closer and digging his fingers into my bare flesh.

I say drily, "My, aren't we handsy all of a sudden."

"I'm only getting started. But that's what I wanted to talk to you about."

"I'd like to get drunk first, if you don't mind."

"I do mind. I need you lucid for this."

"That sounds scary."

"I want to fuck you as soon as we get to the hotel, so we need to get this conversation out of the way first."

My face flushes with heat. I chew on the inside of my cheek as he stares at my mouth with undisguised longing.

His voice thick, he says, "I won't force you, I want that to be clear. Just because you're my wife doesn't mean you can't say no."

Feeling as if I've just been run over by a truck, I take a deep breath and blow it out.

"Are you forgetting our pleasant little chat in the back room of the church where you demanded this fake marriage had to include sex or the whole thing was a no-go?"

"I remember that you agreed to it," comes the hard reply.

"Because my niece was about to be shot by her father."

"Okay, let's get into that." He pauses to smirk at me. "You're full of shite."

I say hotly, "He *would've* shot her! And Juan Pablo, too!"

"Mmhmm. And there was no way you could've wrestled the

gun from his hand or distracted him long enough to shoot him yourself, right? Because you're *so* meek and incapable."

The sarcasm in his tone makes me stare at him in outrage. "Are you suggesting I *wanted* to marry you?"

"I'm suggesting that if you really didn't, you'd have figured out how to get a handle on your idiot brother without strutting down the aisle in a wedding dress."

I say through clenched teeth, "I. Didn't. Strut. I *walked*."

"My point is that I saw you stand in front of a man pointing a gun at your chest and you told him to go fuck himself. You said you'd see him in hell, where you'd cut off his balls and choke him with them." His smile is small and hideously smug. "There's no way Gianni scared you."

I lift my chin and sniff snootily. "You're delusional, but you can think whatever you want."

"I will. And what I think is that deep down, you wanted to marry me."

"Your ego is the eighth wonder of the world, my friend."

Ignoring that, he continues in a softer, more intimate tone. "Because you're not a woman who'd give up a freedom that was won at such a high cost."

His gaze is piercing, drilling into mine and daring me to contradict him. He waits for my response, stroking his thumb gently back and forth over my cheek as he holds me.

"This is a terrible thing to say, especially on our wedding day, so please forgive me. But there's no guarantee I won't be back to wearing black before the month is out."

He stares at me in tense, blistering silence.

Then he throws his head back and laughs.

He laughs so long and so hard, I get irritated. I give him a smack on one of his big, stupid pecs.

"It's not like you didn't already know that! You said you'd be taking your life into your own hands!"

"Aye," he agrees, still laughing. "And I am."

"Then what's so funny?"

"I never thought I'd find a threat on my life romantic."

"Oh, shut up," I grumble, shaking my head in disgust. "You're an idiot."

"But I'm your idiot," he says, his laughter fading. His voice lowers an octave. His gaze grows intense. "And you're my viper."

"I hate that nickname."

He growls, "No, you don't, you fucking liar."

He pulls me in and kisses me.

Wrapping his big hand around the back of my neck, he holds me close and drinks deep from my mouth as I fist the lapel of his tux in one hand and cling to his shoulder with the other. He slides his other hand up my thigh to my hip, which he squeezes.

Then he hooks his thumb under the elastic of my panties and tugs on it, sending shockwaves of pleasure through my pelvis as the cotton drags against my clit.

Against my mouth, he murmurs, "You're trembling. I suppose that's fear, right?" He chuckles. "Because you'd never be aroused by such an idiot."

"I hate you."

"The lies never stop with you, do they?"

He takes my mouth again, kissing me harder. I arch into him, my heart hammering and my nipples hardening with every sweep of his tongue against mine. He tugs on my panties again, making me squirm restlessly, then slides his hand between my legs.

"Soaked," he whispers, rubbing my panties. "Sweet little viper, you're already soaking wet."

"I was thinking about poisoning your coffee," I say raggedly.

"You were thinking about riding my dick."

"How are you so awful?"

"You bring out the bastard in me. Now let's see if I can get you to do something with that mouth other than slice me to ribbons."

He slips his fingers under my panties and gently pinches my swollen clit.

I gasp, stiffening.

When he slides one thick finger inside me, I close my eyes and moan.

"Perfect," he murmurs. "What if I do this?"

He presses his thumb against my clit and slowly works his finger in and out, fucking me with it. I shudder, dropping my head against his shoulder and biting my lip so I don't make a sound.

Until he adds another finger. Then I groan like a zombie crawling out of a grave. It's the most unattractive sound I've made in my life.

But Quinn doesn't think so. He growls in approval, dipping his head to latch onto my throat with his hot mouth. He sucks on my neck and finger fucks me while I helplessly grind against his hand.

He says hotly into my ear, "You want to come like this, baby? Or do you want my mouth?"

Delirious, my eyes rolling back in my head, I gasp, "What the hell is happening?"

"Your husband is fingering your gorgeous wet cunt, that's what."

"Jesus! Quinn!"

He breathes, "Aye, lass. Say my name just like that when you come."

Rocking his hips into me so his erection is pressed right up against my hip, he kisses a path down my neck to my chest, then licks at my cleavage, dipping his tongue into the cleft between my breasts. When I groan again, he lightly bites down on the swell of one breast.

"I need to taste every inch of you," he whispers, his voice dark. "I need to bite every perfect part of your skin. I want to fuck you and spank you and make you take my cock down your throat. I want you to tell me every filthy thing you want me to do to you, starting right fucking now."

He pulls his fingers out of me and slides them lazily up and down through my soaked folds, spreading the wetness around. When he brushes against my clit, I jerk.

"Start talking, viper. What do you want?"

"An annulment."

"Liar."

He bites my hard nipple right through the delicate fabric of the dress.

Panting, I say, "Do you not care that you're giving the poor driver a show?"

"I care that you're flexing your hips to try to get my fingers back inside you."

Horrified that he's right, I drop my head back and squeeze my eyes shut. "Gah!"

Laughter in his voice, he whispers, "So greedy."

"Quinn—"

"Ask me to finger fuck you, viper. Ask me to make you come. I want to hear it."

"You and all your talking! Is this what you learned in therapy? How to break a girl down with your incessant chatter? It's like water torture, only with words!"

Sweeping his fingers back and forth over my throbbing clit, he says, "Tell me you need my cock. Tell me you want me to fuck you. Tell me you've been dreaming about it every night and aching for it every day, the way I have."

When I open my eyes, he's got the most intense look on his face. So intense, it's frightening.

Holding my gaze, he commands, "Tell me."

Then he slides his fingers inside me again.

Arching my back, I suck in a breath. My eyes widen. He crooks his fingers and hits a sensitive spot inside me, rubbing against it with maddening slowness, intently watching every expression that crosses my face.

I can't look away from him. I want to, but I can't.

Somehow, he's got me trapped in the weight of his powerful gaze. A fly caught in amber.

A desperate little insect snared in a hungry spider's web.

And for all my pride and independence, for all the times I swore I'd never allow myself to be owned again, I find it impossible not to give him what he's demanding.

Staring into his eyes and breathing hard, I whisper, "Yes. All of it. I want you to fuck me. I want you to kiss me everywhere. I want your hands and your mouth and every other part of you, and I honestly despise myself for wanting it, but I do. So please make me come now. I'll get back to hating us both after."

"You said you downgraded the hate to dislike."

"That was before I married you. Now, all bets are off."

When he grins, his smile victorious, I snap, "But no spanking. If you ever try to hit me, I'll consider it a declaration of war, and that will be the end of you!"

He growls, "Fuck, it's hot when you threaten to kill me."

Then he crushes his mouth to mine and ravages it as he works his fingers in and out of me, thrusting them deep, moaning into my mouth when I spread my legs wider.

When I come, it's with fireworks behind my eyelids and a full-body jerk that makes one of my shoes go flying. Quinn swallows my moan, humming his approval into my mouth and holding me against him, a Popsicle viper impaled on his huge hand.

I convulse and clench around his fingers until finally, I collapse backward, shaking and spent. He holds me up with that one strong arm around my back, slips his fingers out of me, and slides them into his mouth.

As I watch in dizzy, breathless astonishment, he lazily licks his slick fingers dry, savoring my taste.

Watching me with hooded eyes, he growls, "That's my good girl."

And oh, what that does to me. The golden shimmer of happiness that floods my cells. It's ridiculous how soft and melting I become, as pliant as a green blade of grass under the spring sun.

But I'm not a blade of grass.

I'm a blade. Period.

I'm a strong, capable, grown-ass woman who intimidates Mafia men so much, they can't even look me in the eye.

My voice shaking with emotion, I say, "I'm not good and I'm not a girl. I'm not yours, either."

Chuckling softly, he presses a gentle kiss to my lips. "I'll concede the first two. But you're definitely mine."

Just for an added little fuck-you to make his point, he drawls, "Mrs. Quinn."

That right there tells me all I need to know about how this marriage is going to work.

I never knew before this moment that enemies with benefits is an actual thing.

TWENTY-TWO

SPIDER

I'm glad the hotel is close to the church, because with every mile we drive and minute that passes, Reyna gets closer to a full-blown freak out.

She wants to crawl off my lap, but I haven't let her. Instead, I hold her firmly in place as she hyperventilates and looks around wildly like a caged animal desperate for a way out.

There's no way out for her, though. I'm taking this till-death-do-us-part thing very fucking seriously.

Which means she'll have to kill me to get away.

But I won't give her a reason to. I'll be the opposite of everything her last husband was. I want her to learn that marriage to me isn't the end of her life.

It's only the beginning.

"Where are we going?" she says, staring out the window in rising panic.

I'm going to have to make her come again soon. She needs to calm down.

"The Ritz. I booked the honeymoon suite."

She swallows and moistens her lips. Then she blurts, "Do you snore?"

I have to suppress a laugh at that. "To be honest, I have no idea."

"Nobody's ever told you?"

"Who would tell me?"

"Any woman you've ever slept with."

I quirk my lips. "I don't spend the night."

She looks startled by that. "What do you mean? You've never had a long-term relationship?"

"My relationships can best be described as speedy disasters. Those were few and far between. I haven't been committed to a woman in more than ten years."

She examines my face in silence for a moment. I can see the wheels turning and know she wants to grill me for more information, but she doesn't.

She looks away instead, nervously chewing the inside of her cheek.

"You can ask me anything," I say, stroking my hand up her arm.

"It might be insulting."

"As if that would be new."

"Suit yourself. Here's the question: did you . . ." She pauses to rethink it. "How have you been taking care of your needs for the last decade?"

"How have you been taking care of yours?"

"Romance novels and battery-powered devices."

Her bluntness makes me chuckle. "You can throw them all away. You won't need them anymore."

Her cheeks turn pink. She purses her lips.

I love it when she looks at me like she's a prude old maid.

She says, "Let me just push your ego aside for a sec to mention you haven't answered my question."

I hesitate, because I know exactly how bad it will sound out loud. But she was honest with me, so the least I can do is return the favor.

"I paid for it."

"For sex, you mean."

"Aye."

She sits with that in silence for a while, then nods. "Okay. Thank you for the candor. Can I ask a follow-up question?"

Impressed that she's neither upset nor judging me, I incline my head.

"Do you have any viruses or infections I should know about?"

"No. I'm clean. I'll get tested again so you'll feel better, but in the meantime, we'll use a condom."

The pink in her cheeks deepens to red. "Now's a good time to remind you that you promised I could say no if I wanted."

I lean in to press a soft kiss to her luscious lips. "You don't want to say no. And don't bother denying it, because we both know it's true."

She sighs and mutters, "Part of me wants to say no, just not my vagina."

I don't know why having her so conflicted about her desire for me gets me so wound up, but if my cock gets any harder, it will split open the zipper on my trousers.

Cradling her face in my hand, I lean close to her ear and whisper, "Then let's make a game of it, viper."

After a beat of surprise, she says, "A game?"

"Aye. You can pretend you don't want it, and I can pretend I don't know you do."

She squirms a little in my lap, pressing her thighs together.

She likes the idea.

But of course, she has to act like she doesn't, because God forbid the woman would ever let me get the upper hand.

She says, "How would I know it was a game? It could just be you and your giant ego doing their usual thing."

I kiss her softly under her ear, nuzzling her there, dragging her scent into my nose. She smells like nothing else in the world, no other fragrance or perfume. The scent isn't flowery, cloying, or sweet, because her essence is none of those things.

She smells like some kind of dark, dangerous heaven made of female flesh and poisonous fruit and exotic spices. A garden of deadly delights that a man could wander into and get lost.

A place he could lose his mind along with his heart and soul.

I say, "We'd agree on it beforehand. For a set time in a set place, we'd pretend."

"What if I didn't like it?"

"We'd make a safe word. Like . . . Black Widow, for instance."

She says tartly, "Or I could just punch you in the face."

When I start to laugh, it makes her even more aggravated.

"I'm not your fuck toy, Quinn."

"Not yet, you're not." I bite her throat, and she shivers.

But she doesn't try to push me away. She lets me hold her and kiss her neck as we drive into the underground parking area at the hotel. She lets me fondle her thighs. She lets me squeeze her breasts through the beaded bodice of the gown, and when I pinch her hard nipple, she lets her head fall back so I can take her mouth.

When she curls her hand around the back of my neck, slides her fingers into my hair, and kisses me back eagerly, I know she's as ready for this to happen as I am.

I just can't say that aloud, or I'll be eating a fist sandwich.

We get to the suite via a private underground elevator reserved for wealthy guests who like to stay incognito and can pay for the privilege. As soon as the elevator doors close behind us, I take her mouth again, pushing her against the wall and pressing my hips into hers so she knows exactly what she's about to get.

She pushes me away, gasping. "Wait! I'm not mentally prepared for this!"

"I'll give you two seconds. Go."

"Quinn—"

When I kiss her again, she moans into my mouth. The sound sends such a hot jolt of lust through my veins, I can't help but kiss her harder as I hold her against my body.

She pounds a fist weakly against my chest.

"Quinn, God, please, I need a minute to—"

"The last thing you need right now is time to think," I interrupt. "You've got the next fifty years of your life to do that."

The elevator dings. The doors slide open to reveal the enormous suite. I swing her up into my arms, ignoring her little yelp of surprise, and growl, "If you don't want me to fuck you, just say no."

Bypassing the foyer, living room, and dining room, I head straight to the master bedroom. It's as opulent as the rest of the suite, decorated in subtle shades of cream and blue. One entire wall of the room is floor-to-ceiling windows, showcasing a magnificent view of Boston Commons and downtown. The city lights twinkle against the gathering twilight. The sky is a magnificent shade of violet blue above a golden horizon, but I don't see any of it.

All I see is the woman in my arms, clinging to me in fear and desire.

She's scared, but she wants me.

She hates herself for it, but she wants me.

She's disoriented from the abrupt change in her life from this morning, she's worried about her niece and furious with her brother, she's horrified to find herself married again when she was so against the idea that she had it tattooed right onto her skin, but still . . .

She wants me.

And that's exactly what I'm going to make her focus on for the rest of the night.

I stride up to the king-size bed, drop her onto it, and start tearing off my bow tie.

"Say no if you want me to stop." I toss the tie to the floor and rip open my shirt.

Buttons pop. So do her eyes.

I throw the shirt aside, kick off my shoes, and climb onto the bed, kneeling over her with my hands planted on either side of her head.

Breathing shallowly, she lies beneath me with her hands pressed flat against my chest. She's still wearing the veil. It's spread out all around her head like a lacy halo.

She says faintly, "I don't want you to stop. But you should know that—"

I kiss her before she can finish the sentence.

She fights it for a moment, then melts into it, sliding her hands up my chest and over my shoulders. She pulls me down against her body with a sigh.

And I'm all in. One thousand percent. My body has been aching for this, begging for this, and I won't waste a single second. There's more than a good chance she'll tell me to fuck off in the morning, but tonight, she's all mine.

I kiss her until she's making little mewling noises in the back of her throat and grinding her pelvis against me, then I kiss my way down her neck to her chest. As I nuzzle her breasts, she digs her fingers into my hair and exhales a breath so deep, it sounds as if she's been holding it her entire life.

She whispers haltingly, "I've . . . I've only ever been with one man. And he wasn't exactly interested in getting me ready to . . . what I'm saying is . . . I don't want you to think . . . I mean, I'm probably not very good at this."

I pause to lift my head and look at her. "You think you could disappoint me?"

When she nods, looking ashamed, I almost groan. I rise to my elbows, take her face in my hands, and gaze into her eyes.

My voice husky, I say, "Viper. My lovely, lethal wife. You're fucking perfect, inside and out. Don't ever worry about disappointing me. You couldn't. Even when you're homicidal or hurling insults, you take my breath away."

She swallows hard. Her voice comes out small. "Yes, but you're strange."

I drop my forehead to her neck and start softly laughing.

She smacks me lightly on the back. "Shut up."

"Oh, lass, what you do to me."

I kiss her again, deeply but not hard, letting her relax into it. Bending her knee, she slides her leg up against mine and flexes her hips. I don't think she has any idea how responsive she is, because she'd probably force herself to stop if she did.

"I need you out of this dress," I whisper, forcibly rolling her onto her stomach.

"Wait."

I mutter, "Not this again," and tug on the zipper. The fabric parts under my hands. Reyna stiffens at the same time, saying in a higher voice, "Quinn, please, wait—"

But it's too late.

I've already seen it.

The tattoo is large and vivid, snaking all the way down her spine from her nape to the small of her back. It's a twisting, thorny vine of red roses and delicate black leaves, branching out from the center in all directions.

It's staggeringly breathtaking, not only for the intricacy and artistry of the ink, but also for the stalk from which each flower blooms.

A scar.

Her entire back is covered in raised white scars, each a finger's width and about as long.

Horrified, I whisper, "Reyna."

Her voice low but steady, she says, "He liked to use a whip."

I can't catch my breath. I'm so stunned and sick at the realization of what she must have gone through, what she suffered at his hands, that I can barely see straight.

"Jesus Christ. Jesus fucking bloody *Christ*!"

"That's not helping me feel any better."

I roll her over and pull her up, sitting back on my heels on the bed so we're facing each other. Taking her face in my shaking hands, I say, "I'm sorry. I'm so fucking sorry."

She looks at me askance. "Thank you for that, but it's not like you could've done anything. I didn't know you then."

"No. Fuck." I groan, kissing her. "I'm sorry for every stupid, arrogant thing I've said and done since we met. For every time I was rude. For how I've acted. For—fuck!—I don't even know what! For being a *man*! But most of all for forcing you to marry me. Jesus Christ. What have I done. What have I fucking done?"

I leap from the bed, holding my head in my hands.

She sits on the bed and silently watches me pace back and forth for a moment. Then she stands, pulls the veil out of her hair, tosses it to the floor, and steps out of the dress. It slithers down her legs and pools at her feet, sighing softly as it settles against the carpet.

She stands in front of me naked except for a simple pair of white cotton panties.

And more fucking scars.

On her stomach. Across her ribs. Under both breasts. Her arms and legs are smooth and so are her chest and neck, but the rest of her body is marked with the ghosts of her past, a hundred mementos of suffering.

It's like looking at tombstones in a graveyard.

I've never cried in my adult life, but I think I'm about to break that record.

Watching my face with shining eyes, she says softly, "Don't you dare look at me with pity. I'm not a victim. I'm a survivor. I'm alive. There are millions of other women just like me who weren't so lucky."

I exhale a disbelieving breath. "Lucky."

"Yes," she says vehemently. "And grateful. And determined I'll never waste another second of this life I won. So get your Irish ass over here and fuck me, or I'll divorce you so fast, it'll make your head spin."

Later on, I'll look back and realize this is the exact moment I fell in love with her.

But for now, I simply obey my viper's command and take her back down to the bed.

TWENTY-THREE

REY

Lying on top of me with the length of his big, heavy body pressed against mine, Quinn kisses me with a strange sort of desperation, as if he's trying to fit everything I never had into one kiss.

I don't bother telling him he doesn't have to try so hard, because I'm loving the attention.

"My sweet viper," he murmurs against my mouth. Gazing down at me, he says something in Gaelic that I don't understand.

"English, please."

"English doesn't have the right words."

"For what?"

"How beautiful you are."

Part of me wants to tell him he's a cheeseball, but his eyes are shining with emotion and there's a swelling pressure inside my chest. So I simply smile at him and dig my fingers into all his soft golden hair.

He lowers his head to my breasts and sucks a nipple into his mouth.

A lightning bolt of pleasure shoots straight down between my legs. I gasp, arching into him.

"So responsive," he growls, sounding pleased.

He moves to my other breast and sucks that nipple, too, swirling his tongue around and around until it's taut and aching. I close my eyes and slide my hands over his shoulders, learning their shape as my body comes alive under his mouth.

"Your stitches need to come out," I whisper, shivering.

"Aye. Right after I fuck every part of you."

His voice is so guttural with desire, it makes goose bumps form on my skin. He kisses his way down my chest to my stomach, nuzzling and nipping me gently with his teeth. His beard is soft but also scratchy, making a wonderful tickle everywhere it drags.

I want to feel that tickle between my thighs.

"Quinn?"

"Hush," he says firmly. "You're not in charge."

I don't know why the command in his voice makes me sigh with pleasure. I don't know why his words of praise feel as good as a hand stroked over my skin. The only thing I know is that the bulge in his trousers is big and hard, and I want it inside me desperately.

But I bite my tongue and keep quiet, letting him go at his own pace.

Thumbing over my rigid nipples, he kisses his way down my belly, pausing to bite my hip. It's not hard, but it's very dominant, as if he's saying *This is mine*. Moving lower, he bites my inner thighs, too, one after the other, licking and sucking the flesh where his teeth pressed.

It feels so good, I groan.

He whispers, "You like that?"

"Yes."

"What about this?"

He gently bites me between the legs.

I suck in a breath, stiffening. It doesn't hurt, I'm just shocked to feel teeth in such a tender spot. He quickly pulls off my panties, then gets right back between my legs, lapping at my folds with his tongue. I groan louder, pulling his hair.

I hear a soft, self-satisfied chuckle. "Aye, she likes it," he whispers. "Good girl."

I'd be a liar if I told him I didn't like him calling me his good girl, though I really fucking hate that I like it.

My brain hates it, anyway. The rest of my body goes wild.

A violent shiver of pleasure runs all the way through me. My legs open wider. My hips flex, and it feels like all that happens from someplace beyond my control. My body is on autopilot, singing along to every note he's playing with his mouth and hands.

"Look at this pretty pink cunt," he growls. "God, I need to sink my cock in this."

I make a garbled sound of pleasure as he runs his tongue up and down my center. Then, when he pulls back the hood on my clit and flicks his tongue back and forth over it, I moan, long and loud.

He slides his thick finger inside me, and I see stars.

His voice dark and hard, he says, "I want you to come on my face. Then I'm gonna fuck your pussy and make you come again. Then I'm gonna fuck your gorgeous arse and—"

"Too much talking!" I cry, bucking my hips. "Just do it!"

His lips fasten onto my clit. He sucks, shoving his finger deep inside me. I groan, arching against the mattress, my fingers dug into his hair and my bottom clenched as I grind helplessly against his mouth.

Crying out and scratching his scalp with my nails, I climax.

It rips through me. I thrash and buck through the convulsions, delirious at the feel of his hot lips and tongue licking and sucking me and his finger plunging deep. My nipples are so hard, they're painful. A bloom of heat flashes over me. Sweat mists my skin.

The moment the convulsions have slowed and I'm begging him to stop because it's too sensitive, Quinn rises to his knees, rips open the zipper on his trousers, and fists his cock in his hand.

I stare at it with wide eyes. My hammering heart skips a beat, then starts up again, beating even faster.

Thick and veined, the shaft juts out proudly from his fist. The crown is fat and red. The slit on top glistens with a drop of wetness.

His cock is fucking huge. Porn-star sized. He'd make a killing in erotic movies.

"That look on your face is a bloody nice compliment," he growls. Then he positions himself between my spread thighs and slides the head up and down through my pussy lips, wetting it.

I gasp, managing a breathy, "Condom?"

"Wasn't planning on having sex today," he says through gritted teeth, staring down into my wide eyes. "Still time to say no, viper."

I'm so turned on, I can barely think. "You said you were clean?"

"Aye. I promise."

"Then fuck me, Quinn. And don't you dare hold anything back. I want everything you have to give me."

His grin looks feral. With a single, powerful thrust, he shoves that thick beast deep inside me.

My mouth opens, but no sound comes out. I'm stretched wide, impaled on his cock, taking every inch of it as I sink my fingernails into his back and clamp my shaking thighs around his waist.

He leans down, resting his forearms on either side of my head and fisting his hands into my hair. Into my ear, he snarls, "I knew you'd feel like heaven."

Then he snaps his hips again, thrusting hard.

My breasts bounce against his chest, my nipples dragging against the small metal piercings in his. I cry out in pleasure.

Chuckling, he pulls on my hair. His voice dark, he commands, "Ask me to fuck you again, wife."

It comes out in one long, breathless rush. "Please fuck me oh God Quinn fuck me if you stop now I'll kill you as soon as I can!"

He thrusts again. And again. And again. Each time, I sink my nails deeper into his flesh and moan helplessly, lost to sensation.

He starts to speak in Gaelic, a hot stream of words I don't understand, but adore listening to. It's a beautiful language, musical and lilting, but with a hard edge that also makes it sound masculine and sexy as hell.

Just as I'm about to come again, he rolls onto his back, taking me with him. Breathing hard and sweating, I stare down at him in hazy surprise.

His fingers digging into the flesh of my hips, he looks up at me with blazing eyes and orders, "Fuck that cock, baby. Ride me and make yourself come."

I almost pass out from excitement.

Leaning over, I plant my hands on his strong chest and balance myself as I bounce up and down on his thick shaft. He feels incredible. I'm stuffed with his cock, full to overflowing, and I love it more than I should.

I love it more than anything.

I'll worry about that later, but for now, I'm having the time of my life. This is *way* better than any of my toys could ever be.

My eyes slide shut. My lips part. When I dig my fingernails into his chest and release a breathless low moan, he laughs.

It's a gravelly sound. One full of pleasure.

"You're perfect. Look at you, my beautiful wife. Jesus, these tits."

He reaches up and engulfs them in his big hands, squeezing and fondling them as I rock back and forth, grinding my clit against his pelvis. He pinches both my nipples at the same time, and my grinding grows more frantic.

When he sits up, grabbing me around the waist to steady me as he latches onto my nipple with his wonderful hot mouth, it forces his cock even deeper inside me.

My grinding turns frenzied. I start to buck and groan, pulling on his hair.

He bites my nipple, and I come, screaming.

Holding me tightly with his arms wrapped around my waist, he thrusts into me with short, hard snaps of his hips as my pussy clenches around his cock. He throbs inside me, a pulsing, rigid invader, stretching me wide.

I don't realize I'm sobbing his name over and over until he growls hotly, "Fucking hell, woman, keep crying my name like that, and you'll make me come."

I don't know what makes me do it. It's not a rational decision. It just bursts out, blurted from ecstasy and some kind of dark, primal need.

"Yes come inside me please please please *let me feel you come!*"

Hearing me beg like that unleashes something in him. He was carnal before, but now he's an absolute animal, snarling like a hungry beast set free from a cage.

In a move so fast, it makes me dizzy, he flips me onto my back again, throws my legs up so my ankles are hooked over his shoulders, then fucks me hard and fast, leaning over me with locked arms and wild eyes, his teeth bared as he plunges into me.

"Quinn! Oh God!"

He swallows my cries, crushing his mouth to mine and groaning into it as his body shudders and heaves. I feel him throb deep inside me. He jerks, biting my lips.

Then he throws his head back and groans at the ceiling as he makes one final hard thrust and empties himself inside me.

He's beautiful. God, he's so beautiful like this, sweaty and straining, his entire body clenched. I wish I could take a picture to look at later so I won't forget a single detail.

A wave of emotion hits me hard, squeezing my lungs and stealing my breath. I turn my head and close my eyes, bracing against it, but it doesn't help. I still feel it all.

Everything inside me aches and burns. All the cells in my body are screaming.

And they're screaming the same thing:

Quinn.

Quinn.

Quinn.

The name of the man who looks at me like I'm a sunrise and laughs when I threaten to end his life.

The man whose ego is so big, it could flatten a city, but whose heart is so tender, it broke when he saw my scars.

The man I know almost nothing about except that he's sweeter than any made man should be. Under all his macho swaggering, past his comic book superhero good looks and beyond his armor of snark, there lies a soul that aches with loneliness.

Just like mine does.

Or did, until right now.

Panting, he collapses on top of me. His whole body trembles. He pauses to catch his breath, then takes my face in his hands and kisses me deeply.

"Hi," he says gruffly, looking into my eyes.

"Hi yourself."

"Why are you smiling like that?"

"Maybe I'm thinking about pushing you out a window."

His laugh is low and breathless. "Or maybe you're thinking about what a sex god I am."

"Actually, I was thinking that I'm a lot more flexible through the hips than I thought. In case you hadn't noticed, I'm folded in half underneath you."

"Fuck. Sorry."

He lifts his chest so I can pull my legs down, then settles right back on top of me, keeping his cock seated inside me the entire time. I wind my arms up around his shoulders, inhale deeply, then exhale, stretching underneath him like a cat.

He gazes at me from under hooded lids. "I have something to say."

I fling my arms out to the sides and sigh. "Of course you do."

"Don't be so dramatic. It's not bad."

"I'm going to hunt down these therapists of yours and make them change careers. They're turning grown men into Oprah Winfrey."

"Be quiet and listen to me."

"It's not like I have a choice. You weigh a thousand pounds. I'm not going anywhere."

He rolls onto his back, adjusts me on top of him so our bodies are aligned, then tucks my head into the crook of his neck and squeezes me.

"Better?"

Snuggling against his hard chest, I nod.

"Okay. So here's what I want to say."

There's a long, ominous pause.

"Don't break your brain, Quinn. Just say it."

His chest rises and falls with his heavy exhalation. He slides his open hand down my spine, his fingers gently tracing a path around my scars. Then, abruptly, he starts talking.

"I'll kill anyone who ever disrespects you. I'll kill anyone who even looks at you the wrong way. If anyone so much as *annoys* you, I'll put a bullet in his skull and throw his body into the Charles River. You never have to fight your own battles again, viper, understood? I'll fucking destroy any dumb motherfucker who ever dares to even make you frown."

He's so vehement and his words are so unlikely, I start to laugh.

"Wow, Romeo. Does sex always make you this stabby?"

"And she's laughing," he grumbles. "Bloody wonderful."

"Wait . . ." I lift my head and look at him. "Are you serious?"

"Aye, I'm bloody serious!"

"Because that's unhinged. You know that, right?"

"I don't care!"

My brows lifted, I examine his expression. Aside from being insulted that I laughed, he's completely sincere about his threats.

It's a strange mix of disbelief and wonder that I feel.

And worry, too. This man's trigger finger is a little too itchy.

I say softly, "Thank you. That's lovely. Insane, but lovely."

He grumbles something and looks away.

Trying very hard not to laugh, I kiss his cheek. Into his ear, I whisper, "You know, for such a macho man, you're a big softie."

He grouses, "Don't say the word 'soft' when I'm still inside you."

I can't help it now. I drop my head to his chest and laugh until he rolls me back over and kisses me.

Grinning down at me with shining eyes, he says, "What's that hideous noise you're making, lass? I've heard hyenas that sound better."

"Excuse me, but at the moment, I'm stuffed to my larynx with your giant dick. My lungs have probably collapsed."

He beams. "So you like it, do you?"

"Stop fishing for compliments."

He drops his head and puts his lips near my ear. "You love it. Admit it."

"I admit nothing."

When he flexes his hips, I have to stifle a moan. "Wait, how are you still hard?"

"You're naked. So I'm hard."

"But you . . ."

"Came. Aye. Bucketloads."

When I make a face, he chuckles. "Does that offend her lady-ship's delicate sensibilities?"

"Let's just say my sensibilities aren't used to this kind of sex talk." My smile dies. Bad memories assault me, and I have to look away.

After a moment of gazing at me in silence, Quinn says softly, "He doesn't get a place between us, lass. Keep him in his grave where he belongs."

My throat gets tight and my chest starts to ache, and so help me God, if this bastard makes me cry, I'll stick a knife between his ribs.

In a strangled voice, I say, "I want to give you a compliment, but I don't want it to go to your head."

He furrows his brows, waiting.

"I've downgraded the intense dislike I feel for you to a gen-eralized mild loathing. Now hurry up and fuck me again before your ego gets too big and smothers me."

"That's your idea of a *compliment*?"

"Oh, shut up, Quinn."

I pull his head down and kiss him hard, and within seconds, he's forgotten all about it.

TWENTY-FOUR

SPIDER

She thinks I've forgotten about it, but I haven't.

And I won't.

Ever.

Because I know exactly what's behind that non-compliment, and it sets my soul on fire.

It's like when the stray cat you've been trying to feed for months that's always hissed and run away when you approached finally decides one day it will accept your pathetic offering of kibble and allow you to watch from a safe distance as it dines, glaring at you with unconcealed contempt.

It's called progress.

I'm not stupid. I know it will take a helluva lot more than forced commitment and good sex to break down all her walls.

But it's a start.

In the meantime, I'm going to fuck her silly.

TWENTY-FIVE

REY

He withdraws, flips me onto my belly, pulls me up onto my knees, then plunges his still-hard shaft back inside me with a grunt that sounds animalistic. Gripping my hips in both hands, he starts to thrust again.

My face buried in the duvet cover, I sigh in happiness.

His laugh is dark and knowing. "Aye, lass. I love it, too."

I'm jarred by the mention of that four-letter word, but get distracted when he reaches around and starts to fondle my pussy as he fucks me, tweaking my clit and sliding his fingers all around the place we're joined. I moan and close my eyes, desperately pulling at the blankets.

He says something in Gaelic, a brief, growled word, then fucks me harder.

Though I'm fully exposed, scars and all, I feel no self-consciousness. All my awareness is centered on my body and what he's doing to it. The glorious way he's making it feel.

Until he reaches back around and presses his wet thumb between my ass cheeks.

I jerk, stiffening. My eyes fly open wide.

"Easy, viper," he croons gently. "Remember, you can always say no."

"I can always use that pen on the nightstand to puncture your jugular, too."

"Until I hear a no or you communicate what else you'd rather have me do, I'm amusing myself with this perfect arse of yours."

Slowing the thrusts of his hips, he starts to gently stroke his thumb back and forth over the sensitive knot of flesh. Around and around, over and down, he fondles it as I try to decide if it's amazing or if I'm going to buck and kick him under the chin.

After a few breathless moments, I go with amazing.

When he feels me relax, he growls, "Fucking hell, you're gorgeous. My sweet girl. I'd kill an army for you. I'd burn down empires and lay all their gold at your feet."

I shudder and squeeze my eyes shut, hiding my face in the blankets so he can't see how much I love it when he talks like that. How deeply it affects me.

He breaches the knot of muscle and slides his thumb inside me, shushing me with softly spoken words when I gasp. It takes a moment for me to relax into it, but then I'm pushing back against his hand and he's growling his approval.

He reaches around with his other hand and strokes my throbbing clit.

"Tell me what you want, sweetheart," he says, his voice husky.

I answer without thinking. "More. I want more. I want all of you."

I meant to say "it," but "you" slipped out instead. There's a subtle difference in meaning, and he doesn't miss it.

"And you're gonna get all of me, wife," he says, fucking me harder. "Now come on my cock."

He tugs on my clit, sending a shockwave of pleasure throughout my entire body. Panting, I groan into the blankets, my face hot from hearing the sounds we make as our bodies slap together.

Through gritted teeth, he says, "You feel like silk. Wet, hot silk. Christ. Come, baby. Come for me."

With my hard nipples dragging against the covers and his finger and cock filling me up, I orgasm with a sob.

He moans. The motion of his hips falters. His thrusts turn slow and then stop altogether as I clench and convulse around his girth.

He whispers, "Oh, fuck, viper. I can feel that. That's fucking amazing. You're coming so bloody *hard*."

I sob again, jerking, my body completely out of my control. I feel boneless, like the only thing holding me up is the huge throbbing member I'm convulsing around.

He moves the hand that's gripping my hip farther up my body, sliding it under my breast so he can fondle it and pinch my nipple. I buck back against him, begging for more.

A dark laugh in his voice, he says, "You like it when I play with your nipples as I'm fucking you, don't you? You like my cock, and you like to come for me when I tell you to, because you're perfect and you're gorgeous and you're all fucking *mine*."

I don't understand how we got here.

I can't comprehend that this man growling all these filthy things is my husband. I can't grasp the enormity of any of it, because only this morning, I was bracing myself to send Lili off into her married life, but now I'm here, facedown on a hotel bed, getting railed by a sexy, crazy Irishman who I don't even like.

Or at least I'm telling myself I don't.

The alternative is unimaginable.

All of a sudden, out of nowhere, I burst into tears.

I bury my face in the blankets and wail like a newborn baby, pounding my fist against the mattress because I hate myself for it so much.

Then I'm not facedown anymore, because I'm somehow sitting up in Quinn's arms and he's rocking me, murmuring into my hair.

"It's okay, lass. You're safe here with me. You're safe."

He squeezes those big arms around me, holding me tight. I cry all over his chest, hiding my face and burning with shame as I cling to him helplessly. I'm curled up in his lap with his legs crooked around me, so his whole body is curved around mine.

"I'm s-sorry."

Cupping my head in one hand, he exhales and kisses my shoulder. "Don't be a bloody idiot. You don't have to apologize."

"I don't know what happened."

He chuckles. "I'll tell you what happened. I dazzled the swamp witch with my dick, she fell under a sleeping spell, and the real you woke up for the first time in centuries."

Sniffling, I wipe my nose with the back of my hand and heave a ragged sigh. "God, you're an arrogant ass."

He nuzzles my neck, whispering, "But I'm right."

He's right about one thing at least. I do feel safe in his arms. Safe, warm, and like an absolute, undignified moron.

What kind of woman cries during sex?

I'll tell you what kind: a weak one.

In all the years Enzo abused me, I never allowed myself to cry until afterward, when he'd left me alone and bleeding.

"Lass."

"Yes, Quinn?"

"We're gonna need to do more talking."

Exasperated, I say, "Right *now*?"

He pauses. "No. After I feed you and give you a bath."

"I don't need food or a bath."

He lifts my chin and forces me to look up at him. In a gentle but firm voice, he says, "No, you need a lot more than that, but for the moment, you're going to let your husband take care of your basic needs, and you'll do me a big bloody favor if you'll keep that forked tongue in your mouth until I'm finished. Understood?"

"Why are you being so damn bossy?"

He growls, "You're wearing my ring. Your well-being is my responsibility. It's my job to take care of you now. I'm going to do it whether you like it or not. Got it?"

My lower lip quivers until I bite down on it. I don't trust myself to speak, so I simply nod.

He takes my face in his hands, kisses both of my wet cheeks one after the other, then says gruffly, "Good. Now get your sweet arse under the covers and lie here quietly like a good girl until I come back."

Without waiting for me to reply, he peels the covers back, rolls us over so I'm lying down, stands, then pulls the blankets up under my chin. He fluffs the pillow under my head, kisses me on the forehead, and strolls away, whistling.

I close my eyes and pray for a sudden brain embolism.

Death is preferable to having to live with this new, weepy version of me.

Quinn picks up the phone and orders room service. I don't listen to the words, only to the low, soothing cadence of his voice. After he's done with the call, he switches on music, using a remote he found on the console under the television. That's soothing, too. Some kind of Spanish guitar. Then he disappears into the bathroom. I hear water running.

It could also be the sound of my sanity pouring out my ears.

In a few moments, he's back, naked, bending over me. "Food'll be here in thirty," he murmurs, pulling the blankets down. "Which is plenty of time for a bath."

He picks me up and heads to the bathroom, carrying me in his arms.

I rest my head on his shoulder and say to his chin, "I'm trying not to be impressed by how easily you can carry a grown woman, but I have to admit, this is something else."

He scoffs. "You barely weigh an ounce."

"I weigh a few thousand ounces, as a matter of fact. Wait, were we talking about your brain?"

Grinning, he shoots me a sideways glance. "Ah, the swamp witch awakens. Well, it was nice while it lasted. Hullo, She-Devil."

"Hello, Spider-Man. You're much taller in real life than you look in the comics."

"There's a compliment in there somewhere, I'm sure."

"You only think that because you're obsessed with yourself."

Chuckling, he sets me on my feet next to the bathtub. Pulling me against his body, he gives me a firm, closed-mouth kiss. Then he points at the water. "Get in."

When I send him a hard stare, he smiles.

"*Please* get in."

"Woof." I step into the water, wincing because it's hot, but the sting fades quickly, and I sink down with a grateful sigh, closing my eyes.

Quinn murmurs, "Scoot up, sweetheart."

I bend forward. He lowers himself into the tub behind me, causing the water to rise dangerously high. He settles himself in, stretching his legs out on either side of me, then wraps his arms around me and pulls me back against the solid wall of his chest.

He rests his chin on top of my head and gives me a squeeze.

We're silent for a while, just sitting together in the hot water, until he says in a thoughtful tone, "What if we get you a house?"

I wait for him to explain. When he doesn't, I say, "For what, my collection of crowns made of human femurs?"

"I don't think we could find a place so big. No, I meant for *you*."

"For me to do what?"

"To live in."

Frowning, I twist my neck and stare up at him.

He swipes a thumb under my eye. It comes away black with smudged mascara. He dips his fingers in the water and repeats it on the other side, cleaning off what must be an unsightly mess on my face made from the tears mingling with makeup.

Very gently, he says, "You said you'd never lived alone. That you went straight from your father's house to . . . his."

His eyes flash with hatred when he says "his," but he quickly goes on.

"What would you think about getting a place of your own?"

"I don't think I'm understanding the question."

"Just because we're married doesn't mean I'll force you to live with me."

I stare at him in open-mouthed surprise.

"Don't pull such a puss. I'm not that much of a caveman. Now turn around and let me fondle you while you think of clever insults."

He grasps my jaw in his hand and faces my head forward. Then he sweeps all my hair off to one side and kisses my neck as he reaches around and cups my breast in his huge hand.

"Not live with you?" I say faintly. "Were you planning on doing that with Lili, too?"

He snorts. "Christ, no. I doubt the wee lass even knows how to feed herself. Seems like she'd require round-the-clock care, like a puppy."

I'm about to argue with him, but recall the times she nearly burned the house down attempting to cook, and think better of it.

"*You*, on the other hand." He chuckles again, now cupping both my breasts in his hands and pulling gently on my nipples. "Can take care of yourself."

"But . . . you don't want to live with me?"

He pauses his caressing to say in a husky voice, "Aye. I do. But more than that, I don't want you to be miserable."

I'm overwhelmed by the generosity of that offer. Stunned and overwhelmed, and not altogether believing, because how on earth would something like that even work?

"Quinn . . . I . . . I don't know what to say."

"You don't have to know. Just think about it."

Massaging my breasts, he hums with pleasure. Powered by an internal nuclear reactor that never goes offline, his erection digs into my lower back.

He says, "Oh, but don't think you'd be off on the other side of the city or anything. I'd buy you a house right next door to mine."

That makes me smile. "Naturally."

"I'd probably have connecting doors put in to join the bedrooms, too."

"I can't imagine."

Sliding his hands down my rib cage, he squeezes my hips, then slips his hands between my legs. Kneading the tender flesh on my inner thighs, he murmurs, "You can't blame me, lass. You're a goddamn wet dream. You're perfection. Every time I look at you, I think I could go blind."

My heart expanding painfully, I say, "I'm quite average-looking, actually. You just have a thing for mouthy swamp witches."

He breathes, "God, how I do," and sinks a finger inside me.

I turn my head. He takes my mouth, kissing me deeply as he works his finger in and out and plays with my breasts, going back and forth between them.

"You're trembling again."

"And you're talking again. What a surprise."

Our faces are only an inch apart. He stares down at me, his hazel eyes soft and warm. A lock of hair falls across his forehead. I reach up and brush it away, my lids drifting lower as he lazily strokes his fingers over my clit.

He says, "Tell me about these romance novels of yours."

"Why?"

"I'm interested to know what you like about them."

I think for a moment as he gently pinches a nipple and my clit at the same time. The feeling is incredible. Which he knows, because he's intently watching my face from one inch away.

In a breathy voice, I say, "I guess I like that they're written for women. The whole world is made to please the male gaze, but romance novels only care about what we want. What we need. They're specifically for our pleasure. Some of the stories are great escapist fantasies."

He looks intrigued. "Maybe we should reenact one of these fantasies. What's your favorite type of storyline?"

"Oh, that's easy. Reverse harem."

His brows draw together. "What the bloody hell is reverse harem?"

"Where one female has multiple male sexual partners."

He freezes. His nostrils flare. His lips thin, and a dangerous glint appears in his eyes.

He growls, "Two things you should know about me. One: what's mine is mine. Two: I don't share. Three: see numbers one and two, woman."

I laugh. "God, you're easy to provoke. I was only teasing you."

His outraged stare indicates he doesn't find my teasing at all amusing.

"Okay, Mr. Jealous and Possessive, you can stop glaring at me now." I press a gentle kiss to his thinned lips and say more softly, "I have no desire to have multiple men at a time. In real life, they'd all be more concerned about comparing the size of their dicks than pleasing me. And I'm happy that you don't want to share, but I could do without the over-the-top alpha-male pos-sessiveness."

A rumble of displeasure goes through his chest, but he doesn't say anything.

Smiling, I whisper, "And you claim to not be a caveman."

He snaps, "I said I wasn't that much of a caveman, not that I wasn't one at all."

My smile grows wider. I lounge against him, ridiculously satisfied by everything about this conversation.

"Don't gloat," he warns, nipping at my lower lip.

"It's just that I've never had such a beautiful man act so crazy over me before."

When he lifts his brows and drawls, "Oh, *really*?" I know I've made a huge mistake.

I close my eyes and heave a sigh. "Go ahead. Get it over with."

"It's just that I could've *sworn* I heard you call me . . . what was it again?"

I mutter, "Impossible."

"No, that wasn't it. Hmm." He pretends to think. "It could've been 'beautiful.' But perhaps I'm mistaken? Maybe I need you to say it again."

"Or maybe you need to go find a speeding car to jump in front of."

He slides his hand up my chest and encircles my throat with gentle pressure from his fingers. I open my eyes to find him gazing at me with such burning intensity, it makes me catch my breath.

His voice low and his eyes hypnotic, he commands, "Say it, viper. Tell me what you think of me."

The way he's wrapped around my body—legs, arms, and that big rough hand around my neck—should make me feel panicked. Or cornered, at least. Like a hunted fox, staring down its bloody end.

But all I feel is sheltered.

Secure.

As if his body is a shield instead of a weapon that could do me harm. For the first time in my life, a man feels not like war to me, but like home.

I gaze up into his eyes as an ancient calcified rock melts to warmed butter in the center of my chest.

Then I admit something truly horrifying.

"I think you're a brilliant golden sun in a sky that's only ever known the black and starless night."

Through parted lips, he exhales a slow, astonished breath. His burning eyes could light the whole city on fire. When he touches my mouth, his fingers tremble.

I'm rescued from the feeling that I'm about to leap off a terrifyingly high cliff ledge and plunge headlong into a bottomless abyss when room service knocks on the door.

TWENTY-SIX

REY

We eat in silence.

More accurately, he feeds me forkfuls of food as if I'm an invalid, and I chew while neither of us speaks.

I don't know how he's feeling about all this, but I, for one, am terrified about what might erupt from my mouth next.

I'm in danger of composing more hasty and humiliating odes to his godlike beauty, so for the moment, I'm pretending to be a mime.

The filet is delicious. The asparagus is perfectly cooked. The mashed potatoes are pillowy, buttery perfection. All of it slips past my lips in small forkfuls that my new husband provides with the intense concentration of an explosives specialist defusing a ticking bomb.

In between bites, he lifts a glass of wine to my lips so I can sip from it.

It's a testament to my new state of permanent mental disability that I don't find any of that odd.

When I indicate I've had enough with a little flick of my fingers, he feeds himself. It's like watching a National Geographic special about starving lions. It's messy, savage, and over in ten seconds flat.

Then he shoves aside the plates, tears off both our fluffy hotel robes, picks me up, and takes us back to the bed again.

He settles his naked body on top of mine and kisses me ravenously.

"Ow."

He pulls away, panting. "Fuck. I'm sorry."

With my tongue, I test the raw spot on my lip where he bit me. "Am I bleeding?"

"A little." Looking pained, he licks the spot gently, then murmurs another apology. He's about to withdraw from the bed, but I squeeze his shoulders and shake my head.

He says gruffly, "I didn't mean to hurt you, lass."

"I know," I say softly, gazing up into his eyes. "It's okay."

"It's not. It's never okay. I—"

"You're not him," I interrupt. "You'll never be him. That was an accident, which is very different. Okay?"

I know I was right about what he was thinking when he hangs his head and hides his face in my neck. He whispers, "I'll kill anyone who ever hurts you. Including myself."

"I'll remember that the next time your ego flattens me. Also, that's disturbing."

"It's true."

I say crossly, "I don't ever want to hear you talk about hurting yourself. I don't like it. The only person who's allowed to hurt you around here is me."

He lifts his head and peers at me.

I warn, "Don't you dare say another word, Quinn."

"I have to. Because that almost sounded like you care."

I close my eyes and growl in frustration.

He kisses my neck and whispers into my ear, "Tell me you care if I live or die, viper."

Pressed between my legs, his erection is hard, hot, and eager.

I realize with a sudden start that maybe I'm not the only one with a newly discovered praise kink.

My heart begins to pound. My breath hitches. I say tentatively, "I . . . um . . . of course I care if you die."

"Why?" he challenges. "Because you won't have anyone to insult anymore?"

Do I do this? Do I go ahead and try it and see what happens?

What's the worst that can happen, you embarrass yourself a little more? Give the poor man a break, Reyna. He's not asking you to donate a kidney!

I take a breath to steady my nerves. Then I reach up, thread my fingers into his hair, and say softly, "No. Because I won't have this gorgeous face to look at anymore."

He licks his lips. His breathing goes ragged. And I swear to God, that monster dick between us just twitched.

Encouraged, I continue. My hands drift down to his thick shoulders, then to his bulging biceps, which I squeeze. "Or these big strong muscles to touch."

His pupils dilate until his eyes look black.

With a weird thrill running through my body, I move my hands to his back, stroking my palms over his smooth, warm skin. When my fingers graze the hard, rounded swell of his ass, he shivers.

Looking deep into his eyes, I whisper, "Or this beautiful hard body to make me feel so safe and protected."

The groan that escapes his lips is low and guttural. His eyelids drift shut. He rasps, "I don't even care if you're lying. That's the hottest fucking thing any woman's ever said to me."

"I'm not lying. I've never felt safer before than I do right now, here with you. My gorgeous, masculine, badass Irishman who I haven't stopped thinking about since the day we met."

He's wearing an expression I've only ever seen before on people right before they faint.

Hoping to avoid that outcome, I pull his head down for a kiss.

He kisses me back hungrily, sinking his fingers into my hair and rocking his pelvis against mine. We go at it until I'm squirming with need underneath him.

"You're such a good kisser," I say, panting. "I love the way you taste."

He moans. "Jesus fucking holy hell, you're trying to kill me."

"Not at the moment. I'm just enjoying how delicious you are."

His eyes roll back in his head.

"Will you please fuck me with that amazing fat cock of yours now? I love having it inside me."

Very faintly, he says, "I've died and gone to heaven. That has to be it."

The only word I can find to describe the feeling of his reaction to me praising him is power. Giving him what he needs makes me feel strong, bold, and powerful as fuck.

Is this what it feels like for him, too? When he calls me his good girl and I melt, does it make him feel this incredible? This euphoric?

This seen?

When he scrambles down my body, shoves his face between my legs, and starts to feast eagerly on my pussy, I decide it doesn't matter. If he'll do this every time I say something nice to him, I'm going to be a goddamn cookie dispenser from now on.

Sinking my fingers into his hair, I spread my legs wider and whisper, "I love your tongue, Quinn. That feels incredible."

He moans into my flesh. His fingers dig into my hips. Stiff and bobbing, his cock hangs between his bent legs, the crown flushed a deep berry red. Veins stand out all over it. The tip glistens.

In a frenzy, his tongue lashes back and forth over my engorged clit.

Euphoria beating like a heartbeat inside me, I whisper, "Your cock is so gorgeous. So long and thick. Just looking at it excites me."

He grips it in one hand and starts to play with it, pumping his hips as he strokes it from crown to base and back again, stopping once every so often to run his palm over his balls.

Close to orgasm, I moan. My fingers tighten in his hair. My hips move in time to the strokes of his wicked tongue. Making muffled sounds of pleasure as he eats me, he strokes his dick faster.

I arch my back and grind into his face helplessly. My nipples are hard and sensitive, aching for his mouth or his touch. When I tell him that, he moans, his eyes closed and his cheeks hollowed from sucking.

Watching him, I whisper raggedly, "You're going to make me come. Please don't stop that. I love it just like that. It's perfect. You're perfect. Quinn—oh—God—"

My orgasm steals my breath. I bow from the bed, shaking and sweating, loving every hot swipe of his tongue over my clit, though it's exquisitely, almost painfully sensitive. I come and come, pulling his hair and moaning, until he sinks two thick fingers inside me, and I sob.

"You're the most perfect thing I've ever seen in my life," he snarls, finger fucking me as I jerk and gasp. "And you're all mine, aren't you, baby?"

I babble something. I don't know what. Whatever it is, it makes Quinn chuckle darkly.

"Aye, you are. Tell me you want my cock."

"Please yes please give it to me!"

When he sinks it inside me, I'm still coming. I cry out in ecstasy, my pussy clamping around his thick shaft. Convulsing rhythmically around it, like I'm trying to milk the cum right out of him.

He says something in Gaelic. A curse or a praise, I can't tell. But his voice is strained and his hips are snapping. Sitting up on his knees with my legs spread open around his hips and his hands clenched into my ass as he holds me up, he plunges his cock into me over and over again.

He's rough, but because I know it's passion, not anger that fuels his roughness, I welcome it.

His thrusting falters, and he shudders, moaning.

"Yes! Come! Let me feel you let go!"

He surges forward, falling onto his elbows on top of me. He grabs my face. With his eyes wide open, he kisses me, then climaxes with a primal grunt and violent, full-body spasm that shakes the bed.

Buried deep inside me, his cock pulses as he empties himself.

The entire time, we stare into each other's eyes.

He gasps my name.

I wrap my legs around his waist.

And that tall cliff I was worried about earlier?

I just jumped right the fuck over, headfirst.

TWENTY-SEVEN

SPIDER

We lie entangled on the bed in the dark.

I don't know how long we've been like this. Hours, maybe. Days? Years? Who fucking knows. I've lost all sense of time. All I know is that I'm here, in a place I never dreamed I'd be, with a woman who makes me feel like life might be worth living after all.

Her head rests on my chest. Her legs are twined between mine. Her warm hand is pressed flat over my beating heart.

My stunned, achy, battered heart that doesn't have a bloody clue what just hit it.

It's been bitten by a viper with sharp fangs and the sweetest venom.

After a heavy exhalation, Reyna whispers, "What happens now?"

"Now we figure it out, I suppose."

There's a brief but tense pause. "Is it . . ."

"What?"

"Is it always like this for you? I mean, this intense?"

I close my eyes and exhale. My lungs ache, too. "No, lass," I murmur. "Not for me."

"Good. If you'd said yes, I was going to rip out your nipple rings with my teeth."

Chuckling, I comb my fingers through her long silky hair.

Stirring, she presses a soft kiss to my jaw. I turn my head and look at her, stunning even in shadows.

"Did your mother really name you after the artist Winslow Homer?"

"Aye."

"That's nice."

"She was a nice person."

I can tell she wants to say something else, but she doesn't. She just toys with my beard and watches me with those mermaid eyes, glittering in the dark like sea glass under shifting waters.

Feeling a thousand years old, I turn my head and stare at the ceiling. After a while, I say, "I'm thirty-eight."

"Hmm. You don't look a day over fifty."

"I deserve that."

"You do. What else? Tell me more."

"Like what?"

"I don't know . . . What's your favorite song?"

"'God Bless America.'"

She laughs. "That's not your favorite song."

"It is."

"Really?" She digests that in silence for a moment. "How strange."

I shrug. "I like you, too. You can't account for taste."

She laughs again, softly, tugging at my beard. "Good one."

Then, a moment later and sweetly hesitant: "You like me?"

And she calls *me* an idiot.

My sigh is a huge gust of air. "Aye. I like you. But then again, I'm a glutton for punishment, so there's that."

"That's such a weird phrase. 'Glutton for punishment.' What does that even mean?"

"It means you love what hurts you."

A delicate shiver runs through her body. Burrowing closer to me, she whispers, "Don't love what hurts you, Quinn. Whatever hurts you doesn't deserve you. You're made for so much better than that."

A thousand knives carve her name into my heart. Bleeding, barely able to breathe, I say gruffly, "Goddammit. Stop being sweet. I can't handle it when you're sweet."

"Yes, you can, you wuss. C'mon, we'll practice." She lifts up onto an elbow and smiles down at me. "Hi, Homer. I'm Reyna. It's nice to meet you. You look like an orphan's idea of Christmas morning."

Closing my eyes, I take a breath and pray for the Lord to help me.

Not that he's listening. He was done listening to me a long time ago.

She whispers, "I love it that you're this big tough guy who runs around shooting people like it's just another day at the office, but inside, you're all gooey. One little compliment and you melt."

"That wasn't one little compliment. It was a smile that could end wars and the only time you've ever said my first name and a metaphor about how you think of me that felt like a goddamn standing ovation."

"It was pretty good, wasn't it?"

When I turn my head and look at her, she's grinning at me.

She pokes me in the ribs. "Now you do one."

I cup her jaw in my hand and stroke my thumb over the lovely curve of her cheek. Gazing into her eyes, I murmur, "You're a privilege I don't deserve, but I'm going to spend the rest of both our lives trying to be worthy of you."

She's stunned for a moment, swallowing and blinking. Then

she turns her face to my neck, closes her eyes, and says faintly, "If you make me cry again, the rest of your life will be very short."

That makes me chuckle. "Now who's the gooey one?"

Hiding her face, she shakes her head and says nothing.

Rolling onto my side, I gather her in my arms, bury my face in her hair, and inhale deeply. When she slides an arm around my waist and squeezes me, I feel as if someone just handed me a crown and ushered me into my new castle.

After a while, her voice muffled, she says, "I don't know how to be a wife."

"That's okay. I don't know how to be a husband."

"No, I mean, I don't know if I *can* be a wife. In case you haven't noticed, I've got a lot of baggage from the matrimony department."

I stroke a hand over her shoulder and down her back, gently tracing the outlines of her scars. More than ever, I wish that worthless fuck of a dead husband of hers were alive.

Oh, what I would do to him. All the ugly and wonderful things.

"If it makes you feel better, I have zero expectations. If you'd let me look at you naked every once in a while, that would be grand, but other than that, you don't have to do or be anything."

Sounding confused, she says, "Are all Irishmen as easy to please as you are?"

"Are all Italian women as gorgeous as you are?"

"There are a million Italian women who look like me, Quinn. Tits, ass, lots of sass. It runs in the gene pool."

"Hmm. Sounds like I need to book a trip to Italy."

She slaps me on the back, making me chuckle.

"That was a joke."

She mutters, "Better be."

"I'm sorry, is this the same person who accused me of being jealous and possessive? Because hello, pot, meet the kettle."

"I'll put a bullet in that stupid kettle if you don't shut up soon."

My chest shaking with silent laughter, I roll on top of her, brushing her hair off her face.

She glares up at me with flashing eyes.

"My God," I breathe, staring down at her lovely, livid face. "You're a fine thing, Mrs. Quinn."

"And you're crushing me. How much do you weigh, anyway?"

"Dunno. Don't bother with scales much."

"Maybe you should buy one. You're abnormally heavy."

"It's all the muscles."

She sighs, closing her eyes.

"I have an idea."

"The poor thing must be lonely inside that empty brain of yours."

"Stop insulting me for a minute and listen. Let's go shopping in the morning."

She opens her eyes and quirks a brow.

"Do you not recall that the only item of clothing you currently have is a wedding dress?"

"Are you really suggesting I should go shopping for clothes wearing a wedding dress?"

"Hmm. That is a problem. I'll have some things brought up from the boutique downstairs, then we'll go shopping."

"I have plenty of my own stuff to wear, Quinn. You don't have to bother buying me anything."

"Everything you own is black."

"Oh. Right." She pauses, chewing her lip thoughtfully. "And I threw out all my old clothes after I moved in with Gianni."

"So we'll go shopping. While we're doing that, I'll send some lads to your house to pack your things."

I watch her expression carefully to see what she thinks of that idea.

After a moment of processing it, she says, "Because I'm moving in with you."

I dip my head and press a gentle kiss to her lips. "Aye. If you want to."

"Do you want me to?"

"Don't be a bloody moron."

"Is that a yes?"

"It's a yes."

"I just wanted you to say it out loud."

"I already told you before."

Lowering her lashes, she whispers, "I know. But I like hearing it."

It's so bashful and so unlike her, it catches me completely off guard. It also charms the bejesus out of me.

I say gruffly, "I want you to live with me. I want you to sleep with me. I want you to shower with me, feed me, and fuck me every night and four times on the weekends."

"Aha! I knew you were going to make me cook!"

"Really? That's what you got out of all that?"

"No," she says softly, smiling up at me. "I got the other stuff, too."

"And?"

"And . . . it was all very nice."

"*Nice?* You force me to wear my heart on my sleeve and all I get for the bloody effort is a 'nice'?"

"Is Mr. Hyde coming out to play now? I feel like we're about to start arguing. Wait, or is it Dr. Jekyll?"

When I growl, she laughs, thoroughly pleased with herself.

"I'm only getting you back for making *me* wear my heart on my sleeve."

"Fine. We're even. No more getting each other back for anything else, aye?"

Grinning at me, she teases, "Aye."

I flip onto my back and pull her along with me. She settles on my chest with a sigh of satisfaction and runs her toes along the insides of my calves. Wrapping my arms around her, I kiss her hair and close my eyes.

I don't realize I'm smiling until she reaches up and touches my lips.

She says, "You really are incredibly handsome, Quinn. I've never seen a man with a jawline like this. Even with the beard, it could cut steel."

My voice thick with emotion, I say, "Now you're spoiling me."

"Yes. Do you like it?"

"Aye, evil witch. I fucking like it. Which you know. Stop patting yourself on the back about it and keep going."

"Okay. Hmm . . . what if I told you that when I first saw you, my heart skipped a beat?"

"My dick would get hard, that's what."

"It already is."

She's not lying. All this praise she's heaping on me has my balls tight and my cock jacked. It wants to get sunk into her sweet, slick heat again.

Reaching between us, she wraps her hand around my erection. "Would you show me how to kiss it so it feels good for you?"

My eyes snap open. My heart takes off like a rocket.

"Because I don't know how to do that." She exhales a shaky laugh. "Enzo was embarrassed about how small he was, so he didn't like me to even look at it, let alone put it in my mouth."

I'm a sick, sick puppy for how happy it makes me feel to know that a) he had a small cock and b) she never sucked it. Also that she wants to suck mine.

She's right: all that therapy I had was a waste of money. I'm still as fucked up as they come.

Exhaling a slow breath, I say, "You don't have to if you don't want to. I'll never make you do anything you don't want to do.

And you shouldn't feel obligated to do something just because I've done it to you."

"I know. Which are all reasons why I want to do it."

When I only lie there with a hammering heart, trying to figure out if I should kill myself now because this is clearly the highlight of my life and everything can only be downhill from here, she whispers, "I want to make you feel good, Quinn. It makes me feel good to please you."

I groan.

Now I can kill myself.

She slides down my body until she's eye level with my dick. Propped up on her elbows between my legs as I stroke her hair, she muses, "I wonder if all those romance authors I read have been secretly following you around for inspiration."

"Meaning?"

"Meaning oversized dicks are the norm in my books." She looks up at me. "Or is this the normal size?"

Trying to suppress a smile, I say, "I'm no expert, but from what I understand, there are as many different sizes and shapes of cocks as there are men."

"Oh." She stares at my hard dick again. "God, if there are cocks bigger than this, the men who own them must be giants."

"The fact that you're not even trying to give me a compliment makes that the best compliment of them all so far."

"So how do I start? Pretend it's a lollipop?"

I'd have never in a million years believed I'd be trying not to laugh out loud when a woman was about to give me head, but this day just never stops surprising.

"Give me your hand."

I guide her hand to my shaft and curl her fingers around the base.

Wide-eyed, she whispers, "My fingers can't even touch."

"Be quiet now."

Wrapping my hand around hers, I squeeze, then draw her hand up the length of me to just under the crown. I squeeze again there and murmur, "Lick the slit on top."

She laps at it eagerly like a kitten with a bowl of cream. It feels fucking incredible, but we're only getting started. I don't want to come all over her face and ruin the mood.

My voice husky, I say, "Take your time. Suck on it a little, just the crown, then lick again."

When her lips slide over the engorged head of my dick, a low moan breaks from my chest. She sucks, and my eyes slide shut. Her hot, wet tongue swirls over the slit on top, and I shudder.

"Good?"

"Perfect."

I guide her hand down the shaft again, flexing up against the pressure as she continues to suck and lick the crown.

I'm starting to sweat. My breathing is erratic. The hand I've got curled over hers shakes slightly, and the muscles in my thighs and stomach are tensed.

I whisper, "Try to take a little more in your mouth, sweetheart. Go slow."

The entire head of my cock is enveloped in wet heat. It feels so fucking good, I groan again. She licks and sucks and swirls her tongue around and around as I lie on my back, unraveling.

"You're so hard," she whispers, her lips moving against my skin.

She starts to stroke me slightly faster, responding to the pressure of my hand and the flex of my hips. When she leans forward and bobs her head, I warn, "Not too much or you'll—"

She makes a retching sound. My dick pops out of her mouth.

"Gag."

Pausing to catch her breath, she says hoarsely, "Boy, they never mention that in my books."

"You'll have to send a strongly worded letter to the author."

"Damn straight," she mutters. She exhales, tosses her hair over her shoulder, and leans forward again.

God bless a determined woman.

She starts to suck and lick again, setting a comfortable pace. Comfortable for her, anyway. I'm digging my heels into the mattress and grinding my teeth, trying to maintain a semblance of composure. The last thing I want is to lose control and start fucking her mouth like an animal, though that's exactly what my body is demanding I do.

My cock throbs against her tongue. My balls ache. There's a white-hot whorl of pleasure coiling tighter and tighter in my pelvis, and it's all I can do not to clamp my hands on either side of her head and surge up into her perfect wet mouth over and over again until I explode.

I have to be a gentleman.

It's our wedding night, after all.

Her hand and my shaft are slick from her mouth, so every stroke is now deliciously slippery. She's squeezing harder as she strokes me, and it's driving me fucking wild.

Through clenched teeth, I say, "I'm getting close. I'll warn you right before."

"Why?"

"So I don't come straight down your throat."

"Why would that be bad? I want to taste you."

My groan is broken. If I walk out of this room alive, it will be a miracle.

I tip my head back on the pillow, find a strand of her silken hair, and tug on it as she sucks and strokes my cock. "Viper," I whisper raggedly. "My beautiful viper. What have you done to me?"

When she moans around my cock, I feel it all the way down to my balls. Sucking in air through my teeth, I sink my hand into her hair and make a fist.

"Baby. Fuck. I'm there. I'm right fucking there—ah—"

I gasp and jerk, erupting in hot, uncontrollable pulses before I can finish the sentence.

She curls both hands around my shaft and sucks the crown as I come in her mouth, lost to sensation, my heart flying and my entire body shuddering with release.

When it's over and I'm lying there panting and shaking, she gives my cock one final squeeze, sits back onto her heels, licks her lips, and smiles at me.

"You taste like hazelnuts."

My laugh is breathless. "You like hazelnuts, sweetheart?"

"They're my favorite thing."

Maybe God doesn't hate me so much after all.

TWENTY-EIGHT

REY

*W*hen I open my eyes in the early morning, I have no idea where I am.

I lie on my side in the unfamiliar bed, staring out a wall of glass to an unfamiliar view of a city. There's an unfamiliar soreness in my body—especially between my legs.

There's also an unfamiliar but very comfortable warmth snuggled behind me. Like a heated blanket, only with muscles.

A ray of morning light catches the ring on my finger, blinding me with a sudden flash of scarlet. It all comes back to me like a full-body slap.

I'm married.

To Quinn.

My archenemy.

But that doesn't feel right, calling him my archenemy. I've never had an enemy who killed for me or focused all his attention on my pleasure or gave me choices over how to live my life.

Now that I think about it, I've never had a friend like that, either.

Is that what we are now? Friends?

Don't be ridiculous. Married people aren't friends.

Are they?

I don't know. I've never seen a marriage like that, but I suppose it's not impossible they exist. In the "real" world, people marry all the time for love. Those people must like each other, too, I suppose.

Why else would you vow to spend the rest of your life with someone who's going to annoy you half the time you're together?

Or maybe normal couples don't annoy each other.

Maybe normal couples don't threaten to murder each other, either.

Though the murder threats are only coming from my side. I don't want to get ahead of myself, but if Quinn keeps acting so sweet, I'll have to rethink how often I warn I'm going to put a bullet in him.

Stirring behind me, he says in a thick voice, "I can hear the gears turning, lass. You're thinking again."

"I know it's hard for you to understand, but some people like to engage in that activity from time to time."

"The only thing that's hard for me to understand is how such a good-looking woman can sound like a broken lawnmower when she sleeps."

"I have no idea what that means."

"It means you have sleep apnea."

I sigh and roll my eyes. "I don't have sleep apnea."

He wraps a heavy arm around my waist and kisses my nape. "You do. All the wild boars and elephants within a thousand miles heard your scary mating call," he whispers, a smile in his voice.

"Spent much time with wild animals, have you?"

He snorts. "Only my whole life."

Nuzzling his nose into my hair, he inhales deeply, then exhales with a satisfied sigh. He murmurs, "Good morning, Mrs. Quinn. You smell like an enchanted forest."

With a feeling of wonder, it hits me: the man is a romantic.

He's a hardened criminal who lives outside the laws of society, kills people without breaking a sweat, and probably robs banks and enjoys a little arson in his free time, but he's also a romantic.

Dazed by that realization, I murmur, "Good morning to you, Mr. Quinn."

"Did you sleep well?"

"For the most part. There was this big, hard object that kept poking into me at every turn, waking me up, but I managed to get a few hours in."

Quinn flexes his hips, pressing his erection into my bottom. "Whatever could it have been, do you think?"

"There's a broken spring in the mattress."

"Hilarious."

Caressing my breasts, he kisses my neck and hooks a leg over both of mine, pulling me closer. He whispers, "I'd like to put in a request with the home office that my wife always sleep in the nude."

"Hmm. We'll take it under consideration."

Pulling on a nipple, he gently bites my shoulder. His voice grows husky. "I need to fuck you, woman."

That makes me smile. "I think you take too many vitamins."

His hand drifts down my belly, dipping between my legs. "It's not vitamins. It's you. You make my dick so hard, it hurts."

"Sounds like you should seek medical attention for that."

Making small, lazy circles, he rubs his fingers over my clit. He trails his lips up my neck, tickling me with his beard.

He whispers, "You have no idea what it does to me when you shiver like that."

"I can't help it."

"I know. That's why it's so bloody hot. How do you want me to make you come first? Fingers, mouth, or cock?"

Arching my back and grasping his forearm, I eagerly wriggle my butt into his pelvis. "Fingers and cock at the same time, please."

Pleased by that, he growls. "That's my greedy girl. And so polite."

As he delves a thick finger inside my pussy, I breathe, "I was brought up to have good manners."

He sucks hard on the side of my throat, biting down with his teeth. It's dominant and possessive and sends a thrill of excitement through my whole body. My nipples harden to two rigid, aching points.

"You want me to fuck you, don't you?"

Breathless, I nod.

"Say it."

I whisper, "I want you to fuck me."

"Good girl."

Hoisting up to an elbow, he takes his hand from between my legs and uses it to guide the head of his cock to my pussy as I tilt my hips back and spread my legs. He slides the crown between my folds, hissing in pleasure.

I moan softly when he flexes his hips, sliding the head of his fat cock inside me.

"You like that?"

"Yes. You feel so good."

He curls his hand around my hip and sinks in another inch, lowering his head to say into my ear, "And that?"

"Yes. More. Deeper."

"Say please, viper."

Starting to pant, I whisper, "Please. Pretty please. I need it."

"You *need* it," he breathes, sounding elated as he slides deeper inside me.

I cry out, closing my eyes and shuddering at the feel of him sinking into me, filling me up. When he thrusts to bury himself in, I cry out again, louder.

Quinn slides his hand back between my legs and strokes my clit until it's throbbing and I'm begging him to move his hips.

Hovering over me on his elbow, his mouth on my neck and his hard chest pressed to my back, he demands, "Who do you belong to?"

"You!"

He rewards me by withdrawing and thrusting into me again. Then he stills, playing patiently with my pussy as he waits.

"Quinn, please!"

His voice dark and soft, he says, "Give me what I want, wife. You know what it is. Give it to me."

I turn my head and gaze up into his burning eyes. Without pausing to think what I'm going to say, I blurt, "I belong to you. Only to you. I love how you make me feel, and I don't ever want you to stop. Please fuck me. Fuck me and come with me."

He closes his eyes briefly, clenching his jaw. When he opens his eyes again, they burn with a dark, dangerous fire.

He snaps his hips, shoving his cock deep inside me. At the same time, he pinches my clit.

I moan long and loudly. It only stops when he crushes his mouth to mine.

Then he fucks me hard and fast from behind, pumping into me as he slides his fingers back and forth over my aching clit. He swallows my cries of pleasure, taking everything from me as he gives me exactly what I need and I crumble.

When my orgasm hits, I stiffen, sucking in a breath through my nose.

Quinn shudders and groans into my mouth, and I know he's right there with me.

He rolls me to my belly and fucks me straight through his

own orgasm, pumping hard and groaning as I bury my face in the pillow and scream.

He says something in Gaelic. It's broken and breathless, like a plea.

When the motion of his hips has slowed, he lowers himself on top of me and pushes my hair off my face so he can kiss my jaw and cheek.

We lie like that for a long time, both of us speechless and stunned, watching the room grow brighter with the rising sun, until finally, he exhales a heavy breath.

I whisper, "You okay?"

"Aye."

"Why are you lying?"

He lifts my hand and stares at the ring on my finger. Then he turns his face to my neck and breathes me in.

"Just thinking of something someone once told me."

"What?"

"That a man who'd marry a woman for any reason other than love has the soul of a monster."

"Ah. Yes, well, that person was rather annoyed with you at the time."

He pushes the ring up with his thumb, exposing the slanting black line of cursive below. His voice lower, he says, "Aye. But you were right."

Something in his tone sounds an alarm bell in my mind. I don't know the cause, but suddenly, without warning, he's upset. I say gently, "I don't think you're a monster."

There's a brief pause. His voice comes even lower this time. "But you don't know me, do you, lass? You don't really know me at all."

He doesn't speak to me for two hours after that.

We rise from bed. He orders from room service and makes

phone calls. He takes me into the shower and washes my whole body, including my hair. He washes himself, rinses us both, then lifts me up against the shower wall and fucks me.

His silence is especially unnerving then. Even when he climaxes, it's with nothing more than a grunt.

After the shower and breakfast, he makes more phone calls from the other room and continues to ignore me. I sit on the edge of the bed in the hotel robe, disoriented by this abrupt change.

Maybe I was right about the Dr. Jekyll/Mr. Hyde thing.

Maybe he's only wonderful at night.

In bed.

While he's fucking me.

A nocturnal sex vampire who rises at sundown and turns into an irritating, baffling Irishman during the day.

Since he's still pacing around in the other room growling in Gaelic into his cell, I pick up the hotel phone and dial the Four Seasons. The operator puts me through to Gianni's room.

"Hi, Mamma. It's Reyna."

"Reyna who?"

I sigh heavily. "Glad to see you haven't lost your special spark since your only daughter married a stranger and your grandchild ran off to Mexico with the pool boy."

"I'm on my third mimosa. Things are a little fuzzy over here."

"What happened after we left? Have you spoken to Lili? What's Gianni doing?"

"*I'm* fine, thanks for asking."

"Mamma, please. Not today."

She pauses. "How are *you* doing? The Irishman still breathing?"

I throw an irritated glance toward the other room. "He's still breathing."

She chuckles. "Sounds like he won't be for long."

"Tell me about Lili. Did you see her leave?"

"*Sí.* She and her pretty boy left with about ninety-seven

bodyguards in a convoy of limos. Looked like a presidential mo-
torcade. Then Gianni left. I don't know where, because he didn't
go to the reception, and he never came back to the hotel."

I'm relieved to hear Lili left the church with Juan Pablo and
was under protection when she went. That must mean they were
headed to the airport as Quinn ordered. But then I hear a loud
popping sound in the background and frown.

"Did you just open another bottle of champagne?"

"Don't judge me. I'm on vacation."

Feeling a headache coming on, I rub my temple. "I'm going
to arrange for someone to come to the hotel to get my things."

"Don't bother."

"Why not?"

"They were already here."

"Who was?"

"The Irish army, that's who. Knocked on the door twenty
minutes ago, rushed in like a tsunami, packed up your suitcase,
rushed back out again. That barrel-chested one's cute. Kellen?"

"Kieran."

"Mmm. I think I scared him when I told him I've always liked
a nice big man."

"Jesus, Mamma."

"What, a girl can't dream?"

"Since when do you flirt with men?"

She cackles. "Since never, but it was fun. He ran out of here
so fast, he left skid marks on the carpet."

I say faintly, "I don't understand what's happened to my life."

"You'll land on your feet, *stellina*. In the meantime, have a
mimosa. You sound like you could use one. Or five."

"Thanks for that stirring pep talk."

"You're welcome. When Gianni comes back, should I give
him a message?"

"I'll try his cell. I can't believe he left you there alone. How did you get back from the reception?"

"Your cousin Carmine."

"Oh God. Does he still have a driver's license? He's about a hundred years old!"

"You're thinking of your granduncle Carmine. Speaking of which, he was *molto borracho* at the reception. Got cozy with a bunch of young Irish bucks and went shot for shot with them. Then they all started to sing. It was hilarious."

I'm glad I missed it.

When Quinn walks into the bedroom, I say, "I have to go. I'll call you later, okay?"

"*Certo.* And Reyna?"

"Yes?"

Her voice softens. "Give this one a chance. I have a good feeling about him."

"You had a good feeling about Lili going to college, too."

"Maybe she'll go to college in Mexico."

"And maybe I'll become an astronaut and fly to the moon. Talk to you later."

I hang up and distract myself from Quinn standing in the doorway glowering at me by examining my manicure.

I always keep my nails short and painted black. It confuses people. They're not sure if I'm chic and trendy or a dominatrix.

He says, "That was your mother?"

I say archly, "It speaks! I was beginning to think I'd have to take sign language classes."

A grumble indicates my new husband isn't pleased by my sass. He stands in the doorway wearing only a white towel wrapped around his hips. His hair is mussed, his eyes are burning, and he's so damn handsome, it pisses me off.

"I've got clothes coming for you."

He says it like a threat. That pisses me off even more.

"How thrilling. Would you like to tell me what your problem is now, or are we just going to start throwing things?"

We glare at each other across the room until a sharp knock on the door interrupts us.

His jaw clenched, he says, "That'll be Kieran."

I rise from the bed and brush past him on my way to the bathroom. "Good. I hope he brought one of your better personalities with him."

Fuming, I slam the door behind me.

TWENTY-NINE

SPIDER

*K*ieran takes one look at my face when I open the door and bursts into laughter.

I growl, "Shut it. I'm in no mood."

"As if I couldn't tell by that mug yer wearin'." He peers around my shoulder. "Where's the missus?"

"Heating her cauldron. Is that everything?"

"Aye. Just the few bags. She's a light packer."

I mutter, "Must've left all the spell books and potions at home."

When Kieran makes a face at me, I sigh. "Never mind. We'll meet you downstairs in twenty minutes."

"Don't ye want to know how yer party went?"

"Declan already told me."

He purses his lips in dissatisfaction. "Did he tell ye I spent half the night flirtin' with a Mafia lass and the other half dancin' with her?"

"Do yourself a favor, lad. Stay away from the Italians. They're murder on the nerves."

Kieran and I bring Reyna's bags in, along with a fresh suit for me that he picked up. Then he leaves to wait for us in the car. A few minutes later, a hotel employee arrives with the dresses I ordered up from the boutique. I tip her, wondering why her face is red, then realize I've still got nothing on but the towel.

When she's gone and I've dressed, I knock on the bathroom door.

"Your clothes are here."

When Reyna doesn't answer when I knock again, a twinge of panic twists my stomach. I try the handle, but the door is locked.

"Woman, open this door."

Nothing.

I rattle the handle. "You've got five seconds!"

Still nothing.

My brain presents me with a series of awful images, starting with a weeping Reyna sitting on the toilet with her head in her hands and accelerating directly to her lying naked in a pool of blood, her wrists slit, her skin blue, and her eyes wide open as they stare sightlessly at the ceiling.

My heart pounding and my breath coming fast, I rear back and give the door a hard kick.

It flies open and slams against the wall with a crash.

Wrapped in a towel, Reyna leans against the bathroom sink, filing her nails and smiling at me.

"I wondered how long that would take you. The silent treatment can be so annoying, can't it?"

Relieved, frustrated, and angry, I snap, "Don't do that again."

She looks me up and down with an expression like I just staggered in off the street, covered in my own vomit.

I turn and grab her suitcases. I toss those into the bathroom, then go back for the wrapped packages from the boutique. I drop them onto the floor just inside the door.

"Get dressed. You have ten minutes."

"Where are we going?"

"Out!"

Half an hour later, she sashays out of the bathroom with her nose in the air like she's a socialite attending a fundraiser for her least favorite charity.

I'd say something about that bitchy look on her face and how late she is, but I can't speak.

She's wearing a sleeveless red dress. It appears to be at least one size too small, if not two. The neckline is plunging, from which her ample tits are spilling out. Her waist is cinched like she's got a corset on, her legs are bare, her stilettos are sky-high, and all I can see are curves for days.

Gazing at me in cool silence, she raises her brows.

I have to pause for a rough throat clearing before I can talk. "Why didn't you wear one of the white dresses?"

"I hate white."

"It's the color of new beginnings."

"It's the color of innocence." Her smile is lethal. "I didn't want you to get the wrong idea."

I growl, "Nobody could ever mistake you for innocent, viper."

"Good. By the way, what moron thought I wear a size small?"

"This moron."

Holding my gaze, her voice low and smooth, she says, "Dear husband. You should know by now that there's nothing small about me."

We stare at each other across the room. And of course—because I clearly have a problem—my dick starts to get hard.

She glances down at the growing bulge in my trousers, and her lethal smile grows wider.

I cross the room, take her by the arm, and head to the front door, guiding her along.

She pulls her arm from my grip and says acidly, "I'm able to walk without a rabid service animal, thank you."

So we're back to square one. Fucking wonderful.

Opening the front door, I make a grand sweeping gesture, complete with a mocking bow.

She walks past me like a queen past smelly beggars.

Once we're in the car, she decides her hatred of mankind doesn't extend to Kieran.

Sitting forward on the back seat of the SUV, she says to him, "So tell me all about the reception. Did you have fun?"

"Ach, did I! Met one of yer kin that I fancied. Wee lass named Aria?"

"That's Leo's daughter! Oh, she's the prettiest thing, isn't she?"

"Aye." Kieran whistles, his cheeks turning pink. "What a wetser. With the sweetest little arse I've ever seen in my—" He cuts off abruptly, sending a horrified glance over his shoulder. "Sorry, lass. I'm an eejit. Just ask Spider."

She waves a hand and laughs. "Don't be silly. I don't mind."

I growl, "You mind if I breathe in your general direction, but you don't mind about that?"

Ignoring me, she says, "How did everyone get along? Were there any altercations?"

"Altercations? Nah, it was pure craic! Half the lads were ossified, the other half were fluthered! And the Bettys were bleedin' deadly on both sides, so there was plenty of tonsil tennis goin' on. If they weren't on the dance floor, they were in dark corners, wearin' the face off each other."

"So translated that means everyone had fun?"

"Yer bang on they did!"

She exhales a relieved breath and sits back against her seat. "That's good to hear. I was worried. You know how dangerous putting a bunch of oversized egos into one room can be."

I say, "Was that jab about egos directed at me?"

"Not everything is about you, Prince of Arrogance."

"That'll be King of Arrogance, if you please."

After shooting me a sharp glare, she turns her attention back to Kieran. "So where are we going?"

He sounds confused. "Spider didn't tell ye?"

"We're not on speaking terms at the moment. You tell me."

He sends me a look in the rearview mirror. "Er . . . forgive me, lass, but if it's all right, I'd rather stay out of a marital spat. I tried to intervene between my ma and da once and only got a savage slap about for the trouble."

She folds her hands in her lap and crosses her legs. "Then I guess it will have to be a surprise."

We drive through the city center to an industrial area near the docks. It's crammed with warehouses and shipping containers waiting to be filled and sent across the Atlantic. We pull up in front of one of them, a big white brick building with bars over the windows, and Kieran parks.

Looking out the window at the parking lot, Reyna appears bored.

The stubborn woman won't ask me where we are.

But when I say, "You'll want a gun for this," she whips her head around and stares at me.

"For what?"

"We're meeting with the heads of the other four Mafia families."

Ah, that look of shock on her face is so bloody satisfying, heat rushes to my balls.

"*Why?*"

"Dunno. They called the meet. You tell me."

Obviously unsettled, she frowns. "There's supposed to be a vote for the new capo."

"So why isn't Gianni here?"

"How do you know he isn't?"

"They told us he wasn't invited."

She ponders that in silence, then shakes her head. "That doesn't make sense. He's the head of the family. And the vote was supposed to happen tomorrow, not today." She glances out the window again, this time with a wary expression. "Mamma said he didn't go to the reception. He never went back to the hotel last night, either."

Declan's already told me about the vote and that Gianni was missing from the reception, but the news about him not going back to the hotel is new.

In our world, when someone goes missing, it only means one of a few things.

None of them are good.

From the pocket on the back of the driver's seat, I remove a handgun. I check to ensure there's a round in the barrel, then hold it out to Reyna. "You know how to shoot a Glock?"

"It can't be that hard. You know how to do it." She takes the gun from my hand.

When I shrug out of my suit jacket, she says, "What are you doing now?"

"You're not walking into a room full of made men looking like that."

She says coyly, "Like what?"

I give her a hard stare. "Put on the goddamn jacket."

She thinks about arguing, but apparently decides better of it. She shrugs and slips the jacket on, rolling up the cuffs.

"Button it."

She levels me with a look, but I'm in no mood for sass.

"To the top."

"I want you to know the only reason I'm wearing your jacket is because I don't have anywhere to stash the gun in this minuscule dress you bought me."

"Too bad you forgot to bring your bag of skulls. You could've put it in there."

She smiles sweetly at me. "It's only got space for one more. I was saving it for yours." She opens the door and gets out.

After she's gone, Kieran looks at me in the rearview mirror. "I really like her."

"That's because you've got the common sense of a carrot."

"Just because ye don't know how to handle her doesn't mean I can't like her!"

"I know how to handle her perfectly bloody well!"

He smiles. "Sure ye do. Let me get back to ye when my eardrums have healed, and we'll have a lovely chat all about it."

Muttering, I exit the Escalade and walk around the back to where Reyna's waiting. I'm all ready to have a scuffle over her not buttoning my suit jacket, but to my great surprise, she's done it.

"Ready?"

"I'm not sure going in there alone is a good idea."

"We won't be alone. Everyone else is already here."

She quirks an eyebrow at me. "Who's everyone?"

I can't help the smile that lifts my lips. "You're in the Mob now, darlin'. You'll never be alone again."

A flare of emotion warms her eyes. Or maybe I'm imagining it. Either way, she looks away before I can decide.

I expect her to pull away when I take her hand, but she doesn't. She lets me lead her from the parking lot around the side of the building to a door at the top of a ramp. A big bald man in a black suit waits at the top, his hands folded over his crotch, his legs spread apart, and his face as blank as a brick wall.

"Patrick."

He inclines his head respectfully, greeting me in Gaelic. He also inclines his head to Reyna but doesn't look her in the eye. He's three hundred pounds of pure muscle, but he can't bring himself to gaze directly at her face.

Funny how everyone else can sense she's a swamp witch, too.

He opens the door for us. We go inside with Kieran following. It takes a moment for my eyes to adjust to the low light.

Standing in the middle of the shadowy, empty warehouse is

a group of five men. All are in expensive dark suits. All exude an air of danger and power.

Declan's the only one I recognize.

Standing several feet away from the group are more men in suits, but these are soldiers, not leaders. Though they're all Italian, and I've never met any of them, I can spot the difference a mile away.

Lining the walls of the warehouse are our lads.

I wonder how many of them are nursing nasty hangovers from last night.

Declan turns, sees us, and lifts his chin. Hand in hand, we slowly walk toward him.

Under her breath, Reyna says, "The one with all the hair to the left of Declan is Massimo, head of the DeLuca family. He's clever, but he can't be trusted. He's only out for himself. To the right is Tomasi Berlasconi. He's as dumb as a rock. Next to him in the dark gray suit is Alessandro Ricci. He's a good man. Brilliant strategist. Enzo used to call him the General. In the pinstripe is Aldo LaRosa."

The tense note that crept into her tone when she said that last name makes me look at her. "What about him?"

"I'll tell you later."

"Tell me now."

She hesitates. "He can't be trusted, either."

I'd press her for more details, but we've crossed the warehouse and are now standing in front of the group. Kieran stands off to the side with our men.

Relaxed and smiling, Declan says, "Mr. and Mrs. Quinn. Sorry to interrupt your morning."

I expect Reyna to make a smart remark, but she maintains her composure and simply says, "Good morning, Declan." Then she greets each of the Italians by name in turn.

She receives respectful murmurs in response.

Declan gestures to the group. "These lads would like a word with you, Reyna."

He strolls away, lighting a cigarette.

As if it's the most natural thing in the world for her to be summoned to an abandoned warehouse on a Sunday morning in front of the leaders of the Mafia and dozens more armed men without a clue as to the reason why, she smiles and says calmly, "Of course. What can I do for you gentlemen?"

I feel a hot flash of pride and admiration for my wife. She might be a hell demon with a forked tongue and a knack for driving a man to the brink of insanity, but goddamn does the woman live up to the meaning of her name.

The one called Massimo with all the hair glances at me. It's not a friendly look.

"We were hoping to speak to you in private."

I bristle. Before I can say a word, however, Reyna squeezes my hand. Looking at Massimo with steel in her eyes, she says, "My husband stays, or we both leave. The choice is yours."

Watching us from behind the Italians, Declan smiles.

Massimo hides his anger with a practiced smile, but his eyes glitter with malice. "Very well. Then I'll get right to it. We understand there was an incident at your home last week involving armed intruders."

"There was. What of it?"

"Has your brother discovered who they were?"

"Not to my knowledge."

It's a smart answer. She's not committing herself to a yes or a no, and she's also not betraying the head of her family by divulging any details.

It's a sidestep, and a clever one.

She adds, "That's a question for him."

"We would ask him, but we don't have confidence that he would tell us the truth."

"And why is that?"

"Let's just say we've recently discovered some facts that have led us to believe your brother has been keeping secrets."

It sounds like a threat. An insinuation that whatever Gianni's been up to, she's been up to as well. From one second to the next, this has gone from a conversation to an interrogation.

But if she senses that, she shows no outward sign. Her expression is placid. Clasped in mine, her hand is cool and dry.

When Massimo doesn't say anything for a while and only stands there staring at her, trying to be intimidating, she asks politely, "I'm sorry, was there a question I missed?"

A hint of a smile curves Ricci's mouth. He's the one Reyna said Enzo referred to as the General. The oldest of the group, he's got gunmetal-gray hair, a slight paunch, and eyes like a hawk's.

Right now, those sharp eyes are looking at Reyna with the same admiration I'm feeling.

I decide I like him.

Massimo takes a different approach to see if he can rattle her. "When you killed your husband, the families looked the other way."

Without missing a beat, she replies, "My husband is alive and well, Massimo. Perhaps you missed the ceremony yesterday? I thought I saw you in the church, but weddings are always such a whirlwind."

She turns and smiles at me. "Anyway, here he is. I'm sorry for neglecting to introduce you, honey. Everyone, this is my husband, Mr. Quinn."

Massimo looks like he's trying not to swallow his tongue. Ricci looks like he's trying not to start laughing. The other two Italians look like they'd rather be at home in bed than standing in this dusty, echoing warehouse, watching a woman effortlessly run circles around them.

As for me, I'm simply dazzled.

Looking at her, I say in a husky voice, "Pleased to meet you, gents."

Her smile could light up an ocean of darkness.

Through clenched teeth, Massimo hisses, "My point is that you were granted a pass for murdering one of our own in cold blood. The least you can do in repayment is be honest with us."

Reyna's brilliant smile dies a quick death.

In its place blooms a look of such hot, incoherent rage, I almost drop her hand and start running.

She turns to Massimo and burns him to the ground with her eyes.

"I owe you nothing," she says in an icy, even voice. "Especially considering you knew exactly what Enzo put me through, and you always looked the other way. If anything, Massimo, you should count your blessings that you're still here to insult me. Because we both know I could send you to burn in hell with your dead friend without even chipping my nail polish."

Ricci passes a hand over his mouth to hide his smile.

Grinning, Declan tilts back his head and blows a series of perfect smoke rings into the air.

Everybody else just stands there, stunned.

Until one of the Italian soldiers says under his breath, "That bitch needs to be put in her place."

Scalding heat rushes up my neck and burns my ears. Every hair on my body bristles. I say loudly, "Did you just disrespect my wife?"

When he smirks at me, I pull out my gun and put a bullet in his head.

THIRTY

REY

The gunshot is painfully loud. The soldier's head jerks back. A perfect hole appears in the center of his forehead at the same time a mess of bloody chunks flies out from the back of his skull.

He drops to his knees and topples over sideways, dead.

Looking at the body, Declan sighs.

Chaos erupts. Soldiers from both sides surge forward, shouting and waving guns. An infuriated Massimo hollers at Quinn. Tomasi and Aldo are frozen in shock, gaping.

Ricci holds up his arms, turns to the Italian soldiers, and thunders over the fray, "Shut the fuck up and put down your weapons!"

There's a pause in the noise, into which he says in Italian, "Anybody who fires a shot won't walk out of here alive."

Throwing hard glances left and right, the muttering soldiers lower their guns.

Declan makes an aggravated motion with his hand to indicate his own soldiers should do the same. They comply instantly, stepping back.

It's quiet for a moment, except for the sound of Massimo's heavy breathing.

I turn to look at Quinn standing beside me. His eyes are wild. His face is red. A vein throbs erratically in the side of his neck.

"And you have the nerve to call me a land mine. You explode at the drop of a hat."

He shoves his gun back into his waistband and pulls me against his side with one arm. Glaring at Massimo, he growls, "Nobody disrespects my girl."

I am a sick and twisted individual, because this violent display of protectiveness has got me so hot, I want to push him down to the bare concrete and tear off his pants with my teeth.

Instead, I turn back to Massimo and smile. "You were saying?"

He moistens his lips and straightens his tie. He runs a shaky hand over his hair. He glances at Quinn, exhales a hard breath, and pulls himself together.

"There's a vote for the next capo tomorrow."

"I know."

"We want to know if your brother is worthy of the position."

Sensing there's a lot more to it than that, I tilt my head and narrow my eyes at him. "Why don't you tell me what you really want?"

"I just did."

I say softly, "You have ten seconds until we leave. I've got shopping to do."

Massimo opens his mouth, but Alessandro cuts him off. "We understand that you killed some of the intruders?"

I don't know where they're getting their information, but I'm not about to stand here and justify protecting my own home. So I say flatly, "Anyone who comes into my house uninvited leaves in a body bag."

He nods, considering me. "Does that protectiveness extend to the rest of your family?" He makes a slight sweeping motion of his hand, indicating all the other Italians present.

I notice Declan watching me intently but can't concentrate on that. Holding Alessandro's piercing gaze, I say, "Is my loyalty to the family under question?"

He pauses to carefully choose his words. "Forgive the presumption, but your loyalty could now be said to be . . ." He glances at Quinn. "Divided."

"My loyalty extends to those who prove themselves worthy of it."

"Regardless of blood?"

"For fuck's sake, Alessandro. You're smarter than that. Let me put it bluntly: family comes first. Unless they prove themselves untrustworthy; then they're dead to me." I smile. "Or by me. And before you get too excited, I consider the Irish family now, too. They've proven themselves much better friends than I expected."

I pause to glance up at Quinn. "And for that, I'm grateful."

The look in his eyes is all the reward I need.

Looking back at Alessandro, I say, "The bottom line is that I don't consider my loyalty divided. I consider it extended. I'm Italian by birth, and now Irish by marriage. Do with that what you will, but I won't stand here any longer and be forced to explain myself. I've given you enough of my time."

I wrap an arm around Quinn's waist. "You're interrupting my honeymoon."

Alessandro looks at Massimo. After a pause, he gives a curt nod. Then Alessandro glances at Tomasi and Aldo, who also nod.

He turns back to me. "Thank you, Reyna. Always a pleasure to speak with you." He looks at Quinn and chuckles. "Congratulations, Mr. Quinn. And good luck."

When Quinn narrows his eyes suspiciously, I poke him in the ribs to distract him from using Alessandro's face for target practice.

Massimo turns to his soldiers. He whistles and makes a circle in the air with his finger. Everyone falls back and allows the four heads to pass, then they pick up the body and fall in line behind them, headed for a door at the back of the warehouse.

As they file out, Declan issues a command in Gaelic to his men. They walk to another door, leading out the side.

Smiling, Declan turns to us. "That was a grand bit of fun, wasn't it?"

"It was a test," I say, watching the last of Massimo's men leave. The door slams shut behind him. A trail of blood is the only evidence they were ever here.

Declan murmurs, "Aye."

I focus on his face, which is unreadable. "You know what this is about, don't you?"

He lifts a shoulder and flicks his cigarette butt away. "I know all kinds of things, lass. It's the job. By the way, Sloane wants you both over for supper tonight."

Glancing at Quinn's possessive arm clamped around my body, his crystal blue eyes warm with laughter. "If you don't have any other plans, that is."

Quinn says, "I've got all sorts of plans. What time?"

"Six o'clock work for you, lover boy?"

"Aye." He looks down at me, and his voice grows husky. "Hope Sloane won't be serving anything too heavy. I'll need my energy for later."

"You don't have a problem with energy," I say softly. "Are we done fighting now?"

"Probably not."

"Great. Thanks for the heads-up."

When I turn back to Declan, he winks at me before strolling away.

Back in the car, I ask Quinn for his cell phone so I can call Gianni. I left my handbag at the hotel because I was too distracted wanting to rip off Quinn's head when we left.

When I dial the number, it goes straight to voicemail.

"Gianni. Call me as soon as you get this. Shit, forget that, I don't have my cell on me, I'm calling from Quinn's phone." I look at him and say, "What's this number?"

He quirks his lips. "You think I'm giving out my untraceable burner number to your idiot brother?"

Good point.

Into the phone, I say, "Never mind, I'll try you later. And you'd better be back at the hotel with Mamma right now, apologizing for leaving her alone overnight."

I disconnect and hand the phone back to Quinn. As soon as he's stashed it inside his shirt pocket, he drags me across the seat and pulls me onto his lap. He looks at my mouth. His eyes start burning.

I sigh. "Not in front of Kieran, please."

From the front seat, Kieran says, "Don't mind me, lass. I'm blind as a bat up here. Deaf, too, if it makes ye feel any better.'"

Ignoring him because Quinn's sliding his hand up my thigh, I warn, "Don't you dare."

He whispers, "You defended me. In front of all those wankers, you introduced me as your husband and called me 'honey.'"

"Those 'wankers' are my family."

"You said we were your family, too," he breathes, eyes alight. Sinking his fingers into my flesh, he touches his lips to mine.

Pleased by how satisfied he is, I smile at him. "Don't let it go to your head. That's big enough already."

He takes his hand from my leg and clasps it around my jaw. He kisses me again, this time more firmly, but still with no tongue. A thrill in his voice, he says, "You said we were on our honeymoon."

"I was trying to distract everyone from the mess you made. Remember the dead guy on the floor? Brains, blood, sound familiar? Also, back up a second. What the hell was your problem this morning? Were you concerned about this meeting you neglected to tell me anything about?"

His jaw works. He caresses my face for a moment in pensive silence, then shakes his head.

When he doesn't offer any explanation, I say crossly, "I see you've hit the mute button again. I wish I had access to that when you won't shut the hell up."

"Let me have this moment of happiness before you destroy my will to live, please."

When I blink, taken aback, he says, "That was a joke."

I chew my lip and play with a button on his shirt. "Don't joke about your will to live. You've said some things in that regard that worry me."

He exhales, pulls me against his chest, and tucks my head under his chin. Holding me tightly, he says gruffly, "Tell you what. You're the only one in this marriage who's allowed to kill me. How's that?"

Snuggled in his big strong arms, I whisper, "I don't want to kill you. I mean I do, but not right now."

He chuckles, nuzzling my ear.

I close my eyes and breathe him in. "Quinn?"

"Aye?"

"You shot a man because he disrespected me."

"Aye. And you didn't even flinch."

"Is it bad that I found it erotic?"

"The dead guy?"

I know he's only hunting for praise, but I still sigh in exasperation. "The psychotic machismo. Watching you blow out someone's brains because you didn't like the way he talked about me was a real turn-on."

A smile in his voice, he murmurs, "Careful, viper. Another compliment like that and you'll have a hundred bodies laid out at your feet by the end of the day."

I shiver with happiness, burying my face into the crook of his neck. Then, because I know my reaction is all sorts of wrong, I say sternly, "That's awful."

He laughs, squeezing me harder. "Christ, we're a pair, aren't we?"

Over his shoulder, Kieran says, "Look at it this way, lad: yer savin' two other people by bein' together!"

I say, "I thought you couldn't hear anything!"

"Oh. Right. Sorry, lass."

Settling back against Quinn's chest, I say to him, "I have a question for you."

"And I have an answer. Whether I'll admit it or not remains to be seen."

What I wouldn't give for a Taser right now. "You said yesterday, you didn't have a condom because you weren't planning on having sex."

"So?"

"So why weren't you planning on having sex on your wedding night?"

Kieran chuckles. "Because he doesn't fancy little girls, that's why."

At the same time, Quinn and I say, "Kieran!"

He waves a hand apologetically. "Sorry. Mum's the word."

After a pause to glare at the back of Kieran's head, Quinn says, "Lili didn't want it. I didn't want it. There was no need for protection from something that wasn't going to happen."

I'm so confused, my eyes almost cross.

Then, abruptly, I'm angry.

"Let me get this straight. You were going to marry Lili with no expectation of consummating the marriage, but you demanded *our* marriage include sex *and then made me propose to you?*"

He makes a face as if I'm being silly, then brushes me off with, "Let's talk about Aldo. Why don't you trust him?"

I reply with a pointed stare. "Because he's moody, arrogant, and incomprehensible."

"Ah. Then we'll get along just fine."

Kieran tries to stifle a laugh by coughing.

Positioning me more comfortably between his legs, Quinn says, "So where should I take you shopping first?"

"The Neptune Society."

"What's that?"

My smile is acidic. "A cremation company. Did you know they'll pick up a dead body from anywhere in the world?"

"You're being funny again."

"Yes, but you often mistake threats for humor, so there's really no telling."

Dismissing that, he changes the subject. "Speaking of sex—"

"We were talking about where to go shopping!"

"—what kind of birth control are you using?"

Blindsided by that, I stare at him blankly.

He stares back at me with a patient, curious look, waiting for my answer.

My answer which will make not one damn ounce of sense, so I take a page from his playbook and change the subject. "Why do you think Alessandro was so interested in what happened at the house last week? That was strange, wasn't it?"

"Aye. What's even stranger is why you're trying to get out of answering my question about birth control."

"Rewind to the part in the conversation where you said you'd have an answer for me, but might not admit it, and we'll go from there."

He furrows his brows, gazing at me with growing concern, then murmurs, "Oh."

"What do you mean, 'Oh'?"

He glances out the window and gives me a squeeze, saying softly, "It's all right. We don't have to talk about it."

"I can tell you're formulating some kind of bizarre and utterly incorrect hypothesis in that lump of coal you call a brain, Quinn. Stop thinking so hard. It doesn't suit you."

He glances back at me, his look wary. "So there's not a big *reason* you don't want to tell me?"

I sigh. The man is hopeless. "Just tell me what the big reason is that you've manufactured, and I'll tell you if it's right."

Hesitating, he licks his lips. "Are you . . . ?"

I lift my brows. "Breathless with anticipation? Yes. Spit it out before I faint."

He sends a furtive glance to my lap, then looks at my face again. When he winces, I know what he's thinking.

"No, I'm not infertile."

His pause is so loud, I need earplugs. "Did you have your tubes tied?"

"No."

"So everything is in good working order. Down there."

I say drily, "I'll have my gynecologist send you the records, Doctor. You can pore over them yourself."

Looking relieved and also a little sheepish, he admits, "I just didn't know if you . . . if Enzo did something . . . fuck." He looks out the window again, his cheeks ruddy.

Horrified to realize his meaning, I say softly, "Oh God, Quinn, no. Nothing like that. I was on the pill the whole time I was married."

He exhales, nodding. "Okay. Sorry, I'm just . . ." He stops short, then looks me in the eye. "So you're saying you're still on the pill?"

I feel heat creeping up my neck, but there's absolutely nothing I can do about it. "No. That's not what I'm saying."

His gaze turns intense. "Then what kind of birth control are you on, woman?"

Looking at the roof of the car, I crinkle my nose and say, "Um . . ."

With the speed of two fingers snapping, he devolves from an

adult human male with a fully functioning frontal lobe to a cave-dwelling primate composed of 99 percent penis.

A growl rises from deep in his throat. His arms tighten around me. His intensity level ratchets up a few thousand notches, and his eyes turn black. His energy crackling hot, he stares at me as if I'm about to be devoured.

In a guttural voice that raises all the hairs on the back of my neck, he says, "You're not using anything."

I nervously lick my lips. "Don't go all George of the Jungle on me. I simply didn't know I'd be needing anything because I didn't know I'd be getting married."

His savage grin is reminiscent of how an animal bares its teeth. His eyes gleam with a disturbing light. And his erection is now the fourth passenger in the car, quickly sucking out all the oxygen.

"You never mentioned that, viper. You let me fuck you and—"

"Keep your voice down!"

"—begged for me to come inside you. *Begged* me. And the whole time, you weren't on birth control." He bites my throat, then says hotly into my ear, "What does that mean?"

Shivering, I whisper, "That I have brain damage and should be taken to see a specialist immediately."

He wraps a hand around my throat and takes my mouth.

The kiss is consuming in its intensity. He thrusts his tongue into my mouth and ravages it passionately until I think I'll pass out. When he breaks away, we're both panting.

But he's the only one laughing.

Low, rough, and thoroughly pleased, his laughter is a victory lap around the race that I've obviously just lost with my admission.

"Quinn?"

"Aye, viper?"

"Don't talk to me for the rest of the day, okay?"

Still chuckling, he kisses me again. His mouth is possessive, his embrace is tight, and his eyes are living fire.

"Whatever my queen wants."

Looking away from his triumphant face, I wonder how soon is too soon to start marriage counseling.

THIRTY-ONE

REY

Quinn takes me shopping at the most expensive stores in the city, one by one. Not only at the couture clothing ateliers, but also for shoes, handbags, perfume, cosmetics, lingerie, and luggage.

It takes the entire day.

He arranges for most things to be delivered to his home address, but what doesn't get delivered, poor Kieran lugs to the car with the patience of a saint.

When I ask Quinn why he doesn't help him, he grins.

"I'm on my honeymoon."

And because the man has a highly developed sense of the absurd, our last stop is at Cartier.

When we pull up in front of the building, I frown. "What's this?"

He chuckles. "Did you think a ring would be the only piece of jewelry I'd ever buy you?"

"It's not as if I've had oodles of time to think about it."

"I'll spare you the effort. I want you covered in pretty spar-kling things. The more, the merrier. You'll look like a bloody Christmas tree by the time I'm done with you."

Just to be subversive, he carries me across the threshold of the store in his arms.

We spend more than an hour in there. When we emerge, I'm the new owner of a few million dollars' worth of luxury baubles and am more than a little dazed.

Dazed and dismayed, because this feels much too one-sided.

"What's that sour puss for?" he asks the moment we're back in the car.

"It's just that you've bought me all these wonderful gifts, and I haven't given you anything. You even had to buy your own wedding ring."

He gathers me into his arms, smiles at me, and plants a kiss on my lips. His voice soft, he says, "You've given me everything, you bloody daft woman."

"Really? Because it seems like all I've given you are headaches and a constant barrage of death threats."

"Aye. Those, too. Don't worry about it. I'll make sure you make it up to me later tonight."

His sensual smile leaves no doubt as to what kind of "making up" I'll be doing.

By the time we drop everything off at the hotel and head to dinner, we're half an hour late. The house is on the outskirts of Boston in the wealthy suburb of Westwood.

And when I say "house," I'm being ironic.

Declan and Sloane live on a forty-acre parcel with its own stream-fed pond, infinity pool, pool house, boat dock, and guest-house. The estate is a masterpiece of contemporary design, with twenty-foot ceilings, entire walls of glass, and ten thousand square feet of understated opulence.

Its sleek elegance makes Gianni's house look like a bad dream.

When we're inside and I tell Sloane how much I love it, she smiles.

"Hopefully, this one's a keeper."

"What do you mean?"

She says vaguely, "We've moved around a lot. By the way, I *love* that dress."

Standing beside me in the living room, Quinn puffs out his chest. "I picked it out."

Smiling, I say, "You made a phone call. A hotel employee picked it out."

"It still counts!"

Sloane grins. "Yes, it does, Spider."

She seems fond of him, which I like. I like her, too. She's smart, sophisticated, and the center of a room without trying. She also has a gorgeous husband who obviously worships her. Declan's blue eyes track her every move with unconcealed adoration.

We have cocktails on the patio overlooking the pool and miles of manicured lawn. Though we only met once at the wedding rehearsal, Sloane and I settle into an immediate easy familiarity, chatting about topics as varied as shoes to current events.

There's no bullshit with her. She says exactly what she thinks. She doesn't give a damn about trying to impress.

Which is good for her, because the meal she serves is awful.

Seriously god-awful. I wouldn't even feed it to starving rabbits, which seem to be the target demographic.

Sitting at their huge rectangular glass dining table, I stare down at my plate loaded with inedible, unidentifiable nubby twiggy things and wonder how poor Declan manages to keep so much muscle on his frame.

If I had to guess, he probably eats out a lot.

"Try the soy seaweed cakes," she suggests, pointing with her fork to an ugly oblong greenish-brown lump on her plate. "They're super good for your colon."

I spear the tempeh—whatever in God's name that is—with my fork and nibble on it.

It tastes like what a filthy piece of driftwood from an old shipwreck might taste like: salty, soggy, fishy, disgusting.

"Mmm. Yummy."

Watching me from across the table, Declan pulls his lips between his teeth to keep from laughing.

Sloane beams. "Right? I just love tempeh. It's so versatile. Do you cook, Reyna?"

"Like a bloody Michelin chef," says Quinn, warily eyeing a poisonous-looking fleshy gray lump on his own plate that could be a mushroom of some sort. Or possibly a boiled toad.

"Really?" says Sloane, intrigued. "What's your specialty?"

"Sicilian cuisine in particular, but Italian food in general. My mother was born in Sicily, so many of my favorite recipes are handed down from her."

With a hint of pride in his voice, Quinn says, "She makes everything from scratch."

Declan says forcefully, "Don't tell me you make homemade pasta!"

When I nod, he groans. "Spider, you lucky bastard!"

With arched brows, Sloane turns to Declan. "Why, exactly, is he so lucky?"

Avoiding her searing gaze and an answer that might cost him a testicle, he takes a long drink from his wineglass.

Tactfully hiding my smile, I intervene. "I've always loved to cook, even when I was little. Then, when I got older, food became even more important. It's really the only pleasure I have in my life."

Reaching for my wineglass, I send a warm look in Quinn's direction. "Had, I mean."

When I set my glass down after sipping from it, I realize everyone is staring at me.

But only Quinn's eyes are blazing.

Declan saves me from what could be a rogue attack from Mr. Handsy sitting next to me by asking, "What's your favorite thing to make?"

I laugh. "Oh God. That's like asking a mother which is her favorite child. Five-cheese lasagna with spicy sausage, truffle risotto, saltimbocca, Sicilian stuffed flatbread, the list goes on."

With wide eyes, Declan says faintly, "Bread."

"You should taste her carbonara," brags Quinn.

Even fainter, Declan says, *"Bacon."*

Sloane gives him a smack on the shoulder.

We make it through the rest of the meal with small talk as I try to move things around on my plate so it looks as if I've eaten them. For dessert, Sloane serves vegan ice cream made without cream, eggs, or sugar, or anything else resembling actual food.

But at least it's bland and tasteless, so there's that.

Then the men excuse themselves to speak in Declan's office while Sloane and I sit on the sofa in the living room with our wine.

Thank God she likes wine, or I'd already have jumped into the pond.

"So. Reyna. How are you?"

With her bare long legs stretched out and propped up on the coffee table, Sloane gazes at me with the intensity of a professional interrogator.

I smile. "I'm fine. Thank you for asking."

After a beat of silence in which she examines every minute expression on my face, she says bluntly, "Bullshit."

"You'd be surprised. I've got many years' experience compartmentalizing my feelings."

"Swallowing them, you mean."

I tilt my head in a gesture that's neither a yes nor a no. "An unexpected arranged marriage isn't the worst thing to ever happen to me. I'll survive."

"I bet you will." She spends a while in thought, then says, "So it doesn't bother you, the arranged marriage thing?"

"'Bother' is one of those words that can have many different meanings."

After a moment watching me over the rim of her wineglass as she takes a swallow, she pronounces, "You would've made an excellent politician."

That makes me laugh. "I'm the ranking female of one of the Five Families of New York. I *am* an excellent politician."

She pulls her legs off the table and leans over to peer more closely at me, propping her elbows on her thighs. "You like him, don't you?"

I have to pause to decide how to answer. Then I go with the truth. I say softly, "For the most part, yes."

When she grins, pleased, I add, "His mood changes are pretty rough, though."

She waves a hand in the air. "He's been through a lot lately."

I can tell she regrets that instantly.

Sitting back against the sofa, she crosses her legs and drinks her wine, gazing up at an abstract painting on the wall that suddenly seems to fascinate her.

From someone so forthright and self-confident, this avoidant behavior tells me that whatever it is Quinn has been through lately, she doesn't want to tell me about it.

Which, of course, makes me desperate to know.

I say, "I understand you're his friend. I won't ask you to put yourself in a position where you feel you'd be being disloyal by betraying his confidence. But if there's anything you can tell me that might help me understand him, I would appreciate it."

She slides her gaze in my direction. She takes a moment to

gather her thoughts. Then she says, "It's his story to tell, but I can tell you this: he's been hurt."

I nod. "He told me that himself. It's the reason he wanted an arranged marriage."

Looking encouraged that I already know that, she uncrosses her legs and turns her body toward me.

"So he told you about my sister, Riley?"

I have a split second to decide how to answer.

I remember what Gianni told me the night of the home invasion about the sister of the wife of the Mob boss getting impregnated by her Russian kidnapper, and decide to walk the gray line between truth and lies.

Looking down at my hands, I say, "I know she's pregnant by the boss of the Moscow Bratva."

"Yes. Which Spider blames himself for."

Startled by that, I look up. "Why does he blame himself?"

"He was her bodyguard when she got kidnapped. Plus, you know, he had feelings for her . . ."

She trails off, then makes a face. "You didn't know about that part."

I keep my expression completely impassive when I say, "How long ago was this?"

She wrinkles her nose. "I feel like maybe I've already said too much."

Ignoring that, I think it through. If her sister is still pregnant, that means whatever happened, it was within the last nine months.

So *this year,* Quinn was so devastated by the woman under his protection being kidnapped and impregnated by the Russian that he took the drastic and life-altering measure of agreeing to an arranged marriage with a stranger in response.

He was in love with her.

He's *still* in love with her.

That's what this morning was about. His mood change, his silence, his inexplicable scowls.

He married me and made love to me and woke up with me, a stand-in for the woman he actually wants.

I feel sick. Foolish, ashamed, and sick to my stomach.

A week ago, this wouldn't have hurt. I wouldn't have felt a thing. But last night seemed so real to me. All the passion and emotion we shared felt so damn *real*.

It felt good.

For the first time in my life, I felt wanted.

Protected.

Safe.

Right now, I feel as if I'm the butt of a vicious cosmic joke.

Because no matter how I might feel about my new husband being in love with another woman, I'm basically shit out of luck. I can't do anything about it.

There's a contract.

In front of four hundred witnesses, vows were made.

To make matters worse, I traded my freedom and Quinn let Lili walk away with Juan Pablo like it meant nothing to him. He would've done it anyway. Because I know him a little better now, I understand that if only he'd known about Juan Pablo before he married me, he would have canceled the contract and walked away.

All of us would've been free.

I made myself a sacrificial lamb for nothing.

All that goes through my head within heartbeats. Sloane waits for my reaction with a worried look, but I put on a smile and reassure her.

Because, like she said, I would've made an excellent politician.

I can lie and smile and wave, when inside, I feel like dying.

"It doesn't matter. What's past is past. Thank you for your

candor." I lift my hand and wiggle my ring finger at her. "Can we talk about diamonds now? Because I noticed you've got a rock the size of a skating rink. That thing is gorgeous! Did you pick it out, or does Declan just have exquisite taste?"

She laughs, holding out her hand to gaze down at her ring. "Yeah, it's pretty sweet, isn't it? He likes to spoil me."

We go from there. The conversation flows naturally. If she notices anything strange about me, she doesn't mention it.

About twenty minutes later, I ask where the restroom is.

"Down that hall, third door on the right."

"Thanks. Be right back."

"Should I pour us more wine?"

"Absolutely!"

I head down the hall, desperate for a moment of privacy, but get distracted as soon as I put my hand on the powder room door handle.

I hear voices coming from farther down the hall.

It's Quinn and Declan in his office.

I hesitate, trying to talk myself out of it, but ultimately give in and creep down the hallway toward the cracked-open door. A foot outside, I stop and listen, holding my breath.

". . . can't have had anything to do with it. That was twenty years ago, lad. And you killed him. People don't come back from the grave."

Quinn sighs heavily. "Aye. I know. But I can't help thinking I'm cursed."

"That's your guilt talking, not your good sense."

"If you say so."

"I do say so. Forget about it. Now tell me about your wife. How's the situation?"

I lean closer, my heart thudding as I wait to hear how Quinn responds.

When there's only silence, Declan prompts, "Remember what you said to me when you first asked me to set up the meeting with Caruso?"

"No, what?"

Declan chuckles. "You said, 'There's nothing like new pussy to get over the old,' you cold-blooded bastard."

That feels like a knife plunged through my solar plexus. I don't wait to hear the rest.

I turn and walk away, cursing myself for being so foolish as to let him in.

Women can never trust men. They only want to fuck things or break them.

THIRTY-TWO

SPIDER

I was being an idiot," I reply, shaking my head.

"Aye, I know that. I'm just glad you realize it. So, tell me. How is the infamous Black Widow?"

I say crossly, "I'm not going to tell you how she is in bed, for fuck's sake."

"Get your head out of the gutter. That's not what I'm asking."

"Then what the bloody hell *are* you asking?"

He gazes at me for a moment before saying, "She likes you, you know."

Heat creeps into my cheeks. I say gruffly, "You think so?"

"Aye. Dimwit."

"How can you tell?"

"The way she looks at you. The way she speaks to you. The way she told her own kin to fuck off when they tried to get you to leave the meeting."

"Massimo," I say, my mood darkening at the memory of him. "I don't like that fucker."

"Who does? My point is that your new wife's got your back."

His eyes glimmer with laughter. "Must've been some wedding night, boyo."

"I knew you were talking about that!"

"Ach, be quiet. You're wound up again. I should've forced you to take some time off."

"I already had time off after the whole debacle in Russia, remember? And I'm wound up about that damn dream, like I told you. I haven't dreamt of Shannon in years."

Kicking his feet up onto his desk, Declan takes a swig of his scotch and considers me, sitting across from him in one of his big leather chairs.

"I don't think this needs to be said, but Reyna isn't Shannon. She can take care of herself."

"It's my job to take care of her now!"

He waves that off. "And just because Caruso hasn't discovered who the intruders were doesn't mean it has anything to do with Urosevic."

Agitated, I rise from my chair and start to pace. "They were mercs, Declan. Hired hands who were totally untraceable. That wasn't just your average kidnapping attempt. Something bigger was behind it. Some*one* bigger. And the fact that Caruso can't find anything out about them proves it."

Watching me pace in agitation, Declan says gently, "You put a bullet in his brain, lad. He's been dead and buried for half your life. It wasn't him."

"Then who the fuck was it?"

"I made it my business to find out. You'll have all the information within a few days."

"How?"

His smile is mysterious. "I'm me, that's how."

"You mean you called Killian Black."

His smug look sours. "You can be a real pain in the arse, you know that?"

I mutter, "Now you sound like my wife."

"Speaking of wives, we'd better get back out there before they hatch a plot to rule the world and make us obsolete."

He's right. Leaving a pair of women like Sloane and Reyna alone in a room together is dangerous. Depending on their moods, we could find ourselves missing a few important limbs when we wake up in the morning or discover they'd commandeered our soldiers to serve under new, all-female leadership.

When we return to the living room, they're cozied up together on the sofa, drinking wine and laughing like two old pals.

Declan says, "You two look like you're having fun."

Sloane grins up at him. "Just girl talk. Come sit."

Eyeing Reyna, who's sitting with her bare feet tucked under her and those gorgeous tits falling out of the neckline of her dress, I say, "I think it's time to call it a night. We had a busy day. I'm sure my wife would like to get to bed."

Sloane laughs. "I'm sure one of you would."

My ears are hot, but I can't look away from Reyna. She's gazing up at me from under her lashes with an inscrutable look in her eyes. Like maybe she's got a secret.

I hope that secret involves my hard cock, because it's already stirring.

She turns to Sloane. "Thank you so much for having us over. You're a wonderful hostess. I hope we see more of each other soon."

Sloane says, "Babe, we'll be seeing a *lot* more of each other. By the way, do you think you'd be interested in a girls' trip to Paris? Me and my bestie, Nat, were thinking of going for fashion week in September."

Declan says, "You're not going to bloody Paris without me."

Sloane smiles at him. "Okay, honey." She turns back to Reyna. "We'll stay at the Hôtel Costes, which is where all the cool celebrities stay. They have this *amazing* luxury suite that's like five thousand euro a night and worth every penny. It's the size of an apartment. We can all stay there together and order room service for every meal."

Declan repeats loudly, "You're not going to Paris without me!"

"I know, honey. So I'll call you with all the details, okay, Reyna?"

"Sounds great," Reyna replies, rising. She sets her empty wineglass on the coffee table as Sloane stands, then they hug.

I don't know why the sight of them embracing makes my chest tight and a lump form in my throat, but it does.

Judging by Declan's expression, he's not feeling quite so misty-eyed about the situation.

Poor bastard. He'll spend the next few days trying to dissuade Sloane from the Paris trip idea, which we all know will fail miserably.

We say our goodbyes and head to the car.

As soon as we're settled in and Kieran's driving us down the winding road from the estate, Reyna turns to me.

"I'm worried about Lili. Can you find out what's happening?"

I take her hand and say softly, "She's fine, lass. They got to Mexico safely."

"You talked to her?"

"No. I talked to one of the men who took them."

"When?"

"This morning."

The sun set hours ago, so the light is low, but I can still see her face well enough to catch the flash of anger in her eyes.

"This morning," she repeats, her voice cool. "When you were so distant."

I drag a hand through my hair, sighing. "Aye. I'm sorry about that."

Swallowing, she looks away. After a moment of silence, she says, "You don't have to apologize."

"I should apologize when I've been an arse."

She shakes her head. "You don't have to explain, either. I understand."

Something in the tone of her voice—and in the way her hand is sitting passively in mine, like a dead fish—makes me nervous. "What is it you understand?"

"I just meant that you deserve privacy. You're not obligated to share every little thought on your mind. I know you need space."

When she gently pulls her hand from mine, I grab her chin and turn her head toward me.

Her expression is blank. Her eyes have a distant look in them. She's withdrawn into herself, somewhere she doesn't want me to reach her.

Fuck that shite.

"What's wrong?"

"Nothing."

She swallows again. I think it's a tell for when she's emotional but trying not to show it.

I'm having none of that fucking nonsense. I grab her and drag her onto my lap.

She exhales and closes her eyes, muttering, "Here we go."

"You're bloody right, here we go! Kieran, shut your ears, mate!"

He gives me a thumbs-up and turns on the radio.

Holding Reyna, I give her a squeeze and a little jostle, growling, "Talk to me, viper. What the fuck is going on in that mind of yours? And don't say 'nothing' again, or I'll give you a spanking."

Her eyes flare. She hisses, "Try it, Irish. I'm in the mood to spill some blood."

Though I'm anxious about what's eating her, I grin. "There's my She-Devil. Now start talking."

"What is this pathological need you have to discuss everything?"

"It's called being an adult. Now quit hiding from me and spill your guts, woman."

As stiff and prickly as a cactus in my arms, she glares at me. "I'm going to take you up on your offer to let me live in my own place."

That stuns me. Hurt, I say, "Why?"

"I don't owe you an explanation."

Okay, *now* I'm bloody angry. If she wants a fight, she's getting one.

Through gritted teeth, I say, "Aye, viper. You do. I'm your bloody husband, remember?"

Her eyes could freeze me to an ice cube. She says flatly, "As if I could forget."

"Don't try me, woman."

"Or what?"

I'm well aware that we could go back and forth like this all night, so I take matters into my own hands and kiss her.

She resists me at first, pushing against my chest and trying to get away. But I don't let her. I hold her and kiss her until she's pliant and shivering and my dick is screaming at me for release from my trousers.

"Now fucking talk," I say against her mouth, breathing hard. "And give me the consideration of being honest."

"Like you were honest with me about being in love with another woman?"

That feels like a slap across the face. "What the hell does that mean? Who am I supposed to be in love with?"

"Riley."

From the front, Kieran lets out a low, astonished whistle.

Ignoring him, I demand, "How do you know about Riley?"

I realize that's the wrong approach when all the fight drains out of her. Reyna swallows again and looks away. "Please let me go."

"Goddammit, woman. You're not going anywhere. Look at me."

Of course she won't, so I take her face in my hand and force her to. Looking into her eyes, I say deliberately, "I'm not in love with Riley."

"You know what? It's really none of my business if you are."

"Stop fighting me. I'm not letting you go. And don't close your eyes, goddammit!"

"Will you stop shouting into my face, please?"

I put my mouth right next to her ear and say hotly, "Your jealousy is misplaced. I'm not in love with anyone else."

"I'm not jealous!"

She's horrified by the suggestion, which makes me think I'm right.

It also makes me so fucking turned on, I want to rip that dress off and fuck her right here on the back seat.

I grab her head in both hands and kiss her again. She squirms, trying to get away, pushing against me until I pin her wrists together. Then I fist my other hand into her hair and kiss her again, this time groaning into her mouth with need.

"Quinn, stop. Let me go."

"I'm never letting you go. There's a contract that says I can't."

"You heartless bastard."

"Look at me. Calm down and look at me, Reyna."

Breathing hard, she turns her face away but glances back with a hostile, distrustful look.

Keeping my voice low though I'd like to shout at her, I say, "I'm not in love with anyone else. I'll answer any questions you want me to, but first you need to understand that fact. I was infatuated with Riley, yes. I wanted there to be something between us, yes. But there wasn't. I never even kissed the lass. Never touched her. She was under my protection, and I fucked it up so badly, she ended up shot. *By me.* Accidentally, but nevertheless, it was my bullet she took. So you'll have to forgive me for being more than a little fucked up over that, Reyna, but I'm not in love with her. She's not who I want."

I press a soft kiss to her lips. "I have the woman I want, even if she does hate me."

She stares at me in silence. Then, in a voice so low I can barely hear it, she says, "I don't hate you."

My heart pounding, I pull her closer and kiss her again. I kiss her all the way back into the city and right up until Kieran stops the car in the underground garage. Then I take my wife upstairs to the honeymoon suite and lock the door behind us.

I stalk toward her. Wide-eyed, she backs away from me.

"Don't be afraid of me, Reyna. I swear on my mother's grave, I'll never harm you."

"It's just that every time I think I've seen your highest intensity level, you set a new record."

The last thing I want is for her to think I'm in any way as psychotic as Enzo, so I point to a chair and order, "Sit. Fuck, I mean *please* sit down."

I prop my hands on my hips and start to pace, because apparently, it's the only way I know how to blow off steam without shooting something.

Reyna perches on the edge of the leather chair and watches me warily.

I stop in the middle of the room, blow out a hard breath, and close my eyes. "When I was nineteen years old, I fell in love with a married woman."

"You don't have to—"

"Be quiet. You'll get your chance to talk."

I don't even have to look at her to know she's murdering me with her eyes, but it doesn't matter. Right now all that matters is that I clear the air between us. I need to get her naked and into bed, and that won't happen if she's still angry with me.

I walk over to the bar and pour myself a scotch. I chug it, then hold up the empty glass.

"No, thank you."

"Suit yourself." I pour another and drink that, too. Then I set down the glass, turn around, and fold my arms over my chest as I lean against the marble bar top.

I have no idea how to say what needs to be said, so I decide to try to get through it with as few words as possible.

I draw a slow breath, blow it out, then speak.

"Her name was Shannon. She was five years older than I was. We met at a rugby match. She told me she was married, but I didn't care. I pursued her relentlessly. Eventually, she gave in."

My laugh is low and humorless. "I can be very persistent when I want something."

I'm lost in dark memories for a moment, then shake my head to clear it. Reyna watches me in taut, unblinking silence.

"Her husband found out. I don't know how. I also didn't know he was in the Serbian Mafia."

Reyna's lips part. Her hands tighten around the arms of the chair.

She senses what's coming.

I look right into her eyes when I make my confession.

"He killed her for her betrayal. Slit her throat and left her body on my front lawn. Then he went to my parents' house, first thing that same morning. They were still in bed when he put a bullet in both their heads."

I'm keeping it together until the next part, where my voice breaks.

"He killed my little sister, too. Slit her throat the same way he did Shannon's. Police said later she didn't die right away. Took her a while to choke to death on her own blood. Hannah was twelve."

Reyna lifts her hands to cover her mouth.

I close my eyes again so I don't have to see the look of horror in hers.

"Next he went to my grandparents' houses. He bound them

and lit the house on fire, same thing with both. All four of them were burned alive."

Reyna says faintly, "Oh God. Quinn."

"Don't call for God yet. It gets worse. My older sister lived with her husband and three young children. The husband he tied up and bludgeoned to death. All three kids he shot at point-blank range. I won't tell you what he did to my sister. She was a very pretty girl. Then he went through the rest of my family, one by one, picking them off like fish in a barrel. Aunts. Uncles. Cousins. Their kids, husbands, and wives. By the time he was through, forty-two people had been murdered. My entire family tree was wiped out. Because of me."

I have to stop to catch my breath. I didn't realize my voice had gone hoarse as I'd been speaking.

"I was nineteen years old, and responsible for unimaginable carnage."

Reyna says softly, "Quinn, you were just a boy. He was the one who was responsible, not you."

I lift my head and look at her, my warrior wife who survived fourteen years of abuse at the hands of a madman, and feel such an overwhelming wave of worthlessness, I can barely speak. When I do, it comes out in a rasp.

"No. All that blood is on my hands. It started because of my selfishness. So when a Russian assassin who was sent to kill Declan kidnapped Sloane's sister right from under my fucking nose, this innocent girl I was responsible for protecting . . . I went a little crazy. I relived my own personal hell all over again. And when I woke up this morning, I suddenly realized that by marrying you, I might have signed your death warrant. That even though I took my revenge on Urosevic for what he did to Shannon and my family, maybe his curse still followed me after all these years."

I swallow, then say gruffly, "That's why I was upset. Not because I'm in love with someone else. Because I'm responsible for you now. And if something happens to you, it will be the end of me."

She stares at me across the room in silence. Her mermaid eyes drill into me, straight down into my soul.

Then she stands, crosses to me, and throws her arms around my shoulders.

THIRTY-THREE

REY

*H*e hides his face in my neck and squeezes me so tightly, I'm left breathless.

"Thank you," I whisper. "Thank you for telling me that. It's the worst thing I've ever heard, but I'm so glad I know."

His voice cracks when he says, "Why?"

"Because what I want more than anything is to know you. The real you that you keep hidden under all those smirks and that awful macho swaggering."

"Look who's talking. You've got so many ancient hell witch costumes, I can't keep up with them all."

I pull away, frame his face in my hands, and gently kiss him on the lips. Looking deep into his eyes, I say, "They're not costumes."

After a beat, we both start laughing.

It's soft and grim, but laughter nonetheless.

I kiss him again. He drops his forehead to my shoulder and exhales. A shudder runs through his big body. I can tell he's deeply affected by the story he just told me, that saying it aloud was excruciating and brought back horrible memories along with a mountain of guilt. But for the first time, I'm grateful for his insistence on talking things out.

But there's one last item on the agenda that I'm not about to let go.

I pull away from him and wait until he raises his head and looks at me to say, "A small public service announcement: if you ever refer to me as 'pussy' again, I'll break your face."

He pulls his brows together. "What?"

"I heard what you told Declan about me."

After a moment, he understands. "You were earwigging at the door?"

"If that's an obscure Irish word for eavesdropping, then yes."

He raises his voice. "Then you should've heard me tell him that I was being an idiot when I said that."

"I'd already left by then."

"Also," he says, talking over me, "I didn't even fucking know you when Declan and I had that conversation. I was talking about Lili, not you."

"Stop talking, Quinn. You're only digging your grave deeper."

He stares at me for a beat in tense silence. "You're always going to think the worst of me, aren't you?"

"Don't get dramatic. You're telling me I heard something out of context, and I'm accepting that."

His brows shoot up. "But you don't believe it?"

I can tell he's on the verge of another outburst. I don't want a repeat of the episode we had in the car where I get another angry tirade shouted into my face, so I pull away from him and walk slowly over to the windows.

As I stare down at the city lights, an overwhelming sense of exhaustion settles over me.

I'm thirty-three, childless, with no career or work experience. I was raised in an environment of shame and fear by people who didn't love each other. All I've ever known from every man who was supposed to care for me is violence. I'm jaded, cynical, and broken in so many places, there's not enough glue in the world to put me back together.

And I'm starting to have real feelings for a man who might be even more broken than I am.

I say, "I believe both of us have problems that we're not going to fix tonight. I have trauma over my past. You have trauma over yours. Both of us are haunted by bad memories. I believe you wanted an arranged marriage to try to escape all that and find some peace, but you got me instead. A woman who has as many scars as she does demons. I believe we have an intense physical connection, but neither of us knows how to live with ourselves, let alone another person."

I turn from the window and look at him. "I also believe you would've let Lili out of the contract if you'd known about Juan Pablo sooner."

"Aye," he says crossly. "What of it?"

"It just occurred to me that we never signed a wedding license."

Frozen, he stares at me from across the room. I see his mind in action, the mad dash as he connects the dots. Then he passes a hand over his face.

"Fucking hell."

"Yes. We're not legally married."

He turns around and pours himself another scotch. He shoots it, then sets the glass down carefully. Without looking at me, he says gruffly, "So you want out of the contract."

It's not a question. He says it as if it's a foregone conclusion that I wouldn't be in this room if I wasn't legally obligated to be.

But life is never that simple, is it?

"I don't know what I want. The past few days have ruined my ability to think rationally."

He waits, unmoving, staring down at the empty glass on the bar.

My voice low, I continue. "But I meant what I said when I told you I wanted to know you."

He lifts his head. Our eyes lock. A swell of emotion tightens my chest.

"I like you, Quinn. You're smart. You're funny. You're kind. You're protective. You're also completely unhinged. What happened with you and Riley is still fresh. You're still processing."

He growls, "I wasn't lying when I said I'm not in love with her."

"And I believe that. But you can still be fucked up over someone even if you weren't in love." After a moment, I add softly, "Like I would be if this pretend marriage of ours doesn't work out."

His eyes shine. His jaw works. His Adam's apple bobs as he swallows.

Then he crosses the room in a few long strides, takes me into his arms, and kisses me.

It's passionate, bordering on desperate. He holds my head between his shaking hands and drinks deep from my mouth until we're both breathing hard.

He breaks away and growls, "Permission to get rough. I won't hurt you, but—"

"Granted. I trust you. Fuck me, fake husband. We can work out all the other bullshit tomorrow."

His eyelids flutter closed as he exhales on a soft groan.

When he opens his eyes again, Quinn is gone. In his place is my black-eyed monster who comes out to play with me in the dark.

He flips me up and over his shoulder, strides over to the bed, and tosses me down to the mattress. I haven't even caught my breath before he drags me by my ankles to the edge, thrusts my legs apart, flattens his hand on the middle of my chest, and forces me to lie back.

He tears my panties off and shoves his face between my thighs.

I cry out, arching.

He grabs my bottom in both hands and digs his fingers into my flesh as he lashes his tongue back and forth over my clit. Then he shoves it inside me, making me gasp.

I gasp even louder when he slides his finger into my ass.

"Okay, wife," he says in a guttural voice, his mouth inches away from my exposed pussy and his finger wedged deep inside me as he kneels on the floor between my spread legs. "If this is the last time I get to fuck you, I'm gonna make sure you remember it for the rest of your life."

He sinks his thumb inside my pussy, lowers his head, and starts to suckle my clit, filling me with his fingers and fondling me with his tongue.

The sensation is mind-blowing. As he licks, he squeezes his fingers together, then rotates his hand, then squeezes again. He's manipulating me like a hand puppet. It's hot and dirty and fucking incredible.

I dig my hands into his hair and start pulling as I writhe against his mouth with my legs spread as wide open as I can get them.

When I shudder and moan, he laughs darkly.

"My good girl likes to get finger fucked in all her sweet holes while she has her pussy licked, doesn't she?"

I can't form an answer. My eyes roll back into my head. I make an animal whimper of pleasure as I rock my hips frantically in a wordless plea.

"Aye, she does. She fucking loves it. Now come on my face so I can fuck all these tight holes with my hard cock."

I'm going to die. He's going to kill me. This is the way I go out, flat on my back with my legs spread in the honeymoon suite at the Ritz-Carlton Hotel as a crazy Irish gangster showers me in filthy words like a smut baptism.

At least I'll die happy.

Making circles with both fingers, he flattens his tongue and drags it up and down my engorged clit, faster and faster, until I'm groaning and bucking and out of my goddamn mind.

I climax with a primal scream.

He finger fucks me through my orgasm, reaching up to yank aside the neck of my dress and pinch my throbbing nipple. I thrash against his mouth, sobbing incoherently because it feels so intensely, insanely good.

He surges up from his knees and falls on top of me, kissing me ravenously on my mouth, neck, and chest, dragging his beard over my sensitive skin. I taste myself on his lips and can't decide if I should cry or laugh maniacally.

Rearing back onto his heels, he grabs the neckline of my dress and rips it apart with one savage pull. The sound of tearing fabric and the sight of my breasts spilling out seem to flick on his caveman switch.

His eyes flare wide. He snarls, baring his teeth.

Then he tears the rest of the dress off my body, ripping it to shreds like a tissue.

He throws the shredded remnants to the floor, yanks down the zipper on his trousers, fists his erection in his hand, and falls back on top of me, taking my mouth again as I clutch his hips and raise my own.

He embeds himself inside me with a brutal thrust.

Delirious, I cry out. He bites my neck, laughing.

"You're gonna take it hard, sweetheart, and you're gonna fucking love it. Wrap your legs around my waist."

Disobedience is not an option. Even if I wanted to, my body has surrendered completely to his control. The moment the command is past his lips, I bend my legs and wrap them around him, hooking my ankles together in back.

He growls, "Good girl."

I almost pass out.

His first thrust makes me groan. His second makes me whimper.

Then, when he starts to fuck me hard, plunging into me over and over as he snaps his hips and growls something in Gaelic, I lose the ability to make a sound altogether.

All I can do is feel.

His hard chest against mine. The smooth fabric of his shirt dragging against my tight nipples. His hot breath on my neck and the cool leather of his belt biting into my thighs.

His beard on my skin.

His voice in my ear.

His rough moans of pleasure, all over me.

I hear a chant from somewhere far away, a raw and plaintive repetition of *please, please, please.* It takes a moment before I realize it's coming from me.

"I love it when you beg for me," Quinn says hotly, squeezing my breast. He pulls on my nipple, chuckling when I plead for his mouth.

He lowers his head and sucks hard on my rigid nipple, then slides his hand down my hip and under my bottom. He strokes my ass as I buck and moan underneath him.

I come, crying out his name.

"Aye, baby. Tell me who you belong to. Say it again for me, lass, and make me believe it." His hips thrust harder. His voice drops until it's nothing but a deep, resonant command.

"Make me believe you're mine."

In that moment, it's all I want. It's everything I've ever lived for. I claw his back and cry his name and give him every part of me, body and soul, holding nothing back as I convulse around his cock and hear his words of praise that blend together until they're only sound, husky noises of approval and adoration.

I don't have to speak the language to understand what they mean.

You're beautiful.

I worship you.

You're mine.

He withdraws and rolls me onto my belly. He wraps an arm around my waist and hikes me up to my knees. He sinks a hand into my hair and pulls on it so my neck is arched.

Holding me like that, he uses his other hand to slide his wet cock back and forth over my ass, nudging the crown at my entrance.

"Yes or no, wife?"

The need in his voice sets my nerves on fire.

I see our reflection in the dark windows. A naked woman on all fours on the bed. With an air of absolute dominance, a fully dressed man stands behind her.

And I know that no matter how it might look, the man in this image isn't the one in control of the situation.

It's a funny thing, power. As easily as it can corrupt, it can also be humbling.

Knowing that Quinn will do only what I allow, and do it all only to please me, gives me a feeling of power so absolute, I burn with it.

Trembling all over, I lick my lips. "Yes. Whatever you want, just for tonight, the answer is yes."

He makes a sound I've never heard him make before, some needful, primitive sound that rises from deep within his chest. Then he flexes his hips, driving his hard cock inside me.

It's so painful, I can't even scream.

My eyes fly wide open. I claw my fingers into the blanket. My lips part, but no words come out.

When he hears the strangled gasp I make, he freezes. "I'm hurting you."

"Yes! Fuck! Don't stop!"

"Reyna—"

Whatever he was going to say is cut off as I rear back hard, taking the entire length of him inside me.

He barks out a groan that's even louder than mine.

When he releases my hair, I collapse facedown onto the bed, pulling the covers and gritting my teeth. I have to keep blinking hard to clear my eyes of water.

Panting, he grips my hips in both hands to steady me. I feel the cool metal of his zipper on the back of my thighs and shudder.

"I can't do this if I'm hurting you."

Through gritted teeth, I say, "Goddammit, gangster. You better fuck that ass, or I'll find someone else who will."

As I knew it would, those words make him go ballistic.

He thrusts and withdraws, then does it over and over again. His balls slap against my pussy. His growls of pleasure and fury fill the air. His fingers dig into the flesh of my hips until I'm sure I'll be bruised in the morning.

If tomorrow ever comes. We might fuck each other to death tonight, there's really no telling.

He pauses his fervent thrusting to reach around and slide his fingers over my clit. When I jerk, sucking in a breath through my teeth, he breathes, "Your cunt is drenched."

"And your cock is throbbing. Are we doing a play-by-play, or are you fucking me?"

I can tell his jaw is clenched when he replies. "Careful, woman. You told me I could never spank your arse, but you said nothing about this sweet pussy."

He gives my wet folds a firm tweak, making me yelp. It also makes my ass muscles clench around him.

He groans. Then he decides to try it again.

It's my turn to groan. His fingers are hard and calloused, and though the pinch is firm, it doesn't hurt. If anything, it's a lovely distraction.

I whisper, "So spank it, then."

Breathing raggedly, he pauses for only a second before sliding his fingers all over my folds, up and down, even to the outside, over my thighs. I hear the noise it makes, his fingers covered in my slickness, and feel my face burn.

I forget about my burning face when he slaps me smartly between the legs.

"Ah!"

The sting of it is quickly replaced by a flood of heat that makes my muscles loosen and my jaw go slack. After that, a steady pulse of pleasure throbbing outward from my core makes me shiver.

Sounding triumphant, he whispers, "You liked it."

"Yes."

"Say it."

"I liked it."

He laughs. "Of course you did. Do you know why?"

"Because I'm sick."

"No, sweet girl. Because you're mine."

My breath hitches. My heart pounds. I feel shaky and buzzed and so very alive. So alive, I'm flying.

My face half-buried in the blankets, I whisper, "Come in me like this, Quinn. Fuck me hard and spank my pussy and come inside me. I need to feel you unravel. I want us to unravel at the same time."

Fondling my aching clit with one hand, Quinn slides his other up my back to my nape, then down again, his fingers gently tracing the outline of my scars.

In a reverent voice, he says, "I started to unravel the first moment I laid eyes on you, viper. And even if tonight is all I get, I'll never be wound right again."

He pumps into me, starting off hard and continuing even harder as he plays with my pussy, stopping every once in a while to give it a brisk slap that makes me sob and lose my mind.

The motion of his hips only falters when he grits out, "I'm there."

"Me too."

"Ah, fuck, viper—"

"Quinn! Quinn!"

We groan loudly together, so loudly, it echoes off the walls. He shoves his finger deep inside my pussy. I rear back against him, clenching and clenching, shuddering uncontrollably.

Still pumping into my ass, he leans over and rests his forehead between my shoulder blades as he spills himself inside me.

Pressing his lips to my spine, he breathes my name on a long, low moan.

Any chance I thought I had of not falling for this man evaporates into thin air.

Whatever happens when the sun rises, my cold little heart is now in his hands.

THIRTY-FOUR

REY

*W*e lie tangled on the bed together like victims of a plane crash. Neither of us speaks. It's only when I hear my cell phone ringing from inside my handbag on the other side of the room that I sit up.

Slowly, because I'm dizzy.

Quinn murmurs, "I'll get it."

He swings his legs over the edge of the bed and rises, tucking himself back into his briefs. Walking across the room, he zips up his trousers. He returns in a moment with my phone, two aspirin, and a glass of water.

The phone has stopped ringing, but the number on the screen is Gianni's.

"Here. Take these."

Quinn hands me the aspirin. I pop them into my mouth, accept the glass of water, and drink deeply, all while avoiding his eyes.

I feel as if my heart is exposed, beating outside my chest. Like every nerve has been stripped of its protective lining. I've never felt more naked in my life.

Quinn takes the empty glass from me and sets it on the nightstand. Then he kisses me on the forehead and pulls the fuzzy folded blanket off the end of the bed. He wraps it around my body, nuzzling my neck and sitting beside me to pull me into the warm, safe circle of his arms.

I close my eyes and let him hold me while I sniff his neck and wonder how to politely excuse myself so I can go to the bathroom.

He saves me from embarrassment by picking me up and taking me there himself.

He sets me in front of the counter, kisses my forehead again, then murmurs, "I'll give you a minute. Don't lock the door."

As if I could operate something as complex as a door handle lock right now. I couldn't even tell you what year it is.

He closes the door, leaving me alone with my stunned reflection in the mirror. Flushed and splotchy, my hair tangled and my eyes hazy, I almost don't recognize myself.

I turn away from the stranger in the mirror. I use the toilet and wash my hands. I wrap the blanket around my shoulders again and dial Gianni.

He picks up on the first ring, sounding chipper and relaxed, as if he's enjoying a lovely Caribbean vacation. "Reyna! How are you, *sorellina*?"

"Where have you been?"

I don't know if it's the flat, disaffected tone of my voice that makes him pause, or if he can tell that I've just been used in the most brutal, beautiful way, but he takes a moment before replying.

"I'm at the Four Seasons with Mamma."

"That's not what I asked. Listen carefully. Where have you been?"

Irritation creeps into his carefree holiday tone. "Since when do I answer to you?"

"Since I married an Irishman to save the family. I'll only ask one more time, then I'm sending that Irishman over to break your kneecaps. Where have you been?"

He snaps, "Taking care of business."

"What business?"

"*My* business, that's what. Just because you're married now doesn't mean I need to give you an itinerary."

"Maybe not. But you will give me a copy of that marriage contract. Email it to me. Right now. I want to know the terms you negotiated."

Indignant that I'm issuing commands, he starts to sputter something about being the head of the family, but I ignore that and speak over him.

"I met with Alessandro."

Silence. I hear him breathing on the other end of the line, but other than that, he doesn't say a word.

"Massimo, Tomasi, and Aldo, too."

"When? Why? What did they want?"

"This morning. They contacted Declan O'Donnell and arranged it. They seemed very interested in what you might be up to in your spare time. You know, like when you mysteriously go missing."

Another silence, this one fraught. I feel his nervousness as plainly as if he'd reached out and grabbed me with a trembling hand.

"What's happening, Gianni? What have you gotten yourself into?"

"Nothing. Don't be stupid. I have everything under control."

I say softly, "I have half a mind to tell Quinn a nasty lie about something you said about me and send him over there to rearrange your face, so you'd better stop bullshitting me or this conversation is over."

He snarls, "Twenty-four hours with him and suddenly you think you're in charge of this family?"

"I've always been in charge of this family. I've just been letting you hold the reins for a while. Now talk to me before things get out of hand."

"Fuck you, Reyna. I'm not telling you anything."

We sit and breathe angrily at each other for a while, until I decide he's not worth getting upset over. Whatever it is he's into will come out in the wash eventually.

"Lili and Juan Pablo made it to Mexico safely. In case you're interested."

He mutters an oath in Italian. "I'm not interested. I no longer have a daughter."

"Do you still have a mother? Because she's been sitting alone in a hotel room all day and night. I've been worried."

"Are you joking? She's been having the time of her life. When I got back to the room, she was hosting a party for the housekeeping staff. I've got a two-thousand-dollar room service bill sitting here with her signature on it."

That makes me smile. And I suppose I shouldn't have worried about her. She's been through as much as I have and is still surviving.

"We're leaving for New York in the morning. What are your plans?"

"They're in development. I'll let you know. By the way, you're welcome."

He pauses. "For what?"

"Jesus Christ, Gianni. You're a fucking asshole. Don't forget to send me the contract."

I disconnect and set the phone on the counter. When I open the bathroom door, Quinn is right there, leaning against the wall with his arms folded over his chest.

He says, "You could've asked me for the contract."

"Earwigging, were you?"

"Aye. I don't like not knowing what's going on."

"Really? What a stupendous surprise."

His smile is as soft as his eyes. "I ordered room service. Thought you might be hungry."

"Oh, thank God. I really like Sloane, but I've never had a worse meal in my life."

"She's very into her health."

"Is she into Declan's health? Because it seems like her poor husband could starve to death eating that shredded cardboard she calls food."

He reaches out and brushes a strand of hair off my cheek, tucking it behind my ear. "Declan would eat broken glass if that's what Sloane was serving."

I recall how his eyes tracked her every movement and smile. "He does seem a little obsessed with her."

Quinn pulls me against his chest, wraps his arms around me, and stares down into my eyes. "Aye," he says gruffly. "The Irish take love very seriously."

Don't melt. You have a lot of important things to get to. If you melt, you won't get to any of them.

I think he can tell I'm flustered by that comment, so he changes the subject. "Declan says he'll have information for us within a few days."

"About what?"

"Who came into the house after Lili."

I furrow my brow in confusion. "How can Declan get that information?"

His smile is mysterious. "He's got friends in low places."

"Well, that's good. Though I doubt Gianni will care at this point. He just told me he doesn't have a daughter anymore."

"Let's stop talking about your idiotic brother now."

"Deal. What should we talk about instead?"

He considers me in thoughtful silence for a moment, then swings me up into his arms and takes us back to the bed.

Stretching out beside me, he slides a heavy arm over my waist and puts his nose into my hair. With his eyes closed and his voice rough, he says, "Think about what you want. What you really want, not what you think needs to happen. Let's talk about that."

I lie there, my mind blank. "I've never had anyone ask me what I want before."

"I'm asking."

"I wouldn't know where to start."

"Start with what a good day would look like. Your perfect day. Picture it."

"Then what?"

"Then I'll make it happen."

I squeeze my eyes shut, take a deep breath, and try to talk around the frog in my throat. "Quinn, you don't have to take care of me."

"Someone has to do it. Might as well be your fake husband."

I wrap my fingers around his hard biceps and shiver in delight. He makes me feel as if a red carpet has been unrolled under my feet, stretching out in front of me as far as I can see. And when I walk down it, I'll be showered in rose petals from the choir of singing angels floating overhead.

"Okay . . . my perfect day." I think for a while, trying on different scenarios. "It would start with breakfast in bed. That someone else made for me."

Quinn makes a soft noise of encouragement.

"Then I'd get a massage. At home. From a very good-looking young man who was getting paid an enormous sum of money to pamper me."

"You wouldn't have to pay him anything. Men would line up in the street for a chance to get their hands on your naked body."

"Shut up, please. This is my fantasy."

"Right. Sorry."

"Where was I?"

"Naked on a massage bed with a handsome young man."

"I can tell by your tone that idea doesn't please you."

"It doesn't. He'd leave the house with an imprint of my fist on his face."

I sigh. "Anyway. After the massage, I'd have a lovely long hot shower."

"Alone?"

"Will you shut up?"

A grumble of displeasure is my answer.

"Then I'd get dressed in something that made me look ten pounds thinner."

"You think you're overweight? That's daft!"

"For fuck's sake. This is going to take forever."

"Sorry. Go ahead. My lips are sealed."

"Ha! As if that would ever happen."

Stifling laughter, he squeezes me and nuzzles my neck.

"As I was saying before I was so rudely interrupted, I'd get dressed. Then I'd . . ."

I have to stop. The image that presented itself to me is so unexpected, it's shocking.

Inconveniently being a man with finely tuned antennae, Quinn senses the change in me. He lifts his head and stares at my profile.

"Then you'd what?"

My heart pounds. It's hard to catch my breath. Staring up at the ceiling, I say in disbelief, "Then I'd wake up the kids and get them ready for school."

Every ounce of relaxation flees from his body so fast, it's as if he's been replaced by a robot.

A scorching hot sex robot with burning eyes and a dick of steel.

"Don't say anything, Quinn. Please. I don't think I can handle whatever's about to come out of your mouth."

He stares at my profile with the heated intensity of a thousand suns.

Suns that are melting my ovaries to the consistency of warmed butter.

I close my eyes to try to hide from him.

He demands, "You want children?"

Oh fuck. Here we go. Why didn't I just keep my damn mouth shut?

"I never really thought about it."

"Until now," he says instantly, his body as taut as a live wire beside mine.

"Not exactly. Not before—"

He barks, "What?"

I open my eyes and glare at him. "Dial it down! This isn't an interrogation!"

He lowers his head until our noses are touching and I'm trying not to go cross-eyed because he's so close. His voice deadly soft and his body vibrating tension, he commands, "Finish. That. Sentence."

I swallow and moisten my lips, wondering if this is what a mouse feels like when it spots the hungry cat about to pounce on it. Very softly, I admit, "Not before I met you."

Pressed against my hip, his erection throbs.

Seriously, the man takes too many vitamins.

He grips my jaw in his big hand. He slides a heavy leg over both of mine. Holding me in his searing gaze, he says, "So what I'm hearing you say, Reyna Caruso, is that you want to have children . . . *with me.*"

I snap, "Not if they're going to have your scary intensity gene. They'll terrorize all the other kids at school."

"Say it. You want to have my children."

"Quinn—"

"How many? Tell me."

"Can we please—"

"If you think I'm letting you out of this room before we finish this conversation, you're bloody mad."

I say through gritted teeth, "Fine. If you must know how many fantasy offspring I'd like, the answer is five."

His blazing eyes flare wide. In an elated, astonished whisper, he says, *"Five."*

My God. I've created a monster. If I thought his ego was big before, now there will be no containing it. We'll have to move out to the country on a hundred-acre farm to give it enough space.

I say tartly, "Or maybe none. I'm just winging it here. You put me on the spot."

He rolls on top of me and grips my head in his hands. He kisses me. So wildly, it's as if he wants to eat my soul right out of my body.

I try to push him off, but the man weighs a ton. And there's that erection to contend with. The thing has a mind of its own, not to mention the appetite of a teenage athlete.

When he finally breaks the kiss, he's breathing hard, his eyes are ablaze, and his expression can only be described as exultant. He looks as if he just returned from a trip to heaven where he took a personal meeting with God himself.

"You want my children."

I cover my eyes with a hand.

He pulls it away and insists, "You want me to get you pregnant."

I groan.

He laughs, and it sounds crazed. "That's why you begged me to come inside you, baby. *You want me to knock you up.*"

"What I really want is to go back in time to before we had this stupid conversation."

"Oh, no," he says, still laughing. "That cat's out of the bag, lass. You might not want to be my wife, but you want to grow my babies in your belly. *Five* of them."

"I feel like this is a good time to remind you that I'm perfectly capable of murder."

He kisses me again, then rolls onto his back, flings his arms out, and laughs at the ceiling. He laughs and laughs, shaking the bed, until I rise, pulling the fuzzy blanket around me.

With as much dignity as I can muster, I say, "I'll be in the bathroom until room service arrives. Enjoy this moment, funny boy. Laugh it up. Because when you wake up in the morning, your lips will be sewn together."

I slam the bathroom door to the sound of Quinn's gloating laughter ringing in my ears.

THIRTY-FIVE

SPIDER

$\mathcal{B}$y the time the food arrives, I've calmed down to the point where I feel as if I've only snorted half a key of coke, not the entire thing.

She wants to have my babies.

She can deny it all she wants. She can make up any kind of lie. But the expression of longing on her face when we started talking about it will be seared onto my memory forever.

I let the room service lad into the room and sign the bill. I tip him 400 percent, because holy fucking baby Jesus on a buttery Ritz cracker, Reyna Caruso wants me to get her pregnant.

I'm lightheaded. My heart is palpitating. I have to guzzle two entire glasses of water before my mouth starts to feel normal again.

When I knock on the bathroom door, Reyna opens it reluctantly.

"Are you done cackling in glee yet?"

"I'm done," I say, grinning. "When do you want to start working on getting you knocked up? Because I was thinking right now would be bloody grand."

A flush of color spreads over her cheeks. She mutters, "I regret every decision in my life that has led me to this moment."

I grab her and plant a hearty kiss on her mouth. When I pull away, she sighs.

"Ugh. You're going to be really unbearable now."

I pick her up. She's still wrapped in the blanket, and makes a comfy, fuzzy weight in my arms. Setting her carefully onto the edge of the bed, I roll the room service cart over to her and start removing lids from dishes.

"Okay. We've got steak. We've got chicken. We've got veggies."

She says, "And we've got two hundred side dishes. What happened, were they having a sale?"

"I couldn't decide what I wanted, so I got one of everything."

"Of course you did. And stop smiling like that. You're blinding me."

"Don't be so grumpy. It's bad for the baby."

She flops onto her back on the bed and hollers incoherently at the ceiling.

"So dramatic," I tease, feeling like an overfilled helium balloon. "Oh—is it too soon to start picking out names? Because I've got a bunch of ideas."

Closing her eyes, she mutters, "Where's a good asteroid strike when you need one?"

I make my voice firm. "And I want you to eat a lot of this steak. You'll need the iron. Developing fetuses have high iron requirements."

"Quinn?"

"Aye, lass?"

"You're insane." When I grin at her evil glare, she adds, "Certifiably. There's a padded cell somewhere out there with your name on the door."

My grin grows wider. "Casa de Spider. Love it. Now sit up and let me feed you."

"I'm not an invalid!"

"Be quiet, or I'll put something else in your mouth to shut you up."

If a man could be killed with a look, I'd be dead a thousand times over.

I can't remember ever feeling this happy in my entire life.

THIRTY-SIX

REY

We eat. And by that, I mean Quinn feeds me small portions of carefully cut-up food, making sure to include all the veggies he can coax into my mouth as he drones on and on about the nutritional needs of infants.

After supper and the first of what I fear will be many forthcoming lectures about eating for two, he takes us into the shower, washes us down with the enthusiasm of a Labrador on its first outing at the doggie park, then heads right back to bed with me in his arms.

When he's lying on top of me, searing my retinas with the brightness of his jubilant smile, I decide it's time to make an adjustment to the situation.

"Pardon me for interrupting your gloat-a-thon, but has it occurred to you that I might need a rest?"

He draws his brows together. "Rest?"

"Let me put it to you this way: if I inserted an object the size of a bowling pin into your behind, do you suppose you could go right back to business as usual afterward? Would you be riding around the moors of Ireland on horseback, leaping over streams and galloping around full-speed while your poor, raw bottom took the brunt of all that jostling in the saddle?"

He looks appalled. "I knew I was hurting you!" Then, after a beat: "A bowling pin?"

When his grin returns, I give up. I close my eyes and sigh heavily.

"All right, lass," he says, his voice warm, his mouth close to my ear. "We'll have a rest. We'll get a good night's sleep. You'll need it, because growing babies requires a lot of energy."

"Will you stop talking before I throw myself out the window, please?"

He rolls over, drags me on top of him, and hides his face in my neck as he laughs.

I must be more exhausted than I realize, because I fall asleep on top of him almost immediately.

The dream begins with fire.

All over me, all around me, even underneath my skin. I'm being burned alive from the inside out, and there's no escaping it.

Except it's not really fire. It only feels like fire.

Because that's exactly what being repeatedly lashed with a leather whip is like.

I'm naked, screaming, crawling away over a cold marble floor on my hands and knees, sobbing and pleading for mercy. My tormentor gives me none. Following closely behind as I scramble for safety, he cracks the whip over and over, separating my flesh. Blood splatters the marble. It's warm and slippery under the palms of my hands.

A vicious kick to the ribs sends me tumbling sideways. I lie on the cold hard floor on my back with my arms out, panting, desperately begging *no no no no* as he looms over me, a tall figure with a shadowed face and an arm raised to strike.

As it falls, the whip parts the air with a vicious hiss like a thousand snakes descending with their sharp fangs bared, prepared to bite.

I scream at the top of my lungs, knowing no one will hear me.

"Reyna! Wake up, baby! Wake up!"

Quinn is shouting at me. Holding me in his arms and shouting.

I'm blinded for a moment, seeing nothing but blackness and hearing only my pounding heartbeat and that terrible hiss that always came right before the pain exploded over me.

When I inhale a sharp breath, I come back to myself slowly. Inch by inch, the darkness withdraws. The warmth of the room and Quinn's arms seep in, soothing me.

I'm safe. In a hotel room in Boston, not at home in New York with Enzo.

Enzo is dead.

He can never hurt me again.

Except he can, because that sick son of a bitch lives on in my memory.

Sweating and trembling, I lower my head to Quinn's chest.

"You're okay, love," he says, sounding shaken as he rocks me in his arms. "You're okay. I've got you."

The sheets are in tangles all around us. I must've been thrashing. I wonder how long it took him to wake me up.

He kisses my head, then takes my face in his hands. His eyes search mine.

"You were having a nightmare."

My voice raw, I say, "Enzo."

He winces. "Ah, fuck."

He gathers me into his arms and holds me until my ragged

breath has slowed to normal, and I'm no longer quaking with dread.

"What can I do?"

"Just this. I'll be okay in a minute."

He exhales heavily, then pulls the blankets up, holding me with one arm. He settles us back against the pillows, tucking my head under his chin and wrapping his arms and legs around me so I'm cocooned in his warmth.

We lie like that in the dark, breathing together, for a long time. It could be minutes or hours, I don't know.

Eventually, an odd feeling overtakes me. After examining it for a while, I realize it's peace.

I've never felt peace before.

In all my thirty-three years, I've never known what it's like to find shelter from the storms that always followed me. I've been lost at sea for so long, I thought that's what it meant to be living.

It isn't until now, with a glimpse of a golden-haired man waving at me from shore in the distance, that I realize the storms might be behind me. My sails are full, the seas are smooth, and the wind at my back is soft and easy.

I might finally be coming home.

In a low voice, I say, "Epinephrine."

"What?"

I pull away from Quinn, rolling over and sitting up to swing my legs over the side of the bed. I put my head in my hands and exhale a breath I've been holding my whole life. It shudders out of me, heavier than gravity.

"I said epinephrine. Normally, it's used in emergency treatment for allergic reactions. But in large enough doses, it will stop the heart. And because it's a hormone that occurs naturally in the body, it doesn't automatically get flagged on the coroner's report."

Quinn lies perfectly still and silent, listening.

I lick my dry lips. "Enzo was diabetic. He had to inject himself with insulin before every meal."

After a long moment, Quinn says softly, "You replaced his insulin with epinephrine."

I look out the windows at Boston sparkling like a jewel in the night and think I could already be pregnant. I could already have this man's child growing inside me. I didn't insist he use protection. If I'm honest with myself, I didn't even give it a second thought.

I wanted him from the start. Long before I could admit it to myself, I wanted everything he could possibly give me.

I say, "No one else on earth knows that. The official cause of death was sudden cardiac arrest. Diabetes is a risk factor for it. He also had a fatty liver and elevated cholesterol levels, so the coroner didn't open an inquest. He was cremated, but the coroner's office keeps biomarker tissue samples for five years. If they knew to look for elevated adrenal hormones, I'd be in prison."

I look at him over my shoulder. "So you've got two years left of excellent blackmail material."

He gazes at me with a look of deep admiration.

Which is more proof of his insanity, considering I just confessed to murdering the prior man in his position.

He says, "Antivenom."

"Am I supposed to know what that means?"

"I have a severe allergy to spider antivenom. I was bitten by a spider when I was ten years old. The bite was bad, painful and swollen. My mother took me to the hospital, and they gave me antivenom. I would've survived the bite just fine, but the antivenom almost killed me. I went into anaphylactic shock."

"Why are you telling me that?"

"So both of us know something about the other that no one

else does. So that you don't feel like I have something to hold over you. And so you know I trust you with my life."

His voice drops and his eyes shine. "Now ask me what the only thing was that saved me from dying of anaphylactic shock."

My heart pounds painfully hard. I whisper, "Epinephrine."

Holding my gaze, he nods.

I shut my eyes and bury my face in my hands.

Then his arms are around me, pulling me close. Into my ear, he says, "We should name the first baby Epi."

My laugh is part sob. "That's sick."

He pretends to be serious. "You're right. How about Nephrine? Epine? Rin?"

"Oh God. We're both going to hell."

"For sure. We'll have front row seats." His voice warms. "But we'll be together."

He drags me back to the center of the bed and holds me tightly, kissing me all over my face. I lie in his arms, enveloped by him and a huge sense of wonder at how strange the world is.

"So is that what your tattoo and nickname are about?"

"Aye. After I came home from the hospital, all the neighborhood kids started calling me Spider. It stuck. The tattoo is a reminder to let things be as they are. That sometimes struggling against what is can make things worse. And that the real danger is never what you think it is, so keep your eyes sharp and your mind open before you make a decision that could change your life. Because everything is connected, linked in a delicate chain, like the web of a spider."

"Oh no," I say, my voice cracking. "I'll never be able to think your tattoo is dumb again."

He chuckles. "Most people think it means I've spent time in prison, so having you only think it's dumb is an upgrade."

"I didn't know spiderweb tattoos were symbolic for prison."

"Traditionally, aye. But they can be symbolic for lots of things. A struggle you've had to overcome. Longing to break free from a trap. Time spent away from family."

He adds sourly, "Or, in my case, a reminder that if I ever get bitten by a spider again, not to get the bloody antivenom."

I start to laugh and can't stop. I lie in his arms and dissolve into helpless laughter until my sides ache and my face feels as if it's stuck.

When I've finally calmed down and am sighing, Quinn kisses the top of my head.

"Go to sleep now, lass. And no more bad dreams, understood? You never have to be afraid of anything again. You've got me to watch over you now. I'll never let anything hurt you."

I fall asleep with the image of a huge golden spider rocking me gently in its web as it stands vigilant lookout in the dark, ready to give a deadly bite to anything that threatens me.

In the morning, Gianni calls in a rage, demanding to know what I said to the other family heads to get them to postpone the vote for capo.

When I tell him sweetly that he's forgotten I'm only a stupid, powerless woman, he hangs up on me.

Quinn shows remarkable restraint by not pouncing on me the moment I open my eyes. Instead, he suggests we go to his home so I can decide if I'd like to live there or move to the other side of the world and live in a hut so he can't find me.

He's trying to be funny, but I can tell how nervous he is about it.

I still haven't committed to living with him. Or to signing a wedding license to make the church marriage legal.

The only thing we're both on board about so far is the meeting of sperm and egg.

"Yes, I'd like to see your home. But first, I'd like to see the marriage contract."

He quirks his lips. "You're very interested in that contract, aren't you?"

"There might be a few items I'd like to renegotiate."

"Hmm."

"What a safe response. Show me the contract, Quinn. Let's get it over with."

He pulls it up on his laptop.

It's twenty-seven pages long.

Scrolling through the document, I say faintly, "What the actual fuck?"

Pacing behind me with his arms folded over his chest, Quinn says, "Did you think the terms joining two international criminal empires would be scribbled on a napkin?"

"No. I didn't think it would be the Magna Carta, either."

"Keep reading."

I do. It goes into remarkable detail about trade routes, payment terms, assigned territories, who reports to whom, how disputes are to be handled, termination triggers, jurisdictions and the hierarchy of said jurisdictions' managers. Among other things.

It's possibly the most complicated prenuptial agreement ever created.

"What's this section about someone named Stavros? It's very ambiguous."

Quinn peers over my shoulder to read. "It's a condition Gianni agreed to fulfill as part of the bargain."

"So what is it?"

He straightens and looks down at me. "Gianni has to kill Stavros. Personally. And show proof."

"I see. And what did this Stavros do that Declan wanted it in the contract?"

"He's Sloane's ex."

"Was he abusive?"

He snorts. "Stavros couldn't manage to abuse a wasp that was repeatedly stinging him in the face."

I furrow my brows. "So why does Declan want him dead?"

"It's a long story."

I say firmly, "Then I'll settle in as you tell it."

Sighing, Quinn turns away and starts pacing again. "A man named Kazimir Portnov is in control of the Bratva here in the U.S. He goes by Kage."

"Yes, I've heard the name."

"Declan asked for Kage's help when Riley was kidnapped and taken to Moscow. In return, Kage got a marker from Declan. He had to do Kage a favor, no matter what it was, no questions asked."

"Okay. I'm following."

"Kage's marker was that Declan had to kill Stavros."

"Why did Kage want Stavros dead?"

"Because he's Russian. They're crazy."

"Says the crazy man. Not good enough. Keep talking."

After an aggravated growl, Quinn says, "Declan can't kill Stavros himself because he promised Sloane he never would. And Kage, being the psychopath that he is, thought it would be bloody great fun to make his marker something Declan had promised his wife he'd never do and see how he'd handle it."

"Okay. But why did Kage want Stavros dead in the first place?"

"Disloyalty. At least that's what Declan told me. It could really be nothing more than Kage being Kage."

"Stavros is Russian?"

"Aye."

Mulling that over, I turn my attention back to the computer screen. "So Sloane doesn't know about this marker?"

"Not what it was called in for."

I don't like the sound of that. Even though we're not close yet, Sloane is someone I could see being a good friend. And I know enough about her to know she wouldn't like this kind of backdoor dealing at all.

"Which also means she doesn't know that Declan put it in the marriage contract."

He chuckles. "It's not like he'd tell her, lass. If Sloane found out Declan had broken his promise, he'd be short two balls."

Just as I thought. It's a brilliant piece of strategy on Declan's part, but if Sloane found out about this clever chess move of his, she'd rightly feel betrayed.

These men think they're so smart.

But if they were really intelligent, they'd be much more afraid of their wives.

I move on to other items, asking Quinn to explain and elaborate. I get an education in the technicalities and logistics of how drugs and weapons are moved across borders, how money changes hands, how law enforcement is used to aid illegal activities or avoided where it can't be bribed.

By the end of it, I have a good sense of the terms of the contract.

And an even better sense of where it needs to be changed to the Mafia's benefit.

Closing the laptop, I say, "Thank you. That was helpful. Let's go see your home."

"That's it?"

"Are you the man in charge of contract negotiations?"

Quinn's expression darkens. "Declan is."

"Then that's it. Let's go."

He says firmly, "Lass. The contract can't be changed. It's been signed already."

I smile at him. "But the marriage license hasn't. And without a legal marriage, the contract isn't binding. I saw that in section 18b."

"Gianni isn't going to ask for more concessions. He's already over the moon about what he got."

Yes, but I'm not. And I find myself feeling quite ambitious this morning.

I say, "We'll see about that," and head to the door.

THIRTY-SEVEN

REY

*T*he place Quinn calls home is a penthouse in a skyscraper in the middle of the city that looks as if it were designed by Morticia Addams at the height of a depressive episode.

Decorated entirely in shades of gray and black, the place is dark, sophisticated, and freezing. It's somewhere a coven of vampires might feel cozy and welcome.

Not a single speck of color enlivens the place. There isn't a throw pillow, photograph, or plant in sight. There isn't any carpeting or warm fabrics to soften the space, either. It's all glass, marble, steel, and cold reflective surfaces.

Looking around the echoing living room, I say, "My, how delightful. If I were a cyborg, I'd plug myself right in."

"Used to be Declan's before he got married," says Quinn, strolling past me with his hands in his pockets.

"So it's a Mob bachelor pad. That explains its lack of a pulse."

Quinn turns to look at me. "I take it that means you don't like it."

Feeling his gaze on me as I go, I wander into the kitchen.

There's an enormous marble island in the middle of it, accompanied by a host of stainless steel appliances lurking around in the gloom. They glare suspiciously at me. Even the microwave seems hostile.

I don't want to be mean, so I look around for something to compliment.

"The stove is nice."

"Tell me what you think of the bedroom."

He casually strolls away down a hallway. I peek into the enormous dining room and library before I follow, deafened by the sound of my heels clicking on the marble floor, fracturing into a thousand echoes that bounce back to assault my ears.

When I enter the master bedroom, I find him leaning against a wet bar with a book in his hands. To the right of him, a stack of large cardboard boxes rests against the wall.

"What are all those boxes?"

"Your belongings from your bedroom."

"My bedroom at Gianni's house in New York?"

"Aye. I told you I'd send the lads to pick up your things."

I stare at the boxes in shock. "How did they get everything here so fast? And how did they get in the house when we weren't there?"

He smiles, thumbing through the book. "My friend Bettina the housekeeper let them in. Sweet lass. I think she fancies me."

"And I think she needs to get fired."

He chuckles. "It's not her fault I'm so handsome and persuasive. By the way, this book of yours is *very* interesting." He holds it up, displaying the cover, which showcases a busty, half-naked woman swooning in the arms of a muscular warrior.

Ravaged by a Rogue. It's one of my favorites.

Quinn clucks his tongue. "Did it win the Nobel Prize in Literature? It looks very highbrow."

My cheeks heating, I demand, "Where did you get that?"

He gestures toward a box with its top open beside him. "One of them was labeled 'naughty bits.' So of course I went straight to it. Interesting how dog-eared this book is. It's even got highlighted sections. Oh, here's a good one."

In a theatrical voice, he reads a passage aloud.

"He repeatedly speared his turgid manhood into her velvet channel, excited by her lusty cries of pleasure and the sight of her voluptuous breasts and their taut, rosy nipples lurching in his hands."

Smirking, he looks up at me. "I had no idea nipples could lurch."

I'm horrified by the realization that not only has my cherished collection of vintage erotica been packed up and delivered here—which means Quinn's men had to go through it to pack it up—but also that my cherished collection of battery-powered toys must have been discovered and shipped along with the books.

I picture half a dozen Irishmen in my bedroom, chortling and making dirty jokes as they toss my favorite vibrators around like Frisbees.

I might be in danger of vomiting.

"Ah, don't make that face, lass. I'm sure nobody will think less of you that you enjoy such literary treasures as . . ." He reaches into the box and pulls out another paperback. *"Glazed by the Gladiator."*

When he looks at me with his brows lifted, I say, "In my defense, that one is really well written."

"Oh, I can imagine. The parts about how he glazed her must be majestic."

"As a matter of fact, they are. But my favorite part's on page sixteen."

As he flips the pages, he murmurs to himself, "She's got it committed to memory."

He finds the page and starts reading. After several moments of silence, he glances up at me.

Weirdly excited, I say, "Her husband is a rich old man with erectile problems. And she's desperate to have a child. So when the most famous, handsome, and virile gladiator in Rome gets arrested and thrown into a dungeon below the Colosseum, she decides to pay him a little conjugal visit to try to get some of his super sperm for a baby."

"Why was he arrested?"

"Who cares? That's not what's interesting about the story."

"No, what's interesting is that this scene where a robed mystery woman enters the dungeon and tries to talk her way into the gladiator's good graces so she can harvest his superior genes for her future child takes place in the *first chapter*. What the bloody hell happens in the rest of the book?"

"More of that. Except later, he breaks out of the dungeon to find her because he's madly in love with her by then."

Quinn looks down at the book. "She had him blindfolded by the guards before she entered the cell. How did he know who to look for?"

"By the sound of her voice."

He glances back up at me, and now his tone is droll. "I see. So he breaks out of a dungeon to search all of Rome for a woman he's never seen before. Excellent plan. Your gladiator is an idiot."

I feel unreasonably smug to inform him otherwise. "But he found her, so he's not."

Exasperated, he says, "How did he find her? Telepathy?"

"He was in the market and overheard her talking to the tomato vendor."

When he stares at me in disbelief, I smile. "So, Maximus Aurelius Tiberius . . . how strong is your sperm?"

His eyes sharpen. His energy charges. I swear I see his canines elongate.

Setting aside the books on the bar counter, he says gruffly, "If you want to harvest it, Antonia Octavia Flavius, you'll have to do it the old-fashioned way."

I sashay toward him, holding his predatory gaze. "But I brought this special terra-cotta urn to collect your seed in, gladiator. I'm married. I simply *couldn't* betray my wedding vows."

As soon as I'm within arm's length, Quinn reaches out and grabs me. He pins my arms behind my back, pulls me against his body, and stares down at me with blazing eyes.

"If your husband is too old to fuck you properly, your wedding vows are already broken."

I coyly bat my lashes. "But sir, I'm a lady of the upper class. I could never fornicate with a mere soldier. A vicious criminal. A man condemned to death for his crimes."

Looking at my mouth, he licks his lips. "You can't have my seed unless you do."

When I wriggle against him, rubbing my breasts against his chest, he growls. His eyes darken. His growing erection presses against my hip.

I'm not sure who likes this game better, him or me.

I say breathlessly, "You're supposed to be tied to a chair and blindfolded."

He looks around the room. Releasing me, he strides over to a desk on the opposite wall and pulls the chair out from under it. He sets it in front of me, sits down on it, whips off his tie, and holds it out.

When I take it, he rips off his suit jacket and dress shirt and flings them to the floor. Stripped to the waist, he sits there staring up at me in fiery intensity with his chest rising and falling and all the tendons in his neck standing out.

"Hands behind your back, gladiator."

He instantly clasps his hands behind the chair.

I might lose consciousness from excitement.

Stepping behind him, I wind the tie around his head, covering his eyes, and knot it in back. I bend down and kiss his neck, whispering into his ear, "Will you be a good gladiator and keep your hands behind you, or do I need to find something to bind them with?"

"I'll be good," he says, practically panting.

As a reward, I kiss his neck again, gently biting him, then licking the sting away. He groans softly, fidgeting.

When I straighten, I feel lightheaded. I walk around to his front and straddle his lap. Between my legs, his erection is enormous.

Scratching my nails lightly over his shoulders, I whisper, "You're the most gorgeous gladiator I've ever seen. So strong. Look at all these beautiful muscles."

He leans forward, blindly hunting for my mouth. I give it to him, thrilling at the animal sound he makes when our lips meet. We kiss deeply, until my nipples are aching for his mouth and the throbbing between my legs is unbearable.

I stand, unzip my dress, and shimmy out of it. I remove my panties and kick off my heels. Then I kneel down in front of Quinn and unbuckle his belt.

When I've got his zipper down, his hard cock is proudly jutting out from the top of his briefs.

"Ooh, gladiator. You're as talented as I've heard."

I spread my hands over his thighs and lick the engorged crown. He moans, flexing his hips. All the muscles in his stomach clench.

I take his cock in both hands and lick it all over, swirling my head around the crown and sucking on it, then trailing my tongue up and down the pulsing vein underneath. When I've got him good and slick, I straddle him again, pressing my bare breasts against his chest.

His hard cock is trapped between us, wedged in my wet folds. I slide back and forth on it, barely moving my hips.

He says through gritted teeth, "More. Inside."

Kissing his neck, I smile. "You're not in charge here. You're a prisoner, remember?"

"Fuck."

Flexing my hips back and forth, I take his face in my hands and guide his mouth to my breast. He latches onto a nipple with a sound of relief, sucking so hard, his cheeks hollow.

"That's so good," I whisper, threading my fingers into his hair. "I love your mouth."

I give him my other breast and he does the same thing, licking and sucking greedily. Every pull of his lips is an arrow of pleasure shot down to my pussy. I'm so wet, the friction so delicious, I moan as I glide back and forth over the length of his rigid cock.

I say breathlessly, "I think I should go, Maximus. This is a dangerous plan. If we're found out, my husband will kill me."

He snarls, "I'll kill your husband before he finds out. Then we can be together."

"But you're locked up in this dungeon!"

"Not for long. Now take my big fucking gladiator dick inside your pretty high-class cunt and ride it until I give you what you came for."

Laughing in euphoria, I dig my nails into his shoulders and sink down onto his giant cock.

He thrusts up into me with a grunt, making my breasts bounce. Balancing on my toes and holding on to his shoulders, I slide up and down on his shaft, my hard nipples skimming his chest, until we're both moaning loudly.

Panting, he says, "Are you ready to take my cum?"

"Yes! Give it to me!"

He grabs my hips and pulls me down as he thrusts up, swearing and jerking so hard, the chair jumps.

I feel him spill himself deep inside me. I follow him over the edge into oblivion, convulsing around him as I helplessly cry out his name.

"Take it, baby," he commands hotly into my ear. "Be a good girl and take every fucking drop."

A wave of emotion overtakes me. I sob and lower my head, hiding my face in his neck. He slides his hands up my back and holds me as he grinds himself into me, growling in pleasure, my mobster who let me blindfold him and played such a wonderful gladiator.

I think I might actually like this bachelor pad after all.

THIRTY-EIGHT

REY

*W*e spend the night there. We act out two more scenes from the book. I decline to participate in one scene Quinn found particularly fascinating, where the gladiator demonstrates exactly how the title of the novel was inspired.

I prefer not to have an ejaculate facial, thank you very much. My skin is quite moisturized already.

In the morning, I make breakfast from the single overripe avocado on the counter, the three eggs in the fridge of indeterminate age, and the loaf of sourdough bread in the pantry, half of which is moldy. I throw out the worst and pick off a few spots from the other pieces, then fry them up with butter in a pan.

"Avocado toast with fried eggs," I say to Quinn, who's sitting shirtless at the kitchen island. "It's possible it will kill you. When was the last time you went shopping?"

"For food?"

"No, for uranium."

"I usually eat out."

"Ah. You and Declan must have big restaurant bills."

"Oh, aye. We've got big . . . bills." He grins, biting into his toast.

"Grow up."

"You love it, viper."

I do, but I won't admit it. It will only encourage him.

His cell phone rings. Still grinning at me, he digs it out of his pants pocket and answers.

"Hullo." He listens for a moment, then glances up at me. "We'll be right over."

When he disconnects, I say, "Who was that?"

"Declan. He's got news about the break-in. Says you'll want to hear it in person."

We shower and change clothes, then head out to the palace Declan calls home. As soon as we're seated in his office, Declan says, "Before we get down to business, Sloane made me promise to make another date for supper with you. So let's work that out."

"Oh. Supper."

I glance at Quinn, sitting beside me with a bland smile. His digestive tract is probably more prepared to deal with Sloane's culinary adventures than mine is, having most likely been subjected to them before.

"Actually, let's back up a sec. Let's talk about your promises."

Declan lifts his brows.

Quinn warns, "Reyna."

I smile at both of them and go right ahead with what I was going to say. "We need to remove the section in the contract about Stavros."

Declan leans back in his chair and folds his hands over his stomach. He drawls, "Do we now."

"Yes. And please don't be patronizing. That's literally my least favorite thing."

He glances at Quinn, who looks like he'd rather be anywhere else than in this room, then looks back at me. "The contract has already been signed."

"But it doesn't take effect until my dear husband here and I have both signed a wedding license and filed it with the county clerk. Until then, it's just a bunch of paper."

When Declan draws down his dark brows and glowers at me, I say innocently, "Or am I incorrect?"

Quinn's sigh is heavy.

Declan gazes at me with a calculated look in his icy blue eyes. I'm sure if I were a man, he'd be terribly frightening, but right now, all I'm feeling is determined.

I want that section out of the contract, and I want to negotiate some better terms for my side, and I'm not leaving this office until both of those things are done.

"Look. Either you take that section out, or I'll tell Sloane it's in there. Your choice."

In a clipped tone, Declan says, "I could just cancel the whole bloody thing."

So he wants to play dirty. Well, I'm up for that.

I sit back in my chair, cross my legs, and shrug. "Okay by me."

Groaning, Quinn leans over and drops his head into his hands.

"Does your brother know you're making demands on his behalf?"

Holding Declan's freezing blue gaze, I say calmly, "I'm making demands on behalf of my family and my new friend Sloane, not Gianni. If he had half a brain, he would've negotiated a better contract himself, but since I'm the one sitting here with a wedding ring on my finger, I'm the one you're dealing with."

After a long moment of silence, Declan smiles.

"All right, lass. We'll take out the Stavros section."

"Thank you. Now, concerning section 24a. We're going to need a better payment schedule on those overseas shipments."

Into his hands, Quinn mutters, "Dear God in heaven."

But Declan doesn't seem at all surprised to hear I'm not finished making demands. He simply says, "Why don't you put it all in writing and send it over? We'll have the attorneys draw up a new draft and we can go over it then."

Quinn lifts his head and stares at Declan as if he's lost his mind.

"I'll do that. Thank you."

"Any other surprises you'd like to spring on me?"

"Not at the moment."

"Can we get to the reason you're here now?"

"There's no need to be snippy."

Declan looks at Quinn, who puts his hands in the air and shakes his head.

Declan takes the laptop sitting to one side of the desk and turns it around so the screen is facing us. He hits a button, and a video starts to play. It's a black-and-white picture of what seems to be the security camera feed at an empty loading dock in a warehouse.

"What am I looking at?"

"Just watch."

Frowning, I watch a white van back up into the dock. Its rear doors open. From somewhere off camera, seven men emerge. All of them are in identical black uniforms of combat boots, tactical pants and vests, and long-sleeved shirts.

They're all also wearing black ski masks and carrying rifles.

The hair on my arms stands on end.

The men enter the van. The back doors close. The van pulls away from the loading dock.

I glance up to find Declan watching me closely. He says, "Notice the sign over the door in the background."

I squint at the screen. There's a door off to one side of where the van pulled up. The sign above it reads, CARUSO INDUSTRIES. EMPLOYEES ONLY.

Something dark and ugly forms in the pit of my stomach.

I say quietly, "No."

Declan doesn't respond. He hits another button. Now I'm looking at a white van racing down a country road. It's the same van from the video. The view this time is from above.

The screen splits into four different views, all of the same van speeding down roads, driving erratically.

In Scarsdale.

Away from the house.

Declan says, "Traffic cameras. Recognize the area?"

With dawning horror, I whisper, "He wouldn't. He couldn't have."

"Look at the time."

There's a time and date stamp on the bottom right side of each picture. All show the day and time of the home invasion.

Declan hits another button. Now I'm listening to a recording of a man's voice I don't recognize.

"Mission Charlie Foxtrot. Oscar Mike."

Declan says, "That's military slang for the mission was a clusterfuck, I'm on the move."

"Mission," I repeat faintly, feeling sick.

"The message was left on your brother's voicemail five minutes after the time stamps on the traffic cameras."

"It can't have been. Gianni has excellent encryption. All his communications, his email, everything is secure . . ."

I trail off when Declan hits the button again and a new screen shows up. It's an email, dated two weeks ago. Sent to Gianni from someone named Hangfire. The body of the email says only: *Funds received. The balloon has gone up.*

"That means trouble is coming," says Declan, watching my face. "That date at the end is when the op was to go live."

It's the same date on the videos of the white van.

The same date the men in black invaded the house.

My heart thudding against my rib cage, I say, "This doesn't make sense. Why would Gianni set up an attack on his own home?"

Declan's voice is level when he says, "Why does your brother do anything?"

He's not asking a rhetorical question. And I don't have to think very long before I come up with an answer.

I whisper, "Money. Oh God."

"The plan was to kidnap Lili and hold her for ransom."

"But he'd be putting up his own cash for ransom!"

"Unless I offered to pay it," says Quinn quietly. "Which I would have."

Declan says, "Then that money would've gone right back to Gianni. So either he made a calculated guess Spider would put up the money or he didn't care if he did, because there was a bigger target."

"What target?"

When Declan only stares at me in silence, I know what the target is.

Or rather, who.

And I'm truly sick now, because I know without a shadow of doubt what Gianni was after.

I close my eyes and try very hard not to scream.

"Enzo had a ten-million-dollar life insurance policy on me. I didn't know about it until after his death. I kept paying the insurance premiums but changed the beneficiary to Gianni. At the time, Lili wasn't yet eighteen, or it would've been her."

Quinn says, "Ten million? Why would he go to all that trouble for only ten mil?"

I open my eyes and find Declan staring at me with the answer in his own.

He already knows.

"That was only the cherry on top. The real money is what I inherited on Enzo's death."

Declan says softly, "Two hundred and forty million dollars."

In shock, Quinn turns to me. *"What?"*

"Aye, lad. Your wife's rich."

After a moment of pensive silence, Quinn says, "Except she's not really my wife, is she?"

I can't look at him. There's a note of finality in his voice, as if he's just now realizing that this non-marriage of ours is skating on very thin ice.

I say, "That doesn't change anything between us, Quinn."

Declan says, "What if you were named capo of the Five Families? Would that change anything?"

Stunned, I stare at him with my eyes wide and my heart palpitating. My brain starts to race.

I think of the strange meeting with the heads of the other four families that day in the warehouse, the way I sensed there was something more going on than what they said, and get a tingling feeling all the way down my spine.

I also know I have to tread very carefully here, because I have no way of knowing if this is a trap, if I'm being recorded, or how Declan O'Donnell came to have all this information in his hands.

When it comes right down to it, the Mob and the Mafia are still enemies. Without that marriage license, our relationship doesn't exist.

I say, "What-if is a dangerous question. And here is where I point out that I have no proof any of this information is real. All of it could have been easily manufactured by someone with very little skill."

Gazing at me with the kind of cool composure that belies nothing, Declan says, "There was a vote this morning, Reyna."

"Gianni said the vote had been postponed."

"They told him it had been, but it went on without him."

"Why?"

"Because they'd already decided he was no longer welcome in the family."

My voice rising along with my anger, I say, "What the hell does that mean?"

"It means they were provided indisputable proof that Gianni has been funneling money away from the family operations for years, in addition to many other acts of disloyalty."

I say flatly, "Let me guess. You provided them the proof."

"Not me."

"Who, then?"

"An interested third party."

I can tell that's all I'll get there, so I change gears. "I need to speak with my brother about all this."

After a pause, Declan says quietly, "I'm afraid that's not possible."

It sounds like a threat.

The air goes static. My heartbeat surges. Every muscle in my body tenses.

Beside me, Quinn has also tensed, looking back and forth between us with his hands white-knuckled around the arms of his chair. Every cell in his body is ready to spring into action, primed to the crackling stress in the room.

It hits me with a blast like a nuclear explosion.

If Declan tried to harm me, Quinn would kill him.

His boss, his friend, a person he once described as the best man he's ever known. He'd kill him to protect me.

The emotion I feel is so raw and overpowering, I have to inhale several slow breaths before I can speak again.

"Why not?"

"Because Gianni's dead."

When I leap from my chair, Quinn moves at the same time, jumping up to stand in front of me protectively with a blistering snarl and a threatening scowl in Declan's direction.

Declan regards us with his eyebrows raised and a look of incredulity on his face. "What the bloody hell is wrong with you two?"

Quinn growls, "This woman could be carrying my child. If you want to get to her, you've got to go through me first!"

Declan's laugh is short and astonished. He looks at me as if he's wondering what kind of spell I've put on his friend, then looks back at Quinn. He shakes his head and exhales.

"Sit down, you barmy bastards. I wasn't threatening anyone. Jesus, Mary, and Joseph, I've got a mutiny on my hands. I knew today would be shite."

He reclines back into his big leather captain's chair with a sigh and waves a hand at us like we're being ridiculous.

"Sit!"

Quinn looks to me for direction. I nod, and we both carefully take our seats.

Declan says crossly, "For fuck's sake, lad, don't be staring at me with such a black glower! Last I heard, I'm still in charge of you, so show some bloody respect!"

Grinding his molars, Quinn grudgingly settles into his chair.

Declan cuts his gaze to me and says accusingly, "What have you done with him? He's even more strung out than usual!"

"He's fine. Let's get back to business, please."

He mutters to himself, "I need a bloody drink and it's not even ten o'clock in the bloody morning." Then, overly dramatic, he says, "Now that we're all civilized adults again, I'll continue."

He clicks around on the laptop for a second, searching for something. Then a video begins to play.

Gianni is tied to a chair in the middle of an empty room. His eyes are closed. His head lolls to one side. His face is bruised and bloody. More blood stains the front of his white dress shirt and the floor beneath the chair.

I lift my hand to my mouth, inhaling sharply.

Declan says, "I won't show you the worst of it. Alessandro sent this over after he told me about the vote."

A man walks into the frame. It's Massimo, smoking a cigarette as he circles Gianni. He says, "So you stole money from us. Your own family."

Gianni mumbles something incoherent. Massimo kicks the chair, and Gianni jumps.

"Yes. I did. But you have to believe me, I—"

Massimo kicks the chair again. Gianni falls silent.

"Don't bother with excuses. We know about the money. We know about the stolen product. We know about the bribes you paid to try to keep everybody's mouth shut. But somebody always talks, Gianni. You should know that by now. Somebody *always* talks."

Massimo paces, shaking his head in disbelief. "And your own daughter? *Ma dai!* You set up your own daughter to get kidnapped? That's just fucking sick. Who does that? I'll tell you who. A big piece of shit."

He kicks the chair again. Gianni moans, babbling apologies. Then Massimo looks right into the camera.

"Hey, shitbag. Tell your sister what you had in mind for her, eh? Tell her how you were gonna let a bunch of cowboys mess around with her before they slit her throat. How you promised them they could use her."

A low, dangerous rumble goes through Quinn's chest, but other than a deep sense of unreality, I feel nothing at all.

Massimo turns away from the camera, smoking and circling again. "We got that driver, by the way. Made him talk same way we did you. *Mannaggia a te!* Hope you didn't pay them too much money. What a fucked-up job that was. Ah, well. Any last words?"

From beneath his jacket, Massimo pulls out a pistol.

Gianni starts shrieking. "My daughter ran away with a Mexican! She's useless! Nobody cares what happens to her! And my sister's a bloodthirsty whore!"

I say softly, "Oh, Gianni. You always were a sad little prick."

I reach over and stop the video. It cuts off just as Massimo is raising his gun.

I sit with my eyes closed for a while, listening to the silence in the room and thinking of my brother. Trying to remember a time when we were close.

The memory doesn't come. Gianni and I were related by blood, but no other ties of friendship or love ever bound us.

As with Enzo, I was nothing more to him than a thing to be used for personal gain.

I feel Quinn's touch on my arm and open my eyes.

He murmurs, "You okay?"

I'm not sure how to answer that, so I don't. I look at Declan instead.

"My mother?"

"She's on a plane home to New York."

I nod, thinking. "So the bottom line, if I understand it correctly, is that my brother betrayed the Cosa Nostra and his own blood and was shot because of it."

"Aye."

I nod again. "And there was a vote for the new capo this morning."

"Aye."

"And you're asking me to believe a male-dominated institution hundreds of years old just decided out of the blue they should have a woman as their leader for the first time."

"The vote was split. Not everyone was on board."

"Let me guess. Massimo."

Declan lifts a shoulder. "Some lads still aren't living in the twenty-first century."

"Why didn't they just elect someone else? Alessandro, for instance?"

"They can explain better themselves, lass, but you're the one who stood up in front of four hundred witnesses and God himself and vowed to love and obey this nutty bugger here so you could save your niece from getting shot. You're the one who also spared Juan Pablo from getting shot, and guess whose uncle Alvaro now only wants to make an accord with the woman who saved his dear nephew's life?"

My lips curve upward. "That would be me, I take it."

"That would be you." His voice grows quieter. "You're also the lass who withstood fourteen years of brutality without complaint—"

"As if anyone would have listened."

"—and managed to pull the wool over every law enforcement official's eyes when she surgically disposed of her abuser."

I say automatically, "I didn't kill my husband."

Declan smiles. "And is a mighty fine liar, to boot. Why *wouldn't* they want you in charge?"

"Oh, I don't know. My vagina?"

He chuckles at that. "I did tell them I wouldn't renew the contract with anyone else, so there's that."

My feeling of unreality grows bigger. I'm disconnected from my body, as if I'm seeing this all unfold from somewhere overhead. "But I haven't signed the contract. Gianni did."

Quinn and Declan just sit there and look at me.

"And you knew when I walked into this room that Gianni was dead. You only gave me the concession about Stavros and told me to send over the other changes because you already knew I'd been named capo. You even knew back at that meeting at the warehouse with Alessandro and the others that they were testing my loyalties. You knew the night we came for supper that the woman who agreed to marry this man next to me was a potential candidate for the most powerful position in the Cosa Nostra. You've known an awful lot all along, Mr. O'Donnell."

He says evenly, "You can't blame a leopard for its spots, lass."

"Or a tiger for its stripes."

Quinn's tension is rising again. Even without breaking Declan's gaze, I can feel him growing more agitated, and I know the reason why.

He just realized that if I'm capo, there's no need for me to legally marry him at all.

We don't need a marriage license to make the contract valid. If I'm the head of the Caruso crime family now, I'm free to negotiate my own contracts without selling my body as an asset to anyone.

I'm free to walk away from this non-marriage and still get everything I want.

I'm just . . . free.

I look at Quinn. He looks back at me, all of it written all over his face as plain as day.

In a gruff voice, he says, "I'll have your things sent anywhere you like."

He rises from his chair and stiffly walks out of the room.

THIRTY-NINE

SPIDER

I stand outside with my face upturned to the sky and my eyes closed, feeling the warmth of the sun on my skin and the freezing coldness inside my heart.

I should have known it was too good to be true.

I should have known.

Footsteps approach. I don't turn or open my eyes.

I want to remember this moment. I want to brand every thought and feeling into my memory, so if I ever think things might have changed for me, if I ever make the mistake of having hope again, I'll look back and feel myself burning to the ground and turn away from that hope because it's a lie.

It's always been a lie.

There's no hope for me.

There's only misery.

Declan says gently, "What are you doing, lad?"

"What does it look like I'm doing?"

"Feeling sorry for yourself."

"With all due respect, boss, piss off."

He chuckles and claps a hand on my shoulder. "Don't tell me you're falling in love with your wife."

"Fallen, past tense. It already happened. And she's not my wife."

"Everything's so black and white with you. Try looking at the shades of gray once in a while. It'll do you a bit of good."

I open my eyes to glare at him. Standing next to me in the garden, he's smiling. Looking at me like I didn't just get kicked off the bliss train I'd been riding since the wedding.

"That's your advice for me right now? Look at shades of gray?"

"Aye. Also maybe stick around for the end of a conversation before you go storming out in a dramatic teenage huff."

"I didn't storm! And I'm not dramatic!"

He takes a moment to let the hair settle back around his face before saying, "Oh no. Not you. You're as calm as a bloody Buddha."

Muttering, I look away and cross my arms over my chest.

"So what's your plan, lover boy? Stand out here in the garden glaring at the poor flowers until it gets dark?"

"I don't have a plan."

"Then maybe you could come back inside. The girls are having champagne."

I snap my head around and stare at him. "Champagne?"

He smiles. "Sloane thought a toast was in order. Considering your wife is the first female head of the Cosa Nostra."

My heart starting to beat faster, I say, "She's not my wife."

He shrugs and slides his hands into his pockets. "If you say so." He turns and strolls back toward the house, whistling "Here Comes the Bride."

My hands start to shake. I break out in a cold sweat. My heart decides now would be a good time to test its limits to see how fast it can beat in a ten-second span.

Don't do it. Don't even think it. Don't get your hopes up, you bloody wanker.

This is just another setup for fate to laugh its arse off at you.

I stand rooted to the same spot for five minutes, arguing with myself, until Reyna appears in a window.

Dark hair, red lips, olive skin.

A low-cut dress.

Acres of cleavage.

And eyes that glitter silver in the morning sun like the flash of coins at the bottom of a wishing well.

My pounding heart lets out a primal scream.

The first time I saw her in a window, the day I went to meet Lili in New York and sign the contract, Reyna looked at me with those mermaid eyes like she wanted to slit my throat.

Now she's looking at me like I'm the answer to every question she's ever asked herself.

She smiles and crooks a finger. Then she turns away, disappearing from sight.

I almost faint.

Instead, I bolt toward the house, pumping my legs as fast as they'll take me.

FORTY

REY

I'm sipping from my champagne flute when Quinn crashes through the front door, hollering my name.

Standing in the kitchen with Sloane and me, Declan smiles. "Ah. The groom has arrived."

Eyes wild, his color high, Quinn skids around the corner and makes a beeline for me.

Sloane says, "Man, he's intense."

"You have no idea. Oh, hi, honey."

Sloane removes the champagne flute from my hand an instant before Quinn grabs me in a bear hug and crushes me against his chest.

His heart pounds against mine. His big arms tighten around my ribs until I can barely breathe.

I laugh, hugging him back. "Long time no see, Dr. Jekyll. Or is it Mr. Hyde? I can never remember."

Against my neck, he says gruffly, "Viper."

I whisper, "It's Antonia Octavia Flavius to you, gladiator."

A shudder runs through his chest. He hugs me tighter.

Declan clears his throat. "We'll give you two a minute."

When Quinn finally releases me from the bear hug, we're alone in the kitchen. Leaning against him, I smile at the expression of adoration, hope, and dread on his face.

"You're an emotional wreck, dear husband."

He swallows. He licks his lips. He says, "Husband," as if he's not sure he heard me correctly.

Stroking his beard, I say, "So there's this part in all my romance books that's called the black moment. Heard of it? No, of course you haven't. Cavemen don't spend much time reading. The black moment is when all seems lost, like the couple can never work out their problems and it's the end of the road for them. Are you paying attention? You seem to be spending a lot of time staring at my cleavage."

"I'm listening," he says in a thick voice while staring at my cleavage.

I sigh. "Anyway. In real life, people do this thing called communicating. Now, I know you've heard of that, because you've worn my ears out doing that exact thing. Except for some reason, you decide at a very important juncture in our relationship that you'd rather storm off and break things than talk to me."

He thunders, "I didn't storm! And I didn't break anything!"

I pet his beard and smile at him, my insane Irish mobster with the beautiful hazel eyes.

"There's no need to rupture my eardrums, dear. As I was saying. The black moment. I don't want to have one, because this isn't a romance novel, it's real life. So if there are any questions you'd like to ask about what happened in Declan's office or thoughts you'd like to share—in a normal volume—please do so."

I go up on my toes and press a soft kiss to his lips. "Because I have a date with a gladiator later, and I really hope he shows up."

He exhales and folds himself around me again, burying his face in my hair.

"I take it that's a no," I murmur, stroking my hands up his back. "But just so we're clear, Quinn, whatever happens next, I want you by my side. Marriage license or not, contract or not, head of the Cosa Nostra or not, I want you."

I laugh softly. "You and your superior gladiator seed with which I'd like to make babies."

He groans. He hugs me harder. Then he whispers into my ear, "Five of them."

"You ready for that?"

"I've been ready since the first second I laid eyes on you."

"Good answer. Time to kiss me now, Quinn."

He pulls away, his eyes shining and his expression one of pure devotion. "Are you going to always be this bossy now that you're in charge of the Cosa Nostra?"

My smile grows into a grin. "Oh, I'm going to be the *worst*."

With a chuckle, Quinn lowers his head and kisses me.

It's soft, deep, and everything I could ever ask for. It feels like a promise made, a promise stronger than any signature on a legal document or vow spoken in front of four hundred witnesses in a church.

It feels like a field of flowers opening their buds to the sun after a long winter.

It feels like coming home.

That night, I meet with the four heads of the other families.

Aldo, Tomasi, and Alessandro greet me with respectful hand-shakes and smiles. Massimo greets me the same way, but his smile doesn't reach his eyes.

I'll have to be careful with that one. He's just as selfish as Gianni, but far more clever.

We spend three hours discussing the past, present, and future of the Cosa Nostra in the States. In addition, Alessandro provides me with a digital file of all the evidence they collected about Gianni's betrayals. Nobody apologizes for his death or offers me condolences on the loss of my brother.

I didn't expect such pleasantries. All made men know the price of disloyalty.

Made women know, too.

Blood in, blood out. It's been our way of life for centuries.

There's a formal swearing-in ceremony. I'm given a gold signet ring bearing the family crest to wear. It's too large for my pinky, so I wear it on the index finger of my right hand.

It still has Gianni's blood on it.

I decide on the spot I'll never clean it off.

At the end of the meeting, when the goodbyes have been said and the others are filing out of the back room of the restaurant, Massimo lingers behind. Twisting his pinky ring around with his thumb, he gazes at me in thoughtful silence.

"Speak your mind, Massimo," I say, standing on the opposite side of the table.

After a moment, he says, "Enzo and I were close. You know that."

"I do. I also know you were aware of what he did to me."

"What's between a husband and wife is their business."

"What's your point?"

He removes his cashmere wool overcoat from the back of his chair and shrugs it on. He takes his time buttoning it. When that's done, he regards me with a calculating look.

"You're going to have to choose a side, Reyna. Us or them. The others might think your marriage is an asset to us, but I don't. I think it's a weakness."

"Because?"

"Because a house divided against itself cannot stand."

A faint smile lifts my lips. "You're quoting Abraham Lincoln. That's unexpected."

"You understand what I'm saying."

"I do. But there's no division."

"No? You'll be able to keep all our secrets from your Irish husband?"

Holding his challenging stare, I say evenly, "I've been keeping secrets my entire life. Including one about you, Massimo. A rather big one."

His eyes sharpen to slits. "Like what?"

I smile at his sudden shift from merely unpleasant to downright hostile. "Like you did a favor for the head of an enemy family that would get you both killed if his men found out. People don't like snakes. Especially the Bratva. They're real sticklers about revenge."

Massimo's pupils dilate, but he shows no other outward sign of emotion. "I don't know what you're talking about."

"That's fine, but you really shouldn't make important phone calls at cocktail parties. Especially on speakerphone. You never know who might be listening at the door."

I see him working it out, trying to decide if I'm bluffing, trying to recall what party we might have attended together where he made a call that should have been more discreet.

Just so we're on the same page, I'll give his memory a helpful jog.

"Murdering Maxim Mogdonovich in return for a marker from the man who took his place could be seen by both the Bratva and the Cosa Nostra as a little underhanded, don't you think? Feathers would definitely get ruffled on both sides. But I'll admit, making it look like he died in a prison riot was a small stroke of genius. I couldn't have done it better myself. I bet Kazimir Portnov appreciated your creativity. Oh, excuse me. You called him Kage. I suppose when you kill someone's boss for him, you get a little friendly."

We stare at each other across the table.

I see the exact moment he decides I have to die and roll my eyes to the ceiling.

Men are so damn predictable.

I slip the lovely red silk wrap Quinn bought me off of the back of my chair and wind it around my shoulders. Then I lift my chin and stare Massimo down.

"I've taken precautions. If anything happens to me, a file will be released to the families. To *all* the members of *all* the families, to be exact, not just the heads. That file contains everything I've seen and heard since I was a child. All the conversations no one thought were important to hide from me because I was female. All my memories and experiences. All the things I've witnessed. Everything has been written down and saved in duplicate. If I die for any reason other than advanced old age, those files go out."

I cluck my tongue. "Just imagine the information I have, Massimo. Daughter of a Mafia don, wife of a Mafia captain, sister of the head of one of the Five Families . . . I'm a fucking *mother lode* of fun information."

Massimo's face turns red. A vein in his temple throbs. He snaps, "Bullshit."

My smile grows wider. "Is it? I guess time will tell. But there's one thing we both know for sure, and it's that you've always underestimated me."

I hold his infuriated stare for a beat before I turn my back and walk away, leaving him alone at the table.

FORTY-ONE

REY

PARIS

SEPTEMBER

*W*hat the fuckedy-fuck is *that* thing?"

"It's called haute couture, Riley."

"If 'haute couture' is code for garish and ridiculous, then I get it, Hollywood. Seriously, where in the world could you go out in public wearing a giant balloon dress? Unless there's a flood, then I suppose that hideous plastic polka-dot concoction could be super great as a floatation device."

Sloane sighs. "I see living in the wilds of a Russian forest has done nothing to elevate your sense of style."

Riley snorts and looks down at Sloane's skirt. "This from a woman who thinks hot-pink tulle miniskirts covered in sequins and bows is the height of fashion."

"Don't you dare diss Betsey Johnson! And couture is magical, Smalls. It's wearable art."

"It's lame is what it is. Can we leave now? I'm starving."

We're sitting in the second row of seats at the Fendi runway show, right behind Victoria Beckham. To my left is Nat, the black-haired beauty engaged to the head of the Bratva in the U.S.

To my right are Sloane and her younger sister, Riley, arguing the merits, or lack thereof, of French couture.

They bicker constantly, but the love between them is obvious. Over the past three days since we arrived in Paris, they've fought as much as they've hugged each other.

We watch the final model strut down the runway, then stand and clap with the rest of the audience when the show is over and the designer walks out to thunderous applause. Then we make our way through the crowd, headed to the after-party at the Musée des Arts Décoratifs.

We're followed by no fewer than two dozen bodyguards.

Armed and eagle-eyed, they're spread out across the room, moving through the well-dressed patrons like sharks through water. The protection was a nonnegotiable condition all our men insisted upon, though not the only one. The list was long.

A girls' trip to Paris is much more than a simple getaway when the "girls" belong to four of the most powerful, dangerous men in organized crime.

Men who hate each other.

They probably hate it even more that there's no stopping us once our minds are made up.

But all it took was a single conference call between the four of us to convince us that a girls' trip was exactly what we needed. If these men of ours are going to be at each other's throats for the next forty years, we'll be the glue that holds this shit show together.

And we're bonding the glue in Paris, buying haute couture and eating haute cuisine.

Nobody ever said politics had to be conducted in dreary surroundings.

Chatting about the show, we travel to the museum in a convoy of armored SUVs with blacked-out windows. We enter through a private elevator in the back of the building. Once we're inside, the bodyguards spread out again, keeping their predatory gazes trained for any hint of danger.

The after-party is held in the nave of the museum, an elegant three-story space of carved arches, white marble columns, and glossy marble floors. Displays of mannequins clad in designer frocks are clustered on raised platforms. The walls glow with purple washes of light. Uniformed waiters pass champagne and canapés on silver trays. I spot four celebrities within the first five minutes of our arrival.

We gather around a tall cocktail table draped in linen at one end of the room and talk, eat, and people watch as more guests arrive.

Until Riley says suddenly, "Uh-oh."

Chewing on a pear-and-gouda tartlet, Nat says, "What's wrong?"

I've already spotted the problem. "Oh, just a little ticking time bomb over there."

Nat and Sloane follow the direction Riley and I are looking.

On either side of the opposite end of the room, two pairs of men stand glaring at each other. On one side are Declan and Quinn. On the other are Kage, Nat's fiancé and head of the U.S. Bratva, and Malek, Riley's fiancé and head of the Bratva in Moscow.

All four of them have their arms crossed over their chests and expressions of murderous rage on their faces as they stare at each other over everyone's heads.

Sloane laughs. "Oh, look. The boys are here!"

Nat says crossly, "I knew they wouldn't stay at the hotel like they agreed to. I think they've been following us around every time we go out."

I say, "Of course they have. They can't help themselves. All that big-dick energy comes with some serious caveman side effects."

"Should we intervene?" asks Riley nervously. "I don't like that look on Mal's face."

The look she's referring to is directed at Quinn, who's glaring right back at Malek with his teeth bared.

It's no worse, however, than the look Kage and Declan are sharing, a glower of blistering hatred that could peel the paint right off the walls.

I say, "Don't worry about them. It's just saber rattling. They know better than to go at it with the four of us as witnesses."

Sloane laughs again. "Right? They know what they'd be in for when they got home, the poor bastards."

"They might be bastards, but poor they're definitely not," says Nat, turning to smile at me. "How many carats is that diamond necklace, anyway? Fifty?"

"Close, but no. And look who's talking. How many carats is that ring?"

"Ten." Nat beams down at her engagement ring, a huge chunk of ice that must've set Kage back millions of dollars. "But he thinks I need something bigger. When he saw Sloane's ring, he got really mad."

"Speaking of engagement rings," Sloane says, elbowing Riley with a smile. "When are you and your giant Russian assassin going to tie the knot?"

"Probably not until after the baby's born," Riley says, caressing her stomach. In comparison to the rest of her petite frame, the small bump she's growing looks big. "Though if it were up to him, it would be tonight. I'm not in such a hurry."

"Why wait?"

She snorts. "Because gangster weddings are such calm and simple affairs, maybe?"

I smile. "Amen."

Sloane waves that off and sips her champagne. "Then go to a justice of the peace or something. They do have those in Russia, I presume?"

"Don't be a snob. Russia isn't the middle of nowhere."

"Except that cabin you live in with your man and his pet crow is literally in the middle of nowhere."

"Pet crow?" I say, interested.

Riley smiles at me. "His name's Poe."

"Ah. After Edgar Allan. Very clever."

"So's the bird. I swear that thing is smarter than most of the guys Sloane's dated."

Nat deadpans, "Wouldn't be hard."

"Very funny, assholes," says Sloane breezily. "I'll have you know I once dated a Rhodes scholar."

"'Once' being the important word in that sentence," says Nat, laughing.

"Besides, nobody's smarter than I am, so why bother dating a smart guy?"

"I'm sure Declan would have something to say about you thinking you're smarter than he is."

"Oh, he knows. I tell him so all the time."

Nat rolls her eyes. "Of course you do."

Inside her cute little blingy handbag, Sloane's phone rings. She unzips the bag, takes out the phone, and sighs when she sees the number on the readout. "Oh, Stavi. Give it up already."

"Stavi?"

Sloane smiles at me. "My ex, Stavros. He wants me to text him a pic of my shoes."

I lift my brows. "He's into women's footwear?"

Her chuckle is dry. "Sis, like you wouldn't believe."

I haven't said a thing to her about the section regarding her ex Stavros in the contract Declan and I negotiated, and I never will. It's enough that he agreed to take it out. And as long as Stavros stays alive, I'll keep my promise to Declan that the whole incident will remain between the two of us.

Politics is tricky, but like I once told her, I'm an excellent politician.

Sloane looks up from her phone at me. "Hey, do you know any single Mafia girls? I promised him I'd set him up with someone. He's super sweet. Cute, too. And very rich."

"And he has a thing for women's shoes."

She scrunches up her nose. "I mean, nobody's perfect."

Riley says to me, "I've been meaning to ask you how Kieran's doing."

"He's doing great!"

Sloane says, "Madly in love with Aria, from what Declan tells me."

That makes me laugh. "Yes, our Irishmen fall fast and hard, don't they?"

Nat says, "Probably not as fast or hard as our Russians do, right, Riley?"

Riley looks pointedly at her sister. "Which isn't as fast or hard as the Keller sisters do."

Sloane nods, sipping more champagne. "But Stockholm syndrome runs in the family, so we really couldn't help ourselves."

I've already gotten the full backstory about how kidnapping was the inciting event that had both Sloane and Riley falling in love with their captors, Declan and Mal. And honestly, after all I've been through in my life, it makes as much sense as anything else does.

Except for Nat's story about how she fell in love with Kage.

I don't think I'd ever be able to love a man who was sent to kill me, no matter how handsome he was.

I guess that's the funny thing about love, though.

Its fire can forge soul mates from even the most bitter of enemies.

My own cell phone buzzes in my handbag. When I look to see who it is, I've got a text from Mamma.

How do you open the minibar in this place? The bastardo *is locked!*

I send her the code, hoping she's not hosting a party in her suite. When I invited her to come with us to Paris, she said she'd only go on the condition she have her own room. With a view of the Eiffel Tower. And a butler. Who was over six feet and under thirty-five.

She was granted all her demands, naturally. I'm not the only Caruso female Quinn can't say no to.

"Girls, I've got to visit the ladies' room. Anybody else?"

I get a round of head shakes for an answer.

"Okay. I'll be back in a sec. And keep an eye on the boys. If things look like they're about to go sideways, I'm counting on you to get control of the situation, Sloane."

She smiles as if she's hoping gunfire will break out at any moment. "No problem, babe. They won't know what hit 'em."

I wind my way slowly through the elegant crowd toward an archway marked MESDAMES. The restroom is down a corridor lined with potted palms lighted purple. I go inside, use the toilet, then wash my hands in the sink.

When I come out, the corridor is empty.

Except for my four bodyguards lying facedown and unmoving on the floor and the man leaning casually against the wall.

Wearing faded jeans, a tight white T-shirt, cowboy boots, and mirrored sunglasses, he has a foot propped up on the wall and his tattooed arms folded over his massive chest. His dark wavy hair brushes his shoulders. His angular jaw is covered in scruff.

He's big, masculine, and exudes an air of danger so palpable, I can almost touch it.

He looks like a mashup of Wolverine, Dirty Harry, and James Bond. On steroids.

I say, "At least take off the sunglasses. It would add insult to injury to be murdered by a man wearing sunglasses. Indoors. At night."

"Not gonna harm you, lass. Just want a word."

His Irish accent is lilting and his tone is gentle, but I don't trust him.

I know a killer when I see one. And this guy's a killer with a capital *K*.

He pushes off the wall, pulls a huge semi-automatic handgun out of the back of his waistband, and holds it out to me. "If it'll make you feel better."

"What would make me feel better is if I knew why an Irishman who thinks he's Dirty Harry assaulted four of my bodyguards."

He smiles. My reflection in his glasses looks very small.

"This conversation needs to be private."

"Are they dead?"

"Do you see any blood?"

"There are so many ways to kill a man that don't involve spilling his blood."

His smile grows wider. Tucking the gun back in its place, he drawls, "Aye, there are. Which you know all about, don't you?"

Someone is coming down the hallway. Two women, chattering, their heads together and their high heels clicking off the marble floor. They see us and the four men lying unconscious and pull up short. Then look at each other. Then they turn around and run off without a word.

Dirty Harry strolls away and turns left around a corner, disappearing from sight. From around the corner he says, "C'mon, Reyna. If I wanted to kill you, I already would have."

Whoever he is, this guy is very irritating.

"Who are you?"

A husky chuckle is my only answer.

"I really don't appreciate the cloak-and-dagger routine."

"Two minutes of your time. That's all I need. Why don't you pull that blade out of the sheath on your thigh and wave it around at me? Might make you feel better."

I glance down at the front of my dress. The waist is cinched and the skirt is full, concealing any telltale lumps or bumps. There's no way he could've known I'm carrying a knife.

"Don't think too hard on it, lass. Clock's ticking."

Curiosity gets the best of me. I walk around the corner, stop a few feet away from him, and prop my hands on my hips. He's leaning against the wall again, as if he thinks it's his job to hold up the entire building.

"You're a rival of Declan and Quinn's, is that it? Am I about to be kidnapped and held for ransom?"

His laugh indicates he's amused by the question.

"Is that a yes?"

"It's a no. I've known Declan for more than twenty years. He's a dear friend."

I eye him warily. "Uh-huh. And does your dear friend know about this clandestine little chat? Because it makes a lot more sense that you'd just talk to me out in the other room with him instead of skulking around women's bathrooms."

He studies me for a moment in silence. I feel his gaze going over me, up and down. One corner of his mouth lifts.

"You remind me of my wife. She stole a truckload of diapers from me. That's how we met."

"Fascinating."

"It was."

"Is there a point you'll be arriving at soon? Because if not, I've got some champagne to get back to."

Ignoring my comment, he says, "You'll meet her. Her name's Juliet. I have a feeling the two of you will get along like gangbusters."

I decide I've had enough. If he's going to kidnap me, let's get on with it. If he's not, I'm bored.

I turn and start to walk away, but stop when he says, "Lili

and Juan Pablo are doing well down in Mexico, don't you think? Sweet love story, that."

My heart starts to pound faster. I turn and peer at him, wondering what the fuck this guy really wants. I demand, "What do you know about them?"

"I know they've decided to make Mexico their permanent home. And I know you met with Juan Pablo's uncle Alvaro last week to discuss a deal between the Mob, the Mafia, and the Jalisco cartel."

"Did Declan tell you that?"

He chuckles again. He seems overly fond of doing that.

"No, lass. I've got my own sources of information. And I have to admit, I'm bloody impressed at the deal you negotiated. You were born to twist men around your pinky finger, weren't you?"

"Enough with the rhetorical questions. I hate rhetorical questions. Who are you?"

Instead of giving me his name, he says cryptically, "An interested third party."

At first, I think he wants to get in on the Jalisco deal. But then I remember something Declan said the day at his office when he showed me the evidence that Gianni set up the kidnapping attempt and home invasion himself.

When I asked how he came by all the information, he said the same thing this Irishman just said. "An interested third party."

All the tiny hairs on the back of my neck stand on end.

I say, "You were listening. That day in Declan's office, you were listening in on our conversation."

"Watching it over a hidden camera in the ceiling, actually. Don't blame Declan for that. He didn't know it was there. But your performance was impeccable. I've never seen a woman handle herself so well. Declan can be very intimidating."

"Not much intimidates me."

"Exactly. Which is why I'm extending you an invitation."

He lets it hang there without explaining what he means.

I say sarcastically, "Here is where you'll offer me riches beyond my wildest dreams or something, right?"

"There's money involved, but that's not why you'll be interested."

I'm about to explode with exasperation but manage to remain calm. "Okay, I'll play your silly game. Why will I be interested?"

After a moment, he removes his sunglasses. Without them, he's even more handsome. He stares at me with dark eyes that drill straight through my skull.

"Because you're a do-gooder, Reyna Caruso. You've got an overdeveloped sense of right and wrong."

It's official: he's nuts.

"Since you obviously know so much about me, you must know that I'm the head of the Cosa Nostra. Tell me how being in charge of an organized crime empire makes me so ethical?"

"You sacrificed yourself to save the lives of your niece and her boyfriend. Do-gooding. You told the other Mafia families that at the upcoming annual Christmas Eve meeting of all the syndicates, the Chinese and the Armenians will be cut off if they continue their human-trafficking operations. Do-gooding."

His faint, self-satisfied smile returns. "You ordered Declan not to kill Stavros because it offended your sense of fair play. Do-gooding."

"That's three things. Big deal. And it's really creepy how much you know about me."

"I know much more than that, but I'm trying to recruit you to join my organization, so I won't creep you out any more by giving additional details."

"What's your organization?"

Stepping closer to me, he holds out a white business card.

I take it from him and look at it. "It's blank."

"Turn it over."

When I do, I find nothing more on the back except a number printed in bold sans serif type in the middle of the card.

I glance up at him in confusion. "Thirteen? What's that?"

"The name of my organization."

"Oh. Okay, that's weird."

He sounds offended. "Why is it weird?"

"Thirteen is a feminine number. The number of blood, fertility, and lunar potency. The number of the Great Goddess." I look him up and down. "You don't exactly look like a Great Goddess to me."

He sticks his sunglasses back onto his face, folds his arms over his chest, and sighs. "It's also the number of the Death card in the tarot."

"So your organization has something to do with the tarot?"

"No. Thirteen is just the number of members we have."

I stare at him for a moment. "I feel like we could stand here until the end of time and go in circles while you avoid telling me anything at all about what this organization of yours does."

His smile is mysterious. "I'll be in touch. In the meantime, don't tell anyone you've spoken to me. That's your first test."

"For the record, I hate tests. And considering I have no idea who you are, I'm not likely to tell anyone about you. I don't even know your name."

He lowers his head and gazes at me over the frame of his sunglasses. In a low voice, he says, "The name's Killian Black, lass. And you'll be hearing from me."

Footsteps sound on the marble floor of the corridor. I glance down the corridor. When I turn around again, he's gone.

Killian has disappeared into thin air.

I say loudly, "That's even more creepy! And if I join your stupid organization, you'll have to change the name to fourteen. You know that, right? Every time you recruit a new member, you'll have to print up new business cards!"

I'm not sure, but I could swear I hear the sound of faint laughter echoing from somewhere far off in the distance.

EPILOGUE

Late that night, I'm lying in bed next to Quinn and staring suspiciously at the ceiling of the hotel suite with a growing sense of unease that a crazy person named Killian Black might have planted a camera in the smoke detector, when Quinn rouses and slides one of his heavy legs over mine.

His voice drowsy, he says, "Strange thing happened tonight."

"What's that?"

"Four of our bodyguards claim they woke up in a back hallway of the museum with no idea how they got there."

I knew they were alive when I left them, because I checked all their pulses. But I haven't quite decided what to tell Quinn about this character Killian Black yet, so I go with a vague "Hmm. That is strange."

We lie in comfortable silence for a while, until he says, "What are you thinking, viper?"

"I'm thinking . . ." I turn my head and look at him. His head rests on the pillow beside mine. His hazel eyes are soft, warm, and full of adoration. I smile at him and touch his wonderful springy beard. "That I'm very happy."

"Aye?" He pulls me closer and nuzzles my neck. "Tell me more."

I have to laugh at that. I see many, many years of heaping praise on my Irishman in the future. "I'm happy that we're here together. I'm happy I've made three amazing new friends. I'm happy that my mother hasn't sexually assaulted the handsome young butler you arranged to wait on her."

Quinn says, "Yet."

"Yes, yet. God, it's disturbing to see her flirt. It's like watching a horror movie in slow motion." I slide my hand up his neck into his hair and whisper, "I'm also happy to see you so happy. I was a little worried seeing Riley would be traumatic for you."

He sighs. "Seeing Malek is traumatic for me. I hate that fucker. I've never wanted to strangle anyone more. But I'm glad Riley's happy. She seems good, don't you think?"

I nod, snuggling closer.

After a moment, he asks tentatively, "Are you jealous?"

"I would be if I thought you still had feelings for her. But it's obvious you don't. Hey, by the way, I've been thinking about something."

"Jesus."

"Oh, don't be scared. It just occurred to me the other day that I've never asked you what this tattoo says."

I trace my fingers over the ink that runs across his chest just under his collarbone.

He exhales and pulls me closer. "It's Gaelic for 'embrace the chaos.' Someone told me that years ago, when I was in a very dark place, and it helped."

"One of your therapists?"

"No. Declan."

I think about that for a while as I trace my fingers over the scrolls and loops inked on his skin. It seems as good a slogan as any to survive this turbulent life of ours.

Pressing a kiss to my temple, Quinn murmurs, "I've been thinking about something, too."

The tone of his voice makes me nervous. "Do I need to have a drink before I hear it?"

"It's about the tattoo on your ring finger."

"What about it?"

He pauses. "I was wondering . . . if it's still how you feel about marriage."

"Oh." I laugh a little, snuggling closer to him. "Actually, marriage in general seems like a terrible idea."

His sigh is soft and defeated. He says, "That's what I thought," and closes his eyes.

This man. He always assumes the worst. I'm going to have to work on that.

"I wasn't finished."

He cracks open one eye and looks at me. I smile up into his frowning face.

"As I was saying, marriage in general seems like a terrible idea . . . but marriage to a certain stubborn, bossy, cranky, possessive insect seems like it might be kinda fun."

His breath catches. His eyes flare. His arms tighten around me. He says gruffly, "Arachnid."

"Yes, excuse me. Arachnid."

After a beat of silence, he rolls on top of me and stares down at me with burning intensity, every muscle in his big body tensed.

"So you're saying you want to marry me. For real this time."

Grinning at him, I say coyly, "I don't know. Maybe you should ask me and find out. Because if memory serves, *I'm* the only person in this room who's proposed. Under duress, I might add.

That doesn't make such a great story we can tell our grandkids. It would be nice if we went about it properly."

Because his chest is pressed to mine, I can feel how hard his heart is pounding. I also feel a sudden stiffness against my thigh and have to bite my lip to keep from laughing.

But then I'm gasping, because Quinn has launched himself from bed, dragging me along with him. He gets me steady on my feet, then sinks to one knee on the carpet in front of me.

Gazing up at me with adoring eyes, he says in a gruff voice, "Viper. I want to spend the rest of my life with you. I want you to have my children. I want to make you the happiest woman in the world. I'll give you everything I have to give and anything you ever ask for. I love you with every part of my dark heart and every piece of my wasted soul. Will you please do me the honor of being my wife?"

His smile is breathtaking. "For real this time?"

My throat tight and my eyes watering, I say, "Yes, my beautiful Irishman. I'll marry you. I'll marry you every day for the rest of forever, because I've never loved anything in my life the way I love you."

He closes his eyes for a moment. He swallows. When he opens his eyes again, they've gone dark.

My monster growls, "Good answer," and lunges at me.

He takes us back down to the bed with the sound of my happy laughter echoing off the walls.

BONUS CHAPTER

Q & A WITH REYNA AND SPIDER

Shortly after the whirlwind events in *Brutal Vows,* I sat down with Reyna and Spider to discuss what's next for them and their families and get an update on Reyna's pregnancy. And *wow,* did things take an unexpected turn! We met on a cold but brilliantly bright day in February in Boston at their home.

J.T.: First, let me thank you for taking the time to answer my questions. I've been dying to find out what's happening with you two.

Reyna: It's our pleasure.

(Sitting in a chair next to Reyna in their living room, Spider smiles at me but remains silent. I'm a little worried that he's still sore at me over the Malek-shooting-Kieran incident, among other things, so I nervously smile back.)

J.T.: How are you feeling, Reyna? (I gesture to her large baby bump, draped under her elegant blue dress.)

Reyna: (gently caressing the bump with one hand) I feel wonderful! Reagan has been very active lately, kicking and rolling over and keeping me up at night, but otherwise, I've been lucky. I didn't even have morning sickness in my first trimester, which I'm told is rare.

J.T.: That's so great! I'm happy for you. Remind me, your due date is Valentine's Day, right?

Reyna: (nodding) Just over a week away.

Spider: And it can't come soon enough!

(Reyna and I are surprised by the force of his statement. She looks at him with her brows raised. I wonder if anything is wrong.)

Spider: (rolling his eyes) The two of you and your frettin' faces. I didn't mean anything bad. (he takes Reyna's hand and kisses it) Just that I'm ready to be a daddy. (slants Reyna a heated look) Then we can get right to work on the next batch of Quinns.

J.T.: Reyna, how do you anticipate juggling motherhood with the demands of your work? Do you see that being challenging for you?

(When they gaze at me as if I'm exceptionally dim for asking, I change the subject.)

J.T.: How's your mom doing?

Reyna: (laughing) She's got a boyfriend, if you can believe that.

Spider: (muttering) The poor bastard.

J.T.: (confused) I thought you liked Mrs. Caruso? Are you two not getting along? Did you have a falling out?

Spider: (exasperated) For fuck's sake, lass, why does everything with you have to be doom and gloom?

J.T.: (wondering if that's a rhetorical question) Because it makes things more interesting. That's just how my brain works. If everything were going smoothly all the time, it would be boring as hell.

Spider: (muttering) I feel sorry for your man.

J.T.: (laughs) I'll tell Jay you said so. He'll appreciate the solidarity. Can you catch me up on what's happening with the other syndicates? Is your agreement to work together still holding?

(Reyna and Spider share a loaded glance.)

Reyna: It is. For now.

J.T.: (excited) That's a no. Let me guess. Massimo's a problem, right? Is he undermining your authority? Did he make a deal with that suspicious Albanian guy to have you taken out? Ooh, or maybe Kage and Mal made a secret accord with the Chinese—

Spider: (loudly) Lass.

J.T.: Yes?

Spider: Put a sock in it. (pauses for a beat) Now why the bloody hell are you smiling?

J.T.: My dad used to say that to me. He was Irish too.

Spider: (deadpan) Congratulations.

Reyna: (squeezing Spider's hand) I only meant that it's just a matter of time before a problem will crop up. When you're working with egos like these, things are bound to get bumpy.

J.T.: (looking back and forth between Reyna and Spider) Why do I feel like you're hiding something?

Reyna: I'm sure it's just that doom-and-gloom brain of yours. (smiles blandly)

J.T.: (narrows my eyes at them)

Spider: (sighs) Jesus, Mary, and Joseph. Fine, we've got a wee situation with the Red Scorpions. Satisfied?

J.T.: I have no idea who that is.

Reyna: They're out of Vancouver.

J.T.: (wrinkles my nose in disbelief) Canadians?

Spider: (chuckles darkly) Aye. Everybody thinks of the sweet wee Mounties with their spiffy red coats and good manners when you mention the Great White North, but this outfit is as lethal as they come. Kidnapping, murder, arms dealing, you name it, they're into it. (after a moment) Ach, don't look so bloody excited!

J.T.: It's just that there could be another book there . . .

Reyna: (shakes her head) Look at those wheels turn. Here we go.

J.T.: (leaning closer) So what are they doing? Trying to recruit members from your ranks? Horning in on your territory?

Spider: (in disgust) *Horning in?*

J.T.: Don't make that face. I'm pretty sure you've said that yourself.

Spider: If I did, remind me to stab myself for being so barmy.

J.T.: (ignoring his caustic aside) Reyna, spill the beans. What's happening?

Reyna: (steely-eyed) Nothing we can't handle.

J.T.: (beaming at them) It's so cute that you guys think I'll let this go. Okay, moving on for the moment. How are Kieran and Aria doing? People have been really interested in Kieran's story.

Spider: They're . . . (searches for a word)

Reyna: Struggling.

J.T.: Oh no. Is it another woman?

Reyna: No. It's another man.

J.T.: (shocked) Aria's cheating?

Spider: No, lass.

J.T.: (baffled) I don't get it.

(Reyna looks to Spider, who runs a hand through his hair before sighing.)

Spider: Well, as it turns out . . . Kieran's a little more flexible in who he fancies than he thought he was.

J.T.: (deeply thrilled) Oh my God. Kieran's *bi*? This is amazing!

Spider: (groans)

Reyna: (sternly) You can't write about that, J.T.. I mean it, this is in *strict* confidence.

J.T.: . . .

Spider: Look who you're talking to, viper! The woman loves nothing more than to traumatize people!

J.T.: (insulted) Excuse me, but that's *not* true. (they stare at me in judgmental silence) Okay, it's a little true. But everybody always gets their happily-ever-after.

Spider: (snorts) Not sure you're familiar with the definition of an HEA, lass. Do you actually *read* your own work? I've met hardened criminals with more mercy than you.

J.T.: (silent but secretly pleased)

Reyna: In any case, you didn't hear it from us. (smiles) Blame it on the Russians.

Spider: Aye. Pin it on Malek, the useless sot.

J.T.: (nodding insincerely) Will do. Any news about Nat and Kage?

Spider: (makes a retching sound)

J.T.: I take it they're doing well. Sloane and Declan?

Reyna: Sloane's been sending a lot of . . . *interesting* baby gifts.

J.T.: Oh no. She's baking for you?

Spider: That's not baking. It's friendship-testing. I'm convinced she's playing a grand prank on all of us, having a go at our patience to see how long it'll take to make us crack. Her last batch of "cookies" stank up the house something fierce. I think they had actual shite in them.

Reyna: Their twins are going to be absolutely adorable, though.

J.T.: I bet. (thinking) Wouldn't it be funny if they had girls? They'll be only slightly younger than Mal's and Kage's boys—

Spider: (thunders) Don't even go there!

J.T.: Oh, that's right. You're having a girl too. Gosh, all the kids will be right around the same age! (smiles innocently)

(Spider and Reyna growl in stereo.)

J.T.: (in a stage whisper) Maybe they'll go to school together. Maybe a Bratva heir will fall in love with an Irish Mob princess!

Spider: (glowering) And maybe a certain pain-in-the-arse author will go missing in the woods near Lake Tahoe.

J.T.: Behave yourself or I'll give you erectile dysfunction in the next book. Reyna, are you okay? You look a little pale.

Reyna: (calm) I think my water just broke.

Spider: (leaps to his feet and stares down at her in horror) What? *Now?* It's too bloody early!

Reyna: (still calm) Yes, love, but here we are. Will you please go get the baby bag so we can head to the hospital?

(Spider sprints from the room, shouting unintelligibly in Gaelic.)

Reyna: (bemused) How long do you think it will take before he comes back in asking where I left it?

J.T.: I give it ten seconds. Are you in pain? Is there anything I can do for you?

Reyna: (shakes her head) I'm fine, thank you.

Spider: (panicked, bursts back into the room shouting) *Where'd you leave the bag?*

Reyna: (smiles at him lovingly) Deep breaths, Quinn.

(Spider pauses to look around wildly, then sprints back out.)

Reyna: Would you please give me a hand so I can get on my feet? If he comes back in here and I'm still sitting, he's liable to pick up the chair and carry me in it all the way to the hospital.

J.T.: (helping Reyna rise) Are you having contractions yet?

Reyna: No, not—(gasps and freezes, squeezes her eyes shut)

J.T.: Oh boy.

Reyna: (panting) Wow, that was a strong one.

J.T.: Do you want to sit down?

(Reyna shakes her head as Spider bursts back into the room.)

(Spider takes one look at Reyna standing, instantly drops the small suitcase he's holding, and runs over and picks her up in his arms.)

J.T.: Don't worry, I'll get the bag!

(J.T. plots more Mafia books all the way to the hospital, where sweet baby Reagan is born six hours later. Mama, daddy, and baby are all doing well.)

(For now.)

PLAYLIST

"Enemy" Imagine Dragons

"Angry Too" Lola Blanc

"Black Widow" Iggy Azalea

"Cold Little Heart" Michael Kiwanuka

"Wicked Game" G-Eazy

"Shivers" Ed Sheeran

"Woman" Mumford & Sons

"Fall Into Me" Forest Blakk

"Mrs." Leon Bridges

"The Joker and the Queen" Ed Sheeran feat. Taylor Swift

"Him & I" G-Eazy and Halsey

"Kings & Queens" Ava Max

ACKNOWLEDGMENTS

The response to the Queens and Monsters series has been overwhelming. I can't explain the gratitude I feel for how enthusiastically readers have embraced my Mafia world and shared it with their friends. I want to give a heartfelt shout-out to Geissinger's Gang, my reader group on Facebook, for being my cheerleaders and emotional support team throughout this process. I also want to thank the countless bloggers, reviewers, BookTokkers, Bookstagrammers, and YouTubers who have taken the time to not only read my work, but also to make incredible edits on social media, leave reviews, share snippets and teasers, ask me for interviews, cajole their friends to read along with them, and make the whole experience of getting my books out into the world so amazing for me.

2022 marks the tenth year since my first novel was published. *Brutal Vows* is my twenty-ninth novel, and one I can say without doubt that I had the most fun writing. I hope the joy I felt creating this world and these characters came across as you were reading it.

If you found this book before reading the three prior installations of the series, the last chapter will probably make more sense if you go back and start with *Ruthless Creatures,* book one. And if you'd like to go back to where it all began, start with the Dangerous Beauty series, then read the Beautifully Cruel duet before crossing over to Queens and Monsters. Many of my series have crossover characters who like to make surprise cameo appearances, so there's a full reading order on my website at www.jtgeissinger.com to help direct you.

Sincere thanks to my PR team, Social Butterfly PR, for all their help. Specifically to Sarah Ferguson, who never fails me, thank you so much for all you do. I appreciate you.

Thank you to Linda Ingmanson, editor extraordinaire, for your attention to detail and for hitting all my ridiculous turnaround deadlines.

Thank you to Letitia Hasser of RBA Designs for creating my incredible covers, and also for your quick turnarounds. And for accommodating all the changes I come back to you with, which probably make you pull out your hair.

Big thanks to Denise Black and Marnye Young of Audio Sorceress for making my audiobooks come to life so fantastically with your magic! I love everything you've done for me, and my readers love you, too.

Also huge thanks to Troy Duran, Brooke Daniels, Michelle Sparks, Tara Langella, and Tess Hanna for your incredible talent.

Thank you to the first acquisitions editor I ever had, Eleni Caminis of Montlake Romance, for buying the Night Prowler series, becoming a wonderful friend, and making my dreams of becoming a published author come true.

Thank you to my sweet new friend Charles for insisting Stavros shouldn't die. You're going to have to explain to Declan how he's supposed to fulfill his marker to Kage now, but I'll stay out of it.

Thank you to Jay, my husband, best friend, and best human I know. Without you, I'm nothing. Well, okay, not *nothing*, but not much. Or at least not as happy. Or maybe just not as crabby? I don't really know, but my point is that I think I'll keep you around for another twenty-five years, if you'll let me. (Which you will, because let's be honest, my crazy matches your crazy. You're welcome.)

Thanks to my mother for being half Queen Elizabeth and half Margaret Thatcher, with a side order of Jerry Seinfeld and a dash of the entire *Jersey Shore* cast. You are missed.

And Dad, I'm so sorry you bought all those copies of my first book and shared them with your friends and discovered that fatherly pride is no match for the surprise horror of learning your dear daughter writes smut. In my defense, I did try to warn you. I love you and miss you every day. Until we meet again.

PS: *Ravaged by a Rogue* and *Glazed by the Gladiator* are figments of my imagination.

PPS: I have no idea if I will write a series about the Thirteen, but Killian Black will probably continue to show up in future books, because he's bossy that way. If you're intrigued by the idea of him being all espionage-y, check out the Dangerous Beauty series and the Beautifully Cruel series, where he does his thing.

ABOUT THE AUTHOR

J.T. GEISSINGER is a #1 international and indie bestselling author of thirty-one novels. Ranging from funny, feisty rom-coms to intense erotic thrillers, her books have sold more than fifteen million copies worldwide and have been translated into more than twenty languages.

She is a three-time finalist in both contemporary and paranormal romance for the RITA Award, the highest distinction in romance fiction from the Romance Writers of America. She is also a recipient of the PRISM Award for Best First Book, the Golden Quill Award for Best Paranormal/Urban Fantasy, and the HOLT Medallion for Best Erotic Romance.

Find her online at www.jtgeissinger.com.